William Harrison Ainsworth

# Boscobel, or, the Royal Oak

A Tale of the Year 1651

William Harrison Ainsworth

**Boscobel, or, the Royal Oak**
*A Tale of the Year 1651*

ISBN/EAN: 9783337122133

Printed in Europe, USA, Canada, Australia, Japan

Cover: Foto ©Andreas Hilbeck / pixelio.de

More available books at **www.hansebooks.com**

| | | |
|---|---|---|
| Watch. | Laura Everingnam. | Only an Ensign. |
| Mary of Lorraine. | Captain of the Guard. | Adventures of Rob Roy. |
| Oliver Ellis ; or, The Fusiliers. | Letty Hyde's Lovers. | Under the Red Dragon |
| Phantom Regiment. | Cavaliers of Fortune. Second to None. | The Queen's Cadet. |

Published by GEORGE ROUTLEDGE.

# NOVELS AT TWO SHILLINGS.—*Continued.*

## By FIELDING and SMOLLETT.

| FIELDING. | SMOLLETT. |
|---|---|
| Tom Jones. | Roderick Random. |
| Joseph Andrews. | Humphrey Clinker. |
| Amelia. | Peregrine Pickle. |

The Ladder of L[              ]a Million of Money.

By Mrs. [        ] FERRIER.

Night Side [        ]iage.
Susan Hopl[       ]ritance.
Linny Lock[       ]iny.

Life of a Sailor. [        ] Jack Adams.

By CHARL[     ] LOVER.

Arthur O'Le[       ])'More.
Con Cregan[       ] Andy.

Two Midshipmen [        ]Young Commander

By Mrs. [        ]y C. LONG.

Mothers and [        ]utenant's Story.
Soldier of L[        ].d Ashton.

## By Rev. G. R. GLEIG.

| Country Curate. | Waltham. | The Hussar. |

## By GERSTAECKER.

| A Wife to Order. | Feathered Arrow. |
| Two Convicts. | Each for Himself. |

## By W. H. MAXWELL.

| Stories of Waterloo. | Hector O'Halloran. | Wild Sports in the Highlands. |
| Brian O'Linn; or, Luck is Everything. | Stories of the Peninsular War. | Wild Sports in the West. |
| Captain Blake. | Captain O'Sullivan. | |
| The Bivouac. | Flood and Field. | |

## By LANG.

| | By EDMUND YATES. |
| Will He Marry Her. | Running the Gauntlet. |
| The Ex-Wife. | Kissing the Rod. |

## By THEODORE HOOK.

| Peregrine Bunce. | The Widow and the Marquess. | Passion and Principle. |
| Cousin Geoffry. | Gurney Married. | Merton. |
| Gilbert Gurney. | Jack Brag. | Gervase Skinner. |
| Parson's Daughter. | Maxwell. | Cousin William. |
| All in the Wrong. | Man of Many Friends. | Fathers and Sons. |

**Published by George Routledge and Sons.**

# BOSCOBEL; OR, THE ROYAL OAK.

## 𝕭ook the 𝕱irst.

### THE BATTLE OF WORCESTER.

## CHAPTER I.

#### HOW CHARLES THE SECOND ARRIVED BEFORE WORCESTER, AND CAPTURED A FORT, WHICH HE NAMED "FORT ROYAL."

DURING the Civil Wars, the old and faithful city of Worcester suffered severely for its devotion to the royal cause. Twice was it besieged— twice sacked by the Parliamentarians. In 1642, the Earl of Essex marched with a large force against the place, stormed and pillaged it, and sent several of the wealthier citizens prisoners to London. Four years later—namely, in 1646—the city again declared for the king, and being captured by the Roundheads, after an obstinate defence, under- went harder usage than before. Besides plundering the inhabitants, the soldiers of the Commonwealth, exasperated by the resistance they had encountered, did much damage to the public buildings, especially to the cathedral, the interior of which magnificent edifice was grievously injured. According to their custom, the troopers stabled their horses in the aisles, and converted the choir into a barrack, and the chapter- house into a guard-room. The organ was destroyed; the rich painted glass of the windows broken ; many monuments mutilated ; and the ancient records preserved in the library burnt. The exquisitely carved stone cross in the churchyard, from the pulpit of which Latimer and Whitgift had preached, was pulled down. Before this, John Prideaux, somewhile Bishop of Worcester, had been deprived of his see, and the dean and prebends dismissed—Church of England divines having given place to Presbyterian ministers, Independents, and Anabaptists.

But notwithstanding their sufferings in the good cause, the loyalty of the Worcester Cavaliers remained unshaken. Heavy fines and im- prisonment could not subdue their spirit. To the last they continued true to the unfortunate king, though any further attempt at rising was checked by the strong garrison left in charge of the city, and com- manded by Colonel John James, one of the strictest of the Republican leaders.

After the terrible tragedy of Whitehall, the Cavaliers of Worcester

 *Contents.*

## BOOK VII.—TRENT.

## BOOK II.—WHITE LADIES.



## BOOK III.—THE ROYAL OAK.

# CONTENTS.

Trent—a most interesting old house. Moseley Hall is still extant: but, alas! Bentley House and Abbots Leigh are gone.

Finer figures do not appear in history than those of the devoted Jane Lane and the stalwart and loyal Penderel Brothers. " The simple rustic who serves his sovereign in time of need to the utmost extent of his ability, is as deserving of commendation as the victorious leader of thousands." So said King Charles the Second to Richard Penderel after the Restoration. It is pleasant to think that several descendants of the loyal family of Penderels are still in existence. With some of them I have been in correspondence.

Good fortune seems to have attended those who aided the fugitive monarch. Many representatives of the old families who assisted him in his misfortunes are to be found—Mr. John Newton Lane, of King's Bromley Hall, near Lichfield, a lineal descendant of the Lanes ; Mr. Tombs, of Long Marston ; Mr. Whitgreave, of Moseley ; the Giffards, of Chillington ; and the ennobled family of Wyndham.

In describing the King's flight from Worcester to White Ladies on the night of the fatal 3rd of September, I have followed exactly the careful topographical description furnished by the Rev. Edward Bradley, Rector of Stretton, Oakham, to *Notes and Queries*, June 13th, 1868. Mr. Bradley has been the first to trace out the King's route, and to him all credit is due.

In describing the old and faithful city of Worcester at the time of the Battle, I have received very great assistance from a distinguished local antiquary, which I have acknowledged in its place.

Never did Charles bear himself better than after the Battle. Though vanquished he was not overcome. Truthfully, though in somewhat high-flown strains, has Cowley sung of him :

> " Yet still great Charles's valour stood the test,
> By fortune though forsaken and opprest.
> Witness the purple-dyed Sabrina's stream,
> And the Red Hill, not called so now in vain.
> And Worcester, thou who didst the misery bear,
> And saw'st the end of a long fatal war."

The Tale closes with the King's departure from Heale. How he journeyed from Salisbury to Brightelmstone, and embarked safely on board Captain Tattersall's bark at Shoreham, I have elsewhere related.

HURSTPIERPOINT, *October* 9, 1872.

# PREFACE.

In his letter to Mr. Hughes, the then Bishop of Llandaff describes King Charles the Second's Wanderings after the Battle of Worcester "as being by far the most romantic piece of English history we possess."

I have always entertained the same opinion, and after reading the "Boscobel Tracts," so admirably edited by Mr. Hughes, I resolved to write a story on the subject, which should comprehend the principal incidents described in the various narratives of the King's adventures ; but not having at that time visited any of the hiding-places, I deferred my design, and possibly might never have executed it, had I not seen a series of Views depicting most graphically the actual state of the different places visited by Charles, and privately published by Mr. Frederick Manning, of Leamington.

Stimulated by these remarkable sketches, I at once commenced my long-delayed Tale.

An enthusiast on the subject, Mr. Manning has collected all the numerous editions of the "Boscobel Tracts," and has printed a list of them, which is exceedingly curious.  The collection is probably unique. His nephew, Mr. John E. Anderdon, whose death occurred while this work was in the press, was also an enthusiastic collector of all matters relating to Boscobel and the King's escapes, and from both these gentlemen I have derived much valuable assistance.

I am under equal obligations to my excellent friend, Mr. Parke, of the Deanery, Wolverhampton, who has furnished me with many curious tracts, prints, plans, and privately printed books relating to Boscobel, Brewood, and Chillington.  I shall always retain a most agreeable recollection of a visit paid to Chillington in company with Mr. Parke and the Hon. Charles Wrottesley, and of our hearty reception by the hospitable Squire.

Among the various works relating to Boscobel that have come under my notice is a charming little volume written by the Rev. George Dodd, Curate of Doddington, Salop, the village where Boscobel is situated, who has ascertained all the facts connected with the story.

Boscobel House, I rejoice to say, is in very good preservation, and I sincerely hope it may not be altered, or *improved*, as is the case with

# BOSCOBEL

OR

## THE ROYAL OAK

A TALE OF THE YEAR 1651

BY

# WILLIAM HARRISON AINSWORTH

AUTHOR OF "THE TOWER OF LONDON"

---

In that fair part where the rich Salop gains
An ample view o'er all the Western plains,
A grove appears which BOSCOBEL they name,
Not known to maps; a grove of scanty fame.
And yet henceforth no celebrated shade
Of all the British groves shall be more glorious made.
COWLEY's *Sylva.* Book VI.

---

LONDON

## GEORGE ROUTLEDGE AND SONS

THE BROADWAY, LUDGATE

NEW YORK 416 BROOME STREET

# NOVELS AT TWO SHILLINGS.—*Continued.*

## By G. P R. JAMES.

The Brigand.
Morley Ernstein.
Darnley.
Richelieu.
The Gipsy.
Arabella Stuart.
The Woodman.
Agincourt.
Russell.

The King's Highway.
Castle of Ehrenstein.
The Stepmother.
Forest Days.
The Huguenot
The Man-at-Arms.
A Whim and its Con-
sequences.
The Convict.

Gowrie.
The Robber.
The Smuggler.
Heidelberg.
The Forgery.
The Gentleman of the
Old School.
Philip Augustus.
The Black Eagle.

## By RICHARDSON. (2s. 6d. each.)

Clarissa Harlowe. | Pamela. | SirCharlesGrandison.

## By Mrs. TROLLOPE.

Petticoat Government.
Widow Barnaby.
Love and Jealousy.

Widow Married.
Barnabys in America.

## By VARIOUS AUTHORS.

Caleb Williams.
Scottish Chiefs.
Torlogh O'Brien.
Hour and the Man,
by Miss Martineau.
Tylney Hall.
Ladder of Gold, by
R. Bell.
Millionaire (The) of
Mincing Lane.
Colin Clink.
Salathiel, byDr. Croly
Clockmaker. (2s. 6d.)
Manœuvring Mother.
Phineas Quiddy.
The Pirate of the
Mediterranean.
The Pride of Life.
Who is to Have it?
The Bashful Irishman.
Deeds, not Words.
The Secret of a Life.
The Iron Cousin; or,
Mutual Influence.
The Young Curate.
The Greatest Plague
of Life, with Cruik-
shank's plates.
The Green Hand.

The Attaché, by Sam
Slick.
Matrimonial Ship-
wrecks.
Lewell Pastures.
Zohrab, the Hostage.
The Two Baronets.
Whom to Marry, with
Cruikshank's plates.
The Man of Fortune.
Letter Bag of the
Great Western.
Black and Gold.
Vidocq, the French
Police Spy.
Singleton Fontenoy.
Lamplighter.
Gideon Giles, the
Roper.
Guy Livingstone.
Sir Victor's Choice.
Outward Bound.
The Flying Dutchman
Dr. Goethe's Court-
ship.
Clives of Burcot.
The Wandering Jew.
Mysteries of Paris.
Land and Sea Tales.

Cruise upon Wheels.
False Colours, by
Annie Thomas.
Nick of the Woods; or,
the Fighting Quaker
Stretton, by Henry
Kingsley.
Mabel Vaughan.
Banim's Peep-o'-Day.
—— Smuggler.
Stuart of Dunleath, by
Hon. Mrs. Norton.
Adventures of a Strol-
ling Player.
Solitary Hunter.
Kaloolah, by W. S.
Mayo.
Patience Strong.
Cavendish, by author
of "Will Watch."
Will Watch, by ditto.
Reminiscences of a
Physician.
Won in a Canter, by
Old Calabar.
Mornings at Bow
Street, with plates
by Geo. Cruikshank

---

**Published by George Routledge and Sons.**

transferred their allegiance to the eldest son of the royal martyr and heir to the crown. All the principal citizens put on mourning, and every countenance, except those of the soldiers of the garrison, wore a sorrowful aspect. A funeral sermon, the text being, " Judge, and avenge my cause, O Lord," was preached by Doctor Crosby, the deprived dean, to a few persons assembled secretly by night in the crypt of the cathedral, and prayers were offered up for the preservation of Prince Charles, and his speedy restoration to the throne. The service, however, was interrupted by a patrol of musketeers, and the dean was seized and lodged in Edgar's Tower, an old fortified gate-house at the entrance of the cathedral close. Never had Worcester been so gloomy and despondent as at this period.

Nor did the hopes of the loyal citizens revive till the middle of August, 1651, when intelligence was received that Charles, who had been recently crowned at Scone, had escaped Cromwell's vigilance, and crossing the border with a considerable army, had pursued the direct route to Lancaster. Thence he continued his rapid march through Preston to Warrington, where he forced the bridge over the Mersey, in spite of the efforts of Generals Lambert and Harrison to arrest his progress. The young king, it was said, was making his way to his faithful city of Worcester, where he meant to establish his head-quarters and recruit his forces before marching on London.

The news seemed too good to be true, yet it obtained ready credence, and it was evident Colonel James believed it, for he forthwith began to put the fortifications in order. The commandant, in fact, had received a despatch from General Lambert, informing him that he and General Harrison had failed in preventing the young King of Scots from passing the bridge over the Mersey at Warrington, and had been disappointed in their expectation that he would give them battle on Knutsford Heath, where they awaited him.

Favoured by night, the young king had continued his march unmolested, it being understood from prisoners they had taken, that he was making for Worcester. Charles Stuart's forces, Lambert said, had been greatly reduced by desertions since he entered England, and now amounted to no more than eight thousand infantry and three thousand horse, and he was only provided with sixteen leathern guns. As yet he had obtained few recruits, the country gentlemen holding aloof, or being prevented by the militia from joining his standard. But the Earl of Derby had undertaken to raise large levies in Lancashire and Cheshire, and had been left behind by the king for that purpose. It was to defeat the earl's design that the two Parliamentary generals deemed it expedient to remain where they were rather than pursue the royal army. Many malignants, Papists, and Presbyterians, ill affected towards the Commonwealth, would doubtless join Lord Derby, who, unless he were speedily discomfited, might become formidable. But discomfited he assuredly would be, and his forces scattered like chaff, since the Lord would fight on the side of his elect. This good work achieved, the two generals would hasten to the relief of Worcester. Speedy succour might also be expected from the Lord General Cromwell, who was in close pursuit of the Scots' king, at the head of twelve thousand cavalry and infantry. Colonel James was, therefore, exhorted to hold out

General Lambert further stated in his despatch, that Charles was accompanied by the most experienced leaders in the Scottish army—by the crafty and cautious Colonel Lesley, who had so long baffled Cromwell himself — by Generals Montgomery, Middleton, Massey, and Dalyell, and by the valiant Colonel Pitscottie, with his Highland regiment. Besides these, there were several English and Scotch nobles, the Dukes of Buckingham and Hamilton, the Earls of Rothes, Lauderdale, Carnworth, and Cleveland; Lords Spyne, Sinclair, and Wilmot; Sir John Douglas, Sir Alexander Forbes, and others.

While scanning this imposing list, and reflecting that the royal forces numbered at least eleven thousand men, Colonel James asked himself how he could possibly hold out against them with a garrison of only five hundred? He was ill supplied with cannon and ammunition, and the fortifications were ruinous. Moreover, the citizens were hostile, and so far from lending him aid, were ready to rise in favour of the king. He should have to contend against foes within as well as enemies without. His position seemed desperate, and though as brave a man as need be, he was filled with misgiving.

Before proceeding it may be proper to ascertain how far the old city was capable of defence. Five years previously it had stood a lengthened siege, but the circumstances then were wholly different, for the citizens were arrayed against the besiegers, and fought obstinately. The walls were much damaged at that time, and had only been partially repaired, consequently the towers and bastions were in a dilapidated state. Outside the walls, on the south-east, there was a strong detached fort of recent construction. The castle, which in days of yore rose proudly on the south side of the cathedral, completely commanding the navigation of the Severn, had long since been pulled down, the only vestiges of it left being some fragments of the donjon. The mound on which the mighty fabric once stood could have been easily fortified, if time had permitted, and would have formed an important work. The city, which was of great antiquity, had four gates, each flanked with towers. The strongest resembled a barbican, and commanded the quay and the ancient stone bridge across the river. On the north was the Foregate, "a fair piece of work," as it is described by old Leland, and not far from it was St. Martin's-gate. On the south was Sidbury-gate, giving access to the London-road. The Sidbury-gate was covered by the modern detached fort to which reference has already been made. Deep dykes, supplied by the Severn, strengthened the defences on the east and south-east, but the suburbs constituted a danger, since the habitations would afford shelter to an enemy. Thus it will be seen that the city was not in a condition to stand a siege, and the commandant might well despair of holding out, even for a few days, against the royal forces.

No city can be more charmingly situated than Worcester on the banks of England's noblest river, in the midst of fair and fertile plains, abounding in orchards and hop-gardens, and in full view of the lovely Malvern Hills; but in the middle of the seventeenth century it was eminently picturesque, as well as beautiful. It was then full of ancient timber houses, with quaintly carved gables and open balconies, from the midst of which rose the massive roof and tower of the venerable cathedral, and the lofty spire of St. Andrew's Church. The old walls, grey and ruinous as they were, the fortified gates, the sculptured crosses, and the antique stone bridge, with its many-pointed arches, contributed to its beauty. The noble episcopal palace, the group of old buildings near the cathedral, and the ruins on the Castle Hill—all formed a striking picture when seen from St. John's on the opposite side of the river.

"The wealth of Worcester standeth most by drapery," quoth old Leland, who wrote in Henry VIII.'s time, amd the place had long been noted for its broadcloths and gloves. But many of the wealthiest drapers, glovers, and hop-merchants had been ruined by the heavy fines inflicted upon them by the grasping Parliamentarians, and the city had scarcely yet regained its former prosperity.

Almost simultaneously with the arrival of General Lambert's despatch, a letter was brought by a secret messenger to Mr. Thomas Lysons, then mayor of Worcester, and an avowed Royalist. It came from Captain Fanshawe, the king's secretary, and gave a very different version of the affair at Warrington from that furnished by Lambert.

According to Fanshawe his majesty had displayed great personal courage on the occasion. He found the enemy, consisting of about seven thousand men, united under Lambert and Harrison, in possession of the bridge across the Mersey, which they had partly broken down, and he immediately attacked them with his advanced troops. His impetuosity proved irresistible. A passage being forced, the whole army followed, and the enemy retreated in great disorder, and with heavy losses. During the night, upwards of three thousand of the "rebellious rogues," as Fanshawe styled them, disbanded. The Parliamentary generals did not venture to attack the king again, but allowed him to continue his march towards Worcester without further interruption. The faithful citizens might, therefore, prepare to welcome their sovereign, who would soon be with them.

The mayor immediately called a public meeting in the Guildhall, and read Captain Fanshawe's letter to the assemblage. Great was the enthusiasm excited by it. The hall resounded with cries of "Long live Charles II.!" The joyful intelligence quickly spread throughout the city, and crowds collected in the High-street, shouting "Down with the Commonwealth! Up with the Crown!" The concourse was dispersed by Colonel James and a troop of horse, but in the conflict several persons were wounded, and some killed. The mayor and the sheriff, Mr. James Bridges, were seized, and detained as hostages for the good behaviour of the citizens—the commandant threatening to hang them both if any further disturbance occurred. Luckily for the two gentlemen, the city remained tranquil throughout the night, for most assuredly the commandant would have been as good as his word.

Next day—Friday the 22nd of August, 1651—the scouts sent out by Colonel James reported that the first division of the royal army, commanded by the young king in person, was close upon Red Hill—already described as a woody eminence about a mile distant, on the south of the city.

Shortly afterwards, the enemy's cavalry skirmishers could be distinguished on Perry Wood. Then the advanced guard appeared—the helmets and corslets of the cuirassiers glittering in the sunbeams. Thousands of loyal citizens, who were forbidden to mount the fortifications, climbed to the roofs of the houses, and to the tops of the churches, to obtain a glimpse of the royal army, and could not restrain their enthusiastic feeling when they beheld it.

Colonel James, who had been actively employed throughout the whole night in making the best defensive preparations in his power, had seen that all the engineers on the ramparts were at their posts, and he now proceeded to the detached fort near the Sidbury-gate.

Mounting to the summit, which bristled with cannon, he turned his spy-glass towards the brow of the hill opposite to him, and presently beheld a company of richly accoutred officers ride out of the wood that clothed the eminence, and proceed to reconnoitre the fortifications from various points. That the foremost of the troop was the young king himself he had no doubt, as well from the splendour of his accoutrements, and the white plume in his hat, as from the deference paid him by his attendants. Evidently his majesty's brilliant staff was composed of the general officers and nobles mentioned in General Lambert's despatch. That they were planning the attack of the city was clear.

While watching the young monarch's movements and gestures narrowly through his glass, Colonel James saw him sign to one of his aides-de-camp, a fine-looking young man, and remarkably well mounted, who instantly rode up at the summons.

Major Careless, the aide-de-camp in question, was as brave as he was handsome, though somewhat rash, and an especial favourite of the king. Having received his majesty's orders, he promptly obeyed them. Accompanied only by a trumpeter bearing a flag of truce, he galloped down the hill, shaping his course towards the Sidbury-gate, and, within fifty yards of it, he halted, and the trumpeter blew a blast so loud that the old walls rang again.

A shower of bullets from the battlements would have answered the summons, if Colonel James had not previously sent word that the flag of truce must be respected.

The men eyed the insolent Cavalier sternly, and one of them called out, "If thou hast any message for the commandant of the garrison, he will be found in yonder fort."

Thereupon Careless moved off, glancing haughtily and contemptuously at the artillerymen on the ramparts as he rode along.

On reaching the fort, he descried Colonel James stationed near the edge of the parapets, and leaning upon his sword. Half a dozen musketeers in their steel caps, buff coats, and bandileers, were standing behind him.

" Are you the commandant ?" he called out.

" Ay," replied Colonel James. " What wouldst thou with me ?"

" Thus much," said Careless, in a loud authoritative voice : " In the name of his majesty, King Charles II., who is on yonder hill with his army, I require you to deliver up this his city of Worcester, which you unlawfully hold as deputy of a presumptuous and rebellious parliament. His majesty is willing to extend his clemency towards you, and if you at once throw open the gates, and lay down your arms——"

" Hold !" interrupted the commandant, sternly. " I do not recognise the authority of him whom thou stylest king. The house of Jeroboam, who sinned, and who caused Israel to sin, has been cut off. I will not deny that the young man, Charles Stuart, has been crowned in Scotland, but in England he hath no rule. His proclamation has been burnt by the common hangman in London, and a counter-proclamation published by the Parliament, declaring him, his aiders and abettors—of whom thou, thyself, art one—guilty of high treason against the State, and punishable by death. Shall I, an officer of the Commonweath, and intrusted with the charge of this city, open its gates to a proclaimed traitor ? Shall I command my men to lay down their arms to him ? Not so. I utterly disregard thy king's summons, and though he be backed by the whole Scottish host, yet will I not yield the city to him, but placing my trust in the Lord, will maintain it against him."

" Provoke not the king by your obstinacy," said Careless, losing patience. " If you force us to storm the fortifications, you can expect no quarter. We will put you all to the sword."

Perfectly unmoved by the threat, Colonel James answered, in the religious jargon then habitually adopted by the Republican soldiers :

" The Lord of Hosts is with us. The God of Jacob is our refuge. I doubt not we shall have timely succour."

" From whom ?" demanded Careless, with a sneer.

" From the Lord General Cromwell, who is hastening hither with his legions."

" The city will be ours, and thou and thy rebel horde will be destroyed ere that arch-traitor and parricide can arrive," cried Careless, fiercely.

" Keep guard upon thy tongue, or I will not answer for thy safety," said the commandant, checking the musketeers behind him, who were preparing to give fire. " Take back my answer to the king, thy master. I have nothing to add to it."

" We will soon be with you," shouted Careless.

And, shaking his hand menacing'y at the soldiers, he rode off with his attendant.

While this interview took place, Charles remained on Perry Wood with his generals. He was not in the least surprised to learn from Careless that his gracious offer had been rejected by the commandant.

" Let the attack be made at once," he cried. " I will lead it in person."

" I admire your majesty's spirit," observed General Dalyell. " But I pray you not to run so much risk."

" Risk, say you ?" cried Charles, gaily. " Faith, Tom, you would have all the credit of the affair. But you shall not rob me of it. I mean to be first to enter yonder fort."

Generals Middleton and Montgomery likewise attempted to dissuade him from his purpose, but ineffectually.

The general officers then rode off to give the necessary orders for the attack. Trumpets were sounded, and shortly afterwards the sides of the hill were covered with troops in rapid movement. Ere they got half-way down, the guns of the fort opened upon them, but did not check their progress. Presently the artillery of the Royalists returned the fire of the Republicans, and the king, who was at the head of the advanced guard, saw the cannon pointed.

His majesty being recognised, the commandant directed the mus-keteers on the ramparts to make him their mark ; but he really seemed to bear a charmed life, for though an officer close beside him was hit by a round shot, and his own horse was killed under him, he himself was uninjured.

The leathern guns of the Royalists were worked so well, that three of the fort guns were speedily silenced, and Charles then ordered instant preparations to be made for the assault.

Scaling-ladders were placed against the walls. Several men were struck down while executing this perilous task, but no sooner was it accomplished than Charles caused the trumpet to be sounded, and sword in hand, mounted the nearest ladder.

A soldier, armed with a pike, strove to hurl him from the ladder, but the man was shot by Careless, who followed the king closely.

Again, while springing over the parapets, Charles was opposed by a musketeer, but he cut him down, and next moment the heroic young monarch was joined by Careless, and instantly afterwards by a dozen of his body-guard, and their number was quickly augmented.

Charles was now master of the fort, for the Republican soldiers, after an ineffectual resistance, were put to the sword.

In the struggle, Colonel James discharged a pistol at the king, but missed his mark, and in his turn was attacked by Careless.

"I told you we would soon be with you," cried the Cavalier. "Yield, and I will spare thy life."

"I would not accept life at thy hands," rejoined the commandant. "Look to thyself!"

And beating down Careless's point with his heavy blade, he stepped quickly backwards and disappeared. He had, in fact, dashed down a narrow staircase communicating with the lower chambers of the fort, and secured his retreat by pulling a trap-door over the entrance.

Meanwhile, Charles had torn down the flag of the Commonwealth, and replaced it by the royal standard. As soon as this signal of victory could be distinguished by his forces loud cheers were raised. Possession was immediately taken of the fort, but no prisoners were made, for Co-lonel James, and the few of his men left alive, had evacuated the lower chambers. They had fled, it appeared, by a covered way, and had entered the city through a postern near the Sidbury-gate.

By-and-bye the general officers came to congratulate the king on his victory and express their admiration of his prowess, and it then became a question whether the siege should be continued—General Dalyell being of opinion that the city could be captured before night, if an immediate attack were made upon the fortifications ; but Charles decided on waiting till the morrow.

" I have done enough for the day," he said.   " Since I am master of this fort, the city is at my disposal, and I can occupy it at my leisure."

" Very true, my liege," observed Dalyell.   " But the garrison will take advantage of your forbearance to escape."

" I will not molest them if they adopt that prudent course," said the king, laughing.   " They have ceased firing from the walls."

" But the men are still at their posts."

" If they give us any further trouble, we can turn these guns upon them.   Hark ye, gentlemen.   Henceforth this fort shall be known as Fort Royal."

" A fitting designation, since your majesty has captured it," said Dalyell.

" Let the tents be pitched," said Charles.   " The day's work is over. We can take our rest after our long march.   To-morrow we will enter the city in triumph."

All happened precisely as Charles had foreseen.   Not another shot was fired by the Republicans.   The Royalists encamped quietly on the hill.   But though no apprehensions were entertained of an attack, those within Fort Royal were kept on the alert through the night.

Colonel James, however, had other designs.   Convinced by what had happened that the fortifications were no longer tenable, he decided on abandoning them.   With the whole of his men, he quitted the city secretly at dead of night, taking the mayor and the sheriff with him as prisoners.   Crossing the bridge over the Severn, he rode off in the direction of Gloucester.

The Royalists were aware of his retreat, but, in obedience to the king's injunctions, did not seek to interrupt him.

---

## CHAPTER II.

SHOWING HOW THE MAYOR OF WORCESTER AND THE SHERIFF WERE TAKEN TO UPTON-ON-SEVERN, AND HOW THEY GOT BACK AGAIN.

FATIGUED by his long march of three hundred miles and upwards, Charles slept so soundly in his tent on Perry Wood, that neither the beating of the drum at daybreak, the challenging of the sentinels, nor any of the customary camp sounds, disturbed him.   The men themselves answered very reluctantly to the reveillé.   However, the fresh morning air soon revived them.   A day of ease and enjoyment lay before them. No more toilsome marches, no more skirmishes, but rest—for that day, at least.   Two-thirds of the infantry were without shoes, but being hardy Scots they did not count this an inconvenience.   They all bemoaned the ragged and weather-stained condition of their uniforms, but they had heard that Worcester was famous for broadcloth, and the king had promised them better garments when they reached the city.

The morn was lovely, and gave promise of a splendid day.  At that early hour the view from the heights of the old and picturesque city, with the broad river flowing past it, was enchanting, and delighted even the rough soldiers who gazed at it.  The fair Malvern Hills, however, chiefly called forth their admiration as reminding them of their native mountains, though they admitted that few of the Scottish valleys could compare with the fertile vale of the Severn.

While many a greedy eye was fixed on Worcester, and many a cunning tongue was talking of its wealth, and the plunder it would yield, if they were only allowed to pillage it, the attention of the soldiers was attracted to the walls, which had now become thronged with the citizens and their wives and daughters, while all the church bells—and no church in the old city lacked its proper complement of bells—began to ring forth joyous peals.  It was clear that the city was now awake and astir, and the half-famished soldiers hoped that immediate preparations would be made for their refreshment, and on an extraordinary scale.

It was about this time that Major Careless, who had attired himself rather hurriedly, being excited by the prodigious clangour of the bells, entered the king's tent, and found the young monarch fast asleep—fast as a top.

"Zounds!" mentally ejaculated the aide-de-camp; "his majesty must sleep soundly, since this din does not disturb him—but no wonder. I'll give him another hour."

And he turned to depart, when Charles suddenly ceased breathing hard, and opened his eyes.

"What sound is that?" he cried, raising himself on his elbow and listening.

"The bells of Worcester ringing for your majesty's glorious victory—that's all," replied Careless.

"And enough too," cried the king, looking well pleased.  "What has happened to the garrison?"

"Evacuated the fortifications—taken to flight."

"Just what I expected—just what I desired."

"But your majesty did not expect—nor, I presume, desire—that Colonel James would take the mayor of Worcester and the sheriff with him."

"'Sdeath!" exclaimed the king.  "Has he had the audacity to do so?"

"Even so, my liege.  No doubt they were specially obnoxious to him on account of their loyalty, and he might wish to hold them for ransom. 'Tis lucky he didn't carry off others.  There are several prisoners of note in Worcester—Lord Talbot, Sir John Pakington, and Colonel Mervin Touchet.  But the rascal contented himself with the mayor and the sheriff. At what hour will it please your majesty to enter the city?"

"At noon," replied Charles.

"Not till noon! why, we have no rations," cried Careless, in dismay. "Your army has nothing to eat.  Will your majesty keep the men fasting till noon?  If you could only see how hungry they look, you would feel some pity for them."

"They shall all have a good breakfast in Worcester—that I promise them."

" There will be plenty of grumbling at the delay."

" Bah ! they always grumble.   I must give my loyal subjects time to decorate their houses and make all necessary preparations for my entrance, or I shall disappoint them of their anticipated spectacle."

" Your hungry soldiers will pray that twelve o'clock may come."

" Let them listen to the bells.   How blithely they sound !"

" Excuse me, sire.   When we are enduring the pangs of hunger the sweetest sounds become a mockery.   Spare us this aggravated torture."

" Leave me ; and let it be announced by sound of trumpet throughout the lines that we shall make our triumphal entrance into Worcester at noon."

As Careless went forth on his errand with a dissatisfied look Charles sprang from his couch, and with the aid of a groom of the chamber and a page, for he had brought a large retinue of servants with him on his march, proceeded to dress himself, bestowing infinitely more care on the decoration of his person than he had done since he left Scotland.

His tall, fine figure was well displayed in doublet and hose of crimson velvet and white satin ; his yellow maroquin boots were deeply fringed with lace, and he wore point-lace at his wrists and around his throat. His shoulder-knot was enriched with diamonds, his sword-hilt glittered with gems, and his plumed hat was looped up by a large diamond brooch. His long black locks were worn in the true Cavalier fashion, and fell over his shoulders.   All his princely ornaments were put on for the occasion, the Garter, the George of Diamonds, and the Blue Riband.

Charles was then in the heyday of his youth, being just twenty-one. Though his features were harsh—the nose being too large, and not well-shaped—and his complexion swarthy as that of a Spanish gipsy, his large black eyes, full of fire and spirit, gave wonderful expression to his countenance, and made him, at times, look almost handsome. His manner was singularly affable and agreeable, and very different from the cold, repelling stateliness of his ill-fated father.

The young king was adjusting his mantle before the little mirror hung up in the tent preparatory to going forth, when a noise outside attracted his attention.

Next moment Major Careless entered the tent, his looks beaming with satisfaction.

" How now, Will !" cried the king.   " Have you found a breakfast that you look so gay ?"

" No, my liege, but I have found the mayor and the sheriff, and that is more to the purpose.   They have escaped from the commandant, and have ridden up from Worcester to pay their homage to you, and relate their adventures."

" Are they without ?"

" Just alighted, sire.   They are in a sorry plight, but in their zeal to attend upon your majesty they would not tarry to change, and hope you will excuse them."

" Excuse them ! marry will I !   I shall be delighted to receive them. Bring them at once."

The two gentlemen were then introduced, and their habiliments undoubtedly bore traces of the hardships they had undergone. But Charles was better pleased to see them thus than if they had been in their robes of office, and said so.

Mr. Lysons, the mayor of Worcester, and a wealthy draper of the city, was a middle-aged man, but strong and active, and had a ruddy, pleasant countenance. Mr. Bridges, the sheriff, and by trade a glover, was a few years younger than the mayor, and not quite so stout. Both of them had looked exhausted when they arrived, but they brightened up wonderfully as they entered the king's presence.

Charles advanced to meet them, and gave them his hand to kiss in the most gracious manner possible. After congratulating them heartily on their escape, he inquired, with an air of much interest, how they had contrived it.

" Your majesty shall hear," replied the mayor. " It will always be a feather in our cap to have escaped from Colonel James. With what particular object he carried us off we know not, but it is certain he meant to take us to Gloucester. Shortly after midnight we were brought out of Edgar's Tower, where we had been imprisoned, and were strictly guarded by the troopers as we rode out of the city, but no attempt whatever at rescue was made by our fellow-citizens. Probably no one knew at the time that we were being carried off. Little did we dream as we rode across the bridge that we should be back so soon.

" A dreary ride we had, and our thoughts, which were not very pleasant, were disturbed by those psalm-singing Puritans. They did not speak very respectfully of your majesty. But we told them a day of reckoning was at hand, and that you would drive them all before you. ' Let him first set your worship free, and his honour the sheriff,' said one of the troopers—a snuffling rogue, whom his comrades called Ezra. ' Ay, let him follow us to Gloucester,' observed another, who was very appropriately named Madmannah. ' Be sure that he will follow, and force you to evacuate the city, as you have done Worcester,' I rejoined. In such pleasantries the time was passed.

" A halt was made at Upton-on-Severn. Now the Roundheads have no especial dislike to ale and cider, and do not hold it sinful to indulge in those liquors if good. Knowing the drink they delight in was to be had in perfection at the Red Lion, at Upton, they roused the house, and compelled the host and tapster to broach a cask of stout March ale, and another of cider. The troopers then dismounted, and tied up their horses while they emptied their cans, leaving us to the care of Ezra and Madmannah.

" Apparently, no one suspected us of any attempt to escape ; yet we were already meditating flight, if any favourable opportunity should occur. By the light of the lanterns we could see the men filling their cans. The temptation soon became too strong for Madmannah. He joined the others, but soon returned with a bottle of cider for Ezra. While they were enjoying the pleasant drink, we suddenly broke away and plunged into a hop-garden that adjoined the inn-yard. Both musketeers fired at us, but did us no harm. Fortunately the night was dark, and we were screened by the tall hop-poles.

" Alarmed by the firing, several other musketeers joined in the pur-

suit, but they got into each other's way, and created great confusion, in
the midst of which we reached a wood, and being well acquainted with
the locality, made our way for the meadows on the banks of the Severn.
Then we were safe.

"After keeping in these meadows for two or three miles, we ventured on the high road, and galloped off at full speed for Worcester,
without hearing anything more of the troopers or their commander.
We caught sight of the old city just at daybreak.   'Here we are back
again, after only a few hours' absence,' I remarked, as we passed
through the barbican at the head of the old bridge.   'Who would have
thought it!'   'Not I,' replied the sheriff.   'We are in ample time for
the rejoicings on his majesty's glorious victory.'   'What if we ride up
to the camp on Perry Wood, and seek an audience of him?' I remarked.
'Not in this plight,' said Mr. Bridges.   'His majesty will excuse us,'
I replied."

"Ay, that I will, my good friends," cried Charles   "I am truly glad
that you came to me at once.   With such subjects as you I shall never
stand upon ceremony.   I have long known you both as two of the king
my father's most faithful adherents."

"We are equally devoted to the king, your father's son, my liege,"
rejoined the mayor.   "And now, having been honoured by this audience, we will return to the city and prepare for your majesty's
reception."

"Before you take your departure, gentlemen," interposed Careless,
"permit me to remark to you that the entire army is without provisions.   The sooner, therefore, you can prepare for us the better."

"We will expedite matters as much as possible," said the mayor.
"But I am afraid we shall require three or four hours."

"His majesty's forces number eleven thousand men, as I understand,"
said the sheriff.   "It will be impossible to provide for so many without
some little delay."

"Quite impossible," observed the king.   "I will only beg you, as
my loving subjects, to treat my Scottish soldiers hospitably, even if you
make a great sacrifice."

"Your majesty shall have no ground of complaint," said both magis-
trates.

"There is a point on which I must address a caution to you," pursued Charles.   "The greater part of my army, as you are doubtless
aware, is composed of members of the Scottish Kirk.   They are bitter
sectarians, ever ready to dispute on religious questions, and to reprove
those who differ from them.   Prevent, if you can, all quarrels among
them and your fellow-citizens."

"We have had plague enough already with those Anabaptists,
Presbyterians, and Independents," said the sheriff.   "I am happy to say
there are very few left in faithful Worcester now we are rid of the garrison.   We will not quarrel with the Scots, since they have come hither
with your majesty.   At noon all shall be ready for your reception."

Making a profound reverence to the king, the two gentlemen then
withdrew, accompanied by Careless.

The king had lost his favourite charger at the attack on the fort on the previous day; but another steed, in no respect inferior, had been supplied him by the Duke of Buckingham, and mounted on his new acquisition, he now proceeded to make an inspection of the camp. He was attended by all his general officers, and by the nobles who had accompanied him in his march from Scotland.

The men had begun to strike the tents at Perry Wood; for it had been decided by his majesty, after consultation with Lesley, Middleton, and Massey, that the main body of the army should be moved lower down the hill, and not far from the Sidbury-gate, while Dalyell, with his brigade, should fix his quarters at St. John's on the right bank of the river, and Middleton, with two thousand men, should encamp on the Pitchcroft, a large plain, extremely convenient for the purpose, on the north of the city, and on the left bank of the Severn.

Having completed his tour of inspection, Charles rode down with his staff to Fort Royal; and he was surveying the scene of his late brilliant exploit, and receiving fresh compliments from his attendants, when he was surprised to see Careless come forth.

" What are you doing here ?" he demanded.

" Breakfast is served, sire," replied the aide-de-camp.

" Breakfast !" exclaimed Charles.

" By St. George ! I am glad to hear it," cried the Duke of Buckingham, Lord Wilmot, and several others. " I hope there is enough for us all."

" Enough and to spare," replied Careless.

Amid general exclamations of satisfaction the king and those with him then dismounted, and were conducted by Careless into a large chamber, where a plentiful repast awaited them.

---

## CHAPTER III.

HOW CHARLES MADE HIS TRIUMPHAL ENTRY INTO WORCESTER ; AND HOW HE WAS PROCLAIMED BY THE MAYOR AND SHERIFF OF THAT LOYAL CITY.

MEANWHILE, an almost indescribable scene of bustle and confusion was taking place within the city.

The pealing of bells, which, as we know, commenced at the earliest hour of morning, continued almost without intermission. Great fires were lighted on the Castle Hill, in the cathedral close, on the quays, and at Pitchcroft, at which huge joints of meat were roasted— barons of beef, entire muttons, barbecued hogs. All loyal citizens were enjoined by the mayor to provide the best food they could, and in the greatest quantity, for the king's army. It would be a lasting disgrace to them, it was said, if any of their brave deliverers should be stinted.

While part of each household was busily dressing food, the others were engaged in decorating the habitations. The balconies were hung with tapestry, gaily-coloured cloths and carpets, and the crosses were adorned with flowers. The royal standard floated over the Sidbury-gate, as well as on the summit of Fort Royal, and flags were flying from all the steeples.

Such extraordinary zeal and activity were displayed, that, long before the appointed hour, all the preparations were completed, and the good folks began to be impatient for the coming of their sovereign.

The entire host was now gathered on the hill-side, and presented a magnificent spectacle, as viewed from the city walls, which were densely thronged. The Sidbury-gate was thrown wide open, a guard of halberdiers being drawn up on either side of the entrance; while the mayor, the sheriff, and the aldermen, in their full robes of office, were stationed beneath the archway.

At length the sound of martial music was heard, and a squadron of glittering cuirassiers was seen riding down the hill. Then came Charles, attended by his staff, and followed by Colonel Pitscottie's regiment of Highlanders. The strange, picturesque garb, and unusual weapons of these stalwart mountaineers—their claymores, dirks, and targets—filled the beholders with amazement. Nor were the citizens less astonished by the shrill, warlike notes of the bagpipes, which they heard for the first time.

As soon as it was perceived that the king had set out, a loud discharge of cannon took place from the walls; and this, if possible, heightened the general excitement. Regiment after regiment—cavalry and infantry—were now moving down the hill—colours flying, bands playing—the accoutrements of the cavalry flashing in the sunbeams like so many mirrors.

The splendour of the king's staff produced an immense effect—some of the nobles being singularly fine-looking men. Indeed, the Duke of Buckingham, who rode at the head of the brilliant cortége with the Duke of Hamilton, was accounted the handsomest and most accomplished Cavalier of his time. Lord Wilmot was also a noble-looking personage—tall and well-proportioned. Foremost among the military leaders rode General David Lesley, who commanded one division of the Scottish army. Thin and stern-looking, he had a thoughtful cast of countenance. With him was Major-General Montgomery, who had strongly-marked features and a keen eye, and looked like a thorough soldier. Then came Lieutenant-General Thomas Dalyell, who had served with distinction under Charles I., and in whom the young king placed much confidence. With Dalyell was Vandrose, a Dutch general. Generals Middleton and Massey brought up the list.

Despite the rich apparel of the nobles and the splendid accoutrements of the general officers, none of them pleased the beholders so much—especially the female portion of them—as Colonel Pitscottie, who, as he rode at the head of his Highlanders, look the beau ideal of a Scottish chieftain. He was strongly built, with a red beard, and light blue eyes of extraordinary power. Pitscottie was as brave as a lion, and as true as his own sword. Such were the distinguished persons on whom the spectators gazed from the city walls.

The whole space between the Sidbury-gate and the ancient Commandery was thronged, but a space was kept clear for the king, and for the passage of the troops, by halberdiers placed at frequent intervals.

Here Charles was detained for a few minutes by the enthusiastic demonstrations of the crowd, who would scarcely allow him to proceed. They shouted, stretched out their arms towards him, and hailed him as their rightful sovereign and their deliverer. He could not fail to be touched by such manifestations of loyalty. Though the sun was pouring down his fiercest radiance upon his jet-black locks, he remained uncovered all the time, and bowed round repeatedly with the grace peculiar to him.

As soon as he was able to move forward, the mayor, with the sheriff and aldermen, advanced from the gateway to meet him, and, bowing reverentially, bade him welcome to the city.

" The city of Worcester has ever been faithful to you, sire," said the mayor, " though constrained to yield to superior force. We now joyfully open our gates to you and your victorious army, and pray you to enter the city."

" I thank you heartily for your welcome, Mr. Mayor and gentlemen," replied Charles. " I never doubted your loyalty and devotion. The king, my father, always spoke of Worcester as his ' Faithful City.' I shall never speak of it otherwise. Again I thank you for the reception you accord me. It is precisely what I expected from you."

Loud acclamations followed these gracious words, which were delivered with admirable effect by the young monarch.

With the utmost despatch, the mayor and the civic authorities then mounted their steeds, which were in readiness for them, and preceded the king as he entered the city, the mayor carrying the sword of state before his majesty.

Trumpets were blown, drums beaten, and the bells, which had been silent during the ceremonial at the gate, began to peal joyfully again as the royal cortége moved up Sidbury-street, and shaped its course to the High-street, which it speedily reached. This long and handsome street, which runs through the centre of the city from the cathedral to the Foregate, is now totally changed in appearance, though it occupies pretty nearly the same ground as heretofore. The ancient street, however, being incomparably more picturesque and striking than the modern thoroughfare, its demolition cannot but be regretted. The houses, as already mentioned, were built of oak, painted black and white, in the charming fashion of the period, though not according to any uniform design, so as to avoid a monotonous effect. In many instances they were richly ornamented with curious and elaborate carvings. One peculiarity belonging to them, and constituting a great charm, was the possession of open balconies ; and these were now, for the most part, filled with well-dressed dames and damsels, some of whom boasted considerable personal attractions. Worcester, it is well known, has been at all times famous for pretty women. The rails of the balconies were hung with tapestry, carpets, and rich stuffs, and these decorations gave the street a very lively appearance. The concourse on the footways contented themselves with cheering the king as he passed along, and did not attempt to press upon him, while the damsels waved their kerchiefs from above. Had Charles been the handsomest young prince in Christendom (which he certainly was not), he could not have captivated more hearts than he did as he rode along the High-street, and gazed at the well-filled balconies on the right and left. Each fair nymph on whom his eye rested for a moment fancied herself the special object of his admiration, while many a one— perhaps with some reason—believed she had been distinguished by a bow from his majesty.

In this manner Charles rode on—receiving fresh homage from all classes of his subjects as he proceeded—till he came to the Guildhall, where the civic authorities had already halted, and where he himself alighted, in order to sign certain warrants. Like almost all the other edifices in the street, the Guildhall has been rebuilt, and though we have every respect for the modern fabric, we should have been better pleased if the ancient structure, with its recollections of the past, had been preserved. Allowing the mayor and his fellows to conduct his majesty into the great hall, we shall leave them there, having more to interest us outside.

Troops were now pouring into the city, and were marching in different directions; some regiments being taken by their officers to the Castle Hill, others to the cathedral close, aud others to the quays—at all of which places good eatables and drinkables, and in the greatest abundance, were provided for them. On that day, in all parts of the city, thousands of hungry soldiers were feasted—every house being open to them. And to the credit of the Scots, it must be stated, that they in no wise abused the hospitality shown them.

While his majesty was signing the warrants in the Guildhall, a halt took place in the High-street, and when thus seen from above, the various regiments of horse and foot, with their flags and banners, now forming an almost solid mass, presented a splendid spectacle. A good deal of animated conversation between the officers and the damsels in the balconies took place during this interval, and some amusing incidents occurred, one of which must be related.

Among the spectators collected nearly opposite the Guildhall were an elderly dame and an exceedingly pretty damsel—the old woman's grand-daughter, as it turned out. They evidently belonged to the middle classes. With them was a sallow, ill-favoured personage, whose closely-cropped black hair, steeple-crowned hat, plain Geneva band, and black cloak, proclaimed him a Puritan. It was certain that he was passionately enamoured of the damsel, whom he addressed by the name of Mary, for he watched her every look with jealous eyes; but it was by no means equally certain that she returned his passion. Rather the contrary, we should say.

Urso Gives, for so was pretty Mary's suitor named, was more than double her age, and far from well-favoured, but he was tolerably rich, and this was enough for Dame Rushout, Mary's grandmother.

Urso Gives was a tailor, and had prospered in his business. For a knight of the thimble, he was not devoid of mettle, and somewhat quarrelsome and vindictive. He was decidedly a Republican, and in religion an Independent. As may be imagined, this was a bitter day for him, and he would not have come forth upon it had it not been to watch over pretty Mary Rushout, who was determined to see the young king. So he was compelled to place Mary and her grand-dame in a good position opposite the Guildhall, and there they had an excellent view of the young monarch, and saw him dismount.

Mary Rushout was enchanted. Never had she beheld any one so graceful, so majestic as the king. How royally he bestrode his steed! How beauteous were his long black locks!—Urso must let his own hair grow long. And then how his majesty's diamonds sparkled! She could not help calling out " Long live the king!" Charles noticed her, and told her, with a smile, " She was the prettiest girl he had seen that day, and deserved a better lover." Was not this enough to turn her head? Was it not enough to madden the irritable and jealous Urso? The by-standers, who were staunch Royalists, laughed at him, and this exasperated Urso beyond all endurance. He broke out against the king, called him the chief of the malignants, and the favourer of heresy and profaneness, and would have gone on in the same strain if he had not been soundly buffeted on all sides.

Mary Rushout and her grand-dame screamed, and their cries attracted the attention of an aide-de-camp, who was waiting his majesty's return. It was Major Careless. Seeing a pretty girl in distress he pushed forward his steed, and quickly extricated her and the old dame, while Urso took advantage of his interference to escape.

A cavalier so gallant as Careless we may be sure did not retire after such an introduction, and he found Mary Rushout very willing to flirt with him. He soon learned all about her and about Urso Gives, and that they both dwelt in the Trinity, and continued chatting with her till Charles came forth from the Guildhall.

The royal cortége was once more put in motion, and proceeded to the large open place near the Foregate, in the midst of which stood the antique sculptured cross previously mentioned. The place was now filled with people, but the assemblage was no farther disturbed than was necessary to allow the troops to form a square round it.

The mayor and the sheriff having made their way to the cross, trumpets were sounded, and, amid the silence that ensued, the mayor, in a sonorous voice, proclaimed Charles King of England, Scotland, France, and Ireland. Tremendous acclamations followed, and guns were fired from the top of the Foregate.

Even then the assemblage did not move, nor did the troops quit their position.

Trumpets being again sounded, a Manifesto was published in the king's name, declaring a general pardon to all the inhabitants of the city as should henceforward conform to his authority ; and also announcing that warrants had just received the royal sign-manual in the Guildhall, whereby his majesty summoned, upon their allegiance, all the nobility, gentry, and others, of what degree and condition soever, of the county of Worcester, from sixteen to sixty, to appear in their persons, and with any horses, arms, and ammunition they had or could procure, at Pitchcroft, near the city, on Tuesday next, being the 26th of August, 1651, "where," pursued the king, "ourself will be present to dispose of such of them as we shall think fit for our service in the war, in defence of this City and County, and to add to our marching army."

On the king's return to the city, the mayor ceremoniously conducted him to his private residence, where a grand collation had been prepared, of which his majesty and his suite partook.

## CHAPTER IV.

### HOW CHARLES WAS LODGED IN THE EPISCOPAL PALACE ; AND HOW DOCTOR CROSBY PREACHED BEFORE HIS MAJESTY IN THE CATHEDRAL.

THE ancient episcopal palace—which had been prepared, as well as circumstances would permit, for the reception of the king and his suite —was a large and stately pile, and, from its size, grandeur, and the number of apartments it contained, was well fitted to be the temporary residence of a monarch—even had that monarch been firmly settled on the throne—and, indeed, it was again occupied by royalty at a later date, when George III. and his queen visited Worcester in 1788. By far the most important mansion in the city, it occupied a commanding position on the left bank of the river, and from its fine bay windows presented a very imposing façade. The roof was lined with battlements, towers, and belfries, and on the highest of these towers the royal standard now floated, while sentries were stationed at the river gate, and at the upper gateway. The palace was surrounded by high embattled walls, within which was a garden laid out in the old formal style, and boasting a broad terrace. The garden had been utterly neglected by the Roundheads, and the terrace was covered with grass. Internally the mansion, which was erected probably about the beginning of the sixteenth century, contained a noble hall, with a richly carved screen, an exquisite chapel, a carved oak staircase of great beauty, conducting to a long gallery, the deeply embayed windows of which, while they embellished the exterior, commanded fine views of the country, and the broad intermediate tract once known as Malvern Chase, but now a most fertile district, through which, as Dyer sings,

——the wide
Majestic wave of Severn slowy rolls.

Considerable damage had been done to the gallery and the rooms opening from it by the Roundheads, who had torn down the fine old tapestry once adorning the oak panels, and injured the carvings. Most of the old furniture, being of oak, had withstood a great deal of barbarous usage, and an immense ponderous bedstead, in which many a bishop had reposed, was prepared for his majesty. A good many other beds had to be provided for the king's suite, and for his large retinue of servants, but this was satisfactorily accomplished, and luckily there were rooms enough to accommodate all. Fortunately, also, the mansion possessed a vast kitchen, having no fewer than three large grates, whence hospitality had been dispensed by the worthy prelates in the olden time. At these three grates cooks had been at work, roasting and boiling, throughout the day.

The first persons presented to the king on his arrival at the palace were Lord Talbot, Sir John Pakington, and Colonel Mervin Touchet, who had been kept prisoners by the commandant of the garrison. Lord Talbot and Sir John said they had only waited to see his majesty, and were about to depart instantly to raise recruits for his service, but Charles would have them stay and dine with him. Another person whom the king was delighted to see was Doctor Crosby, the loyal divine, who had suffered imprisonment for his zeal in his majesty's behalf.

Dinner was served in the great hall, and what it wanted in ceremoniousness was more than compensated for by abundance of viands and excellence of wine. Not much form was observed. The mayor occupied a seat on his majesty's right, and the sheriff on the left. Grace was said by Doctor Crosby. We shall not particularise the dishes, but we must mention that a Severn salmon of prodigious weight—quite a regal fish, that had allowed itself obliging'y to be captured for the occasion—was set before the king. Moreover, the stewed lampreys were an entirely new delicacy to his majesty, and pleased him greatly.

Charles was in high spirits, and laughed and jested in the most good-humoured manner with those near him. Of a very sanguine temperament, he had never doubted the success of his expedition, and the events—unimportant as they were—that had occurred since his arrival before Worcester heightened his confidence. For the first time he had been victorious, and had been warmly welcomed by his subjects. He had been assured that a great number of recruits could be raised in the county before the general Muster took place at Pitchcroft, and he felt certain Lord Derby would bring him large levies from Lancashire and Cheshire. He would then give battle to Cromwell, defeat him, and march on triumphantly to London. His confidence seemed to be shared by all the nobles and general officers present—even by the cold and cautious Lesley. While quaffing their claret and burgundy, they predicted the utter defeat of Old Noll and the destruction of all rebels.

Next day, being Sunday, was comparatively calm after the great previous excitement. Not that the city had by any means resumed its ordinary aspect—that was clearly impossible with a large army encamped outside the walls, and many regiments quartered within them—but the Scottish soldiers, being strict observers of the Sabbath, conducted themselves in a very orderly and decorous manner. Much preaching was there in the camps at Red Hill and Pitchcroft, and officers might be heard reading the Bible and holding forth upon sacred texts to their men, who listened with the profoundest attention.

All the churches—and Worcester, as we know, abounded in churches—were filled with congregations in which the military element predominated; but the cathedral—as might be expected, since it was known that the king would attend divine service there—collected within it all the principal personages of the city, all the chief officers of the army, and as many regiments as the vast pile could contain. Never, perhaps, before or since, has the interior of this grand old edifice presented such a striking sight as it did on this memorable occasion. Its marble monuments and effigies, its chantry and lady-chapel, had been mutilated, as we have already told, by the Roundheads, but these injuries were now concealed from view by the throng collected within the aisles of the choir and the retro-choir. Owing likewise to the attention being directed to other objects, the loss of the splendid painted glass in the windows was scarcely noticed. The majestic pillows lining the broad nave rose up amid a mass of troops that not only occupied the body of the fane, but the aisles. Seen from the entrance of the choir, paved with steel caps, and bristling with pikes, muskets, and carabines—for the men all carried their arms—the nave presented an extraordinary coup-d'œil. Stationed within the south transept, Pitscottie's Highlanders contributed materially to the effect of the picture. All the nobles in attendance upon the king, with the general officers, occupied the stalls in the choir —Charles being seated in the bishop's throne.

As this was the first time on which the service of the Church of England had been performed within the cathedral since its desecration by the Parliamentarians, it may be conceived with what satisfaction the members of that religion were enabled to resume their own form of worship within it—and this satisfaction was heightened by the circumstances under which they came back. The organ was gone, but the military music substituted seemed not inappropriate to an occasion when hymns of triumph were sung. Certes, the drums, trumpets, and other martial instruments, resounding from the roof, produced an extraordinary effect.

The sermon was preached by Doctor Crosby, and was a most eloquent and fervid discourse. The pale countenance of the venerable dean flushed, and his eyes blazed as with fire, while he denounced the murderers of the martyr king, and declared that the vengeance so long delayed would speedily fall upon them. Rebellion, which had stalked unchecked through the land, would be crushed, and the monarchy restored. To Charles he attributed the highest spiritual authority, and spoke of him as " in all causes, and over all persons, next under God, supreme head and governor"—expressions at which his Presbyterian hearers took great offence. The earnestness, however, of his manner could not fail to impress them with a conviction of his sincerity.

A council of war was subsequently held within the palace, and it was decided that the fortifications should at once be thoroughly repaired, so as to enable the city to stand a siege, if necessary, though no tidings had yet been heard of Cromwell. After an early repast, Charles rode forth with his retinue into the city, and was surprised to find the High-street so empty, and almost all the houses shut up; but his surprise ceased when he reached the camp at Pitchcroft, and found that the vast plain was covered with people, and resembled a fair. The Scottish soldiers were quiet, and took no part in the profane recreations of the dissolute Cavaliers, who were everywhere swaggering about, and making love to all the pretty damsels

Charles was enthusiastically received, but he did not stay long on Pitchcroft. After riding through the principal line of tents, he returned and crossed the river to St. John's, where Dalyell's brigade was placed to protect the approach to the bridge. Lower down, on the meadows on this side of the river, Pitscottie's Highlanders were encamped, and the king passed them on his way to Powick, which he desired to see. From the Highlanders' camp, which was almost opposite the episcopal palace and the cathedral, the finest view of old Worcester could be obtained, and he paused for some minutes, enraptured by the charming picture.

A delightful ride of a mile, or somewhat more, along this bank of the Severn brought the king and his attendants to the Teme at its point of junction with the larger river, and then following its deeply-ploughed channel, and watching its swift-flowing current through the fringing trees, they rode on to Powick.

Near Powick there was a woody island of some little extent, round which rushed the river—here, as elsewhere, too deep to be forded. The island was gained by a bridge from either bank, and the importance of the point was so obvious, that the king determined to place a battery upon it.

---

## CHAPTER V.

HOW CHARLES RODE TO MADRESFIELD COURT; AND HOW MISTRESS JANE LANE AND HER BROTHER, WITH SIR CLEMENT FISHER, WERE PRESENTED TO HIS MAJESTY.

NEXT morning another council of war was held at the palace. No tidings as yet of Cromwell—no despatches from the Earl of Derby. After an hour's deliberation the council broke up, and the king proceeded to the Castle Hill, which was being fortified under the superintendence of Lord Rothes and Sir William Hamilton.

The city walls, in the reparation of which hundreds of men had been employed since midnight, were next inspected by his majesty, who was well satisfied with the progress made. He then visited both camps, and while riding along the High-street with his escort, attended by Major Careless, was loudly cheered. Ever since the king's arrival at Worcester the weather had been splendid—a circumstance that contributed in no slight degree to the gay and festive air that prevailed within the city. The taverns were full of roystering Cavaliers, smoking, drinking, dicing, and singing bacchanalian songs.

On his return from the camp at Pitchcroft, Charles paid a visit to the mayor at his private residence, and had a long conference with him. Having given all the instructions he deemed necessary, and feeling that his presence was no longer required, Charles, anxious to escape from the ceaseless applications by which he was beset, crossed the river, and, still attended by his escort and Careless, rode in the direction of the Malvern Hills, his destination being Madresfield Court an old fortified mansion, buried in the midst of thick woods of oak, beech, elm, and other trees, stretching almost from Malvern to the banks of the Severn.

The day, as we have said, was splendid, though excessively hot; but shaded by the trees, which sheltered him with their mighty arms from the oppressive summer heat, Charles found the ride through the forest enchanting. He seemed to breathe more freely now that he was away from the crowded city and the bustling camps.

A lovely sylvan scene, such as he had not for some time contemplated, was offered to his gaze. Madresfield Chase, which formed part of the old forest of Malvern, boasted some trees of great age and vast size. Generally the chase was flat, but occasionally a knoll could be discerned, crowned with timber. A long and beautiful glade of some miles in extent led towards the ancient mansion, which could not, however, be distinguished. Rising in front, above the trees, appeared the lovely Malvern Hills, and their summits, bathed in sunshine, looked so exquisite that Charles wished he could be transported to one of them.

" I never look at a mountain top," he remarked to Careless, " without desiring to ascend to it."

" 'Tis a natural wish I think, my liege," replied the aide-de-camp. " At least, I have the same feeling. Those hills are not difficult of ascent, and command a magnificent view. The highest of them, and the nearest to Malvern, is the Worcestershire Beacon ; the other is the Herefordshire Beacon. Both noble hills."

" Can we ride to the top of the Worcestershire Beacon ?"

" Easily, sire."

" Have you ever made the ascent on horseback ?"

" Never—either on horseback or on foot, sire."

" Then you know nothing about it. However, the difficulties, if there are any, won't deter me. I cannot resist the inclination to ride up to the beacon. We will make the ascent in the evening, when it grows cooler. 'Tis too sultry just now."

" Very true, sire. I should be loth to quit these trees for the bare hill-side."

They then rode on till they came in sight of the grey old structure, which was a very good specimen of a castellated mansion, being strongly built, embattled, flanked with towers, surrounded by a broad, deep moat, defended by a drawbridge, and approached by a grand embattled gateway.

During the Civil Wars, Madresfield Court had been alternately in the possession of the Royalists and the Roundheads. Strongly garrisoned by Charles I., taken by Colonel Fynes at the first siege of Worcester, retaken by the Royalists, and again captured in 1646, it had remained, until within the last few days, in the quiet possession of its owner, Colonel Lygon, who prudently acted with the Parliamentarians. On the arrival of Charles at Worcester, Colonel Lygon was driven forth, after an ineffectual attempt at resistance, and his mansion seized and garrisoned for the king. It was now in a condition to stand a siege, being already well victualled, and well provided with arms and ammunition. Falconets were placed on the gateway, and larger ordnance on the battlements.

Charles was well pleased to see the royal standard displayed from the roof of the old mansion, and to note the preparations for defence. Trumpets were sounded and drums beaten on his approach. The drawbridge was lowered, and the officers and men prepared to turn out and receive his majesty. Charles, however, halted beneath a spreading oak that grew on a wide lawn in front of the mansion, and was contemplating the ancient edifice with some pride in being once more its master, when Careless drew his attention to three persons on horseback, who had just issued from an avenue on the right. From their attire, and from their steeds, the equestrians looked like persons of distinction. One of the party, who specially attracted the king's attention, was a young lady, slight in figure, and extremely graceful. Even beheld at that distance, it might be safely asserted that she was lovely, and when she drew near, she more than realised any notions the king had formed of her beauty. Her companions were Cavaliers undoubtedly—both fine-looking young men, distinguished by their military bearing.

"Know you whom they are?" inquired the king of Careless.

"Unless I mistake not, sire, he in the black velvet doublet, slashed with white, is Colonel Lane of Bentley Hall, in Staffordshire——"

"The Lanes are staunch Royalists?" interrupted Charles.

"Staunchest of the staunch, sire. With the colonel is his sister, Mistress Jane Lane, one of the fairest damsels in the county, and devoted to your majesty. He on the roan horse, and in the green jerkin, laced with silver, is Sir Clement Fisher, of Packington Hall, in Warwickshire."

"Jane Lane's suitor, I'll be sworn!" cried Charles.

"Your majesty has hit it," replied Careless, with a smile.

While this brief colloquy took place, the party had stopped, as if awaiting permission to advance.

"Bring them to me, and present them," said Charles.

Careless, who was a *preux chevalier*, executed his task with infinite grace. It was a charming sight to witness Jane Lane's presentation to the young king. There was an ingenuousness in her manner that delighted Charles. She seemed to possess great spirit and force of character, and yet she had all the most agreeable feminine qualities. As to her beauty there could be no question. Brighter black eyes, features of greater delicacy and refinement, tresses more exquisite, Charles had never beheld. Though she coloured deeply when she first encountered the king's gaze, she manifested no embarrassment.

There was a certain likeness between Colonel Lane and his sister, though the colonel had strongly-marked traits, a firm mouth, and a bold, determined look. But he had dark eyes like Jane, and in them resided the expression that constituted the likeness. Sir Clement Fisher was an admirable specimen of a Cavalier—handsome, brave, chivalrous, he seemed formed to win a fair lady's heart. Whether he had won that of Jane Lane will be seen.

"How is it I have not yet seen you at Worcester, gentlemen?" inquired Charles.

"We are on our way thither, sire," replied Colonel Lane. "You will see us at the Muster at Pitchcroft to-morrow. We have not been lukewarm in your majesty's cause."

" Even I have done something for you, sire," said Jane. " This morning I have secured your majesty forty horse ; and I hope to render you still better service before the day is over."

" My sister is zealous, you perceive, sire," remarked Colonel Lane, with a smile.

" Were there a hundred like her I should soon have an army," observed Charles, highly pleased. " But what is the great service you hope to render me ?"

" Nay, sire," she rejoined, playfully, " you must allow me to keep my secret. 'Twill be a surprise to you to-morrow."

" Then I will ask you no further questions, yet I would fain know why you came here. You could not have expected to find me at Madresfield."

" Pardon me, your majesty, I *did* expect to find you here."

" Oddsfish ! you must be a witch," cried Charles, laughing.

" There is no sorcery in the matter, sire. Have you not sent a messenger to Mr. Thomas Hornyold, of Blackmore Park, commanding him to attend upon you at Madresfield this afternoon ?"

" And you have seen the messenger ?"

" I have, sire. I have read the message, and I told Tom Hornyold I would come in his stead, and make his excuses. The blame of his disobedience of your majesty's order must rest entirely with me. I have sent him to Sir Rowland Berkeley."

" Indeed !" exclaimed Charles.

" He will do more good with Sir Rowland than here. But that is not all. He has promised me to see Sir Walter Blount, Sir John Winford, and Mr. Ralph Sheldon of Beoly. Will you forgive now for my great presumption, sire ?"

" Forgive you ! I am beyond measure indebted to you."

" Sire !" she cried, with a look that bespoke her conviction of the truth of what she uttered, " I believe that I am destined to render you a signal service. My brother will confirm what I am about to say. It was foretold of me when I was a child, by a famous astrologer, that I should save a prince's life. The prophecy must refer to you."

" It may be so," said Charles, smiling at her enthusiasm. " At all events, I shall look upon you as my guardian angel."

" My heart beats only with loyalty, sire. I have no other feeeling in my breast."

" No other feeling, fair mistress ?" said the king, glancing towards Sir Clement.

" It is perfectly true, sire," observed the young baronet, with a somewhat despondent look. " Mistress Jane Lane vows she will never wed till your majesty is seated on the throne."

" And I will keep my vow," cried Jane.

" Then I trust ere long Sir Clement may be in a position to claim you, and that I may be present at your nuptials," said Charles. " But whither you go ?" he added, seeing they were preparing to depart. " Will you not enter the house ?"

" We must pray your majesty to excuse us," said Colonel Lane, bowing. " We have much to do. We are going to cross the hills into Herefordshire."

" Nay, then you must stay till the heat of the day is abated, and I myself will bear you company for part of your journey, for I design to ascend the Worcestershire Beacon. 'Tis not fit your sister should be exposed to this fierce sun."

" I am not one of those damsels that care for my complexion, sire," observed Jane, laughing. " The sun will not melt me."

" Nay, then I will not detain you," rejoined Charles. " I shall see you to-morrow at the Muster at Pitchcroft. You must not be absent, fair mistress."

" Be sure I will not, sire," she replied.

Bending reverentially to the king, she rode off with the others.

" A noble girl!" exclaimed Charles," gazing after her with admiration. " She is the incarnation of loyalty."

---

## CHAPTER VI.

### HOW CHARLES ASCENDED THE WORCESTERSHIRE BEACON ; AND OF THE AMBUSCADE PREPARED FOR HIM AS HE CAME DOWN.

AFTER examining the preparations made for the defence of the old mansion, Charles sat down with Careless and the officer in command of the garrison to a repast prepared for him in the great hall. When he had finished it he ordered his horses. The officer asked if his majesty required his escort.

" No," replied Charles. " I am not about to return to Worcester. I am charmed with this place, and shall sleep here to-night. I mean to ride to Malvern. Major Careless will attend me."

So his majesty set forth, accompanied only by his aide-de-camp. A pleasant ride through the woods brought them to the foot of the giant hill, on a ridge of which stood the little secluded village of Malvern. Yes, the little secluded village of Malvern. Where terraces of well-built houses now spring above each other on the hill-side—where countless white villas peer from out the trees, contrasting charmingly with the foliage, and helping to form one of the prettiest towns in England—a town as healthful as pretty—nothing was then to be seen but a few small habitations, in the midst of which rose the old priory church and the beautiful gateway adjoining it. The priory was pulled down at the Dissolution of the Monasteries, and with it the glory of Malvern had departed. Devotees were still attracted by the Holy Well, and marvellous cures were said to be wrought by its waters, but such pilgrims were rare, and Malvern remained an obscure, unfrequented village, until its beauties and salubrity were discovered in the early part of the present century.

Charles and his attendant halted on the ridge on which this charming town is now built, and surveyed the extensive prospect it commands. They were not aware that they were watched from behind a tree by a tall, ill-favoured man, in the garb of a Puritan. This eaves-dropper, who had followed them cautiously for some minutes, ascertained their purpose, and as soon as they began to ascend the hill, he hurried down to the little inn near the priory gate.

All difficulties in the ascent of the lofty hill, known as the Worcestershire Beacon, have now been removed, and well-made paths enable even invalids to reach its summit almost without fatigue. But at the time when Charles and his attendant mounted it, it had a stern, solitary air, and its silence was unbroken by any sound except that of the sheep-bell, or the cry of a bird of prey. Sheep-tracks alone led up its rugged sides, and conducted the pedestrian through the broad patches of furze, or past huge protruding rocks, to the smooth turf above. Charles being a daring horseman, took the nearest road, and not unfrequently came to places where it was too steep to proceed with safety, and had to retrace his course and seek a less dangerous ascent. The only person in sight was a shepherd tending his flock, and he was far off. At length the king and his attendant gained the rounded summit of the hill, which was covered by turf smooth as velvet, and fragrant with thyme.

Hitherto, both Charles and Careless had been too much occupied by the difficulties of the ascent to pay much attention to the vast panorama opening upon them as they mounted the hill. But as they now gazed upon it, they were lost in admiration, and quite forgot the trouble they had experienced.

It boots not to describe the thoughts that passed through the king's breast, as his eye ranged over that astonishing prospect, which, comprehending as it does nine or ten counties, showed him a large portion of his kingdom, and that perhaps not the least beautiful portion. How many towns and villages—how many noble mansions—could he count in that wide-spread landscape! On the left, and almost as it seemed at his feet, lay the old and faithful city of Worcester, with his army encamped around it. Two other cathedral towns, with their church towers and steeples—Gloucester and Hereford—could likewise be distinguished. Charles sought the Severn for some time in vain. Owing to the height of its banks, it could only be here and there discerned.

He hung long upon this incomparable prospect, and then turned to the Herefordshire side of the hill, whence the view was almost equally fine, three distinct mountainous chains, of beautifully varied form, meeting his gaze.

On quitting the green sward the perils of the descent commenced, and they were obliged to proceed with caution, the ground being covered with loose stones and fragments of rock. They proceeded singly, Charles taking the lead, and were skirting a huge mass of granite that obstructed their course, when suddenly half a dozen men, armed with muskets, whose steel caps and buff coats showed they were Parliamentary soldiers, and who had evidently been lying in ambush behind the rocks, sprang forward, one of them seizing the king's bridle, and two others forcibly preventing him from using his arms. Careless was treated in precisely the same manner, and the capture was so quickly executed that it was perfectly successful.

At the same time two persons appeared on the top of the rock, which rose to some little height above them. In one of these Careless recognised Colonel James ; the other, who kept back, was the spy we have previously mentioned.

" Release me, villains !" cried Charles, furiously, as he vainly attempted to free himself from the grasp of the soldiers who held him.

" Not so," said the leader of the ambuscade from above. " The Lord hath delivered thee into my hand, as He delivered Jabin, King of Canaan, into the hands of the children of Israel. I will not put thee to death, but will take thee and thine officer as prisoners to the Lord General, to deal with ye as he may see fit. With thy capture the invasion of the men of Moab is at an end."

Scarcely were the words uttered than a loud report was heard, and he dropped on the rock, apparently mortally wounded.

" The Amalekites are upon us !" shouted the spy. " Save yourselves !"

So saying, he jumped down on the other side of the rock and disappeared.

Supposing their commander killed, and not knowing what force might be upon them, the soldiers did not dare to carry off their prize, but sought safety in flight.

Next moment, from among the rocks beneath issued Sir Clement Fisher, who had fired the shot, while close behind him appeared Colonel Lane and his sister.

" Heaven preserve your majesty !" shouted the two Cavaliers, raising their hats ; while Jane, whose dark eyes flashed, and whose face was radiant with delight, echoed the loyal aspiration.

Charles heard them, and raised his hat in response.

" Haste thee to Madresfield Court," he said to Careless. " Bring a detachment of horse to scour these hills. I will have the villains who have dared to lay hands upon me."

" Your majesty——"

" Obey me. I shall have Colonel Lane and Sir Clement Fisher witn me. Away ! Spare not the spur."

Thus enjoined, Careless dashed down the rocks at the hazard of his neck.

Charles then descended to his preservers, who had moved to a less rugged spot, and thanked them heartily.

" The prophecy is fulfilled," he said to Jane. " You have saved my life."

" Nay, it was Sir Clement who delivered you, sire," she replied. " But I may, at least, claim the merit of having perceived your majesty's peril."

" You may claim more," remarked Sir Clement Fisher. " Had it not been for your coolness and self-possession, we could not have succeeded in effecting his majesty's deliverance."

" I said you are my guardian angel, and so you are." cried Charles.

" But I must learn what took place. Let me have the description from your own lips."

" Since your majesty commands me, I must speak, though Sir Clement could better explain the matter," she rejoined, blushing. " Then, thus it was, sire. We had accomplished our errand, and were returning through yonder pass hetween the hills, when we observed your majesty and Major Careless near the beacon. We could see you both quite distinctly, and our gaze never quitted you till you were about to commence your descent. I then begged my brother to quit the lower road, in order that we might meet you as you came down. Your course lay towards those rocks, and while gazing in that direction, I noticed some armed men moving stealthily about among them, and pointed them out to my brother and Sir Clement, who at once recognised them as rebel soldiers, and felt sure that an ambuscade had been placed there. What was to be done? Impossible to warn you. A plan occurred to me. I showed my companions how, by keeping among the rocks, we could approach the ambuscading party unperceived, and they followed my counsel, as it seemed the sole chance of saving your majesty. We got near enough to enable Sir Clement to bring down the leader of the troop."

" And luckily not another shot was needed," said Sir Clement.

" I know not whether you were my deliverer or Sir Clement," said Charles. " But I am equally indebted to you both. And now you must all accompany me to Madresfield Court. I shall need your escort, gentlemen."

<hr>

## CHAPTER VII.

HOW COLONEL LEGGE BROUGHT IMPORTANT NEWS TO THE KING, AND HOW HIS MAJESTY PAID A VISIT TO SEVERN END.

CARELESS was able to execute the king's commands much more quickly than he expected. Encountering a small party of dragoons near Malvern, he ordered them to scour the lower part of the hill, while he himself reascended the heights. The Roundheads, however, had made good their retreat. They had hidden their horses, it appeared, in a deep chasm, on the hill-side, and after their unsuccessful attempt, had descended into the plain, where they were lost among the woods.

A singular discovery was made by Careless. On visiting the rock, on which the commandant had fallen, he found the spot stained with blood, but the body was gone. By whom had it been removed? Not by the Roundheads—that was certain. In all probability Colonel James had not been mortally wounded, as was at first supposed, but had recovered sufficient strength to crawl off. The search made for him proved ineffectual, and Careless was obliged to return to Madresfield Court without having effected a single capture. The king having by this time recovered his good humour, laughed at his aide-de-camp's ill success.

" Oddsfish !" he exclaimed. " I had nearly lost my crown by that foolish ascent of the Worcestershire Beacon—rather too high a price to pay for a fine view."

His majesty was alone, Colonel Lane and those with him having proceeded to Worcester.

Next morn, Charles arose betimes, broke his fast lightly, and had just mounted his charger with the intention of setting off to Worcester, when his departure was stayed by the arrival of Colonel Legge, one of his most gallant and trusted officers, and familiarly called by his majesty " Honest Will."

Colonel Legge brought very important news. He had been with a reconnoitring party to Evesham, and had captured a couple of Round-head scouts, from whom he had obtained information respecting the enemy's movements. Cromwell was approaching with a large army, having seventeen thousand horse and foot under his own command ; while the regiments of Lord Grey of Groby, Fleetwood, Ingoldsby, Lambert, and Harrison, together with the militia that had recently joined the Parliamentary forces, swelled the amount to upwards of thirty thousand.

" Nearly treble my force," exclaimed Charles. " But were they forty thousand I should not fear them."

" 'Tis well you are prepared, sire," remarked Legge.

" Much has yet to be done," replied the king. " The passes of the Severn and the Teme must be looked to. Upton, Powick, and Brans-ford Bridges must be broken down. Haste thee to Worcester, Will. Summon a council of war to meet me three hours hence. By that time I shall have visited Upton and Powick, and perhaps Bransford. Is Massey at Upton ?"

" Massey's head-quarters are at Severn End, sire, the residence of Judge Lechmere. The judge sides with the Parliament, but I suspect he is a time-server, and will always support the party in power. If your majesty is victorious, he will throw himself at your feet. Severn End is a fine place, and Massey seems to like his quarters. Judge Lechmere's nearest neighbour is loyal Tom Hornyold, whom you will assuredly see at Pitchcroft to-day."

" Oddsfish ! Judge Lechmere must be an astute fellow from thy ac-count of him, Will," replied Charles, laughing. " I will go first to Severn End. Perchance I may see the judge. If so, I will have a word with him."

" Fine him heavily, sire, or imprison him, if he will not join you," said Legge.

" Humph ! I like not to have recourse to harsh measures," rejoined Charles. " Still, an example ought to be made of such a man. Now, off with thee to Worcester, Will. Say to all that thou hast left me in good spirits."

" I can say so with truth, my liege," replied Legge.

Careless undertook to conduct his majesty to Severn End, being well acquainted with Judge Lechmere's residence. Their course lay through the loveliest part of the chase, but Charles was too much preoccupied to notice the beauties of the scene, and Careless did not venture to disturb the profound reverie into which his royal master had fallen, and which lasted till they came to the precincts of a large, well-timbered park, in the midst of which stood a fine old house embosomed in a grove of rook-haunted trees.

" Is this Severn End ?" asked Charles.

" No, my liege ; this is Blackmore Park, the abode of your staunch adherent, Captain Thomas Hornyold."

" And a charming place it is," observed the king ; " I would all my staunch adherents were as well housed !"

After skirting the moss-grown park pales for a few minutes, they came upon a long and stately avenue, down which a troop of horse was riding, with their leader at their head.

" As I live that must be Tom Hornyold's troop !" cried Charles, halting, while Careless signed to the king's escort to stop.

Seeing Careless ride towards him, and comprehending the aide-de-camp's object, Captain Hornyold put his troop into a trot, and presently drew up before the king.

Tom Hornyold's manly bearing, open countenance, frank manner, and steady look prepossessed the king in his favour.

" I trust your majesty will pardon my inattention to your summons yesterday," said Hornyold, after making an obeisance. " Here are forty good men and true, who will fight well for you, and I have had barely time to get them together."

" Mistress Jane Lane explained all to me, Captain Hornyold," rejoined Charles, graciously. " You did quite right, and I thank you heartily. By my faith, you have brought me some famous recruits."

As he moved towards the troop, he was welcomed with a shout that startled the clamorous rooks overhead, and put to flight a herd of deer that had been couching beneath the trees.

Well pleased with the appearance of the recruits, many of whom were remarkably fine-looking young men, and all well accoutred and extremely well mounted, the king thus expressed his satisfaction :

" Good men—good horses—good weapons, and strong arms to wield them—those you have brought me, Captain Hornyold, and I thank you once more. Gentlemen," he added to the troopers, " I cannot tarry longer with you now, though I fain would say something more, but I have much to do, as you are aware. I shall see you again at Pitchcroft. Au revoir !"

Bowing graciously to Captain Hornyold, he then rode off, attended by Careless and followed by his escort.

On quitting Blackmore Park, the king approached another equally well-wooded domain, which he did not need to be told belonged to Judge Lechmere.

It was, in sooth, Severn End, and their road towards the house led them for a short distance near the bank of the river. The grounds contained many noble trees, amongst which were several towering elms and broad-armed oaks that delighted Charles, as did a remarkably fine service-tree, which he pointed out to his attendant.

As they drew near the picturesque old mansion, it was easy to perceive that it was under military occupation—sentinels being placed at the entrance, while small parties of dragoons were gathered on the terrace, as if awaiting orders; and a troop of cavalry was drawn up on the lawn. A soldier was walking a powerful charger to and fro before the porch.

Drums would have been beaten, and trumpets sounded, but the king would not allow any announcement of his arrival to be made. Leaving his escort at the extremity of the lawn, he rode up to the portal with Careless. He then dismounted and marched up the steps, merely returning the salutes of the officers he encountered.

Loud and angry tones were audible as he crossed the hall, and guided him to the room in which General Massey could be found. The door being partly open, Charles pushed it aside and entered a large chamber with a somewhat low roof, panneled with black oak, ornamented with several full-length portraits.

This was the dining-room, and in the midst of it stood General Massey, booted and spurred, with his hat on, and his riding-whip in hand, evidently prepared to mount his charger.

A fine, tall, broad-shouldered man was the general, and well became his rich accoutrements. His back being towards the door he did not notice the king's entrance. Full of wrath, as we have intimated, he was pouring his fury on the head of a grave-looking personage in a black velvet gown, and having a black skull-cap on his head, who was standing calmly before him.

Perhaps this individual, whom Charles had no doubt was Judge Lechmere, recognised his majesty. If so, he gave no sign, but kept his keen grey eye steadily fixed on the irate general.

"Hark ye, judge," thundered Massey. "'Tis you, and such as you, supporters of this rebellious Parliament, who ought to suffer most, and by Heaven you *shall* suffer. You shall be forced to contribute largely to the expenses of the war you have compelled his majesty to undertake for the recovery of his throne. You are fined five thousand pounds."

"By whom am I fined that large sum?" demanded Lechmere, in a calm tone. "Not by the king, I am well assured. He would not commit such an injustice."

"You are fined by me—that is sufficient. I have his majesty's warrant for all I do."

"Not his written warrant," said the judge.

"I need it not," cried Massey. "What doth your Lord General, as you style him? I do not desire to imitate his ruthless and robber-like proceedings. I do not intend, like him, to plunder churches, hospitals, and private dwellings. I do not mean to break open chests and carry off gold by the sack, and plate by the cartload, as he did at Worcester, after the first siege. But I will imitate him in one thing. I will punish wealthy offenders like yourself by fines proportionate to their means. You have amassed money, I know, and, though a lawyer, I hope have come by it honestly. Had you been loyal you might have kept your money. But since you are a rebel, and a favourer of rebels, you shall disburse your gains for the king's use. You shall pay me the five thousand pounds I demand."

" And yet you affirm that you design not to plunder me," observed Judge Lechmere, still with perfect calmness. " What call you this but plunder on the greatest scale?  Better strip my house of all it contains —better carry off my pictures and my plate—than fine me in a sum so large that I cannot pay it.  Again I say, I am certain the king would not allow this demand to be made."

" His majesty will approve of what I do," rejoined Massey.  " But I will not bandy words with you.  You are now in my court, judge, and my decision holds good here.  I will have the sum I have named—no less.  Two thousand pounds—the first instalment—must be paid before noon on Thursday.  That will give you two days to raise it.  If you fail, I will have you shot in your own court-yard.  You hear!  No excuses will avail.  Till then you are a prisoner in your own house."

" If I am a prisoner, how am I to raise the money, general?" asked the judge.

" That is your concern," rejoined Massey,  " Have it I must—or you die!"

As he turned to quit the room, he perceived Charles standing behind him.

" Ah! sire," he exclaimed.  " I did not know you were here."

" Am I indeed in the king's presence?" exclaimed Judge Lechmere, with well-feigned astonishment.

" You are in the presence of the sovereign to whom your allegiance is due, my lord judge," rejoined Charles, with dignity.

" Whatever my feelings may be towards to your majesty," said Lechmere, " I cannot consistently——"

" You dare not declare yourself in my favour, eh, judge?" cried Charles.  " Well, I will give you till Thursday for reflection.  Naturally you are included in the general pardon I have published, and if you then return to your allegiance, I shall be disposed to forget the past, and will remit the heavy fine imposed upon you by General Massey. Nay, I will do more ; I will take you into my favour."

" I thank your majesty for your goodness. I will perpend the matter."

" Methinks it requires little consideration," observed Charles, somewhat sternly.  " You have to choose between your lawful king and a usurper.  You will best consult your own interests in serving me."

" I am inclined to believe so, sire—nay, I am certain—yet give me till Thursday."

" I have said it," rejoined Charles.  " I now leave you in General Massey's hands."

With a grave bow to the judge, who had rushed forward as if to throw himself at his majesty's feet, but stopped suddenly, he quitted the room, followed by Massey.

As he crossed the hall he laughed heartily.

" Your judge will turn Royalist on Thursday, if nothing happens to-morrow," he said.

On quitting Severn End, Charles accompanied General Massey to Upton.

They rode through Hanley, where a stately pile belonging to the Earls of Gloucester once stood, and wnere Massey's troops were now encamped.

The general had with him a detachment of five hundred horse and a regiment of dragoons, and he assured the king that he felt confident of preventing the enemy's passage at Upton Bridge, come in what force he might.

Together they carefully examined the fine old bridge, which, like the bridges of Worcester and Powick, was somewhat narrow, but had deep angular recesses. It was strongly built of stone, and had several arches.

Charles advised its total destruction, but Massey was of opinion that it would suffice to break down the central arch; and the king giving his assent, a large body of men was at once set to work upon the task.

After witnessing the commencement of the operations, Charles took leave of Massey, urging him to be more than ever vigilant, as the safety of the army now depended on him, and rode on with his escort to Powick.

The security of this important pass seemed to be guaranteed by the presence of General Montgomery and Colonel Kirke, with two battalions of foot and a regiment of horse, and Charles, with a mind very much quieted, crossed the river to Worcester.

---

## CHAPTER VIII.

### OF THE COUNSEL GIVEN BY COLONEL LESLEY TO THE KING.

When Charles arrived at the palace, the war council was already assembled. Several general officers, however, were necessarily absent.

A long and anxious discussion ensued, and great diversity of opinion prevailed—jealousies having sprung up amongst the commanders. His grace of Buckingham hated the Duke of Hamilton, and derided his plans; but his own rash counsels were rejected.

Charles felt sure, he declared, that he should be largely reinforced by the levies which the Earl of Derby was bringing from Lancashire and Cheshire. But he cared not if his army should be inferior to that of the enemy in number.

"There is no fear of treachery," he said. "The loyalty of the citizens of Worcester is unquestionable. They will fight for me as bravely as they have fought for the king, my father. No defeat will subdue them. But why do I talk of defeat? Let us speak of the victory, that is certain."

"The next battle must be decisive, sire," remarked the Duke of Hamilton. "We must conquer or die."

"We will conquer," cried Charles, energetically.

"We will," cried several voices.

Having remarked that Lesley took no part in the conference, the king drew him aside and inquired the meaning of his sombre looks.

"Are you afraid of Cromwell?" he asked.

“ I am afraid of my own men, sire,” replied Lesley.   “ They are discontented, and do all I can, I am unable to remove their dissatisfaction.”

“ Of what grievance do they complain ?” asked Charles.

“ I need not remind your majesty, that  nearly five thousand Scottish
soldiers have  returned  to their own country  since we crossed the Border——”

“ Deserted, if you please, colonel,” interrupted Charles.

“ Well, deserted, sire.  But they had this excuse.  Being zealous Presbyterians, they had conscientious scruples against establishing the Episcopal government in  England by force of  arms ; and  like  sentiments
prevail, to a great extent, among the remainder of the troops.  Since our
arrival at Worcester their discontent has perceptibly increased.  They do
not like to fight with the Cavaliers.  For  this reason, they are not
pleased with the Muster about to take  place to-day, neither do they
desire to be joined by the levies promised by the Earl of Derby.”

“ They fear that  my devoted adherents  may  become too strong for
them.   Is it not so, colonel ?” asked Charles, coldly.

“ They deem that a preponderance of the royal party—strictly so
called—though we are all Royalists—would be contrary to the true
interests of Scotland, and to the welfare of the Kirk.”

“ Ah, I see !” exclaimed the king.  The Committee of the Kirk of
Scotland have troubled their consciences — meddlesome fools that they are !
But you *must* keep your men in good humour, Lesley.  They *must* fight
this battle.  Assure them that I am  a  zealous partisan of the Covenant,
and that when  I  ascend the throne I will  ratify  all  the  conditions imposed upon me.”

“ Humph !” exclaimed Lesley.   “ I may  give them these assurances,
but they will not believe me.  So critical do I consider the position, that
if I dared to offer your  majesty a counsel, it would be to return to Scotland without hazarding an engagement.”

“ Return to  Scotland ! — never !” exclaimed  Charles, indignantly.
“ How dare you make a proposition so dishonouring to me, Lesley ?  I
have not advanced thus  far into my kingdom to go back again without
a blow.”

“ I knew my advice would be distasteful to your majesty, but I deemed
it my duty to give it.”

“ No more !” cried the  king.  “ Quell  this mutinous  spirit in your
men, Lesley—quell it, by whatever means you can.  Mark well what I
say, and fail not to repeat it.  When  we have  routed the rebels—and
we *shall* rout them—those why have  fought best for me shall receive the
highest reward.”

Before Lesley could make any reply, Pitscottie approached his majesty.

“ Where  are your Highlanders, colonel ?” demanded Charles.

“ Drawn up in the college green, sire.  I await your orders to march
them to the place of Muster.”

“ Have they heard that Cromwell is at hand ?”

“ Ay, sire ; and they are eager to meet him.”

“ No discontent among them—ha ?”

“ Discontent !  No, sire.  They were never in better spirits.  All

hey desire is to prove their zeal to your majesty, and use their broad-
words against the foe."

" Brave fellows !" exclaimed Charles, glancing significantly at Lesley.
' They shall serve as my body-guard to-day."

## CHAPTER IX.

### OF THE GRAND MUSTER AT PITCHCROFT.

EVER since the old city of Worcester was built and encircled by walls,
Pitchcroft has afforded its inhabitants a delightful place for exercise and
recreation. On this broad, flat plain, bounded on the west by the
Severn, and completely overlooked by a natural terrace on the further
bank of the river, many a grand tournament has been held in the days
of our earlier monarchs. Magnificent pavilions and galleries have been
reared upon the wide mead—splendid cavalcades have come forth from
the city gates—nobles, knights, squires, jesters, and fair dames—and
many a lance has been splintered at the royal jousts of Worcester. In
1225, these displays incurred the displeasure of the Church—a grand
tournament being held on Pitchcroft in that year, when all the noble
personages concerned in it were excommunicated by Bishop Blois.
Sports and pastimes of all kinds have been familiar to the plain from
time immemorial—games which, by a pretty figure of speech, have been
described as Olympian, and which, we rejoice to say, are not altogether
discontinued. Not only has Pitchcroft been the scene of many a
knightly encounter and many a festive meeting, but when the loyal
city was invested, it witnessed frequent conflicts between Cavaliers and
Roundheads, and one well-fought action, in which the fiery Rupert took
part.

On the morning appointed for the Muster, Pitchcroft was even more
thronged than it had been on the previous Sunday, and presented a far
gayer and more animated appearance. A great number of troops was
assembled there, while the new levies were continually pouring into the
plain through Foregate-street.

Before proceeding to the place of rendezvous, the recruits entered the
city, and halted for a time in the area near the Cross, where their numbers were registered by the mayor and the sheriff, who acted as commissioners.

Among the principal names inscribed on the muster-roll were those
of Lord Talbot, Sir John Pakington, Sir Walter Blount, Sir Ralph Clare,
Sir Rowland Berkley, Sir John Winford, Mr. Ralph Sheldon of Beoley,
Mr. John Washburn of Witchinford, and Mr. Thomas Hornyold.

Lord Talbot's troop, which was far more numerous than any other,
was composed almost entirely of gentlemen, whose accoutrements and
horses were far superior to those of ordinary cavalry. The regiment was
commanded by Lieutenant-Colonel Mervin Touchet, and subsequently

proved exceedingly efficient.    Every Cavalier who came singly to Worcester was included in some troop or other.

These arrangements were made by Colonel Lane and Colonel Legge, assisted by Sir Clement Fisher.    As quickly as one troop was filled up, it was sent off to the place of Muster.    It was calculated that two thousand Worcestershire Cavaliers, including of course retainers and servants, answered the king's summons on that day.

The sight of so many recruits tended materially to dissipate the alarm not unnaturally excited by the rumours of Cromwell's near approach. Having begun to distrust the Scottish soldiers, the citizens were glad to have some defenders on whom they could confidently rely.    For this reason, as well as for their gallant bearing and handsome equipments, the recruits were lustily cheered as they appeared on the plain.

A large concourse was collected in Foregate-street, and on the northern walls, to see the new troops come forth.    The Scottish regiments of cavalry and infantry excited but little curiosity; the chief objects of interest being the numerous small bodies of horse, extending for a quarter of a mile on the left—each little troop with its officers in front.

The effect of this arrangement was extremely good, and delighted the spectators on the city walls and those on the west bank of the river.

The last troop had just got into its place, when the shrill notes of the pibroch were heard, and the Highlanders, with Colonel Pitscottie at their head, marched forth, and were received with cheers by the crowd assembled in Foregate-street.

Acclamations greeted the king.    His majesty looked extremely well, and charmed the beholders, as he always did, by the extreme affability of his demeanour.    On this occasion he was only attended by Careless and Colonel Blague.    The recruits instantly attracted his attention— their numbers giving him manifest pleasure—and he expressed his satisfaction at beholding them audibly to his attendants.

He had not proceeded far, when the mayor and the sheriff advanced to meet him.

Opening a scroll which he held in his hand, the mayor in a loud voice recited the long list of loyal gentlemen of the county who had responded to his majesty's summons.    The king looked highly gratified, and repeated each name as it was given out.

When the mayor had made an end, Charles rode towards Lord Talbot, who was nearest him on the left, and while surveying his splendid troop with admiration, called out, so that all might hear him:

" Why, my good lord, these are all gentlemen.    Better mounted better equipped Cavaliers, I would not desire to see."

" They are *all* loyal gentlemen," replied Lord Talbot, bowing ; " and as such I am proud to present them to your majesty."

" Long live the king ! Confusion to his enemies !" shouted the gallant band, brandishing their swords.

The shout was caught up by the next troop, which was commanded by Sir John Pakington, and was echoed far and wide.

After a few complimentary observations to Colonel Touchet, Charles moved on, inspecting in turn all the newly-raised troops. Had loyalty been chilled in any breast, his majesty's gracious manner would have kindled it anew—but all were loyal. The king could not help noting that in almost every troop gentlemen had joined, and horses and accoutrements were generally so good that officers could scarcely be distinguished from privates.

Captain Hornyold's troop was stationed near the Scottish cavalry—Sir Clement Fisher acting as second captain. But the real commander, in the king's estimation, was Jane Lane, who was posted in front on her steed.

A glance of triumph lighted up her fine eyes as Charles addressed her :

" You only want arms to become a veritable Amazon."

" I will wear them if your majesty commands."

" No, you have brought me so many recruits that it is unnecessary. How many troops have you helped to fill up ?"

" I have done my best, sire, but I have not brought you half so many as I could desire. The Worcestershire gentry are loyal, but irresolute and cautious—I will not use stronger epithets. They try to excuse their lukewarmness on the ground that they suffered so much from fines and sequestrations during the Civil Wars. But, as I tell them, that is no excuse. They ought to risk all—sacrifice all, if need be—for their sovereign. Many have come here to-day. But," she added, with a look of mingled grief and indignation, " some, on whom I fully counted, are absent."

" I scarcely miss them. When I have won a battle, they will hasten to rally round my standard, but I shall know how to distinguish between late comers, and those who have been true to me in the hour of peril."

" All here are true men, my liege. I would not say as much for yon Scottish soldiers." Then lowering her voice so as only to be heard by the king, she added : " Do not trust Lesley, sire. He may play you false."

" Why do you entertain these suspicions ?"

" From what I hear of the conduct of his men, and of his own discourse. Heaven grant my fears may prove groundless !"

" If Lesley proves a traitor I am undone, for he commands the third of my army, and his men will obey no other leader. But I will not believe him false."

" What news has your majesty of the Earl of Derby ?" asked Jane, still in the same whispered accents. " Pardon the question. 'Tis prompted by the deep interest I feel——"

" No messenger from the earl has arrived as yet. But I have no apprehensions of a reverse. Doubtless, he is marching hither with the levies he has obtained, but has been compelled to turn aside from the direct route to avoid Cromwell."

" Would he were here now !" exclaimed Jane, earnestly.

" I would so too," responded Charles, with equal fervour. " But he will not fail me at the right moment, and will cut through any opposing force to join me."

" Is it not strange you have not heard from him, sire ?"

"Not so strange—since the enemy is between us.  Besides, if he has not effectually disposed of Lilburn, he may be harassed by him in his march.  A few hours, I trust, will bring me tidings of the friend on whom I reckon most."

Banishing the gloom that had gathered on his brow during his converse with Jane, he turned to Captain Hornyold, and delighted that loyal gentleman by his praises.

Having completed his inspection of the new troops, Charles proceeded towards the centre of the plain, where Pitscottie and his Highlanders were drawn up.  Here he stationed himself, and immediately afterwards it became evident, from the movement that took place, that the recruits were about to march past.

With as much promptitude and precision as if they had belonged to the regular cavalry, Captain Hornyold's troop came up.  By the side of their leader rode Jane Lane, but she proceeded no further, being called upon by the king to take a place beside him.

Each little troop rode past in rapid succession—each being commended by the king in no measured terms—and they all deserved his praises, for a finer set of men were never got together.

Almost all of them were in the full vigour of manhood, and the ardour displayed in their looks and bearing, and in the shouts they could not repress, formed a striking contrast to the sullen visages and moody silence of the Scottish soldiers, who seemed to regard their new comrades with aversion.

But the coldness of the Scots was more than compensated for by the genuine enthusiasm of the citizens, who put no bounds to their rapturous delight, and shouted lustily as the new troops rode by.  Every officer, and indeed almost every one in each company, being known, they were familiarly addressed by name, and cheered individually as well as collectively by the spectators.

After defiling past the king, the troops were formed into four regiments of five hundred each—respectively commanded by Colonel Mervin Touchet, Colonel Legge, Colonel Wogan, and Colonel Lane.

Attended by Lord Talbot, Sir John Pakington, Sir Walter Blount, Sir Ralph Clare, Sir Rowland Berkley, and Sir John Winford, the king rode slowly past them—ever and anon raising his hat—and manifesting by his looks the high gratification he felt.

Amid the loud and reiterated cheers of the concourse, his majesty then returned to the city—preceded by Colonel Pitscottie and his Highlanders, and attended by the gentlemen we have just mentioned.

---

# CHAPTER X.

### THE BIVOUAC ON THE PLAIN.

SHORTLY after the king's departure, two of the newly-raised regiments proceeded to the quarters temporarily assigned them in the city.  Next day they encamped on the west side of the river. The regiments left behind remained where they were, and commenced their experience of military life by bivouacking on the plain. They did not undergo much hardship, since the night was fine and warm, and the moon being nearly at the full, every object was as distinctly visible as during daytime.

As far as eatables and drinkables were concerned, the newly-enrolled troops had no reason to complain. Plenty of provisions and an abundant supply of good liquor—ale, perry, cider, canary, sack, and other wines, were sent them by the mayor and sheriff. Though novices in the art of war, the new soldiers were adepts in drinking, and could empty their cups as well as the oldest campaigner. Every Cavalier was welcome to a share of their runlet of sack or claret—but they did not invite the Scottish soldiers.

Though the night was fine and warm, as we have described, they kept up their fires, and sat around them to a late hour. These groups, with arms piled, and horses picketed beside them, lent a very picturesque appearance to this part of the plain. Further on could be seen the tents of the Scottish soldiers, bathed in moonlight, but few were stirring near them except the sentinels. It would almost seem as if the Scots had retired to rest earlier than their wont to avoid hearing the songs and laughter of their roystering comrades. A great noise was undoubtedly made, for a dozen Cavalier ditties were chanted at the same time by different parties. At last, however, the recruits grew tired of singing, and began to talk of the war. Round each fire were collected individuals who had fought at both sieges of Worcester, and these now favoured their companions with their recollections of those stirring times.

" Nine years ago," said a burly-looking young man, who had been addressed as Martin Vosper, " I was just nineteen—so you will readily guess my age now—and I was then 'prentice to Mr. Lysons, the present worthy mayor of Worcester. The city, as you know, has always been loyal, and for that reason was regarded from the very first with especial disfavour by the rebellious Parliament. In 1642, our faithful Worcester, for I love to call it so, declared for the king, opened its gates to Sir John Biron and the three hundred Cavaliers he brought with him, and fortified its walls. The Roundheads did not leave us long alone. Lord Say and Colonel Fynes, with a large force, laid siege to the city ; whereupon the king sent word from Oxford that he would bring fifteen hundred horse and twice as many foot to raise the siege. Our satisfaction at this agreeable intelligence was damped by hearing that Lord Essex was marching against us with fourteen thousand men ; but just as we were beginning to despair, Prince Rupert, with his brother Maurice, threw themselves into the city with a large body of troops. Then we felt able to set Old Noll himself at defiance. Two successful stratagems were practised. But I must first describe an action that took place on this very plain. Determined to strike a decisive blow before Lord Essex could bring up his forces, Prince Rupert, on the morning after his arrival, with fifteen troops of horse, marched forth upon Pitchcroft, and, sounding his trumpets loudly, challenged the enemy to battle. A gallant sight his troops made, I can assure you, when drawn up on the plain, for I watched them from the northern walls. A word about the prince. Never did I behold a fiercer-looking man. His eye went through you like a rapier. But to proceed. At first the enemy appeared to decline the challenge, but they were ready enough to fight, as it turned out, only their forces were dispersed. Lord Say and Colonel Fynes were elsewhere, as I shall presently explain, but Colonel Sandys and Colonel Austine brought up their regiments, and the conflict began. 'Twas a splendid sight. What tremendous charges Prince Rupert made! How he mowed down the Roundheads! Still he could not break their ranks. The fight lasted for a couple of hours with varying success, but the advantage seemed to be with the prince, when a troop of horse was descried coming from the Blockhouse fields, and a cry arose that it was the Earl of Essex with his reinforcements. The alarm proved false, for the troops were those of Colonel Fynes, but on seeing them, the prince ordered an instant retreat, and dashed precipitately into the city, whither he was followed so quickly by the Republicans, that the gate could not be shut, and a desperate fight ensued, which lasted till midnight, the streets resounding all the time with the rattle of musketry and the clash of steel. Many a Cavalier died that night, but not before his sword was reddened with the blood of his adversaries. The corn-market was full of wounded and dying. Prince Rupert might have succeeded in driving out the Republicans, if they had not been strongly reinforced by Lord Say. At length the prince was compelled to abandon the city, but he rode at the rear of his troops and drove back the Roundheads who sought to follow him across the bridge."

"Those confounded Parliamentarians *can* fight, it must be owned," remarked one of the listeners. "But what were the stratagems you spoke of just now, Vosper ?"

"You shall hear, Simon Terret," replied the other. "But first give me a cup of sack to drink the king's health, and confusion to all rebels. From what I am about to relate you will perceive that the conflict on Pitchcroft was part of a cleverly-devised scheme, that ought to have succeeded better than it did. Prince Rupert having ascertained from his scouts that Lord Say had taken a detachment of a thousand men to Powick, while another equally large detachment had been taken by Colonel Fynes to Perry Wood—the object of the two Republican commanders being to surround the prince, as his highness perfectly understood—he endeavoured to out-manœuvre them. With this design a clever spy was sent to Powick, who represented himself as a servant to the Earl of Essex, and stated, with an air of great plausibility, that Cromwell had entered Worcester—and that, if Lord Say advanced immediately, the retreat of the Royalists would infallibly be cut off. Duped by the man's apparent sincerity, Lord Say acted on the advice, and fell into an ambuscade that cost him five-and-twenty men. Colonel Fynes was imposed on in much the same manner. A messenger galloped up to Perry Wood and informed him that Prince Rupert was advancing with ten thousand men, whereupon he fell back four miles. But he found out the stratagem rather too soon. It was his force that subsequently alarmed Prince Rupert and caused his highness to retreat into the city. Had not this discovery occurred, the prince would have beaten the enemy in detail."

" I think I have heard that those two clever spies were hanged," remarked Terret.

" Ay marry, were they," replied Vosper. " They were hanged with several other good citizens and staunch Royalists on a gallows as high as Haman's, which was set up in the market-place by Old Noll."

" Would Old Noll were hanged on a like gallows!" cried several voices.

" The *Jus Furcarum* was an enviable privilege," remarked one of the circle. " If I possessed the right, as did the old priors of St. Mary, I would hang every Roundhead rogue of them all."

" Ha! ha! ha!" laughed the others.

" Ah! never shall I forget the barbarities practised by Essex's soldiers when they took the city," observed Vosper. " Heaven preserve us from a repetition of such dreadful usage. But all these severities did not check the loyal spirit of the citizens. You recollect the second siege in 1646, Trubshaw," he observed to another person near him, " when Worcester was invested by Sir William Brereton and Colonel Birch ?"

" Ay, Colonel Henry Washington was governor at the time," replied Trubshaw — " as brave a man as ever drew sword, and as loyal.* Several skirmishes occurred outside the walls, but there was an affair at St. John's in which I, myself, took part. The Parliamentary generals had blockaded the city on that side, lining the approaches to St. John's with musketeers, and quartering a large force behind the tower. Determined to dislodge them, Governor Washington sallied forth one night with a couple of hundred horse, of whom I myself was one, and five hundred foot. Tybridge-street, which you know leads to the bridge from St. John's, was strongly barricaded by the enemy, but we drove back their advanced guard to Cripplegate, where being reinforced by horse and foot, they made a stand, but they could not resist our brave commander, who attacked them with such vigour that he quickly routed them, and would have put them all to the sword if they had not sought refuge in the church. We set fire to the houses in Cripplegate, so they could no longer find shelter there. In this sortie we killed a hundred of the enemy, and took ten prisoners. Our own loss was trifling. Governor Washington gained much credit by the achievement."

" Not more than he deserved," remarked another of the interlocutors named Barkesdale. " Governor Washington was a man of undaunted resolution, as his answer shows, when he was summoned to surrender the city. ' It may be easy,' he wrote to General Fairfax, ' for your excellency to procure his majesty's commands for the disposal of this garrison. Till then I shall make good the trust reposed in me. As for conditions, if necessitated, I shall make the best I can. The worst I know, and fear not.' "

" A brave answer!" cried Vosper. " Did you know Captain Hodgkins? ' Wicked Will,' as he was called by the Roundheads ?"

---

* An uncle of this brave Cavalier was an ancestor of the great General Washington, President of the United States.

"Know him! ay," rejoined Barkesdale.  "Captain Hodgkins drank deeper, and fought harder, than any Cavalier of his day.  One night, after he had emptied half a dozen flasks of claret, he crossed the bridge with a small band of boon companions, surprised the enemy's guard at Cripplegate, drove them back as far as the Bull Ring, which you know is close to St. John's, and put several of them to the sword. In returning, he fell from his horse in Tybridge-street, and not being able to walk, was tossed into a boat and rowed across the Severn.  In another sally, being somewhat more sober, he brought back seven prisoners."

"Seven prisoners! ha! ha!" laughed the whole circle.

"'Tis a pity he did not die a soldier's death," observed Trubshaw. "His body was found in the Severn below the city, near Bunshill Whether he was accidentally drowned, or thrown into the river, is uncertain."

"Wicked Will's death was a judgment," observed a deep voice behind them.

Trubshaw and some others turned at the remark, and perceived a tall, thin man, moving away in the direction of the river.  Hitherto this person had eluded observation as he had been standing among the horses.

"A spy has been amongst us!—a Roundhead!" cried Vosper, springing to his feet.

"Seize the rogue and make him give an account of himself," cried Trubshaw, likewise starting up,  "What ho! stand!" he shouted.

The spy paid no heed to the summons, but speeded towards the river. The Scottish sentries were too far off to challenge him, and did not fire.

Vosper and Trubshaw started in pursuit.  But the spy reached the river before them, and jumped into a boat, which he had doubtless moored to the bank.

When his pursuers came up he was pulling vigorously across the stream.  A pistol was fired at him by Vosper, but without effect.

With a mocking laugh he then altered his course, and rowing down the stream, soon disappeared beneath one of the narrow arches of the bridge.

---

## CHAPTER XI.

COLONEL ROSCARROCK RELATES HOW THE EARL OF DERBY WAS ROUTED
AT WIGAN.

ILL news came to Charles on the morrow.

He was in his cabinet with his secretary, Captain Fanshaw, when Careless entered and informed him that Colonel Roscarrock was without.

"Roscarrock!" exclaimed the king, struck by Careless's looks.  "What news brings he from the Earl of Derby?"

"Ask me not, I beseech you, my liege," rejoined Careless, sadly.  "The colonel will tell his own tale.  I grieve to say he is wounded."

Comprehending at once what had occurred, Charles merely said, "Bring in Colonel Roscarrock."

And as the aide-de-camp departed, he arose and paced the cabinet with anxious steps, trying to summon his firmness for the painful interview.

Presently Careless returned supporting the colonel, whose left arm was in a sling.

Roscarrock was a tall, soldier-like, handsome man, but loss of blood and excessive fatigue gave a haggard expression to his features. The dusty state of his apparel and boots showed that he had ridden far.

" Alas, sire, I bring you bad news !" he exclaimed, in dolorous accents.

" Be seated, colonel, and I will hear you," said Charles, aiding him to a chair. " We have sustained a defeat, I perceive, but ere you enter into details, relieve my anxiety respecting the Earl of Derby."

" His lordship is sore hurt," replied Roscarrock, " but he is in safety, and will be with your majesty ere many days."

" Thank Heaven for that !" exclaimed Charles, earnestly.

" You have lost many loyal subjects and brave soldiers, sire," pursued Roscarrock. " Lord Widdrington is mortally wounded, if not dead. Sir William Throckmorton cannot survive. Sir Thomas Tildesley, Colonel Boynton, Colonel Trollope, and Colonel Galliard are slain."

" Alas ! brave Widdrington ! Alas ! brave Tildesley ! have I lost you ?" ejaculated Charles, mournfully. " Where did this dire disaster occur ?"

" At Wigan, in Lancashire, my liege," returned Roscarrock. " At first everything promised success. As your majesty's lieutenant, the Earl of Derby had issued his warrant commanding all your loyal subjects to meet him in arms at Preston, and he had collected six hundred horse and about nine hundred foot. With this force he marched to Wigan, with the design of proceeding to Manchester, where he not only hoped to surprise Cromwell's regiment of infantry but expected to obtain five hundred recruits. I need not tell your majesty that I was with his lordship. In a lane near the town we encountered Colonel Lilburn with a regiment of horse. Our men shouted loudly as we dashed upon the enemy, and fought so well that they drove Lilburn to the end of the lane. But a reserve of horse coming up changed the fortune of the day. What could our raw recruits to do against Lilburn's veterans ? Owing to the earl's reckless daring, he was wounded early in the conflict, which lasted upwards of an hour. How can I relate the disastrous issue ? Suffice it, the rout was total. Our men were panic-stricken, and could not be rallied. Hundreds were slain in flight. Pursued by a party of horse, the earl dashed into Wigan, and turned into a narrow street. Observing an open door, he flung himself from his steed and entered the house. A woman recognised him, and barred the door, enabling him to escape through a garden at the back before the Roundheads could search the house. By a miracle almost the noble fugitive got out of the town. which was filled with Parliamentary soldiers, and shaped his course towards the south. I was proceeding slowly in the same direction, when Providence—for I like not to call it chance—brought us together near Newport. At the house of a Royalist gentleman named Watson, we met another true man, Mr. Snead, who volunteered to conduct us to a lonely house called Boscobel, standing on the borders of two counties—

Shropshire and Staffordshire—where we could remain safely hidden till
our wounds were healed.  We gladly accepted the offer.  I rested one
night at Boscohel, when feeling ahle to proceed to Worcester, 1 came on.
Lord Derby was too weak to accompany me, but bade me say that your
majesty may count on seeing him in a few days."

"I thought to see him with two thousand men at his hack," exclaimed
Charles, in a melancholy and somewhat despondent tone.  "But the
hope ought never to have been indulged.  Treat it as we may, Roscarrock, this defeat at Wigan is a heavy blow to our cause.  'Twill en-
courage the enemy, and dishearten our own troops.  Lilburn will join
Cromwell."

"He has already joined him, sire, with his regiment of horse," remarked
Roscarrock.  "I should have been here before, had I not experienced
much difficulty in getting nigh Worcester, owing to the enemy's numerous outposts.  Would I had a sword like Widdrington's, and an arm
like his to wield it !" he continued with a grim smile.  "Widdrington
cut down half a dozen dragoons ere he was overpowered.  In losing him
your majesty has lost the tallest of your subjects, and the strongest."

"But not the bravest, while hardy Ned Roscarrock is left me," said
Charles.  "But you need refreshment and rest, colonel, and you must
have both, or you will never be able to fight for me, and I may call upon
you to attack Lilburn again before long."

"Your majesty will find me ready, call on me when you will," returned Roscarrock.

With Careless's assistance he then arose and withdrew, leaving the
king alone with his secretary.

---

## CHAPTER XII.

### HOW URSO GIVES WAS WEDDED TO MARY RUSHOUT.

AMID his manifold distractions, Careless had not forgotten pretty Mary
Rushout.  Twice had he seen her at her grandmother's dwelling in
Angel-lane, but on the second occasion she prayed him with tears in her
eyes never to come to the house again.

"We must part," she said ; "and it would have been better if we had
never met.  Urso, you know, is exceedingly jealous, and keeps the
strictest watch over me.  He saw you enter the house last night, and
waited outside till you departed."

"He must have waited long," remarked Careless, smiling.

"Ah ! it's no laughing matter, I can assure you," cried Mary.  "Urso
is a terrible man.  I won't tell you how bitterly he reviled you, but he
said you had better look to yourself if you came to Angel-lane again.
I shouldn't wonder if he is on the watch now.  Ay, there he is of a
surety," she added, stepping towards the little lattice window, and peep-
ing out into the lane.

"Heed him not," cried Careless, drawing her back.  "I was going—
but, to punish him, I'll stay an hour longer."

"No, no—you mustn't—indeed you mustn't!" she exclaimed. "It will drive him frantic, and when he is in one of his rages, he is capable of killing me. You must go immediately,"

"Impossible, sweetheart. I have much to say to you. Don't trouble yourself about this jealous Roundhead. Leave me to deal with him. I'll crop his ears still more closely to his head. Why don't you give him up?"

"Unluckily, I've plighted my troth to him, or I would."

"Never mind that, sweetheart. I'll liberate you from your pledge."

"You graceless Cavaliers will swear anything, and care not for breaking your vows—that's what Urso says."

"Truce to Urso. You will believe me, when I swear that I love you."

"No; because I find you do not regard an oath."

"Bah! promise to love me."

"No; because it would be sinful to make such a promise. Urso himself would say so."

"Urso again!—confound him! I must find means to free you from this tie—even if I sever it with my sword."

"That won't make me love you—rather hate you. But you must really go. Pray do not quarrel with Urso."

"If he stops me, I shall assuredly chastise him. Adieu, sweetheart! Expect me at the same hour to-morrow."

"No, no—you must not come—indeed, you must not."

But she seemed so little in earnest, that Careless construed her prohibition in the opposite sense, and believed she wished him to come.

As he went forth, Angel-lane—a narrow street running nearly parallel with the walls on the north of the city, in the direction of All Hallows —appeared quite deserted, and he thought that Urso Gives was gone. But he had scarcely reached the church, when a tall figure stepped from behind a buttress and barred his path.

"Out of my way, fellow!" he cried, haughtily, feeling sure it was Urso.

"Not till I have spoken with you," rejoined the other, maintaining his ground.

The Independent then continued, in a stern, menacing voice, "On the peril of your life, I forbid you to re-enter the house you have just profaned by your presence. You have beguiled the damsel who dwells there by your false speeches, and have sought to corrupt her. You cannot feign ignorance that she is my affianced wife, for I myself heard her tell you so."

"Since you have been playing the spy, you might easily have learnt that I am coming again to-morrow night at the same hour," rejoined Careless, in a mocking tone.

"Think it not," rejoined Urso, fiercely. "Since you will not be deterred from your evil courses by the warning given you, look to yourself!"

And suddenly drawing forth the long tuck-sword which he held under his cloak, he placed its point at the other's breast.

Careless sprang back and so saved his life, and drawing his own sword, their blades were instantly crossed.

Notwithstanding his eminently peaceful vocation, Urso proved no contemptible swordsman, and Careless failed to disarm him as soon as he expected.   The clash of steel roused the inmates of the houses, and some of them opened their doors, but when they perceived that an officer of rank was engaged with a Roundhead they did not interfere.

Mary Rushout, however, came forth, screaming with terror, and reached the combatants just as Careless, having knocked Urso's weapon from his grasp, seized him by the throat, and forced him down upon his knees, exclaiming :

" Sue for mercy, caitiff hound, or I will despatch thee !"

" Spare him, gentle sir !—spare him !" cried Mary, seizing the Cavalier's arm.

" He owes his worthless life to your intercession, sweet Mary," cried Careless, spurning Urso from him.   " If he is not sufficiently grateful for the obligation, let me know, and I will sharpen his gratitude.   Adieu, till to-morrow !"

And sheathing his sword, he strode away.

Quite crestfallen at his discomfiture, and eager to escape from the jeers of the neighbours who had come forth, Urso picked up his tuck-sword and hurried back to the house with Mary.

What passed between them need not be recounted.   It will be sufficient to state the result.

Not till the second evening after the occurrence just described, did Careless return to Angel-lane.   His duties to the king had detained him in the interval.

 After tapping softly at the door of Mary's dwelling, he raised the latch, but the door was fastened, and he was compelled to knock more loudly.   Still, no answer to the summons.   He listened intently, but not the slightest sound was to be heard within ; neither was any light visible through the little lattice window.

While he was making another ineffectual attempt to obtain admittance, a glover, who lived next door, came forth and told him that Dame Rushout and Mary were gone.

" Gone ! whither ?" cried Careless.

" That is more than I am able to inform your honour," replied the glover ; " but you are not likely to see Mary again, since Master Gives has taken her away."

" 'Sdeath ! did she consent to go with him ?"

" She could not very well refuse, seeing that she has become his wife," responded the glover.

" Amazement !" cried Careless.   " I could not have believed she would wed him."

" No one expected it, though the marriage has been long talked of," said the glover.   " But we think her grandam must have wrought upon Mary to consent—for she herself seemed wondrously reluctant.   Be this as it may, and I cannot speak for certain, she and Urso were married by the Reverend Laban Foxe, an Independent minister, and soon after the ceremony—if ceremony it can be called—Urso and his bride, with the old dame, quitted Worcester."

Careless had heard enough, and strode away to hide his vexation.

## CHAPTER XIII.

SHOWING HOW THE KING HAD FORTIFIED THE CITY.

THE fortifications of Worcester having now been completely repaired and considerably extended by Charles, it may be necessary to take another survey of them.*

On the south, the city was provided with a double enceinte—Sidbury-gate and the Commandery being completely enclosed by the newly raised lines. On the south-east, the outer fence extended from Fort Royal almost to Friars'-gate. On the other side, the new line of fortifications ran towards the Severn, covering the Moat, and the strong old wall behind it—a boundary wall built by a prior of the Convent of St. Mary early in the thirteenth century—and forming an outer defence to the Castle Mound, with which it was connected. The Castle Hill, as we have already had occasion to remark, was strongly fortified, and had become almost as formidable as Fort Royal itself, with which it was now linked by the new line of fortifications. These new fortifications were necessarily not very strong, but they answered their purpose. In the fields opposite Friars'-gate, and facing Perry Wood, stood an old blockhouse, which had more than once fallen into the hands of the former besiegers of the city. Dismantled by Colonel James, the Blockhouse had now been put into repair, and was garrisoned and provided with ammunition, its commander being Colonel Blague, on whose courage and fidelity Charles could perfectly rely. The district in which the old fortress stood is still known as the " Blockhouse Fields." Right and left of St. Martin's-gate, which looked towards King's Hill, as the acclivity was naturally enough designated after Charles's encampment upon it, a new bastion had been constructed. Two more bastions strengthened the northern ramparts, and at the north-west angle of the walls, not far from St. Clement's Church, removed in later times, stood a strong fort, the guns of which commanded the bridge. The tower in the centre of the bridge was well armed and well manned, as was the fort at the western extremity of the bridge. Proceeding along Tybridge-street to Cripplegate, the scene of many a former conflict in the days of

* Evidence of the wonders accomplished by the king in the short space of time allowed him is afforded by the very curious Diary of Judge Lechmere, some portions of which have been given by Mr. RICHARD WOOF, F.S.A., in his " Personal Expenses of Charles II. in the City of Worcester in 1651." Thus writes Judge Lechmere (the personage whom we have introduced in a previous chapter) a few days before the Battle : " The Scots king having sodainly possessed himself of the city of Worcester, in a few daies *fortified it beyond imagination.*" From his position in Worcester, and from his antiquarian researches, no one is, perhaps, so intimately acquainted with the history of the faithful city at the period of this Tale as Mr. WOOF, and the author seizes this opportunity of acknowledging the obligations he is under to him for much valuable information.

Sir John Biron and Governor Washington, and of wild Will Hodgkins's mad exploits, we come to St. John's, where General Dalyell's brigade was quartered—all the approaches to this outwork being as strongly barricaded, as when the dangerous suburb formed a Leaguer for the Parliamentarians in 1646.

From the foregoing hasty survey, it will be seen that the city was now in a thorough state of defence, and was especially strong on the south and south-east. Owing to the active zeal and forethought of the mayor and the sheriff, it was abundantly provisioned and well stored with forage.

On the enemy's approach, as a precautionary measure, it was resolved by the council of war to burn all the suburbs on the north and east—a determination that inspired great terror, since Foregate-street contained a large number of inhabitants, and Lawrence-lane, leading from Friars'-gate to the Blockhouse, was also a populous district.

Fort Royal now mounted some large ordnance, and was regarded by its defenders as impregnable. Including the fortifications, it contained upwards of fifteen hundred men, among whom were the most skilful engineers in the royal army. Fort Royal was commanded by Sir Alexander Forbes, an officer of great experience and resolution, and distinguished as the first knight made by Charles in Scotland. The Duke of Hamilton's head-quarters were at the Commandery—a hospital founded in the eleventh century by Bishop Wulstan, the saintly prelate who commenced the present cathedral. Two centuries later, the Master of the Hospital assumed the title of Preceptor, or Commander, whence the designation of the structure. The Commandery is one of the most picturesque old edifices in Worcester. Of its beautiful refectory, roofed with Irish oak, in which the king dined with the duke on the day before the battle, we shall have to speak hereafter.

The command of the fort on the Castle Mound had been intrusted to the Earl of Rothes, Sir William Hamilton, and Colonel Drummond, who had under them two brigades of Scottish infantry, with some artillery. Colonel Lesley's regiment of cavalry was encamped on the slopes of King's Hill. But the main body of the army, including the newly-raised troops, had now been moved to the western side of the river, where the camp extended for some miles towards Malvern. Pitscottie was stationed at Wick, midway between St. John's and Powick, near a cherry orchard, in which, nine years previously, the ambuscade was successfully laid for Lord Say. Montgomery and Keith were at Powick. Scattered troops were encamped on the left bank of the Severn almost as far as Upton, where General Massey, as we know, was posted to defend the pass.

Such was the disposition of the royal forces—when it was found that Cromwell was pushing his outposts round the city on the south and south-east, and that the main body of the Parliamentary army was between Stoulton and White Lady Aston, which latter place the Lord General himself had made his head-quarters.

Charles was not much disquieted by the intelligence. His spirit rose with the difficulties he had to encounter, and his cheerfulness and gaiety inspired confidence in all with whom he conversed. But he had not overcome his suspicions of Lesley, and these suspicions were almost confirmed by the conduct of the Scottish leader, who persisted in maintaining his post on King's Hill, whence secret communication with the enemy might most easily be held.

Jane Lane still remained in Worcester. Charles entreated her to quit the city before hostilities commenced, but she refused.

" I shall not go unless your majesty commands," she said. " Then I must perforce obey. But I beseech you to let me remain. I may be of some use ; and my brother will take care of me."

Naturally, there was much speculation amongst the Royalist leaders as to where the attack would begin, some mentioning one place, some another ; but Jane ventured to remark to the king that the first blow would be struck at Upton-on-Severn. She had ridden thither with her brother and Sir Clement Fisher, and while they were examining the broken bridge with General Massey, her quick eye detected a small reconnoitring party of the enemy in an orchard on the opposite side of the river. The Parliamentarians were quickly put to flight by a few musketshots from Massey's dragoons, but Jane declared they would return, and in much greater force. And she was right.

---

## CHAPTER XIV.

BY WHAT MEANS GENERAL LAMBERT GAINED THE PASS AT UPTON BRIDGE.

Early next morning—August 28th—Major General Lambert, who had crossed the Avon at Pershore on the previous day, and passed the night at Strensham, advanced with a regiment of horse and three troops of dragoons towards Upton Bridge, with the condition of which he had been made acquainted by the reconnoitring party he had sent on. No information of his movements reached Massey, and as he approached the river he was sheltered by the orchard previously described. On examination he found that, although the central arch of the bridge was destroyed, a plank had been most incautiously laid across the piers for the convenience of foot-passengers. Moreover, not more than three or four dragoons were on guard at the time. How so important a passage, on the security of which the royal army mainly depended, chanced to be so slenderly guarded, seemed inexplicable to him. Nevertheless, he greatly rejoiced, and firmly believed that Providence had favoured him.

At the very time when they ought to have been on the look-out, watching for their active and daring foe, Massey's troops were scattered about the single street, which formed the quiet little town, as careless and unconcerned as if no surprise were to be apprehended, and the fate of a great kingdom did not depend upon their vigilance. General Massey himself was at breakfast at the little hostel, and not a single officer was on duty. It is true they were close at hand, since the street led direct to the bridge, but not near enough, as the event showed.

General Lambert could not have chosen a more opportune moment for his approach. He had taken the Royalists completely unawares, and they certainly betrayed unpardonable negligence. Even the few dragoons on guard seemed half asleep, and were reclining drowsily against the parapets of the bridge.

Nothing could be more peaceful—nothing more lovely than the scene—and yet how soon, how terribly, was its calmness to be disturbed!—its beauty destroyed! Round the tower of the grey old church the swallows were wheeling; some sounds arose from the quiet little town, but they were not unpleasant to the ear; a few barks were moored to the bank below the town, but their owners seemed infected by the general indolence, as did some other persons who were fishing lower down the stream. The smooth, broad river flowed calmly on, save where its current encountered the remains of the broken arch of the bridge, against which it split and struggled. Partly destroyed as it was, the old stone bridge somewhat marred the peaceful character of the scene, yet it did not detract from its effect. Lambert was struck with the beauty of the view as he gazed at it, yet he hesitated not to play the part of a destroyer.

" Look yonder, Corporal Lightbound," he cried to a sour-visaged soldier near him. " Behold how these malignants keep guard. When they should be watchful, they are eating and drinking, or slumbering on their posts. They have broken their bridge to hinder us, yet have they foolishly laid down a plank whereby we may pass over and destroy them. Of a truth this is the Lord's doing. He has delivered them into our hands. Thou, corporal, art chosen for the work. Take with thee a score of musketeers on whom thou canst best rely. Cross over the plank as quickly as thou mayest, and possess thyself of the church. Thou canst easily maintain the post till I come to thine aid. The river must be fordable yonder," he added, pointing to a place below the bridge, where the current was rushing swiftly over a pebbly bed, and where a man who had reached a large stone, almost in the mid-stream, was fishing. The Severn, we may incidentally remark, had not then been dammed up at intervals, as is now the case, to preserve a constant depth of water for trading navigation.

" Truly, a fording party might well cross yonder, general," remarked Lightbound.

" The position yon man has attained proves it. He must have waded to that stone. There I will cross with the whole of my force."

" You will find me within the church with my men, general."

" I nothing doubt it," rejoined Lambert. " Fear not. The Lord is with thee, and will enable thee to surprise the enemy. And now about the work."

A man of great resolution, and appalled by no danger, Corporal Lightbound instantly obeyed. Selecting twenty musketeers, each as stalwart and fearless as himself, and bidding them follow him, he left the orchard.

So unlooked-for was the attempt, that the attacking party reached the bridge, and indeed were only a few yards from the broken arch, before they were discovered by the drowsy guard.

" Let me go first, corporal," said a soldier. " Thy life is more precious than mine."

" Nay, Zachariah ; the command belongs of right unto me," cried Lightbound, sternly and authoritatively. " I may not yield it—and I will not."

But Zachariah pressed forward, and went on to his death.

So offended was Corporal Lightbound at this act of insubordination, that he allowed all the others to pass on before him, whereby his own life was preserved.

Meantime the Royalist guard, aroused at last to a sense of danger, shouted loudly, " Arms! arms!" and sprang forward to dispute the passage.

The foremost of them discharged his musket at Zachariah, who was now crossing the plank, sword in hand. The shot took effect. Zachariah tottered, and fell upon the huge stones lying beneath him, scarce covered by water.

Another shot was instantly fired, and did execution upon the second soldier, who likewise dropped into the river.

The Royalists shouted, but their triumph was short-lived, for the bullets of the musketeers killed them both, and their comrades took to their heels.

By this time the call to arms having been loudly beaten, troopers and dragoons came rushing from the street to the scene of action. But they were not quick enough to prevent the assailing party from gaining possession of the church, the door of which, fortunately for them, chanced to be left open.

Everything favoured them, and they might well think, as their leader affirmed, that Heaven had declared itself on their side.

No sooner had they entered than the church door was closed and barred. Musketeers were placed at each window—with others behind them—and every possible precaution for the defence of the place was taken by Corporal Lightbound. Churches constantly served as fortresses in those days—and very good fortresses they made, as we see.

Cursing his own imprudence, General Massey rushed from the little hostel, sprang on his charger, and galloped to the bridge, followed by a small body of cavalry.

His first aim was to dislodge the detachment that had gained possession of the church, but when he rode into the churchyard with his troopers for this purpose, they were received by a well-directed volley from within, that killed several men and horses, and threw the rest of the troop into confusion. Massey himself was wounded in the hand.

Nothing daunted, the Royalists rode close up to the windows, fired their pistols into the church, and tried to reach their enemies, with their swords, but did them little hurt. The Parliamentarians, on the contrary, returned the fire with deadly effect, being able to aim deliberately at their opponents.

With the second volley, the churchyard was strewn with horses and wounded and dying men. Attempts were made by the Royalists to force an entrance to the church, but the windows were secured by bars, and the door being fashioned of stout oak and clamped with iron, their efforts were futile, and only excited the derision of the enemy.

By this time a regiment of cavalry had come up, and all seemed over with the brave men in the church. Massey ordered the door to be blown open; but ere a petard could be fixed to it, a fresh alarm was given.

The main body of the enemy was at hand.

While the attack on the church was taking place, Lambert had succeeded in fording the river at the place he had indicated, without any loss whatever, and was now hastening with his whole force to support the small detachment previously sent over.

Massey prepared to meet him, but his troops were utterly unable to resist the overwhelming force brought against them. Their ranks were broken on the first charge, and they made a headlong retreat into Upton, all Massey's efforts to check them being vain.

On gaining the street, which, as we have said, led to the bridge, they were reinforced, and faced the foe; but the conflict was of short duration, and ended in the complete rout of the Royalists, numbers of whom were slain.

Massey performed desperate acts of valour, needlessly exposing his life.

Surrounded by a party of dragoons, he extricated himself; and although wounded in the attack on the church, and subsequently hit in several places—two horses being shot under him—he managed to conduct his shattered troops safely to Worcester.

Pursuit was not continued far by Lambert, who was more intent on securing the pass he had gained than anxious to destroy the enemy. He knew the immense importance attached by Cromwell to the possession of Upton Bridge, and he also knew the effect its loss would inevitably have on the young king's fortunes.

Master of the all-important pass, he ordered the bridge to be repaired with all possible despatch.

---

## CHAPTER XV.

### HOW CROMWELL RECONNOITRED THE CITY FROM RED HILL.

No attempt was made by either of the Royalist commanders stationed on the western side of the Severn to repair Massey's disastrous defeat at Upton. The first tidings received of the conflict by Dalyell were from the wounded general himself, and it was then too late to act. Montgomery did not dare to quit his post at Powick, nor to detach Keith with any troops. Early next day, Upton Bridge having been sufficiently repaired to allow them to pass over it, Lambert was joined by Fleetwood, Ingoldsby, and Harrison, with their regiments of horse and foot; so there were now ten thousand Parliamentary soldiers at Upton. The Royalist troops encamped at Old Hills, on Newland-green, and at Lewthorn, drew closer to Worcester, and a new camp was formed between Upper Wick and Pitmarston.

No one profited more by Lambert's victory than Judge Lechmere. Not only did he escape payment of the fine imposed upon him by Massey, which became due on the very day when that general was worsted, but he got rid of his obnoxious guests, and avoided all further pains and penalties, for if Massey had not been compelled to beat a hasty retreat, he would assuredly have carried him off as a prisoner. As soon as he could venture forth with safety, the judge rode over to Upton to congratulate Lambert on his victory. At the same time he begged him to make Severn End his head-quarters. The Parliamentary general willingly accepted the offer, and was installed that night in the room which his adversary had quitted in the morning, with the full intention of returning to it.

Next day, the other generals who had just crossed the river were established at Severn End, and treated by the judge with the greatest hospitality. Whatever personal annoyance he had endured, Judge Lechmere could not complain that his house had been damaged or plundered by the Cavaliers; and this was more than could be said of Captain Hornyold's residence—Blackmore Park—which was stripped by the rapacious Republicans, Colonels Goff and Gibbons. Madresfield Court was summoned by Fleetwood to surrender, but the commander of the garrison refused, and the siege was postponed.

Lambert's victory was in the highest degree satisfactory to Cromwell. The seizure of the pass at Upton Bridge was part of the Lord General's plan, but it had been accomplished more expeditiously than he had anticipated. Though some miles off on the south of the city with the main body of his army, he was in constant communication with his generals, and directed all their movements. On the 28th of August, as we have previously mentioned, he made White Lady Aston, distant about five miles from Worcester, his head-quarters; and on that evening he was joined by Colonel Lilburn, who had arrived with his victorious troops from Wigan, in Lancashire.

The old manor-house of White Lady Aston, which originally belonged to a nunnery of the Benedictine order, situated in the northern suburbs of Worcester, was now occupied by Mr. Symonds, and by this gentleman, a thorough-going Republican, Cromwell was heartily welcomed. Almost midway between this place and Red Hill, until quite recently, had stood another fine old manor-house, belonging to Sir Robert Berkeley, and it was in this large mansion, the position of which perfectly suited him, that the Lord General meant to fix his quarters; but he learnt from his friend Mr. Symonds that the mansion no longer existed —it having been burnt down only three days previously by the Scottish Presbyterians, because Sir Robert Berkeley, its owner, when one of the Justices of the King's Bench in the time of the late king, had given his opinion for ship money.

Judge Berkeley, we may remark, had been very hardly used. Impeached for high treason, he was fined twenty thousand pounds, deprived of his office, and imprisoned in the Tower. His house had been plundered by the Parliamentarians in the first siege of Worcester, and now it was burnt down by the soldiers of the sovereign, whose cause he warmly supported. Nevertheless, his loyalty was unimpaired. It is to this high-minded and charitable man that Worcester owes the Berkeley Hospital.

As Cromwell rode through Spetchley Park, on his way to Red Hill, early next morning, he stopped to look at the blackened ruins of the fine old mansion, with which he had been well acquainted, and though not easily moved, he was touched by its melancholy aspect. A pleasant spot it had been, but it was now an utter ruin—nothing being left standing except the stables.

"These Scots," he remarked to Dighton, an inferior officer of his life guards, who was in constant attendance upon him, "have done worse than the men of Ephraim did, when they threatened to burn down Jephtha's house upon him with fire. 'Tis a mean and dastardly revenge, and they will pay for it. Those stables are large," he said, observing them carefully; "and the rooms connected with them must be commodious. I will pass the night here. Hold thy peace, Dighton. I know what thou wouldst say—but I care not if the rooms have been occupied by grooms."

Dighton gave the necessary orders while the Lord General rode slowly along the noble avenue of elm-trees that led to the place where the old mansion once stood. Within Spetchley Park, which was charmingly wooded, and contained a fine sheet of water, the main body of the Parliamentary army was encamped. Next came Lord Grey of Groby's brigade, and the camp continued, at intervals, to Red Hill, where Lilburn's regiment was now stationed.

As Cromwell approached Red Hill, he heard the sound of cannon, and, quickening his pace, soon learnt that the guns of Fort Royal had opened upon Lilburn's troops while they were taking up a position on the heights.

As no damage was done, Colonel Lilburn did not return the fire. "Let them waste their ammunition if they will," he said to his engineers. "They have not too much to spare."

Cromwell was of the same opinion.

"It would be useless to cannonade them from these heights," he said to Lilburn. "But I will soon get near enough to reach them."

Accompanied by a regiment of musketeers and a train of artillery, he then rode on to Perry Wood, which, as we know, faced Fort Royal, and, in order that the movement might not be discovered by the Royalists, he shaped his course through the Nunnery Wood, so designated because it had once belonged to the old convent we have alluded to in describing White Lady Aston, and entered Perry Wood, where his men could be hidden. He then gave orders that during the night a strong breastwork should be raised on the south of the hill, and a battery of heavy guns mounted, which would command Fort Royal.

This done, he returned as he came, attended only by a small escort; but he halted for a short time at the Nunnery Farm to see what the enemy were about. The engineers on Fort Royal had not made any discovery of the troops concealed in Perry Wood, and were still firing away uselessly at Lilburn's camp on Red Hill.

Throughout the day the Lord General remained with Lilburn, and together they reconnoitred the enemy from various points of Red Hill, examining the new lines of fortifications, which surprised them by their extent, and being much struck by the formidable appearance of the Castle Mount. But they had troops as well as fortifications to examine —the main body of the king's army being now posted on this side of the city.

This was what they beheld. From Friars'-gate on the east to the south-west angle of the fortifications near the river, the city was surrounded by troops. Lesley's brigade had descended from King's Hill, and now occupied the Blockhouse Fields. This Scottish cavalry seemed to give Cromwell little uneasiness, and he smiled as he pointed them out to Lilburn, but he did not regard with equal indifference the large force under the Duke of Hamilton, which occupied the London-road, and commanded the approach to the Sidbury-gate. Nor did either of them think lightly of the regiments respectively commanded by the Duke of Buckingham, Lord Wilmot, Colonel Legge, and Colonel Lane. Lilburn thought General Middleton's brigade likely to give him trouble. Middleton's troops were posted near the river, on the spot where Diglis's Bowling-green was subsequently laid out.

Such was the disposition of the royal forces on the south and south-east sides of Worcester when the two Parliamentary leaders examined them from Red Hill. Cromwell looked upon the troops as already scattered and consumed. But Lilburn was struck by their gallant appearance, and did not refuse them the tribute of a soldier's admiration.

---

## CHAPTER XVI.

IN WHICH MASSEY PROPOSES A NIGHT ATTACK ON THE ENEMY.

THE greatest consternation reigned within the city. Massey's defeat at Upton had been felt as a heavy blow, and the boldest amongst the Cavaliers were much discouraged by it. The appearance of the enemy on the southern heights increased the alarm of the citizens, and some of the most timorous began to think of flight. For the credit of the loyal city, and its brave inhabitants, we are happy to record that these were very few in number. A proclamation was made that all who desired to depart might do so, but none availed themselves of the permission. The excitement caused by the movement of the troops, and the cannonade from Fort Royal, soon roused the spirits of the citizens, and enabled them to shake off their depression. Charles showed no symptoms of misgiving; but on the contrary, seemed full of energy and resolution. He paid an early visit to Massey, whose wounds had detained him at St. John's, but did not reproach the unfortunate general. Massey, however, could not sufficiently deplore his error.

"I have committed a great fault," he said. "Your majesty may forgive me; but I can never forgive myself. Here I am, stretched on this couch, when I ought to be with my regiment! Oh! that Heaven would grant me sufficient strength to meet the enemy."

"Make yourself easy, general," replied Charles, kindly. "You will soon be able to serve me again."

"I trust so, sire," groaned Massey. "I shall die if I am kept here long. Cromwell, I am told, has appeared on Red Hill."

"Lilburn's regiment is on the brow of the hill. Cromwell is at Spetchley," replied Charles.

"And I am here, and cannot face them," cried the wounded man, in a tone of anguish.

"Be patient," said Charles.

"I cannot be patient, sire, when I think what might be done. Were I able to move, I would attack Cromwell in his head-quarters this very night, and either slay him, or sell my life in the attempt. But I cannot do it—I cannot do it," he added, sinking back with a groan.

"A night attack might be made upon Lilburn—or upon an outpost," observed Charles.

"That is not enough, sire," rejoined Massey, raising himself, and speaking with such earnestness that for the moment he forgot his wounds; "Cromwell himself must be reached. I would give twenty lives, if I had them, to win you the crown."

"I feel your devotion," said Charles. "The attempt might be successful, but it is so desperate that none but yourself would make it."

"Yes, sire, there are others—many others—who would not shrink from the task, but the bravest, the most determined, the most trustworthy of your generals, is Middleton. Let him take my place."

"Will he take it, think you?"

"Joyfully, sire. I will answer for him as I would for myself. He will need fifteen hundred of the best horse and foot. Let him take with him Sir William Keith and Colonel Legge. Both can be relied on. Let the word be 'Death to the Regicide!' But they must not return until their work is accomplished."

"I will summon a council forthwith, and lay the matter before them," said Charles.

"I pray you do not, sire," rejoined Massey, earnestly. "If the enterprise is to succeed, it must be kept secret. Confide it only to those you can trust, as the Duke of Hamilton, Colonel Drummond, and Sir Alexander Forbes. Above all, let not Lesley hear of it. One word more, sire, and I have done. The camisade must take place to-morrow—an hour after midnight—when the rebels are lulled to repose. Then Middleton must dash through Lilburn's camp, and cut his way through all other obstacles to Spetchley."

"I am half inclined to lead the attack myself," said the king.

"It must not be, sire. You would throw away your life. The chances are a thousand to one against Middleton's return. But that matters little if he can accomplish his object. Should the enterprise succeed you will forgive me the loss of Upton Bridge."

"I have already forgiven you," replied Charles. "I will see Middleton forthwith."

And, bidding Massey a kindly farewell, he took his departure.

The king had intended to visit the camp just formed at Wick, but his plans being now changed, he crossed the bridge, and sent on Careless with a message to Middleton, who was posted outside the city, opposite Frog Gate, with his regiment, bidding the general attend him without delay at the Commandery, and bring with him Sir William Keith and Colonel Legge. We have already mentioned that the Duke of Hamilton was quartered at the Commandery, and on the king's arrival at the ancient hospital, he found the duke in the refectory—a large and beautifully proportioned hall, with an open roof of richly ornamented woodwork, a minstrel's gallery, and lofty windows, filled with exquisitely painted glass. With the duke was Sir Alexander Forbes, the commander of Fort Royal, and the king remained in converse with them until Careless appeared with General Middleton and the others.

The whole party then adjourned to an inner room, better adapted than the refectory for secret discussion, and Careless was stationed at the door to prevent all chance of interruption.

The apartment looked on a small garden, and the day being extremely warm, one of the windows was unluckily left open—unluckily, we say, for a personage outside, apparently a gardener, contrived to place himself so near it, that he overheard all that passed within. The conference did not last long. General Middleton, as Massey had foreseen, at once undertook the daring enterprise, and both his companions were eager to share the danger with him.

When all had been discussed and settled, General Middleton said to the king :

"Your majesty need not fear that the design will be betrayed. Not till the latest moment shall the men know on what enterprise they are to be employed, and even then they shall not be aware of our precise aim. Before dawn your majesty shall hear that the blow has been struck, and if I cannot come myself, some one more fortunate will bring you the glad tidings."

With this, he took his departure with his compnaions.

---

## CHAPTER XVII.

### HOW THE SUBURBS OF THE CITY WERE BURNT.

EVERY moment of that eventful day had its employment for the king, who had now a most painful duty to perform. Most reluctantly had he given his assent to the execution of the stern decree of the council of war, which enjoined that all persons dwelling without the walls should remove their goods forthwith, and take refuge within the city, since it was necessary that their habitations should be burnt down, in order that they might not afford shelter to the foe. Now, the suburbs of Worcester, as we have already explained, were extremely populous, and consequently great numbers of houses—indeed, several small streets—were

thus doomed to destruction.   The greater part of the luckless occupants
obeyed the mandate without a murmur, though it deprived them of a
home.   The mayor, the aldermen, and the sheriff rendered every assistance in their power, and the goods of the poor folks thus ousted, were
temporarily placed in the churches.   The king expressed his profound
sympathy for the sufferers, and promised them compensation for their
losses.   Alas! it was but a promise.

The occasion called forth the active zeal of Jane Lane, and never had
it been more energetically displayed.   Accompanied by Sir Clement Fisher
and her brother, she rode through all the districts destined to destruction,
and wherever she found a little crowd assembled, or heard murmurs, she
halted and earnestly exhorted submission to the decree.

" Blame not the king," she said, " for this severe measure, but blame
the great rebel and regicide, who has rendered it necessary.   It is Cromwell, the murderer of your martyred sovereign, who comes hither to
ravage your city, and slay your rightful king, that he may set himself up
in his place, who thus drives you from your homes.   Charles, your
king, loves you, and would save you from this ruthless general and his
fierce and fanatical soldiery, who will put you all to the sword if they
obtain the victory.   Resist, therefore, to the uttermost.   Better that
your houses should be burnt down than that they should afford shelter to
such an enemy.   Better your wives should be driven forth than exposed
to the insults of Cromwell's soldiery.   Quit your homes without hesitation and without murmuring, but with the deep determination to be
avenged upon the foe.   'Tis a sacrifice you are called upon to make for
your king—but we all make sacrifices for him.   Right, justice, truth
are on our side : treason of the darkest dye, rebellion and oppression,
are on the other.   Fight for your lawful king.   Place your trust in
Heaven, and you will triumph over these bloodthirsty rebels."

While uttering these stirring words, which produced an extraordinary
impression upon those who heard them, she looked as if inspired.   Her
beautiful features assumed a very different expression from that which
they ordinarily wore.   For the moment they had lost all their softness,
and when speaking of Cromwell, her eyes flashed as with lightning,
her proud nostrils distended, and her delicate lips curled fiercely.   Her
beauty, her energetic language, and fiery looks produced, as we have
said, the strongest effect upon her auditors, and roused within them a
burning desire of vengeance.   No longer they thought it a hardship to
quit their homes, but were eager to fight for the king, and, if need be,
lay down their lives for him.   All feelings of discontent were subdued,
and the greatest enthusiasm for the royal cause was awakened.   Even
the women who listened to her were almost as much roused as their
husbands.   Nor when she had departed did the effect of her eloquence
subside.   Wrath against Cromwell had now taken possession of every
breast.   Old Noll was the real author of the cruel decree.   Old Noll
had driven them from their homes.   Old Noll would burn down the
city itself, and massacre them all, men, women, and children, if he could.
But the king would prevent it.   Long live the king!—Down with the
Republic!

Night had come on before all the necessary preparations were completed. Combustibles having been placed in most of the houses, and bands of men employed to set fire to them at a given signal, the conflagration began simultaneously on every side, and in a surprisingly short space of time the city was encompassed by a semicircle of fire. The spires and towers of the churches caught the red reflection of the flames, and a ruddy glow illumined the massive roof and tower of the cathedral. All the principal buildings were lighted up.

Viewed from the heights, it seemed as if the fire, which burnt with great fierceness, was gaining upon the walls and gates; but this was not so, all needful precautions having been taken to prevent its too near approach. Luckily the night was almost calm. A gentle breeze from the south carried the flames from the city. Overhead hung a c'oud of smoke. The spectacle was magnificent; the soldiers could be seen on the gates and walls, the engineers on the summit of Fort Royal and the Blockhouse, while all the troops outside the city were clearly distinguishable.

The conflagration did the Royalists an unexpected service by revealing the engineers engaged in raising the breastwork in front of Perry Wood. The operations of these men were quickly stopped by the guns of Fort Royal, to which they offered an excellent mark. Two artillerymen and a matross were killed, and the rest dispersed.

The defenders of the fort, having thus learnt that a detachment of the enemy was hidden in Perry Wood, continued their cannonade briskly, and sent shot into different parts of the thicket in the hope of dislodging the Parliamentarians. Little did they think that among those whom they had driven off was the Lord General himself, who chanced at the time to be superintending the construction of the breastwork. One of the artillerymen was killed close beside him.

With the utmost calmness, Cromwell gave orders to the engineers to suspend their work till the fire had burnt out, and then deliberately withdrew to a place of safety, whence he watched the progress of the conflagration, the cause of which he had comprehended from the first. Several shots passed over his head and shattered the trees beyond him, as he stood behind a hedge bank with his constant attendant Dighton. His curiosity was excited, for the fortifications were more completely revealed by this fierce glare than by daylight. He could count the large guns on Fort Royal, and the sakers, demi-cannons, culverins, and falcons on the Blockhouse.

"Ha!" he suddenly exclaimed. "Methinks I see the young man, Charles Stuart, on the summit of yon blustering fort, which he took from Colonel James, and which I shall soon retake from him. Were he wise, he would stop this furious and senseless cannonading. But the noise pleases him. Dost note what he has done, Dighton?"

"He has fortified the city strongly, according to my opinion, your excellency."

"Ay, he has fenced it—doubly fenced it with high walls and bulwarks—he has armed his forts better than I thought he could have done, chiefly yon new fort on the Castle Hill, for this Blockhouse hath no real ordnance—and he hath placed his troops with some judgment; but neither troops nor defences will avail him. There will soon be a breaking down of the walls, and then woe to those within the city that has upheld him. I shall not spare them. England must never again be invaded by a Stuart."

"This pretender to the throne must die on the same scaffold as his father at Whitehall," observed Dighton.

"'Twere better he should die here at Worcester," rejoined Cromwell, sternly. "Then these bigoted fools cannot make a martyr of him. In any case, he must not escape to give me further trouble. I mean not that he troubles me, but the state."

"I quite understand your excellency."

"Mark well what I say to thee, Dighton," pursued Cromwell. "On the 3rd of last September, as thou knowest well, a great victory was wrought at Dunbar; but on the anniversary of that day, now close at hand, a still greater victory will be achieved here at Worcester. The false light that has deluded so many will then be as utterly extinguished as yon fire will be ere long, and nothing more will be heard of Charles Stuart and his pretensions to the throne. But the power of the army must then be recognised, and——" He paused, as if unwilling to complete the sentence.

But Dighton finished it for him, by adding:

"And the ruler of the country can be no other than the Lord General Cromwell."

"I do not desire to rule, Dighton; but I would have my country well governed and wisely."

"And no one could govern it so wisely and so well as your excellency —of that I am assured."

"Thou flatterest me," said Cromwell, not displeased. "But this is idle talk. The decisive battle has yet to be fought."

"I look upon it as already won," rejoined Dighton. "As the Lord instructed Joshua how to take Ai, so will he instruct a greater general than Joshua how to take this rebellious city."

"That the great work will be perfected I nothing doubt," said Cromwell. "But I have seen enough of yon burning houses, and will tarry here no longer. I must visit all the outposts, in case a sally should be made; though, judging from appearances, I do not think aught will be attempted to-night."

He then made his way through the wood, closely followed by Dighton, and ere many minutes reached a sheltered spot where his escort awaited him. Mounting his charger he next proceeded to the camp at Red Hill, where he found Colonel Lilburn and Lord Grey on horseback and attended by several officers. They had been watching the conflagration which was now almost extinguished. Cromwell and Lilburn visited all the outposts, after which the Lord General rode through the park to Spetchley.

## CHAPTER XVIII.

### HOW URSO GIVES HAD AN INTERVIEW WITH THE LORD GENERAL IN THE STABLE OF SPETCHLEY MANOR-HOUSE.

VIEWED by torchlight, as Cromwell beheld it on his arrival there, the large stable-yard of Spetchley manor-house presented a very curious sight—being full of musketeers, cuirassiers, lancers, and dragoons, with their horses. Closely adjoining the stable-yard, and forming not the least interesting part of the striking scene, were the blackened walls of the ancient mansion, now silvered by the rays of the moon.

As Cromwell rode into the yard, attended by Colonel Lindsey and Dighton, he remarked an elderly personage, guarded by two musketeers.

"Ah! you have a prisoner yonder I see, Cornet Hardiman?" he observed to the officer who came up to him. "Where was he taken?—and who is he?"

"He was found in a summer-house in the garden, your excellency, and refuses to give his name," replied the cornet. "As he may be a spy, I have detained him till your return."

"You have done right," said the Lord General. "Bring him to me."

"Advance, prisoner!" cried the officer.

And as the prisoner was brought forward, Cromwell was struck by his grave looks and deportment.

"This man cannot be a spy," he thought, after a moment's scrutiny. "Who art thou? And what dost thou here?" he demanded.

"Truly it would appear that I am an intruder," replied the prisoner, somewhat haughtily. "Yet I once was master of this mansion."

"If so, you are Sir Robert Berkeley," rejoined Cromwell, surprised.

"Your excellency has said it," rejoined the other. "I am that unfortunate man."

"Had you declared as much from the first, you would have been set at liberty," observed the Lord General.

"I am not so sure of that," replied Sir Robert. "I do not think my word would have been taken. But be that as it may, I cared not to answer questions rudely put to me by your soldiers. Mistake me not—I make no complaint of ill-treatment. Such explanation as I have to offer your excellency I give readily. My habitation having been burnt down, my stables occupied, I had no place of refuge except my summer-house, where I sought shelter for the night. There I was found, as hath just been stated."

"You have only yourself to thank for the detention, Sir Robert," rejoined Cromwell. "Though your nephew, Sir Rowland Berkeley of Cotheridge, is an avowed malignant, and you yourself are known as an active partisan of Charles Stuart, I will not discredit what you tell me. You are free; and, furthermore, are free to speak of all you have seen or heard. You shall be conducted to the nearest outpost, or, if you desire it, shall be taken to White Lady Aston."

"I will rather sleep beneath a tree than under Mr. Symonds's roof," replied the old judge. " If I might ask a favour of your excellency, it would be to be allowed to pass the night in my summer-house."

" You seem to like the spot," remarked Cromwell, somewhat suspiciously.

" 'Tis all that is left me of the old place," replied the judge.

" Well, I will consider of it," said Cromwell. " Have you supped, Sir Robert ?"

" Neither dined nor supped."

" You have fasted too long for a man of your years. You shall sup with me."

This was said in a more cordial tone than the Lord General had hitherto adopted.

Dismounting, he gave his horse to a soldier, and ordered Cornet Hardiman to show him the rooms prepared for him in the stables.

" Come with me, Sir Robert," he added to the old judge, who, of course, complied with a request amounting to a command.

The stables being full of horses, it seemed at first that there could be but little accommodation for the Lord General, but the cornet mounted up a ladder-like flight of stairs, that brought them to a room which might have been a hay-loft, but which was now furnished with a table and a few old-fashioned chairs saved from the wreck of the ruined mansion. On the table were placed cold viands and a couple of flasks of wine. Covers were laid for four, in case the Lord General should invite any of his officers to sup with him, as was occasionally his wont. A lamp set on the table scarcely illumined the loft, but its glimmer showed the cobwebbed rafters overhead.

" Let Dighton wait below," said Cromwell. " I shall require no attendance."

As the cornet withdrew, he took off his casque and gauntlets, and pronounced, with considerable unction, a very long grace, during which he kept Sir Robert standing. Grace ended at last, he bade him sit down and fall to—setting him the example. Though the old judge had fasted so long, he ate little in comparison with his host, and drank only a single glass of wine. Cromwell, however, partook with right good appetite of the plain fare set before him, and emptied a large flagon of sack. While thus employed, he scarcely spoke a word, but he afforded his guest an excellent opportunity of studying his remarkable countenance.

With Cromwell's coarse features, disfigured by a large, ill-formed red nose, against which the Cavaliers never ceased to direct their scurril jests ; with his stout, ungainly figure, utterly devoid of dignity and grace, the reader must be familiar. Yet with all these drawbacks, which have not been in the slightest degree exaggerated, the Lord General's physiognomy was very striking. Chiefly so, on account of its determined and formidable expression. His eye possessed extraordinary power, and few could brook its glances when he was angered, or when his suspicions were aroused. His habitual expression was that of bluff sternness, and he looked like a surly bull-dog, whom no one who valued a whole skin would care to offend, and yet he could put off this morose and repelling look when he pleased, and exchange it for one of rough good-humour. But even when he unbent, he inspired fear. His character has been too much darkened by some writers, and virtues have been ascribed to him by others which he certainly did not possess. Courageous, crafty, ambitious, hypocritical, almost a fatalist, cruel, unjust, and unrestrained by any moral principle, by the sole force of his indomitable will, he overcame every obstacle, and reached the goal at which he aimed. His ambition being boundless, nothing less than sovereign power would satisfy him, though he affected to disdain the title of king, being perfectly aware that the Royalists would never accept a regicide as king. Of marvellous sagacity and penetration, he was rarely deceived in his judgment of men, and always used them, where he could, as instruments in furthering his designs. A profound dissembler, and fully capable of using religion as a mask, had it been needful to do so, it can scarcely be doubted that he was really religious ; though few entirely believed in the sincerity of his religious professions. Cromwell's character is full of striking contrasts. Abhorred by his enemies, he had multitudes of devoted friends. For a time his memory was execrated. In latter days somewhat more than justice has been done him. The great crime he committed has never been pardoned—will never be pardoned. The stain of blood cannot be washed out. As to his high military genius all are agreed. Among great commanders he stands foremost. And he would rank among the greatest of men, if his crimes did not overshadow his virtues.

The accoutrements of the Lord General differed very little from those of an officer of his own body-guard, except that they were somewhat more ornamented, being filigrained with gold. They consisted of an open casque and a very large gorget. But he had neither breast-plate, nor cuisses—the stout buff coat with long skirts which he wore affording sufficient protection to the lower part of his person. A scarf was tied round his waist. His strong buff boots were drawn far up the thigh, and from his broad embroidered shoulder-belt hung a large basket-hilted sword.

He was not unconscious that he was the object of his guest's covert scrutiny, but the circumstance did not trouble him—perhaps rather gratified him. It may be that he designed to win over the old Royalist judge, or at least to produce a favourable impression upon him, for as soon as he had finished supper, he almost compelled Sir Robert to take more wine, and then began a very friendly discourse with him, professing great regret that Spetchley manor-house had been destroyed by the Scottish soldiers, and expressing a hope that it might soon be rebuilt.

Their conversation, however, was interrupted by the entrance of Dighton, who informed the Lord General that a man was without who stated that he had matter of the utmost importance to communicate to his excellency.

"What manner of man is he?" demanded Cromwell.

"I have reason to believe he is a spy from the city," replied Dighton. "He delivered himself up to the vedettes on Red Hill, conjuring them to bring him speedily before your excellency. Accordingly he hath been sent on from the first outpost. He is the bearer of this letter, which he affirms is from Colonel James, somewhile commandant of the garrison of Worcester."

Cromwell took the missive, and after glancing at its contents, said, "The man hath spoken truly. His business is important. I will see him."

"With your excellency's permission I will retire," said the old judge, rising.

"I am sorry to lose your company," said Cromwell; "but this is a matter that cannot be postponed. A bed must be found for Sir Robert Berkeley," he added to Dighton.

"I know not where to find one, unless his worship is content to sleep on straw," was the half-grumbling response.

"If I am allowed to occupy my old summer-house, I shall be perfectly satisfied," replied the judge.

"Be it so, Sir Robert," said Cromwell. "I wish you sounder repose than I myself am likely to enjoy. To-morrow's news may surprise you."

The old judge did not venture to question him, but, bowing deeply, departed with Dighton, and Cromwell was left for a few moments alone.

"What says Colonel James?" he muttered. "'The bearer of this may be trusted. He hath preserved my life, and, with Heaven's grace, may be the happy means of preserving a life in comparison with which mine is as naught.' The import of the message is plain. The life to be preserved is mine own. 'Cursed is the man that trusteth in man,' saith the prophet. Yet in whom can I trust, if not in those who serve me? If there be a plot against me, it were better for him who hath hatched it that he had never been born."

Steps were now heard on the staircase, and the next moment a tall, thin man, whose aspect was that of a Puritan, while his habiliments were those of a Cavalier, was ushered into the presence of the Lord General by Dighton. Behind them came a couple of musketeers, but the guard advanced no further than the head of the steps.

Cromwell fixed a long and searching glance upon the personage thus introduced, who bore the scrutiny firmly.

Apparently satisfied, the Lord General signed to Dighton to withdraw, bidding him, however, wait outside.

"Now, fellow, thy name?" demanded Cromwell of the man, as soon as they were alone.

"Urso Gives, of Worcester, by trade a tailor," was the reply.

"An honest trade. I have naught to say against it," rejoined the Lord General. "Men must be clothed, though it were better they were clothed in sackcloth than in purple and fine linen. Better still they were clothed in the garments of salvation. But enough. Hath thy trade aught to do with what thou hast to declare to me?"

"Nothing. I mentioned it for a reason which I will presently explain to your excellency. I have come hither at the hazard of my life to bring you timely intelligence of a daring and well-conceived design, which, if it were successfully executed, would snatch from you the victory and give it to Charles Stuart. What am I to claim as a reward if I shall prove what I assert?"

“ Go to. Bargain not with me. Thy reward shall be proportioned
o the importance of thy disclosure.”

“ But I may not live to receive it,” rejoined Urso. “ The risk I run
s great. When I depart hence I must return to Rabbah, and I may fall
into the hands of the Ammonites, who will show me little mercy.
What then becomes of the recompense promised me ?”

“ Hast thou a wife ?”

“ Yea, verily,” replied Urso ; “ a fair young wife, whom I have just
espoused. If I perish in my efforts to save Israel, shall she have the
reward ?”

“ Content thyself—she shall. I promise it to thee,” rejoined Cromwell. “ Thou hast great faith in the constancy of women, I perceive, and
it is well.”

“ I cannot with truth affirm that I have great faith in the constancy
of her whom I have wedded,” replied Urso. “ But I love her better
than life.”

“ And she, I trust, will honour thy memory, as it deserves to be
honoured,” remarked Cromwell, in a slightly contemptuous tone. “ But
having made thy conditions beforehand, let me hear what thou hast to
tell. Be brief.”

“ ’Tis not my wont to waste words,” rejoined Urso. “ But first let
me inquire the hour ?”

“ The hour ! Thou shouldst know it as well as I. ’Tis past eleven.”

“ Then in less than two hours’ time General Middleton will sally
forth from the Sidbury-gate with fifteen hundred picked men, all well
mounted and well armed, wearing their shirts above their breastplates
for distinction. The malignant general has vowed to take your excellency, dead or alive, and thus end the war, and he will make every effort
to fulfil his vow. Expecting to find Colonel Lilburn wholly unprepared,
he will pass through the camp without attacking it, and cut his way
through any other opposing force further on, his aim being Spetchley,
where he hopes to find your excellency. Should he arrive, no quarter
is to be given.”

“ Thou art sure of this ?” remarked Cromwell, with forced calmness.

“ I heard the project discussed and settled this very morning at the
Commandery between Charles Stuart, the Duke of Hamilton, General
Middleton, and some others. As I have said, Middleton has vowed to
accomplish your excellency’s destruction, or to perish in the attempt.”

“ And those engaged in the camisade are to sally forth an hour after
midnight, thou sayst ?” observed Cromwell, calmly.

“ That is the hour appointed. I would have given your excellency
earlier warning, had I been able to quit the city. But I could not obtain
an order, and only succeeded in getting out during the burning of the
suburbs.”

“ Thou hast arrived in time. The design can be easily frustrated.
Thy intelligence merits a good reward, and thou shalt not be disap-
pointed of it. If aught befals thee, thy wife shall have the reward.
Moreover, I promise thee ample vengeance.”

Cromwell, who did not seem at all disturbed by the alarming intelligence he had received, but maintained the most perfect composure, put several questions to Gives, and then said :

" Do not suppose that I doubt the truth of thy statement, but I cannot allow thee to return to Worcester till the affair is over."

" The danger to me will be far greater, if I return not before daybreak," pleaded Gives.

" Why shouldst thou return ?  But like a doting fool, thou canst not, I suppose, leave thy young wife."

He then called out for Dighton, who instantly answered the summons, and said to him, " This man will remain here till I return, or until I send an order for his release.  Sit down at the table, friend," he added to Gives.  " Eat and drink and make glad thine heart.  Thou wilt see thy wife again ere long."

While thus speaking he had donned his casque and gauntlets, and he then quitted the chamber, and proceeded to the stable-yard, where he found Colonel Lindsey, the commander of his life guards, and telling him he was about to proceed to Colonel Lilburn's camp, bade him follow with three hundred men.

" The whole regiment must remain under arms throughout the night," he added.  " An attack may be expected."

Without a word more he mounted his charger, which was ready for him, and attended by Dighton and a small party of musketeers, rode at a brisk pace through the woods to Colonel Lilburn's camp.

<hr>

## CHAPTER XIX.

### THE CAMISADE.

Good watch was kept—the sentinels were at their posts—but the quietude of the camp proved that no apprehensions of attack were entertained.

" Kerioth would have been surprised and taken had I not received this warning," mentally ejaculated Cromwell, as he rode up to the commander's tent.

Lilburn had thrown himself on a couch, but hearing Cromwell's approach he sprang to his feet, and met him at the entrance of the tent.

After a brief consultation between the generals, it was decided that neither drums should be beaten nor trumpets blown, lest the sounds should be heard by the enemy, but that the slumbering soldiers should be quietly roused to arms ; and this was done by Lilburn in person.

Meanwhile, Colonel Lindsey had arrived with the life guards from Spetchley, and putting himself at their head, Cromwell rode to the outpost nearest the city.

This outpost was about three hundred yards from the camp, on the slope of the hill, not far from the London road, and was stationed in a field bordered on the north and north-east by high-banked hedges.

The night can scarcely be described as dark, though the sky was covered with lazily-moving clouds, but through these the moon burst occasionally. The old city, with its towers, steeples, and fortifications, could be distinguished through the gloom; but no lights were visible within it, and no sounds from it arose. So profound was the stillness, that it might have been supposed that the inhabitants and their defenders were alike buried in slumber, and that no attacking party could be waiting to sally forth.

As Cromwell, with the life guards, cautiously descended the hill, keeping under cover of the hedges, three-quarters past midnight was struck by the cathedral clock—proclaiming that the hour was close at hand.

The outpost reached by Cromwell was guarded by two hundred and fifty foot and two hundred horse, but three hundred of the best troopers in his army being now added, he deemed this force quite sufficient to repel the attack.

Little time was left, but luckily those on guard at the outpost were on the alert. Having placed his troops with the quickness and skill peculiar to him, the Lord General stationed himself on a small woody mound in the centre of the field, whence he commanded the approach to the Sidbury-gate, and awaited the sortie with some impatience, but without the slightest anxiety. Close behind him were Dighton and a couple of cuirassiers.

He had not to wait long. While the single stroke of the cathedral bell yet vibrated through the air, and was echoed by the clocks of the other churches, the gate yawned wide, and a troop of sheeted spectres— for such they seemed in the gloom—issued forth. The ghostly band formed three regiments—the first being commanded by General Middleton, the second by Sir William Keith, the third by Colonel Legge.

The troops came forth from the Sidbury-gate, and formed in silence. If any orders were given they did not reach Cromwell's ears, though he was listening intently; and the ghostly appearance of the horsemen was fully preserved until Middleton dashed off with the greatest rapidity, when the clatter of hoofs and the jingling of arms proved that the phantoms were substantial soldiers. The second regiment followed instantly, galloping along the London road as swiftly as the first; but a momentary interval occurred before Colonel Legge started. The cause of this brief delay was perfectly intelligible to Cromwell, and he gave some orders to Dighton, who rode off at once to Colonel Lindsey.

Meanwhile, the two foremost regiments came on at full speed, and dashed past the field in which the outpost was stationed, making it evident that their point of attack was Lilburn's camp on the brow of the hill, and showing that the outpost would be dealt with by the regiment that followed.

In obedience to Cromwell's orders not a shot had been fired, and Colonel Legge came on uncertain as to how he would be received by the enemy. Easy access to the field could be obtained at several points known to the Royalists, and small parties of men entered at these places, but the main body, led by Colonel Legge, broke through the hedge skirting the London road, and were received by ranks of pikemen three deep, the front rank kneeling, the centre stooping, and the rear standing upright, and forming an almost impassable barrier. On the flanks, right and left, were posted musketeers, who poured a terrible volley upon the enemy as they gained the field,

Several saddles were emptied.    Neverthcless, Colonel Legge, shouting to his men to follow, charged the pikemen with the greatest intrepidity, but it was impossible to cut through their ranks.    Many horses were killed in the charge, and others so desperately hurt that they bore back their riders in spite of all efforts to force them on.    Colonel Legge's charger, though badly hurt, had still strength enough left to sustain its rider, but would not again face the deadly pikes.

Caught as in a trap, it seemed as if the unfortunate Royalists must all be slaughtered, but turning from the pikemen, Colonel Legge charged the musketeers with a fury that proved irresistible.    Having gained the open field with such of his men as had been able to follow him, he was joined by the others, who having entered at different points had hitherto taken no part in the conflict.    But before they could form they were charged by Colonel Lindsey, at the head of the life guards, and so shattered, that they could not recover, but fled from the field in the greatest disorder, hurrying towards the Sidbury-gate faster than they had quitted it.    Many were shot while jumping the hedges, or pressing through the gates.    Colonel Legge was the last to retreat.    His horse carried him out of reach of the foe, and then dropped.

Cromwell watched tbe conflict from the mound on which he had taken his stand, and did not quit his position during the short time occupied by the conflict.

" It is the Lord God that fighteth for us.    He it is that hath enabled us to scatter them thus quickly," he exclaimed, as the Royalists fled in disorder.    " Pursue them not, but prepare to cut off the retreat of those pestilent malignants who have gone on to attack the camp above—lest, peradventure, they escape the snare laid for them."

It happened as Cromwell had foreseen.    Instead of finding Lilburn unprepared, when General Middleton and Sir William Keith reached the camp on the hill, they quickly discovered that their design had been betrayed.    Duped by stratagems which they ought to have suspected, they entered the camp, but had scarcely done so, when they were completely surrounded by a force more than trebling their own.

Thus entrapped it would seem that nothing was left to Middleton but to surrender.    But the brave general was undismayed by numbers, and when summoned to surrender, answered by a charge so fierce and impetuous that the ranks of the enemy opened, and, ere they could close again, he and his two regiments had passed safely through.

Down the hill they dashed at a headlong pace, and, though hotly pursued by Lilburn, very few of them were captured.    Luckily for the fugitives, Cromwell was not able to get his life guards out of the field in time to intercept them, or their utter destruction would have been inevitable.    As it was, they escaped with very little loss, considering the terrible hazard they had encountered.

On reaching the nearest outpost of the royal army, Middleton found Colonel Legge, and learnt the disaster that had befallen him.

" I cannot carry this bad news to his majesty," said Legge.    " Tell him what has happened."

" The king will not reproach you," said Middleton. " You have done your best. We have been betrayed."

" That is certain," said Sir William Keith. " Lilburn was prepared for us."

" And Cromwell himself was with the outpost when I attacked it," said Colonel Legge. " I knew it not till too late."

" Would I had known it !" cried Middleton, furiously. " He should not have lived to boast of this triumph. One of his spies has served him well on this occasion. I will not rest till I have discovered the traitor."

" Lesley may help you to find him," said Legge.

" No ; Lesley knew nothing of this," rejoined Middleton. " But come with me to the king, and get it over. A word will explain all. We have been betrayed."

---

## CHAPTER XX.

### HOW URSO GIVES WAS ARRESTED.

ABOUT the same time that the interview took place in the stable at Spetchley between Cromwell and Urso Gives, Major Careless, who had been upon the eastern walls to satisfy himself that the fires in the suburbs were completely extinguished, descended from the ramparts at Friars'-gate. This was one of the smaller gates, and derived its appellation from a convent of Franciscan friars that stood hard by—the old religious house having been subsequently converted into a prison.

On quitting the ramparts, as just stated, Careless proceeded to the old hostelry of the Grey Friars, where he knew that several officers about to take part in the camisade would be assembled. The old inn—an ancient timber-built house, with quaint gables, and a projecting upper story—is still standing in Friars'-street.

In the principal room of the old hostel he found, as he expected, a party of Cavaliers smoking, singing, and quaffing sack and claret, as if they had no serious business in hand. They were thus making merry to the last, since among them were Major Knox and some others, who, two hours later, were killed in the attack on the outpost. They were all fully armed with steel caps, gorgets, cuirasses, pauldrons, and taches, but had divested themselves of their swords and pistols. Beside each sword lay a small roll of linen. This was the shirt which its owner meant to wear over his armour, and which, in some cases, proved a winding-sheet.

All the Cavaliers rose on Careless's appearance, and gave him a hearty welcome. He could not help being struck by the enthusiasm they displayed. Not one of them but seemed proud of being included in the dangerous enterprise. Not one but was ready to lay down his life for the king. Careless never afterwards recalled that meeting without heaving a sigh for the brave men who perished in the camisade. However, at the moment, he thought little of the <u>hazard of the</u> attack, and would gladly have joined in it if the king would have allowed him. Sitting down, he emptied the flagon of claret filled for him by Major Knox Shortly afterwards Colonel Legge entered the room, but left again almos immediately, saying, as he departed, to Major Knox :

" Half an hour hence you must all be at the place of rendezvous."

Shortly afterwards Careless took leave of the company, and was pro ceeding along Friars'-street in the direction of the Sidbury-gate, whe he heard his name pronounced in a familiar voice, that instantly awakene tender recollections, and turning, he perceived that he had been followe from the hostel by a young woman whose features were muffled in hood.

Not doubting who it was, he exclaimed :

" Ah ! is it you, Mary ?  I never expected to see you again."

" And you would not see me now, I can assure you, if I had no something of importance to say," she rejoined, partially removing he hood.

" Whatever has procured me the happiness of beholding you once more, sweet Mary, I feel grateful for it," he rejoined.

" Speak not thus lightly," she said.  " 'Tis a grave matter."

" Before you mention it, then, let me ask how you came to throw yourself away upon that detestable Roundhead ?  You must be heartily sick of him already."

" If you persist in talking thus you will frighten me away, and I shall leave unsaid what I have to tell you—and it is very important."

" Nay, by all that is bewitching, I swear you shall not go," he cried, catching her hand.

" Be serious, if you can, for a single instant, and listen to me."

" Tell me you are resolved to abandon Urso, and I will be as serious as you please."

" You put everything out of my head by your trifling talk.  How very different you are from Urso, to be sure !  He is always grave."

" Yes, I warrant me you rarely catch a smile on his sour visage.  But I hope there are few points of resemblance between him and me. Again I ask, how could you marry such a man ?"

" 'Twas all my grandam's doings," she sighed.

" And you have bitterly repented of the foolish step ever since, I'll be sworn.  Confess, and I'll forgive you, though, I own, the effort will be difficult."

" Then pray don't make it.  Unless you listen to my warning, you will fall into a snare that has been privily laid for you."

" Privily laid for me by Urso, eh ?  The Roundhead rogue had better take care of himself, or you will speedily become a widow."

" It is not of Urso I would warn you.  Do not take part in the camisade to-night."

" The camisade !" he exclaimed, in surprise.  " How do you know there is to be a camisade ?  Who has told you of it ?  Answer me that."

All his levity had vanished.  As she did not answer, he repeated the question still more peremptorily.

" No matter who told me," she rejoined.  " If you value your life you will not go.  I have warned you.  Do as you please.  Farewell !"

"Stay! we must not part thus. You spoke of a snare being privily
laid for me. What was your meaning?"

"I will tell you nothing more," she rejoined.

And breaking from him, she flew towards the inn.

Just as she reached the door the Cavaliers came forth in a body.
Some of them tried to stop her, but she pushed them aside and got into
the house.

Careless thought of following her and insisting on an explanation, but
after a moment's reflection he concluded that, since she was lodging at
the inn, she must have overheard the loud and indiscreet talk of the
Cavaliers, and so have ascertained the nature of the enterprise on which
they were engaged. As to the "privily-laid snare" of which he had
been warned, the expression savoured strongly of Urso, and probably
meant nothing in particular.

Having arrived at this conclusion he marched off, with the fixed
determination of paying another visit to the old hostel on the morrow.

But before the morrow came he was undeceived, and he then bitterly
regretted that he had neglected the warning given him.

So well was the secret kept, that only the troops actually engaged in
the camisade were aware of its object. Many heard of the enterprise
and of its failure at the same time. When the attacking party was
driven back, a call to arms was instantly made by the Duke of Hamilton
and all the commanders stationed on the south and south-east, lest
Cromwell should follow up his success by an immediate assault on the
city. But it soon became apparent that he had no such design, and
though the Royalists remained on the alert, they were not disturbed
during the remainder of the night.

To Charles, who had made certain of success, the failure of the enterprise was a terrible disappointment. But he bore it manfully, as he bore
all his reverses. He had remained at the Commandery in order that he
might receive the earliest intelligence of the victory he so confidently
anticipated, and was seated in the refectory, trying to while away the
time in light chat with Careless, when General Middleton, followed by
Sir William Keith and Colonel Legge, entered the hall. Charles read
what had happened in their downcast looks, and for a moment forbore
to question them.

"Fortune has played me another sorry trick, I perceive," he exclaimed, at length. "I thought the fickle goddess would this time have
befriended me."

"All would have gone well, sire, if our plan had not been betrayed,"
replied Middleton. "The enemy was prepared. We found the whole
of Colonel Lilburn's force under arms, and were surrounded, but succeeded in cutting our way through them."

"I have a further proof of treachery, sire," said Colonel Legge.
"Cromwell himself, with his body-guard of Ironsides, was with the outpost when I attacked it."

Charles could not repress an exclamation of rage.

"That we have been bought and sold is certain," he exclaimed. "But
who can have betrayed us?"

"I think I can give a shrewd guess as to the villain who has thus

traitorously discovered the design," said Careless, "and if I am right he shall not escape chastisement."

"Whoever the traitor may be," observed the king, "he must have obtained early information, and have acted with the greatest promptitude, or the enemy could not have been prepared at all points for the attack. Cromwell must have clever and active spies in the city."

"True, sire," replied Middleton. "And I now recollect that, during our conference in the adjoining chamber, a man in the garden approached somewhat near to the open window. At the time I did not suspect his motive, but I now believe he was a spy."

"It may be so," observed Charles.

"Whether General Middleton is right or wrong in his suspicion, I am certain I can discover the traitor, sire," said Careless. "I have a clue to his hiding-place, and before many hours I engage to produce him."

"It will be some satisfaction to hang the villain," observed Charles.

"Your majesty may rely upon having that gratification," replied Careless. "With your permission, I will set about his capture at once. Nor will I rest till I have effected it."

And bowing to the king he quitted the hall.

In the court-yard of the Commandery was the king's ordinary guard. Taking two of the men with him, Careless proceeded to the Sidbury-gate, passed through the wicket with his attendants, and in another minute was in Friars'-street.

So dark was the narrow street, owing to the projecting stories of the ancient timber houses lining it on either side, that Careless was unable to discern any object unless close at hand. A heavy, measured tread, however, informed him of the approach of the rounds, and the next moment the patrol came up.

Captain Woolfe, who was with the guard, immediately recognised his superior officer, and on learning Careless's business, proffered his aid. They proceeded together to the old inn, followed by the whole party.

It would seem that all the inmates had retired to rest, but the knocking of a halbert staff against the door soon caused it to be opened by Master Kilvert, the host, who had hastily huddled on his apparel, and in a trembling voice inquired the meaning of this nocturnal visitation.

No explanation was vouchsafed him. Ordering the guard to post themselves secretly on the other side of the street and be ready to answer any summons, Careless and Captain Woolfe entered the house, shutting the street door after them.

The terrified host conducted them to the principal room, and setting down the light with which he was provided, humbly waited their pleasure to address him.

"Answer truly the questions I shall put, and you have nought to fear," said Careless. "You have a lodger named Urso Gives?"

"Your honour has been rightly informed," replied Kilvert. "Master Gives, the tailor, with his wife and his wife's grandmother, are lodging in my house. Master Gives is a worthy and God-fearing man, or I would not have him as a guest."

"Your description of him is altogether inaccurate. He is a traitor and a spy. Lead us to his chamber instantly, and call him forth," said Careless, drawing his sword.

"I will lead your honour to his chamber," replied Kilvert, now still more alarmed. "But it will be useless to call him, seeing he is not there."

"I must be assured of this," said Careless. "Lead us to the room."

"I shall not need to do so, for here comes his wife, who will confirm what I have just declared to your honour."

And as he spoke Dame Gives entered bearing a light. It was evident from her attire that she had not been in bed. Careless sheathed his sword on her appearance.

"Why have you come here at this hour? What do you want with Urso?" she cried, rushing up to him.

Careless, however, turned away, and said, in a low voice, to Captain Woolfe:

"Explain our errand to her."

"We have come to arrest your husband," said Woolfe.

"Arrest him! What crime has he committed?"

"The highest crime a man can commit," rejoined Woolfe. "He has betrayed the king to his enemies."

"I hope he can disprove the charge—but you will not find him here," she exclaimed. "Master Kilvert will satisfy you that he is not in the house."

"I have striven to do so, but ineffectually," said the host.

"Since it appears that your husband has not returned from his secret visit to the enemy's camp, we must wait for him," said Careless. "Have him we will."

"The house must be searched. He may be concealed within it," said Captain Woolfe. "Show me to the upper rooms," he added to the host.

"Readily," replied Kilvert. "And should you discover him, I will be content to take his place, and that I would not do for a thousand pound. This way, captain! this way!"

As soon as they were gone, Dame Gives exclaimed, distractedly:

"Cruel and ungrateful man! Is this the way you reward me? In my desire to serve you, I have destroyed poor Urso."

"You ought to thank me for ridding you of such a miscreant," rejoined Careless. "You do not seem to comprehend the magnitude of his offence."

"Yes, I do comprehend it," she rejoined. "I regard the crime with horror. But I am his wife. Save him! save him!"

"Impossible!" exclaimed Careless. "I would not save him if I could. I am sorry for you, Mary, but I cannot feel the slightest compassion for the villain you have married. It pains me that his arrest cannot be accomplished without your taking part in it."

"Oh! that I could warn him of his danger," she exclaimed. "If I could only give him a signal!"

"The signal would be useless," said Careless. "A guard is posted outside."

"But he will not enter from the street!" she cried. "The door at the back is left open. I must fasten it."

And she would have rushed forth to execute her design if Careless had not prevented her.

" I cannot allow you to stir, Mary," he said, detaining her.

She besought him to let her go, but he refused.  Just then, footsteps were heard in the passage.

" Ah, he is here !" she exclaimed.

Next moment Urso Gives entered the room, and started on beholding his wife and Careless together.  By an instant and rapid retreat he might, perhaps, have escaped, for the way was then clear, but yielding to a sudden impulse of jealous fury, he drew a pistol and fired.

His aim was Careless, but the shot took effect on his wife, who was slightly wounded in the arm.   Uttering a scream, she would have fallen if Careless had not caught her and placed her in a chair.

The report of the pistol brought Captain Woolfe and Kilvert into the room, and in another moment the guard rushed in from the street. Urso, who attempted no resistance, was seized and secured.

" Is this the man you seek, Major Careless ?" asked Captain Woolfe.

" Ay, this is the accursed traitor," was the reply.   " And now he would have added murder to his other crimes."

" I should be satisfied if I had slain thee," rejoined Urso, fiercely.   " I have wrongs enough to avenge."

" Search him to see that he hath no concealed weapons," said Careless.   " He shall then be taken to the Commandery, in order that his majesty may interrogate him."

" I know well what my doom will be, and am prepared for it," said Urso.   " Before I am taken hence let me look for the last time upon my wife."

Careless signed to the guard to bring him forward.

Poor Mary was still lying in the chair in which she had been placed, and was tended by the hostess and a female servant, who had come into the room.   A handkerchief had been bound round her arm by Careless to stanch the blood.

The prisoner gazed at her for some moments with a look of unutterable affection.

" She will live," he murmured.   " Heaven be thanked I have not killed her !"

" No, thou art spared that crime," said Careless.   " She is not much hurt."

Bending down, Urso kissed her pallid brow.   The contact of his lips caused her to open her eyes, but on beholding him she shuddered, and immediately closed them.

With a sharp pang Urso turned away.

Attended by the guard, the prisoner was taken at once to the Commandery.

Though it was now close upon daybreak, Charles had not retired to rest.   He was so much disturbed by the result of the night attack that, feeling he could not sleep, he remained in converse with Middleton and the two other unsuccessful commanders.

The king and his companions were in the refectory, when Careless entered and informed his majesty that he had captured the spy.

He then explained how the arrest had been accomplished, and after giving the king all needful particulars, the prisoner was introduced.

Urso Gives did not seem at all intimidated by the presence in which he stood, but maintained a resolute demeanour. General Middleton at once recognised him as the eavesdropper he had noticed in the garden.

When interrogated by Charles, the prisoner refused to answer any questions, and though threatened by Middleton with the thumbscrew, declared, with a firmness that carried conviction with it, that no torture should force him to make a confession.

After hearing Careless's relation, confirmed as it was by various circumstances, and, above all, by the discovery on the person of the prisoner of an order in Cromwell's handwriting, Charles could entertain no doubt of Urso's guilt. He ordered him to be hanged at mid-day on the Sidbury-gate, so that the spectacle of his ignominious death might be witnessed by the rebel army.

The prisoner, who heard his sentence without betraying the slightest emotion, was then removed, and taken by the guard to Edgar's Tower, where the king had ordered him to be kept till the hour appointed for his execution.

---

## CHAPTER XXI.

### SHOWING HOW DAME GIVES BECAME A WIDOW.

Careless did not lose sight of the prisoner until he had seen him safely bestowed in Edgar's Tower. With the strictest injunctions to watch carefully over him, he then committed him to the custody of Martin Vosper, who, it may be remembered, was one of the party that bivouacked on Pitchcroft on the night of the Grand Muster. Vosper had since been promoted to the rank of lieutenant. Placed in the strong room in which Dr. Crosby had been confined by Colonel James, Urso immediately threw himself upon the pallet that formed part of the scanty furniture, and being greatly fatigued, soon fell asleep. But his slumber was disturbed by fearful dreams, and his broken exclamations seemed to have reference to some dark deed he had committed. These muttered words attracted the attention of Lieutenant Vosper, who remained with him in the chamber. From the first Vosper had been struck with the prisoner's resemblance to the spy whom he and Trubshaw—now a corporal—had pursued, and he now felt sure he was the same individual.

While the wretched sleeper was muttering some incoherent words, but amidst which the name " Wicked Will " was plainly to be distinguished, Vosper stepped up to the couch and shook him violently.

Thus roused, the guilty wretch started up, looking the picture of horror and despair. His hue was death-like, his eyes stared widely, and cold drops gathered thickly upon his brow.

" Lighten your breast of its heavy load," said Vosper. " When you played the spy on me and my comrades at Pitchcroft, you cried out in a solemn voice that Wicked Will's death was a judgment. But you neglected to tell us who was the instrument of the judgment.   Supply the information now.   Who drowned him in the Severn ?"

" Not I," replied Urso, shuddering.   " If I have talked in my sleep, as I do sometimes, my words must not be taken against me."

" Die not with a lie on thy lips," said Vosper.   " Since thou art certain to be hanged, give yourself a chance hereafter, by confession and repentance."

" I will not confess my transgressions to thee," rejoined Urso.   " If I may have some godly man to pray with me I will lay bare my breast to him.   I would fain see the Reverend Laban Foxe, who hath known me long and well."

" And needs not to be told of thine iniquities, I'll be sworn," said Vosper.   " I know the Reverend Laban, and a cunning old fox he is— his name suits him perfectly."

" A sorry jest, and ill-timed," said Urso.   " Shall I see him ?"

" Content thee—-thou shalt."

" I thank thee," replied Urso.   " In return, I will tell thee how Captain Hodgkins perished.   Though I hated him as a bloodthirsty and wicked malignant, I did not compass his destruction.   One evening, about dusk, he was staggering along the bank of the Severn, raging and roaring from strong drink, when he fell into the river."

" Wretch ! you pushed him in," said Vosper, sternly.

" No," rejoined Urso.   " It happened as I have said.   I was standing by, and could have saved him had I stretched out my hand.   But I hated him, and let him drown.   Ah ! I shall never forget his agonised, imploring looks, for the cold water had sobered him.   I can see him now," he added, covering his eyes, as if to exclude some terrible object.

" With such a crime on thy conscience, no wonder thou canst not sleep soundly," said Vosper, regarding him with mingled pity and abhorrence.

" Thou sayst truly," rejoined the wretched man.   " Since that night I have not been able to lay me down in peace.   But I shall soon sleep the quiet and unbroken sleep of death."

" Hast thou aught more to tell me ?" asked Vosper, after a pause.

" Ay, I will tell thee of another matter, though I feel no remorse for it," rejoined Urso.   " Not many days ago I laid an ambush for thy king on one of the Malvern Hills, which he was foolish enough to ascend in company with Major Careless, whom I bitterly hate.   Had I captured Charles Stuart, as I hoped to do, I should not be a prisoner here ; and, better than all, I should have been avenged of Careless."

" I heard of his majesty's providential escape," said Vosper.   " But I knew not thou wert the contriver of the ambuscade."

" I can talk no more," said Urso.   " I pray thee fulfil thy promise to let me see the godly man I have named."

Lieutenant Vosper immediately opened the door, and conferred for a moment with Corporal Trubshaw, who was standing outside.

This done, he re-entered the room.

Nearly an hour, however, elapsed before the corporal appeared with the Independent minister, and during this interval Urso turned his face to the wall, and maintained a profound silence, which Vosper did not care to interrupt.

The Reverend Laban Foxe was a sour-visaged old man. He wore a tall steeple-crowned hat and a long black cloak, but his attire had nothing of the divine about it.

He seemed much moved on beholding Urso, who rose from the pallet on his entrance, and a sad greeting took place between them.

The minister prayed to be left alone with the prisoner. Vosper assented and withdrew, but after awhile, thinking time enough had been allowed, he returned, and found Urso listening to the words of consolation addressed to him.

He therefore again retired, but returning after another long interval, and finding the exhortation still going on, he deemed it necessary to interrupt it.

" Since you sincerely repent of your sins, my son, I need say no more," observed the minister. " Bear your cross with resignation. Godly sorrow, like yours, worketh repentance to salvation." After a moment's pause he added, " But have you no message for your wife ?"

" May I not see her ?" cried Urso, casting an imploring look at Vosper, who made no reply.

" Alas ! she cannot come to you, my son, even were she permitted," interposed the minister. " Her wound is not dangerous, but she has not strength for the painful interview."

" 'Tis better thus !" exclaimed Urso, in a voice that betrayed profound emotion. " The parting with her would be a greater pang than death itself. Bid her an eternal farewell from me, and say to her——"

And he stopped.

" What must I add, my son ?" inquired the minister.

" Say that I have left her a good legacy," rejoined Urso.

" Know you not that any money you may have bequeathed her will be forfeited ?" remarked Vosper.

" Forfeited to whom ?" demanded the prisoner.

" To whom should it be forfeited except to the king ?" rejoined Vosper.

" I am easy on that score," said Urso. " Charles Stuart will not keep this money from her. The provision I have made is secure. Tell her so," he added to the minister. " She may not understand my meaning now, but she will understand it hereafter."

" Your words shall be faithfully repeated," said the Reverend Laban. " Farewell, my son !"

And with an earnest look at the prisoner, he departed.

When the hour fixed for the execution approached, a strong mounted guard was drawn up in front of the beautiful old gateway. Without a moment's delay, the prisoner was brought forth by Lieutenant Vosper, Corporal Trubshaw, and a party of halberdiers, who marched on either side of him.

Urso was bareheaded, his hands tied behind him, and a rope coiled round his neck. Before him walked the hangman—a caitiff apparently chosen for the revolting office from his savage and repulsive looks. The mounted guard, previously mentioned, rode on in front to clear the way.

As the cortége passed slowly down Edgar-street and along Sidbury-street, Urso's appearance was everywhere greeted with yells and execrations, and if the infuriated concourse could have reached him, the hangman would have been spared a labour. Ever since it had become known that the night attack had been betrayed, the greatest indignation was manifested by the citizens, who demanded that the severest punishment should be inflicted on the traitor. Mere hanging was too good for him. They would have him drawn and quartered, and his head fixed on the Sidbury-gate, that Old Noll might see it.

Though Urso had nerved himself to the utmost, he was not equal to the terrible ordeal he was exposed to, and his agony during the march to the place of execution was far greater than that which he subsequently endured.

At length the Sidbury-gate was reached, and being taken inside the structure, he was for some minutes lost to sight.

The spectators awaited his reappearance with a fierce impatience, which they did not seek to control or disguise. The large area in front of the Sidbury-gate, which has been described as surrounded by the new fortifications, was crowded with soldiers ; the ramparts of Fort Royal, the walls, the towers, were likewise thronged by soldiers. But there were hundreds, nay, thousands, of distant spectators of the tragic scene.

On the top of the Sidbury-gate a gallows had been reared. So lofty was it, that it could be seen from most parts of the city, while it formed a conspicuous object to the enemy on the heights.

Towards this extraordinary gallows every eye was now directed. Deep silence pervaded the vast assemblage.

At length the hangman came forth, and, climbing the long ladder quickly, seated himself astride on the transverse bar of the gallows, and proceeded deliberately to fasten the fatal rope to it.

While he was thus occupied, the prisoner appeared, still guarded by Lieutenant Vosper, Trubshaw, and the halberdiers, and his appearance was the signal for a renewal of the terrible outcries that had before assailed him. He bore them undauntedly, continuing perfectly motionless, until the executioner called out from above that all was ready. He then sprang quickly up the ladder, as if eager to meet his doom.

In another minute all was over, and his body swinging in mid air ; while a universal groan—though not a groan of pity—burst from the spectators.

Thus died the traitor Gives, whose name is still execrated in faithful Worcester.

At the moment when Urso was launched into eternity, the discharge of a cannon from Fort Royal informed Cromwell that the spy he had employed had been punished with death.

Cromwell, who was with Lilburn and Lord Grey of Groby on Perry Wood at the time, could not control his rage.

"The man's execution is justified by the laws of war," he said ; "but it shall cost the citizens of Worcester dear. The great service he rendered us last night shall be requited as he desired. His widow shall have the reward I intended for him."

"How much is it to be ?" asked Lord Grey.

"Two hundred pounds, and a pension of two hundred a year," replied Cromwell.

"A good reward, in sooth," said Lord Grey. "She will be well consoled for his loss."

## CHAPTER XXII.

### HOW THE EARL OF DERBY ARRIVED AT WORCESTER.

THE end of August had arrived. The anniversary of the battle of Dunbar—fought on the 3rd of September, 1650—was close at hand. Cromwell, as we have shown, had resolved to wait for this auspicious day, if he should not be forced by the king to accept a battle sooner. But Charles had been so much discouraged by the failure of the camisade that he hesitated—perhaps too long—before risking a general engagement. A few unimportant skirmishes had taken place between the outposts, sometimes with advantage to one party, sometimes to the other, but these were all.

The interval was employed by Cromwell in making strong intrenchments at Perry Wood, where he had mounted a battery with heavy guns. As this battery threatened Fort Royal and the city, Charles was eager to attack it, but was dissuaded from the hazardous attempt by his generals. The jealousies among the Royalist leaders, already alluded to, had increased in bitterness, and, in consequence of these disputes, which he found it impossible to check, he could form no plan with the certainty of carrying it out. All his designs were frustrated.

Cromwell, on the other hand, took counsel from no one. His instructions were implicitly obeyed. What his precise plans now were could only be conjectured. They were known to Lambert, Fleetwood, Ingoldsby, and the generals stationed at Upton, but to no others.

Charles had recently changed his quarters, and had removed to the ancient mansion belonging to the mayor, where he enjoyed greater privacy than he could command at the palace. The residence he had chosen is one of the largest old houses in the city, and stands at the north end of New-street, looking into the Corn Market. Over the porch is the appropriate inscription, "LOVE GOD—HONOUR THE KING." Here he could retire when completely worn out by the ceaseless toils of the day, certain of being undisturbed.

On the evening of Monday, the 1st of September, he was seated in a large old-fashioned room on the ground floor of the ancient mansion referred to. The dark oak panels were hung with tapestry, and the cumbrous oak furniture was of Elizabeth's time. He had just dined, but had eaten little, and was in a very despondent mood. Careless, who was in attendance, filled a large silver goblet with claret, and handed it to him. The king raised the cup to his lips, but set it down untasted.

" I never saw your majesty so downcast before," remarked Careless. " A cup of wine will cheer you. The claret is good, I'll answer for it, for I have emptied a flask."

" Wine will not rouse my spirits," rejoined Charles, gloomily. " I am quite worn out. I will hold no more councils of war. They are utterly unprofitable. There is no deliberation—no unanimity of opinion —each plan, however promising, is violently opposed. What will be the end of it all ?—certain defeat."

" Yes, I own your generals are difficult to manage, my liege," replied Careless.　" But you humour them too much, and in consequence they presume on your good nature, and disregard your authority.　Enforce obedience to your commands.　That is Old Noll's plan."

" Would you have me resemble him ?" cried Charles.

" Yes, in that particular, my liege.　He would not be where he now is if he were not absolute.　At your next council explain your plans, but do not allow them to be discussed."

" Why summon a council at all, if those composing it are not to deliberate ?"

" Merely that your generals may hear the expression of your will."

" Well, thy notion is not a bad one," replied Charles, smiling for the first time.

" Let no one speak but yourself, my liege, and there can be no wrangling, no contention."

" That is indisputable," said Charles.

At this moment a sound was heard in the passage.

" Some one is without !" exclaimed the king.　" But be it who it may, I will not be disturbed."

Thereupon Careless left the chamber, but almost immediately returned.

" I have disobeyed your majesty," he said; " but I am sure you will pardon me."

As the very distinguished-looking personage who had entered with him advanced slowly towards the king, Charles perceived who he was, and sprang forward, exclaiming :

" Welcome, my dear Lord Derby !　Welcome to Worcester !　Of all men living you are the one I most desired to see.　Once more, welcome ! You have arrived most opportunely.　We are on the eve of a great battle—a battle that must decide my fate !—and I could not have fought it successfully without you."

" Thank Heaven I have arrived in time !" cried the earl.　" I was aware that a battle was imminent, and almost despaired of reaching Worcester in time to take part in it ; but here I am at last, ready to fight for your majesty."

" You can do more than merely fight for me, my lord," said Charles. " You can give me the benefit of your advice.　I sadly want a counsellor."

" I fancied you had already too many counsellors, sire," observed the earl.

" Nay, that is true," rejoined Charles.　" But I want a leader like yourself—entirely devoted to me—one who will not thwart me.　Heaven has sent you to me at the right moment, and my hopes are now revived."

" If I had not been protected by Heaven, I could not have overcome the difficulties I have had to encounter in coming hither, my liege," re- plied the Earl of Derby.

" Have you quite recovered from the hurts you got at Wigan, my dear lord ?" asked the king, anxiously.

" Not entirely, my liege," replied the earl.　Six-and-twenty wounds are not cured in a week.　But I am able to sit a horse, and wield a sword. Finding myself strong enough for the journey, I left Boscobel this morn, attended by Captain Giffard of Chillington and his brother, with a dozen of their retainers. We got on without accident or interruption, till within a few miles of Worcester, and though we had quitted the high road, and taken to the fields and lanes in order to avoid the enemy, we were discovered by a party of skirmishers, and chased almost to the gates of the city. We found the Foregate walled up, and so entered by St. Martin's-gate."

" The Foregate has been walled up as a matter of precaution," said Charles. " But you look pale, my good lord. Be seated, I beg of you. A cup of wine, Careless."

The earl emptied the goblet proffered him.

" That has marvellously restored me," he said. " I did feel somewhat faint and exhausted after my long ride."

The colour was now, in some degree, restored to the earl's pallid countenance, but as Charles gazed at him with deep interest, he saw how severely he still suffered from his numerous wounds.

Never did the spirit of loyalty burn more strongly in any breast than in that of James Stanley, seventh Earl of Derby. This is sufficiently proved by the earl's haughty response to Ireton, when summoned to surrender the Isle of Man to the Parliament. " I have received your letter with indignation," he wrote, " and with scorn I return you this answer, that I cannot but wonder whence you should gather any hopes from me that I should, like you, prove traitorous to my sovereign, since you cannot be insensible of my former actings in his late majesty's service, from which principle of loyalty I am in no way departed. I scorn your proffers ; I disdain your favours ; I abhor your treasons ; and so far from delivering this Island to your advantage, I will keep it to your destruction. Take this final answer, and forbear any further solicitations, for if you trouble me with any more messages upon this occasion I will burn the paper and hang the messenger."

To Charles II. this loyal and chivalrous peer was as devoted as he had been to that monarch's martyred sire.

Born in 1606, the Earl of Derby was still in the prime of manhood, and was endowed with a frame of extraordinary vigour. Skilled in all athletic exercises, brave to a fault, prompt, determined, undismayed by danger, he would have been a great general but for his excessive rashness. Somewhat below the ordinary height, he was powerfully built and well proportioned. His features were cast in a large and noble mould, and his dark, deep-sunk eyes had a grave and thoughtful expression, that harmonised with his sombre and melancholy aspect. Baines, the historian of Lancashire, thus describes him : " His was one of the old Stanley faces which we love to look upon as they darken in their frames, and to associate with deeds of chivalry, as enduring as the history of that country with whose annals their names are so proudly connected."

The Earl of Derby was married to Charlotte, daughter of Claude de la Tremouille, Duke of Thuars, and through this union he became allied to the royal houses of Nassau and Bourbon. The Countess of Derby was exceedingly beautiful, and her high spirit was equal to her beauty. Her heroic defence of Latham House for four months against the Parliamentarian forces is one of the most memorable incidents of the Civil Wars.

Such was the seventh Earl of Derby, not the least illustrious of a long and illustrious line. The earl's tragical end is well known, and it forms one of the darkest pages in the sanguinary annals of the period.

"I must now inquire after Roscarrock," observed the earl. "He is here, I trust. But I have heard nought of him since he left Boscobel."

"He arrived here safely nearly a week ago, and has well-nigh recovered from his wounds," replied Charles. "Go find him, and bring him here at once," he added to Careless.

"I shall only have to tell him that Lord Derby has arrived, and he will hurry hither," replied Careless, who instantly departed on his errand.

Left alone with the earl, Charles acquainted him with the present posture of affairs, and explained his difficulties to him. After listening with deep interest to all that was said by the king, the earl replied:

"I am sorry to find your majesty thus embarrassed, but I trust I shall be able to relieve you from your perplexities. I have some influence both with Hamilton and Buckingham, and I will use it to heal their differences. If they can be reconciled—and this shall be my first business—there will be little difficulty with the others, except perhaps with Lauderdale, but I will endeavour to soothe his wounded pride. This is not the moment for disputes. All quarrels must be settled after the battle."

"You give me fresh heart, my dear lord," cried Charles. "I was in despair, but you have restored my confidence. With my father's best and staunchest friend by my side, I shall yet triumph."

Just then the door opened, and Roscarrock entered, followed by Careless. Joyful exclamations were uttered as the two companions in arms embraced each other. There was something so touching in their meeting that both Charles and Careless were moved by it.

As soon as the excitement caused by seeing the earl was over, Roscarrock made a reverence to the king, and said, in an apologetic tone:

"I trust your majesty will pardon me. I have been carried away by my feelings."

"The warmth of your feelings does you honour, colonel," observed Charles. "I am as rejoiced as yourself at the Earl of Derby's arrival. His presence will animate my troops. He will have the command of a regiment, and you will be with him."

"I thank your majesty," replied Roscarrock, bowing. "Heaven grant we may be more fortunate than we were at Wigan!"

"That disaster will now assuredly be repaired," observed Charles; "though you will have Cromwell himself to contend with. But you said the two Giffards of Chillington accompanied you from Boscobel," he added to the earl. "Where are they?"

"They are waiting to learn your majesty's pleasure respecting them," replied Lord Derby.

"In the street?" cried Charles.

"Ay, in the street, my liege," said Roscarrock. "I spoke with them as I came in.   They have not dismounted.   Your majesty has not two more loyal subjects than Thomas and Charles Giffard."

"That I will answer for," added Lord Derby.   "And they are brave as well as loyal."

"You praise them so highly that I must needs see them," remarked Charles, smiling.   "Bring them to me, Careless.   Boscobel belongs to them, you said, my lord?"

"To Tom Giffard, the elder brother, my liege.   The Giffards are a very ancient Roman Catholic family, and have remained constant to the faith of their forefathers."

"I do not dislike them for adhering to the old religion," said Charles.

"Besides Chillington, they have another seat called White Ladies," pursued the earl.   "Your majesty will understand what Boscobel is like when I mention that it is a secluded recusant's house, full of priests' hiding-places, so wonderfully contrived, that none concealed within them were ever discovered.   I felt perfectly safe there."

"A good place of refuge, no doubt," remarked Charles.   "'Tis well to know of it.   But here come the Giffards."

As he spoke, the two brothers were ushered in by Careless.   Both were handsome, stalwart young men, and their good looks and manly bearing very favourably impressed the king.   A strong family resemblance existed between them.   They were fully armed, as were all gentlemen at that distracted time. The king accorded them a most gracious reception.

"I am glad to see you, gentlemen," he said.   "And since you have come to Worcester, I must, perforce, detain you till after the battle.   I want recruits—above all, such recruits as you."

"We have come to offer our services to your majesty," replied Captain Giffard.

"I accept them," said Charles.   "You shall serve under Lord Derby."

"Your majesty has anticipated the request we were about to prefer," observed Charles Giffard.

"My Lord of Derby," said the king to the earl, "you must take up your quarters here.   For many reasons I desire to have you with me." The earl bowed, and Charles turned to the two Giffards and said : " Gentlemen, you will likewise find quarters here.   The kindness and hospitality shown by you to Lord Derby demand some return.   Nay, nay, good sirs, you will not incommode me.   The house is large, and has plenty of rooms within it.   Major Careless will see you comfortably bestowed."

It need scarcely be said that this gracious proposition was gladly accepted—indeed, it could not be declined.   The Earl of Derby and the two Giffards were lodged that night in the old mansion in New-street with the king.

## CHAPTER XXIII.

### IN WHAT MANNER JANE LANE WAS CAPTURED AND BROUGHT BEFORE CROMWELL.

THOUGH often urged to do so by the king, Jane Lane did not leave Worcester till the last moment, but when it became certain that a battle was imminent, Charles insisted upon her departure. Very early on the morning of the 2nd of September she quitted the city, accompanied by Colonel Lane and Sir Clement Fisher. By riding hard, she hoped to reach her home in Staffordshire before night. Her companions were not going with her further than Bewdley, where they hoped to procure a safe escort for her.

Having selected the road they deemed most secure, the party were galloping along a lane near Hindlip, when they heard a shout, and the next moment a party of musketeers, evidently Parliamentarians, with an officer, came upon them from a cross road. There was nothing for it but instant flight. As they turned back, the musketeers galloped after them, and fired a few shots—luckily without effect.

Thinking to escape more quickly, Jane Lane jumped a hedge on the left, and gained a broad meadow. But neither her brother nor Sir Clement followed her, while the sounds she heard convinced her they were being hotly pursued. She rode partly across the meadow, and then stopped, uncertain what to do, still hoping her companions would join her. But they came not, and fresh firing at a distance added to her fright. What was she to do? She could not proceed on her journey alone, and yet a return to the city was fraught with the utmost peril. Yet this was the course she resolved on after a few minutes' consideration, and she rode down to the bottom of the field, anxiously listening for any warning sounds. The enemy, however, was nearer at hand than she imagined, and she had no sooner got out of the field by clearing another hedge than she was made prisoner by a couple of musketeers. No rough usage was offered her, but seizing her bridle, the men took her to their leader, who was posted beneath a wide-spreading beech-tree, with a dozen troopers beside him.

"Soh! you have captured the Moabitish maiden," observed the leader.

The words and the stern tone in which they were uttered caused Jane to look at the speaker, and she then, to her astonishment, perceived she was in the presence of the Lord General himself. Instead of being alarmed by the discovery, she felt her courage return.

"Thou knowest me, damsel, I perceive," observed Cromwell, perceiving the effect he had produced upon her. "Answer truthfully the questions I shall put, and you have no cause for fear."

"I have no fear," replied Jane, stoutly.

"Who were the malignants with you? Was Charles Stuart one of them? Speak! I will have an answer."

His manner was so authoritative, that she felt almost compelled to obey. Still she remained silent.

"I ask again, was Charles Stuart one of them?" said Cromwell, still more sternly. "I have received intelligence from one not likely to deceive me, that he meditates flight from the city on this very morn. And I am here on the watch for him."

"You have received false intelligence," rejoined Jane. "The king will never leave the city."

"Ah! you have plenty of spirit, I find," cried Cromwell. "But you draw suspicion on yourself by your reluctance to answer. For the third time, who were those with you?"

"My brother, Colonel Lane, and my brother's friend, Sir Clement Fisher," she replied.

"And your own suitor, perchance," remarked Cromwell.

"You are right," rejoined Jane.

At this juncture several of the troopers returned, and Cromwell called out:

"Have you captured the men of Moab? Have you smitten them with the sword?"

"No, your excellency," replied Dighton, who commanded the party. "They have escaped into the city."

"Heaven be thanked for that!" exclaimed Jane. "Then I care not what becomes of me."

Cromwell regarded her fixedly, not without a certain admiration.

"You are a stout-hearted maiden," he said. "'Tis a pity you cannot understand the truth."

"I understand some things," replied Jane, boldly. "I understand treason and rebellion, and I will have naught to do with traitors and rebels. Your excellency is fond of texts. Forget not that it has been said, ' Rebellion is as the sin of witchcraft, and shall be so punished.' Remember also what Rabshakeh said to Hezekiah, ' On whom dost thou trust that thou rebellest?' Lastly, I ask with Nehemiah, ' What do ye? Will you rebel against the king?' "

"There is no king left," replied Cromwell. "The Lord has smitten the house of Ahab, and the seed royal shall be destroyed."

"Not so, thou worse than Athaliah," said Jane. "The blood of the royal Martyr cries for vengeance upon his murderers, and it will not cry in vain. Thou mayst capture yonder city—mayst destroy its brave and devoted citizens, but the king will escape—ay, escape, I tell thee—and mount the throne when thou art dust."

"While I live he shall never mount the throne," rejoined Cromwell.

His brow had grown very dark as he listened to Jane's imprudent speech, but he repressed his wrath, and a seasonable interruption was offered by the arrival of another party of musketeers under the command of Cornet Hardiman.

With them was a young and good-looking woman on horseback, seated on a pillion behind a serving-man. She was habited in deep mourning.

"How is this?" cried Oliver, angrily. "Can ye bring me none but women as prisoners to-day?"

"May it please your excellency," replied Hardiman, "this young dame is not a prisoner. She is the widow of that Urso Gives who was hanged by Charles Stuart. Having heard that you made some promise of a reward to her late husband, she entreated me to bring her before you, and believing her story, I consented."

" Is this the Widow Gives ?" demanded Cromwell, regarding her with attention.

" Ay, marry, your excellency," replied the young dame. " I am the widow of that unfortunate man, who lost his life in your service. I have been informed by the Reverend Laban Foxe—a most godly minister—that your excellency promised Urso a reward, and that if he perished I should receive it."

" It is true, and I will not fail one word of my promise," replied Cromwell. " You shall have the reward, but you must be content to wait for it till the city is in my hands."

" Then I trust she will have to wait for it long," observed Jane.

Cromwell took no notice of the remark, but said to the young widow :

" You are passing fair, and I marvel not at your husband's strong attachment to you."

" Of a truth, poor Urso was greatly attached to me," replied the young widow, putting her handkerchief to her eyes.

" Be constant to his memory, if you can—though I fear 'twill be a hard matter with you to be so," observed Cromwell. " But I have no further time for idle discourse. Since there is no chance of capturing Charles Stuart, I shall not tarry longer here. Take charge of this damsel," he added. " Her friends have left her. But mark me! she must not return to the city. Neither return thither thyself, if thou wouldst live to enjoy thy pension."

" Your excellency's injunctions shall be obeyed," replied Dame Gives, trembling.

" I thought I was a prisoner," remarked Jane, surprised.

" I do not make prisoners of women," replied Cromwell, coldly.

With this he gave the word to Dighton, and immediately rode off in the direction of Perry Wood, followed by his troops.

No sooner was he gone, then Jane said to Dame Gives :

" Notwithstanding the Lord General's prohibition, I must, and will return to Worcester. I must relieve my brother's anxiety on my account."

" Beseech you do not, dear lady," replied the young widow, earnestly. " Come with me to Droitwich, whither I am going, and I will undertake to provide you a faithful messenger, who shall convey a letter or a token from you to Colonel Lane or Sir Clement Fisher."

" You know me then !" cried Jane in astonishment.

" There are very few in Worcester who do not know Mistress Jane Lane," replied Dame Gives.

" But your sympathies are with the enemy—not with us," cried Jane.

The very significant look given her by the young widow satisfied her she was mistaken.

" Major Careless would tell you differently," whispered Dame Gives, leaning forward.

" My doubts are removed," said Jane. " I will go with you to Droitwich."

" You will not find your confidence misplaced," replied Dame Gives. " And it will delight me to be of service to you."

They then rode off at a brisk pace, and were soon on the high road to Droitwich.

---

## CHAPTER XXIV.

WHAT CHARLES BEHELD FROM THE SUMMIT OF THE CATHEDRAL TOWER.

BRIGHTLY dawned the fatal 3rd of September, 1651, as if the day just breaking were destined to be one of peace and rejoicing rather than of strife and bloodshed. But the gladdening influence of the sunshine that gilded its towers, spires, and pinnacles could not dispel the gloom hanging over the devoted city. Men sprang from their restless couches oppressed with the sense that the dreadful contest in which they must of necessity take part was close at hand. Before night the king's fate would probably be decided. If he fell, the city dedicated to his cause would fall with him.

This conviction forced itself upon the minds of all who arose that morn in Worcester. After arming themselves, many of the soldier citizens looked round at their quiet homes as if taking leave of them for ever, or gazed with unspeakable anguish at their wives and children, well knowing the beloved ones would not be spared if the ruthless Parliamentarians should obtain the mastery. Some few were unmanned, but the majority faced the terrible situation resolutely, and conquered their emotion. Of victory they had now but little hope, yet they did not absolutely despair, since in war there is always a chance. Their word had been given to the king, and it must be kept, be the consequences what they might. If they could not secure him the throne they could die for him, and they were determined to sell their lives dearly. As to surrender, such a thought never occurred to these loyal folks, and if advantageous terms had been offered by Cromwell they would have rejected the dishonouring proposal with scorn.

Half an hour before daybreak the reveillé was beaten in the streets, the citizens who belonged to the different corps having been ordered to muster at an early hour on the College Green, at the Cross, and in other places. To these different points they were now marching, and the clank of arms resounded in all quarters.

The men of Worcester were not inexperienced in military service, most of them having been engaged in the two previous sieges of the city. A considerable number were employed on the walls and fortifications to assist the regular artillerymen, but others were formed into companies, each corps being commanded by a skilled officer. These companies were intended as a reserve force. The city being under military rule, the authority of the mayor was to a certain extent superseded, but he had quite enough to do as commander of the mounted civic guard, which being augmented by recruits brought by gentlemen of the county, now formed a regiment four hundred strong.

All the gates of the city were strongly guarded, and, as already intimated, the Foregate, which formed the principal outlet on the north, had been walled up.   No one, without an order, could cross the bridge ; and no boats, except the large flat-bottomed ferry-boats employed for the transit of troops and horses, were allowed on the river.

Grim war had set its stamp on Worcester.   Since the citizens had all become soldiers, there seemed to be soldiers everywhere—none but soldiers.   No women were abroad ; they were afraid to stir forth, and would fain have barricaded their dwellings.   The clank of arms, the beating of drums, the call of the bugle, were the only sounds heard in the streets.

The churches were open, and those who chose stepped in to breathe a prayer—the last, perhaps, they might ever utter.   Alas ! how those sacred edifices were soon afterwards profaned !  The taverns likewise were open—indeed, they had been open all night—and were full of Cavaliers fortifying themselves before assembling for duty with a morning's draught of canary.   A large body of the mounted civic guard was drawn up in front of the Guildhall awaiting the mayor's appearance, while small detachments were patrolling the streets.   In the Corn Market the king's body-guard was assembled, ready to escort his majesty to the cathedral.

As soon as it became light, anxious looks were directed towards the strong intrenchments thrown up by Cromwell on Perry Wood, and to the camp on Red Hill, but no movements were distinguishable at either place.

Charles was as early astir as any of the citizens.   He had slept soundly on the last night he was destined to pass at Worcester, and awoke refreshed and in good spirits, fully prepared for any perils and fatigue he might encounter.   Had he known all he would have to go through during the next twenty-four hours he might have felt grateful for the good night's rest he had enjoyed.

Half an hour before daybreak he was roused by Careless, and after making a hearty breakfast with Lord Derby, put on his armour and rode with the earl to the cathedral.

A council of war had been summoned to meet the king soon after daybreak on the summit of the cathedral tower, whence the whole surrounding district could be surveyed, and the movements of the enemy more easily discovered than from any other post of observation in the city, and his majesty was now proceeding to the place of rendezvous.

Alighting at the northern portal, Charles and the Earl of Derby entered the sacred edifice, and found the Duke of Hamilton, the Duke of Buckingham, the Earl of Lauderdale, Lord Talbot, Lord Wilmot, Lord Rothes, and several other distinguished personages, assembled in the nave.

All being fully armed, they formed a very striking group.   The anxious expression of their countenances, which none cared to conceal, showed how deeply they were impressed with the perilous position of affairs.   Charles appeared far more hopeful than his generals, and returned their grave salutations with a cheerfulness that surprised some of those who expected to find him despondent.

Massey had so far recovered from his wounds that he was able to attend the council, and Pitscottie was likewise present; but Montgomery, Keith, Drummond, Dalyell, and Sir Alexander Forbes, were necessarily absent, and Lesley had sent an excuse.

Several small groups of soldiers were collected within the cathedral, and amongst them were half a dozen Highlanders, who formed Pitscottie's guard.

Inviting the members of the council to follow him, the king proceeded to the north aisle of the choir, in which was the entrance to a spiral staircase communicating with the tower. Two musketeers were stationed at this door. Careless mounted first; the king went next, and the others followed, as they might, in no particular order.

In the belfry, which he soon reached, Charles found Middleton and Colonel Legge, and was well pleased to see them, but being impatient, he scarcely paused a moment, and quickly ascended a second circular staircase, narrower and steeper than the first, and soon gained the summit of the tower.

A wide and beautiful prospect now lay before him, but it was not the beauty or extent of the landscape that attracted him. The lofty post he had attained enabled him to see the whole of the adjoining districts on the south and south-east of the city, Red Hill and Perry Wood, both banks of the river, the junction of the Teme and the Severn, Powick with its church crowning a woody eminence, and all the country skirting the right bank of the Severn, and lying between Powick and Upton.

But before proceeding with our description, let us say a word about the cathedral tower, on the summit of which the king stood.

Some five centuries old, being finished in 1374, this structure, one of the finest in the kingdom, and the richest in embellishment, is upwards of one hundred and sixty feet high, measured from the roof of the central transept from which it springs. Exquisite tabernacle work surrounds the upper stage, and the eastern façade is ornamented by figures, one of which represents Edward III., at the latter end of whose reign the tower was completed. Viewed from all points, owing to the position of the reverend pile it adorns, the tower appears to singular advantage.

About fifty years subsequent to the date of our history, this noble structure was repaired—judiciously repaired, we are bound to add—and the existing pinnacles and battlements were erected. In other respects it is unaltered since Charles II.'s time, except what has been done internally in the belfry and clock-chamber by the unwearied exertions of the Rev. Richard Cattley, one of the present minor canons of the cathedral.*

---

* The whole scheme for the new clock and bells in Worcester Cathedral originated with the REV. RICHARD CATTLEY; and the city is deeply indebted to him for, perhaps, the finest set of Bells in the country, and for a Clock of great power and accuracy. These valuable additions to the ancient cathedral are to be supplemented by very perfect musical chimes, the mechanical appliances of which will be the gift of a great local benefactor, ALDERMAN J. W. LEA.—R. W.

As the battlements at the time of our history were more than six feet high, a wooden platform had been constructed to enable the king and his attendants to look over them without inconvenience.   Above the tower, on a tall flag-staff, floated the royal standard.

Springing up the wooden steps Charles leaned over the south parapet, and gazed eagerly at the posts of the enemy.   In another minute the whole of the battlements were thronged, and a dozen field-glasses anxiously directed towards Perry Wood and Red Hill.

The main body of the Parliamentary army which now occupied the former post remained stationary, but it was evident that some movement was taking place on the western slopes of Red Hill—probably in the direction of the Severn —and thinking this might be so, Charles directed his scrutiny to the near bank of the river, but though he scanned it carefully for a couple of miles he could discern nothing to justify alarm. The river that flowed past the lofty pile on which he stood was nowhere disturbed.   Next following the Teme from its point of junction with the larger river—its course being easily traced by the withes and willows fringing its banks—his eye rested on the old bridge of Powick.   A desperate effort he had always felt would be made by the enemy early in the day, to secure this pass; but he did not foresee, nor did any of his generals foresee, the skilful manœuvre by which its capture would be effected.

Charles had every reliance on General Montgomery's vigilance and bravery, supported as he was by Colonel George Keith.

Viewed from the cathedral tower on that bright morning, Powick seemed close at hand, and though the old bridge was partially veiled in a slight mist arising from the river, Montgomery's brigade could be seen drawn up on Wykefield, a large meadow, close beside it—the helmets and accoutrements of the men flashing in the sunbeams.

Satisfied that Montgomery was on the alert, and that no immediate danger threatened him, Charles continued his inspection, and, with his field-glass, swept the district lying between Powick and Upton.

Suddenly an exclamation broke from him that caused all the other glasses to be turned in the same direction as his own, and it was then perceived by all that a large body of cavalry was skirting the Old Hills.

Almost immediately afterwards another regiment of horse could be descried somewhat nearer the Severn.   Both were evidently advancing upon Powick Bridge.

" That must be Fleetwood's brigade," cried Charles, still keeping his glass fixed on the troops.

" Your majesty is right," observed Massey, who was standing behind the king.   " It is Fleetwood's regiment—Ingoldsby is nearer the river— and with him are Goff and Gibbons.   The troops coming through Woodsfield Copse, if I mistake not, are commanded by General Deane. Montgomery will have enough to do to maintain the bridge against such odds."

" He must be reinforced—and quickly," cried Charles.   " No troops can be spared from the city.   Dalyell must send a detachment from St. John's.   Careless shall take a message to him at once."

" I will go myself, sire," said Massey, " and take command of the detachment."

" But have you strength enough for the task, general ?"

" My strength will return when I meet the enemy," rejoined Massey. Charles did not attempt to stay him, and he departed.

Again the king watched the regiments advancing from Upton. They came on slowly and cautiously, while the skirmishers scoured the fields and lanes.

" How is this?" cried Charles, angrily. " Are they to be allowed to reach Powick without hindrance ?"

" Not so, my liege," replied Middleton, who had taken Massey's place behind the king. " They will meet with a warm reception anon. Look more closely, and you will perceive that the hedges are lined with soldiers. Those are your new recruits, and they are just the men for this sort of work. Ah! they are beginning in earnest now."

As he spoke, firing was heard in the distance, and looking in the direction of the sound, Charles perceived that several of the skirmishers had been shot down, while the riderless horses were careering wildly over the field.

A stronger party was instantly sent on to clear the hedges. But this was no easy task. General Middleton was right. The new recruits understood this kind of fighting. Excellent marksmen, and well posted, they gave their enemies a vast deal of trouble. Driven from one spot, they quickly took up another position, and even while retreating managed to do considerable execution. Their officers knew every inch of ground, and where to place them. Advantage was taken of every lane and defile, and the enemy's progress towards Powick was very considerably checked.

Among the officers who commanded these gallant little bands, which were scattered about the coppices and orchards in order to distract the enemy, and if possible throw him into confusion, were Colonel Lane, Captain Hornyold, and Sir Rowland Berkeley of Cotheridge. Sir Rowland rode a piebald horse, and the peculiarity of his steed caused him to be remarked by Colonel Goff. In Sir Rowland's corps were Lieutenant Vosper and Corporal Trubshaw, both of whom displayed great courage. Half of this brave little corps were cut down ; but the rest—and Vosper and Trubshaw were among them—reached Powick Bridge, and were then posted with Captain Woolfe in a water-mill on the banks of the Teme.

---

## CHAPTER XXV.

### HOW CROMWELL CONSTRUCTED A BRIDGE OF BOATS ACROSS THE SEVERN.

CHARLES and his council were still watching with great interest the desultory fighting previously described, and expressing surprise and admiration at the courage and pertinacity displayed by the recruits, when their attention was suddenly called to a circumstance that materially tended to increase the king's anxiety.

About a mile below the city, on the left bank of the river is a woody acclivity called Bunn's Hill. I+ :-          d the land beyond the summit has a park-like appearance, being ornamented with fine timber and coppices. The high road to Bath, which passes over Bunn's Hill, is distant about half a mile from the Severn. The hill itself slopes towards the river, and there is more rough wood on that side than on the summit. After passing the top, and getting on to the level, the slope towards the Severn becomes somewhat more precipitous, until a place is reached, now called "The Ketch"—about half a mile beyond the summit of the hill. For some distance the bank is then a nearly perpendicular marl rock, some thirty or forty feet in height. Bunn's Hill is not quite half a mile from the confluence of the Teme and the Severn. The appearance of Bunn's Hill was somewhat wilder when Charles gazed at it from the cathedral tower than it is at the present day, but its general features are unchanged.

While looking towards the woody slopes we have just described, the king perceived a large body of soldiers, amounting perhaps to a thousand, issue from a coppice that had hitherto screened them from view. They had with them pontoon-carriages and some cannon, and descending to the banks of the river, selected a favourable spot for their purpose, and immediately began to construct a bridge of boats.

The sight of this operation, which was carried on most expeditiously, greatly excited Charles.

"This must be stopped," he exclaimed. "If yonder pontoon bridge should be completed, Cromwell will cross the river and outflank Montgomery. We ought to have foreseen it."

Then calling to Pitscottie, who stepped towards him instantly, he added, "Haste to your regiment, colonel. Fortunately, it is not far from the spot you have to reach. That bridge of boats must not be completed, or if it should be finished before you arrive, it must be destroyed."

"It shall be done, my liege, if I sacrifice all my men in executing your majesty's order," replied Pitscottie. "Trust me, Cromwell shall never set foot on the west bank of the Severn."

With that Pitscottie disappeared.

In an inconceivably short space of time he was seen crossing the river in one of the large flat-bottomed boats we have before mentioned. His charger and his guard of Highlanders were with him. On reaching the bank, he quickly disembarked. and mounting his steed, galloped off towards his camp, his swift-footed men almost keeping up with him.

Not entirely satisfied with Pitscottie's ability to execute the order given him, Charles was about to send Colonel Legge with a detachment of men to Bunn's Hill to interrupt the pontoniers, but the Duke of Hamilton dissuaded him from the design, saying that the forces round the city must on no account be diminished.

"Rather let a general attack be made upon the enemy on Perry Wood, sire," said Hamilton. "We shall thus most effectually divert Cromwell from his designs on Powick. He cannot be everywhere."

The Earl of Derby coincided with the duke in opinion, but Charles, who had noticed that Fleetwood and Ingoldsby were driving the recruits before them, and drawing near to Powick, became very impatient, and cried out:

"Not till I have conferred with Montgomery and Keith—not till I have seen yon bridge of boats destroyed—must the general attack be made. If Montgomery is forced to retreat, we shall be hemmed in. On my return, we will attack Cromwell's intrenchments on Perry Wood, as proposed, and I will lead the assault in person. To-day will decide our fate. To you, my good Lord Rothes, and to you, brave Sir William Hamilton, a word at parting, as I may not see you again till all is over. To no better hands than yours could the maintenance of the Castle Hill be confided. Hold it to the last. Those who can be spared may accompany me to Powick. The rest must repair to their posts, and hold themselves in readiness for the signal of attack."

Attended by the Duke of Buckingham, the Earl of Derby, Lord Wilmot, and one or two others who eagerly availed themselves of his permission to accompany him, Charles then quitted the summit of the tower.

Hastily descending the circular stone staircase, he passed out of the cathedral. In another moment he was joined by his attendants, and the whole party proceeded quickly to the quay and embarked in one of the flat-bottomed boats we have previously mentioned. Their horses were brought over in a similar conveyance, under the charge of Careless; and in a third boat came half a dozen musketeers of the guard, who did not even dismount as they were ferried across the river. No time was lost in the disembarkation, and in a few minutes more the king and his attendants were speeding towards Powick, followed by the musketeers.

As they rode on, the continuous rattle of musketry was heard in the direction of Bunn's Hill, and they all concluded that Pitscottie was now actively engaged in checking the attempt of the Republican corps to cross the river at this point by means of the bridge of boats.

Such was the king's opinion—such the opinion of the Earl of Derby—but in reality, before the Scottish leader could bring up his regiment, the bridge of boats was completed.

---

## CHAPTER XXVI.

### HOW CROMWELL THREW A FLYING BRIDGE OVER THE TEME.

The first person to cross over was no other than Cromwell himself. Under the Lord General's personal superintendence the pontoon bridge had been constructed with the utmost rapidity, and, strange to say, almost without opposition. He crossed the river on foot, at the head of the column of men we have described, and at once prepared for action, for he saw Pitscottie advancing with his regiment of Highlanders to attack him. With the promptitude which he ever displayed, the Lord General took up an excellent position, and after a sharp conflict, during which he was reinforced by a detachment of horse, he drove back the Highlanders with great slaughter.

Pitscottie retreated towards Pitmarston, and satisfied with routing him, Cromwell marched towards the Teme, his object being to throw a flying bridge across that river, so as to allow reinforcements to be sent to Fleetwood and Ingoldsby during their attack upon Montgomery at Powick.

When this important manœuvre was accomplished, he felt he should be master on the west side of the river, since a quick and uninterrupted communication could be kept up with his generals. His progress, however, towards the Teme was not unopposed, but, on the contrary, was seriously obstructed by the Royalist infantry. He had to pass through a meadow, the hedges of which were lined with soldiers, who fired on his men as they marched on. But these obstacles were removed by the troopers, and the Teme being reached, a flying bridge across it was speedily constructed. Thus Cromwell's able plan was accomplished, and he inwardly exulted at its success.

Without a moment's loss of time he sent Dighton, with a detachment, to Fleetwood, to acquaint that general with what had been done.

"Say to him," he added, "that the enemy is now compassed about, and bid him destroy them in the Lord's name."

Though he had no fear that the flying bridge across the Teme could be reached by the enemy, he left a sufficient guard for its protection, and then returned with the rest of his troops to the bridge of boats across the Severn.

The communication between the two bridges was now unobstructed, the enemy having been completely driven off. Cromwell, however, posted a battalion on the west bank of the Severn to defend this important pass.

Before crossing the river, he awaited Dighton's return. This active messenger brought him very satisfactory intelligence.

Fleetwood and Ingoldsby had reached the village of Powick, and were preparing to attack Montgomery's brigade. Lambert was bringing up his regiment to reinforce them, so that their success appeared certain.

"It is rumoured that Charles Stuart himself, with the Duke of Buckingham, the Earl of Derby, and some others of the malignant leaders, are with General Montgomery," observed Dighton. "From what I could learn they have only just arrived, and will not tarry long."

"They may tarry long enough to see Montgomery driven from the bridge," rejoined Cromwell, with a grim smile. "But no—I do Montgomery wrong. He is brave, and will hold his post as long as it can be held. Colonel George Keith, also, is a good soldier. Mark me, Dighton. Charles Stuart will hurry back to the city as soon as he has given his orders. I will find him employment there."

As he spoke, sharp firing was heard in the direction of Powick Bridge.

"Ha! the attack has commenced," cried Cromwell, to whose ears the sound was music. "Would I were with them. Yet they do not need me. I have no better general than my son-in-law Fleetwood, unless it be Lambert, and he is with him. Together they are resistless."

After listening for a few minutes to the rattle of musketry, which was now mingled with the sound of heavier guns, Cromwell raised his hands, as if invoking a blessing, and exclaimed aloud, so that all might hear:

"The Lord of Hosts go with them, and give them a glorious victory!"

He then crossed the pontoon bridge, and mounting his charger which was in readiness for him, rode up the pleasant slopes of Bunn's Hill, ever and anon turning to look at the conflict going on at Powick Bridge.

Halting for a short time at Red Hill, he gave his final instructions to Lilburn and Lord Grey of Groby, both of whom were arrayed for battle, and then rode on to Perry Wood.

On arriving there, he gave instant orders that the largest guns in the battery should open fire on Fort Royal—preparatory to storming the fort.

The order was instantly obeyed. The engineers on the fort at once replied to the cannonade, and what would now be called an "artillery duel" commenced. The outposts of the royal army were likewise fired upon from other points, but no general attack was made on either side.

---

## CHAPTER XXVII.

### THE FIGHT OF POWICK BRIDGE.

MEANWHILE, a desperate conflict took place between the contending forces at Powick Bridge—hundreds of lives being sacrificed for the possession of this all-important pass.

The grey old bridge still stands, and if the stones could speak, they would have a terrible tale to relate. The situation of the old bridge is singularly peaceful and quiet. At the time of which we treat, there were no habitations near it except a water-mill, and two or three cottages, the village of Powick being about three parts of a mile distant. The bridge is strongly built, and narrow, with angular openings like those of Upton Bridge.

Peaceful as is the spot, it had already been the scene of a bloody conflict between the Parliamentarians and Royalists, in 1642, when Prince Rupert posted himself near a hawthorn-bush on the brow of a bank adjoining Wykefield, and dashed upon the Earl of Essex. But things were now destined to be changed. In front of the bridge, on the road to Powick village, Montgomery's infantry was posted, in ranks, five deep —the men being armed with pikes and carabines.

Attacked by Fleetwood's dragoons, they sustained the onset firmly, killing numbers of men and horses, but on the second charge their ranks were broken, and they were driven across the narrow bridge with great slaughter—many of them jumping into the river to avoid the merciless dragoons who were hewing them down. Deeply dyed with blood, the Teme was almost choked with the bodies of the slain. But it was on the further side of the bridge, at Wykefield, just mentioned as the scene of Rupert's victory nine years before, that the severest part of the contest took place.

On Wykefield, as three or four meadows hereabouts are designated,

Montgomery's main body was drawn up, and when the confusion caused by the retreat of the advanced guard could be set right, a fierce attack was made on the Parliamentarians, and so energetic was it that the latter were driven back, and it seemed as if possession of the bridge would be regained by the Royalists. But the success was fleeting.

Another troop of horse came on—the bridge was cleared—Ingoldsby's regiment passed over—and the fight became general on the meadows, and soon extended as far as Rupert's hawthorn-bush.

Just below the bridge, on the left bank of the river, as we have previously mentioned, was a water-mill, and near it were two or three small cottages. The mill, which with its large wheel formed a picturesque object from the bridge, was occupied by a party of recruits, placed there by Montgomery. The party was commanded by Captain Woolfe, and amongst those with him, as we have already intimated, were Lieutenant Vosper and Corporal Trubshaw. These recruits were excellent marksmen, and being thus advantageously posted, did great execution upon the dragoons during the conflict on the bridge. Orders were given to dislodge them, but this was found impossible, owing to the continuous fire kept up by Captain Woolfe and his men. Nor would they have been driven out if the enemy had not set the mill on fire. The old structure was speedily in flames, and for a short time formed a striking object in the terrible picture. The blazing mill and some wooden outbuildings connected with it, which had likewise caught fire, were reflected on the river already dyed of a sanguinary hue, and filled with dying and dead.

While still burning, the mill was surrounded by dragoons, between whom and the Royalist recruits a desperate fight took place. With the fire at the back, and the enemy in front, no wonder the Royalists fought fiercely. Some few escaped—but the greater number were killed, or thrown back into the flames. Captain Woolfe and Vosper fought their way out, but poor Trubshaw was not so fortunate. His skull was split, and he staggered back into the fire.

Wykefield was now a complete field of battle, in which many marvellous acts of heroism were performed by the Royalists. Small parties of Cavaliers might be seen scattered over the field engaged against fearful odds—but still fighting furiously, and in some cases overcoming their antagonists. With the remnant of his brave regiment of Highlanders, Pitscottie had joined the fight, and lent what aid he could. But despite their gallant efforts to maintain their ground, the Cavaliers were driven back almost as far as Rupert's hawthorn-bush. Still, the fight went on, though the ranks of the Royalists were much thinned, and their ammunition began to fail. On the other hand, the Parliamentarians were being constantly reinforced.

Considering the inequality of the contending forces—the Parliamentarians being now three to one—the duration of the fight at Powick was remarkable. The contest lasted for nearly two hours, and during this time the Royalists held their ground stoutly against their adversaries.

Montgomery was severely wounded, and could with difficulty sit his horse.

Keith, who had thrown himself into the thick of the fray, in the vain hope of turning the tide, had been taken prisoner. Finding all against him, Montgomery, at last, was compelled to order a retreat, and strove to prevent it from being converted into a total rout.

The advance of the victors was somewhat checked by the soldiers who lined the hedges, and fired at the enemy from every sheltered spot.

A stand was made at Pitmarston, but it was brief and ineffectual. The rout of the Royalists was then complete, and all who could escape the enemy's sword fled to St. John's, where General Dalyell's brigade was quartered, and where it was thought that the victorious Parliamentarians would be stopped. But such was not the case.

Earlier in the day, alleging that he could not spare them, Dalyell refused to send a detachment of his men with Massey to Powick, and now after a short resistance, which only reflected disgrace upon him, he ordered his brigade to lay down their arms to Fleetwood.

Having thus carried everything before them on the western side of the river, Fleetwood and Ingoldsby prepared to cross the bridge, and enter the doomed city.

---

## CHAPTER XXVIII.

### HOW THE BATTERY ON PERRY WOOD WAS TAKEN BY THE KING.

THE king was not present during any part of the disastrous conflict just described. On arriving at Powick Bridge with his attendants, he found Montgomery and Keith at their post, and confident of their ability to maintain it. No reinforcements had been sent, as yet, by Dalyell, but doubtless they would soon arrive, and Montgomery declared he did not require them.

Continuous firing having been for some time heard in the direction of the Severn, Montgomery, in obedience to his majesty's command, was about to detach a party of men to support Pitscottie, when a Highland soldier arrived in breathless haste bringing intelligence that his leader had been routed by the enemy. Charles could scarcely credit the news, but on ascertaining the full extent of the disaster, he felt the necessity of immediately returning to the city and preparing against an attack on the south, which might now be expected.

He therefore rode back with his attendants, crossed the river at the palace-ferry, and at once proceeded to the Sidbury-gate, where he found the Duke of Hamilton. From the watch posted on the summit of the cathedral tower, the duke had already heard of Pitscottie's defeat and the construction of the flying bridge across the Teme. He did not for a moment attempt to disguise the perilous position in which his majesty would be placed if Montgomery should be worsted at Powick, and coincided with the king in opinion that the general attack should not be delayed, but advised that a visit should first be paid to Lesley, whom he had not as yet seen that morning.

Acting upon this counsel, Charles, attended by the Earl of Derby, Lord Wilmot, Careless, and a small escort, rode to the Blockhouse fields, where Lesley was stationed with his Scottish horse. He found him with the whole of his large force under arms, and apparently ready for action. But he could not help noticing that Lesley looked exceedingly grave, and not altogether free from uneasiness.

"Is this man really the traitor he is generally thought?" mentally ejaculated Charles. "I will try him. Colonel Lesley," he cried, as he rode up, "I am resolved to take yon battery on Perry Wood. Bid your men prepare for the attack. I shall lead them in person."

On receiving this command, Lesley immediately drew near the king, and said, in a low voice:

"I beseech you not to call upon them to make the attack, sire. They will not follow you."

"Not follow me!" exclaimed Charles, fiercely. "Lesley, you are a traitor!"

"I have already told you, sire," replied Lesley, in the same low voice, "that the men are not to be relied on. They will not fight with your Cavaliers."

"What will they do, then?" demanded Charles, sternly. "Will they utterly desert me in my hour of need? Will they deliver me to the enemy?"

"No, sire; but if, in obedience to your commands, I order them to attack yon battery, not one of them will stir."

Just then the roar of artillery was heard. The battery had opened fire on Fort Royal, and was immediately answered—as we have already described—by the Royalist engineers. The din was heightened by the smaller ordnance of the Blockhouse, which now began to operate—though with little effect—against Cromwell's intrenchments.

"Can you hear this, and stand tamely by?" observed Charles, reproachfully, to Lesley.

"I cannot help it, my liege," was the Scottish leader's answer. "My men are mutinous and will not obey me. Look at them now, and you will be convinced that I speak the truth. But do not, I entreat you, compel me to put their disloyalty to the proof."

Charles cast his eye along the line nearest him, and the sullen and discontented aspect of the men fully confirmed Lesley's assertion.

The Earl of Derby had likewise taken a rapid survey of the regiment, and came to a like conclusion.

"A mutinous spirit evidently prevails among the men," he said to the king, "and may break out at once, if an attempt is made to force them into action. Leave Lesley to manage them. He can do it, if he will."

"'Tis the confounded Kirk Committee that has been at work with them," cried Charles. "Lesley," he added, in a low significant tone to the Scottish leader, "you will gain nothing by deserting me; but much —very much—by standing firmly by me at this critical juncture."

"My liege," said Lesley, earnestly, "if you are in jeopardy, I will bring you aid. I cannot promise more."

Obliged to be content with this, Charles rode off with his attendants and escort, and regardless of the enemy's fire, which was now extending along the heights and increasing in fury, proceeded to visit his various outposts.

Very little impression was produced upon Fort Royal by the heavy cannonade directed against it from Perry Wood, nor was any immediate attempt made by the enemy to storm it.

Lilburn and Lord Grey of Groby gradually drew closer to the Royalist outposts, but seemed to be awaiting the Lord General's signal for the grand attack. And such, in reality, was the case. From the apparent inertness of the enemy it was erroneously supposed by the Royalists that most of the Parliamentary troops had been drawn to the other side of the Severn. Cromwell, however, had a motive for all he did, and if he delayed the attack, it was because he deemed the right moment for making it had not arrived.

Never was he more cheerful than he appeared to be throughout this trying day. Confident of victory, he yet kept a watchful look-out upon the enemy, and seemed surprised that the attack, which he expected the king to make upon him, should be so long delayed. For this attack, come when it might, he was fully prepared; but as evening began to draw on, and no movement was made by the royal forces, he grew impatient.

"Time will scarcely be allowed us for the work," he said to the officers with him, "yet will I not move till I have full assurance that Fleetwood and Ingoldsby are masters of St. John's, and ready to enter the city."

At this moment a messenger rode up bringing the intelligence he so eagerly desired.

Montgomery was utterly routed—Keith a prisoner—Dalyell had surrendered. Fleetwood and Ingoldsby were preparing to cross the bridge, and enter the city. Lambert was marching towards the bridge of boats, and would soon bring his regiment to Perry Wood. Such was the sum of the despatch. The messenger had to take a circuitous route, or it would have been delivered sooner.

Cromwell could not conceal his satisfaction.

"The Lord of Hosts is with us," he exclaimed. "His holy arm hath gotten us the victory. Nothing remains but to finish the work so well begun. On this day twelvemonth, at Dunbar, the word was, ' The Lord of Hosts.' So let it be to-day. The signal then was, ' We have no white about us.' The same signal shall serve now. Make this known throughout the regiments, and then prepare for action."

While issuing these orders, Cromwell had noticed a movement at the Sidbury-gate, and now fixing his field-glass upon the spot he perceived that the main body of the royal army, horse and foot, was coming forth from the gate, evidently for the purpose of attacking him. He was at no loss to discover that the host was commanded by the king in person, and that Charles was attended by several of his most distinguished nobles. Indeed, from a closer survey, he felt certain that the Dukes of Hamilton and Buckingham were with him.

It was a splendid sight to see that gallant host issue forth from the gate, and familiar as he was with such spectacles, Cromwell watched it for some minutes with great interest—noting the strength of each regiment, and making many shrewd observations to his own officers.

"Charles Stuart hath come forth in all his bravery," he said. "But he and all his host shall be utterly discomfited. We ... smite them.

Spare none of the malignants.  As to their prince, take him not captive, but slay him without pity."

Many circumstances had conspired to prevent Charles from making the attack he had meditated upon the enemy until so late in the day. But when he learnt that Dalyell had surrendered he no longer hesitated. but marched forth as we have just described.  He was accompanied by the Dukes of Buckingham and Hamilton, the Earl of Derby, Lord Wilmot, Sir Alexander Forbes, and several other distinguished personages, and had with him his best infantry and cavalry, and his bravest Cavaliers.

The command of the right wing was given to the Duke of Hamilton, that of the left to the Earl of Derby, with whom was Colonel Roscarrock, while he himself commanded the centre.  Perry Wood was to be attacked on either side, while a charge was made on the battery.

The plan was executed with remarkable quickness and precision.  No sooner were the men formed than a general charge was made on Perry Wood, each division taking its appointed course.  Such was the impetuosity of the Cavaliers who formed the central body led by the king, that they drove back Cromwell's body-guard who rode down the hill to meet them, and rushing on with irresistible fury broke through the pickets, forced the intrenchments, and putting the artillerymen to the sword, actually obtained possession of the enemy's largest guns.

For a brief space Charles, who had led this wonderful charge—the most brilliant feat performed at the fight of Worcester—seemed master of the position.  He was on the very spot just occupied by Cromwell himself, and had taken his guns.  The valiant Cavaliers who attended their sovereign raised a shout of triumph, and struck the cannon with their swords.

With the king were Colonel Legge, Colonel Lane, Captain Giffard, Colonel Blague, Marmaduke Darcy, Wogan, and Careless.  They had ridden close behind him, and had shared every danger he incurred. Colonel Legge, indeed, had saved the king's life.  It was a singular sight to see the royal party on the top of the hill in the midst of the Parliamentarian forces.  But their position seemed scarcely tenable, though Hamilton and Derby were pressing on, on either side, to their aid.

Nevertheless, Charles exulted in his brief triumph, and his exultation was shared by his companions.  The hitherto invincible Ironclads had retreated before him, and were still in confusion and disorder, while both Hamilton and Derby, animated by the king's success, were driving all before them.  Moreover, a most important result had been obtained by the capture of the guns. Fort Royal, which had suffered considerably from the ceaseless cannonade of the battery, was now left unmolested.

At this critical juncture, when his fate hung in the balance, and when the Scottish horse might have helped him to victory, Charles looked anxiously down to the spot where Lesley was posted.  He was still there with his troops.  But they remained motionless, although their leader must have been aware of the king's success, and must have felt how important aid would be at that moment.

" Does he move ?—is he coming ?" cried Charles.

" No, sire," rejoined Legge, straining his eyes in the direction of the Scottish cavalry. " He does not stir. Curses on him for a traitor."

" Oh, that Montrose were alive and in his place !" ejaculated Charles, bitterly. " He would not have served me thus!"

" No, sire," observed Careless. " Montrose would have secured you the victory."

It may be that the battle of Worcester was lost by Charles, owing to Lesley's inaction or treachery. If the king's extraordinary success could have been at once followed up, victory might have ensued. Who shall say?

---

## CHAPTER XXIX.

### HOW THE BATTLE OF WORCESTER WAS LOST BY THE KING.

CROMWELL was somewhat disconcerted by the unlooked-for advantage gained by Charles, but he quickly brought his disordered troops to their ranks, and prepared to bring forward his reserves. Like Charles, he looked down to the Blockhouse fields to see what Lesley would do, but was speedily reassured by finding the Scottish horse remain motionless.

" The men of Sechem have dealt treacherously with Abimelech," he said, with a stern smile. " Had Lesley come to his master's aid in time, he might have given me some trouble."

Detaching troops on either side to prevent a junction between the three parties of Royalists, he himself made a determined attack on the king.

The onset was terrible, but Charles and his Cavaliers bore it firmly, and maintained their ground, giving abundant proofs of valour, and showing of what stout stuff they were made, since they could thus resist the attack of Cromwell's veteran troops.

The conflict lasted for a considerable time—much longer, indeed, than Cromwell expected—but when Lambert arrived with his troops it became too unequal, and the Cavaliers were forced to give way. Besides, their ammunition was completely exhausted, and they were obliged to fight with the butt-ends of their muskets. After a most obstinate but ineffectual resistance, they retreated in disorder towards the city.

No junction had taken place between the battalions under the Duke of Hamilton and the Earl of Derby, but neither of these leaders were more successful than the king, though both fought valiantly. The Duke of Hamilton routed a troop of horse, but in a subsequent encounter his horse was shot under him, and he himself was so severely wounded, that he had to be taken from the field, and was conveyed to the Commandery. Sir John Douglas was likewise mortally wounded, and Sir Alexander Forbes, disabled by a shot through both legs, was left in this lamentable condition in Perry Wood during the whole night. Next day he was discovered by the enemy and taken prisoner. Both the Earl of Derby and Roscarrock escaped unhurt, but the battalion commanded by the earl was routed after a gallant fight.

Overpowered on all sides, the Royalists, after sustaining fearful loss, were compelled to retreat into the city. Lesley, who had taken no part whatever in the fight, finding that the day had gone against the king, moved his regiment towards Barbourne Bridge, about a mile on the north of the city, and close to Pitchcroft.

No sooner did Cromwell's engineers regain possession of the great guns than they began to cannonade Fort Royal with redoubled fury. Under this tremendous fire a strong storming party was detached to take the fort, with orders from the Lord General to put all the troops within it to the sword unless they surrendered. The barbarous order was executed. The fort being carried by storm after an obstinate resistance, no quarter was given to its brave defenders. The guns of the fort were then turned upon the city, and being so close to it, caused terrible havoc, and drove all the artillerymen from the walls.

But we must now return to the king. So long as a chance was left him, Charles fought valiantly, and during the retreat, though he failed to rally his disordered troops, he turned several times to face the enemy.

While thus braving the foe for the last time he was left alone, none of his attendants being aware that he had stopped. From the richness of his accoutrements he was at once recognised, and fierce cries were raised :

" 'Tis Charles Stuart !—'tis Jeroboam ! The Lord has delivered him into our hands ! Slay him—slay him !"

Several pistols were discharged at him, but though the bullets struck his armour, no injury was done him. Most luckily his horse was not hurt, but bore him swiftly and safely to the Sidbury-gate. He was hotly pursued by the Roundhead troopers, who would assuredly have cut him down, according to Cromwell's order, if they had come up with him.

On reaching the Sidbury-gate he found, to his dismay, that it was blocked up by an ammunition waggon, which had been overturned there either by accident or design. One of the oxen that had drawn the waggon was killed on the spot.

Without a moment's hesitation, the king threw himself from his horse, and contrived to creep past the waggon. As he entered Sidbury-street, Mr. William Bagnal, a staunch loyalist, who dwelt in that quarter, rode towards him, and, instantly dismounting, offered him his horse. The steed, thus opportunely provided for his majesty, was of infinite service to him in the day, as will be shown.

Once more on horseback, Charles rode up to the High-street, and found it full of soldiers, most of them belonging to the Scotsish infantry. They had all a most dejected look, and on seeing him, many of them threw down their arms, to intimate their refusal to fight any longer. In vain he rode up and down their ranks, with his feathered hat in his hand, addressing them with a passionate eloquence that ought to have roused them.

" Stand to your arms !" he cried. " Fight like men, and we shall yet conquer. Follow me, and I will lead you to victory. Ours is the right cause, and truth and justice must prevail in the end. Follow your king !"

Finding, however, that they would not stir, he called out in accents of bitter reproach, " Recreants that you are to desert me thus. If you will not fight, turn your arms against me. I had rather you would shoot me than let me live to see the consequences of this fatal day."

He then rode slowly off towards the College Green, still hoping some might follow him, but none stirred.

---

## CHAPTER XXX.

### HOW THE ENEMY ENTERED THE CITY, AND HOW THE KING QUITTED IT.

MEANWHILE, a sharp conflict was taking place outside the Sidbury-gate between a party of flying Royalists and a troop of horse under Colonel Pride. The unlucky Royalists were unable to enter the city owing to the obstacle before mentioned, and, after a short struggle, were slain to a man in front of the gate.

The ammunition waggon being removed, a regiment of infantry rushed in through the Sidbury-gate, and encountering no opposition, the men spread themselves through the lower streets of the city, and commenced plundering the houses.

The loyal city was now paying the penalty of its devotion to the king. Terror and confusion reigned everywhere. Doors were burst open, and the most horrible threats were answered by shrieks and cries for pity, but no pity was shown by the ferocious soldiery.

By this time Fort Royal had been stormed, as we have already related, and its guns being turned upon the city, the destruction caused in various parts by the shot heightened the terror of the inhabitants. Desperate fighting was going on in all quarters, and nothing was heard but the clash of steel, the sharp ring of musketry, and the roar of artillery, mingled with shouts and cries.

Fleetwood and Ingoldsby had now forced their away across the bridge, but their entrance into the city was furiously opposed by such forces as could be rallied by Lord Wilmot, Colonel Blague, Colonel Lane, and others, but the contest was too unequal, and could not be long sustained.

As both horse and foot were now continually pouring into the city on all sides, conflicts were taking place in almost every street. There was desperate fighting on the west as well as on the east. There was fighting on the quay — in Newport-street and Dolday — near All Saints' Church—and in Broad-street. There was no fighting near the Cross—for the Foregate, as already mentioned, had been walled up—and, indeed, the enemy chiefly entered the city from the Sidbury-gate, from Friars'-gate, and from the bridge. But there was a great deal of fighting in Friars'-street, Lich-street, and multitudes of armed citizens and artillerymen who had been driven from the walls were running about in different directions. Hundreds of these were killed, for quarter was given to none with arms in their hands, and the streets were full of dead bodies.

The Scottish infantry tamely surrendered, and were shut up in the

cathedral.   They had better have died valiantly, for they were afterwards sold as slaves to the plantations.   But other Scottish regiments
behaved with the greatest resolution, and if all had done equally well,
the result of the day might have been different.   Castle Hill, as we
know, had been strongly fortified, and was held by the Earl of Rothes,
Sir William Hamilton, and Colonel Drummond, with a party of brave
and loyal Scots.   The fortress was attacked by Lambert and Harrison,
but was so obstinately defended that its leaders were able to capitulate
on advantageous terms.

Having thus endeavoured to describe the frightful condition to which
the city was reduced by the entrance of the enemy, we will now return
to Charles, whom we left proceeding in a most melancholy frame of
mind, and wholly unattended, towards the College Green.   So cast
down was he at the moment that he scarcely took note of anything
that was passing around him, when he was suddenly roused from his fit
of despondency by seeing a large troop of horse issue from the college
gates.   It was a party of Cavaliers headed by the Earl of Derby, Lord
Cleveland, Colonel Roscarrock, Colonel Wogan, and Careless, and on
making this discovery he immediately rode up, and was welcomed with
the greatest delight by the Earl of Derby, as well as by his faithful
attendant Careless.   The greatest uneasiness had been felt for his safety,
and it was feared he might have fallen into the hands of the enemy.
Nor were the Cavaliers composing the troop less delighted, and their
enthusiasm quickly raised his drooping spirits.   He put himself at their
head, and, despite the entreaties of the Earl of Derby that he would
seek safety in flight, he led them towards the Sidbury-gate.

But they had scarcely descended Lich-street when Colonel Pride's
regiment of horse was seen advancing, and an instant onset upon it was
made.   As on all previous occasions, the first advantage was with the
Cavaliers, but Pride and his men were not to be driven back.   As soon
as it was discovered that Charles was with the party, an attempt was
made by Pride to capture him, and it would have been successful if Careless had not flown to his rescue.

The Cavaliers still made a desperate struggle, but it was evident they
could not hold out long.   Charles, who had been left for a few minutes
in the rear after his rescue, was again about to place himself at their
head, but Careless earnestly besought him to fly.

"The day is lost, my liege—utterly lost!" exclaimed this faithful
attendant.   "Save yourself, while there is yet time.   We can hold out
long enough to cover your escape.   Fly, I entreat you."

"No.   I cannot—will not—abandon my faithful followers," cried
Charles.

"Your presence unnerves us, my liege," implored Careless.   "See
you not that the enemy is resolved to capture you, or slay you.   Balk
his design by instant flight.   We will prevent all pursuit till you are
safe.   Quit the city by St. Martin's-gate.   'Tis the only safe outlet.
Ride on to Barbourne Bridge, where those of us who are left alive will
join you when all is over here."

Charles yielded to these entreaties, though with the greatest reluctance,
and Careless rushed to the front.   Captain Woolfe and Vosper chanced

to be near the king at the time, and he ordered them to follow him. Divining his intentions, they instantly obeyed.

On the way to St. Martin's-gate, he had to pass the ancient mansion which he had latterly made his private quarters, and wishing to enter it for a moment to take off the heaviest part of his armour, which might incommode him during his flight, and possess himself of some valuables he had left behind, he dismounted, and giving his steed to Vosper, en tered the house.

His imprudence in doing so had well-nigh led to his capture. He did not imagine that his flight had been discovered by the enemy, but he was mistaken. Quick eyes had been upon him at the time. Colonel James, who had recovered from his wounds, was with the Parliamentarians, and seeing the king quit his adherents, guessed his purpose.

But for some minutes pursuit was impossible, owing to the obstinate resistance of the Cavaliers. At length, Colonel James, accompanied by a dozen dragoons, forced his way into New-street, and was galloping along it when he caught sight of Woolfe and Vosper with the king's horse. They instantly disappeared, but he had seen enough. He knew that Charles had made that old mansion his private quarters, and felt convinced he must be within it at the time.

Galloping up, he entered with half a dozen of his troopers, leaving the rest on guard outside. Luckily for Charles, his pursuers had neglected to secure the door that opened into the Corn Market. Before moving off, Woolfe and Vosper gave the alarm. The king had already divested himself of his armour, and was prepared for flight. At the very moment that Colonel James and his troopers entered, he passed out at the back.

Not many persons were in the Corn Market at the time, and the few he encountered being staunch Royalists, would have protected him with their lives, rather than have betrayed him. Woolfe and Vosper were not in sight, but he learnt they had gone out by St. Martin's-gate.

Hurrying thither, he passd through the gate without interference— for the Parliamentarians had not yet placed a guard there—and in another instant was joined by his attendants, who brought him his horse.

Quickly mounting his steed, he galloped off in the direction of Barbourne Bridge. He was not pursued—false information being given to Colonel James, which led him to believe that the royal fugitive had not quitted the city.

After awhile Charles slackened his pace, but just then he heard the trampling of horse behind him, and fancying the enemy was on his track, was about to gallop on, when he discovered that his fancied pursuers were a small party of his own cavalry. He then faced about, and as the troop drew nearer, found that at its head were the Duke of Buckingham and the Earl of Lauderdale. A painful meeting took place between the king and the two nobles. They were seeking safety in flight, and were rejoiced to find that his majesty had escaped.

Soon afterwards, several small parties of Royalists overtook them—no other route being open to the fugitives. Charles, therefore, had no lack of attendants.

On reaching Barbourne Bridge, to his great surprise he found Lesley and his regiment of horse

"Soh! you are here," he cried, furiously.   "I sought for you in vain in the city.   Your men must be fresh since they have taken no part in the fight.   Come back with me at once and help me to retrieve the fortune of the day."

"Sire," replied Lesley, calmly, "the contest from the first has been hopeless, and your troops are now annihilated.   It would be madness to return.   "I have been waiting for you here."

"Waiting for me?" exclaimed Charles.

"Ay, waiting for you, sire.   I knew you would come this way, since none other is open to you.   I am ready to conduct you to Scotland."

"But I will not return thither to be the slave I have been," cried Charles.   "I will rather die in England."

"Humour him, my liege—humour him.   He may be of use now," observed Buckingham, in a low tone.

"You majesty has now no option," remarked Lesley, coldly.   "You must go back to Scotland.   I will insure you a safe retreat.   'Tis for that purpose I have reserved my troops."

"Say you so?" cried Charles.   "Then I must needs go with you. But I must wait here for my friends."

"Your majesty will have to wait long ere some of them will join you," said Lesley.

"At least they have not deserted me," rejoined the king.

---

## CHAPTER XXXI.

### THE LAST STAND MADE BY THE ROYALISTS.

ONCE more we must enter the ill-fated city, which was now completely in the power of the enemy, though many a conflict was still going on within it.   So inflamed with fury were the Cavaliers, that they fell upon the foot soldiers who had been plundering the houses, and were so much encumbered with booty that they could not defend themselves, and slew such numbers of them that Friars'-street was quite choked up with dead bodies.   On neither side was quarter given.

"The hour of vengeance is come," shouted the fierce Cromwellians. "Slay the Amalekites.   Destroy them utterly—so that they may never more rise against us."

"Down with the rebellious sectaries!" cried the Cavaliers.   "Spare them not.   Kill them as you would wild beasts."

Savage shouts like these were heard on all sides, proclaiming the deadly animosity of the combatants which could be satisfied with nothing but slaughter.

The last stand made by the Royalists was at the Guildhall, and a more gallant stand was never made, because success seemed out of the question.

A tolerably strong party of Cavaliers had been rallied by Careless, Sir Rowland Berkeley, Colonel Legge, Colonel Lane, and Captain Hornyold.   They assembled, as we have said, in front of the Guildhall.

With them were the Earl of Cleveland, Sir James Hamilton, Colonel Wogan, and some others. They were attacked on the left by Fleetwood, and on the right by Lambert, with whom was Cromwell in person. In the fierce conflict that ensued, many were slain, and many more taken prisoners, but all the leaders escaped, except Sir James Hamilton, who was severely wounded.

Finding the contest hopeless, and that they should soon be shut up within the city, without the possibility of escape, Careless and the others dashed down Pump-street, and made their way to St. Martin's-gate. Having thus got out of the city, they rode as quickly as they could to Barbourne Bridge, where they found the king.

Deprived of all its defenders, its bravest inhabitants slain, or made captive, the city was then delivered over to the rapacious and fanatical soldiery, who had obtained possession of it. On the frightful atrocities perpetrated during that night upon the wretched inhabitants by the barbarous hordes let loose upon them, we shall not dwell. Suffice it to say that the sack of Rome under the Constable de Bourbon scarcely exceeded the sack of Worcester in horror.

Imagination cannot conceive scenes more dreadful than actually occurred. No soldiers were ever more savage, more ruffianly, more merciless than the Paliamentary troops. Cromwell himself had left the city before the direst deeds were enacted, but he well knew what would happen. He did not expressly sanction pillage and rapine and all other atrocious acts, but he did not forbid them, and, at all events, did not punish the offenders.

On that night, at the very time when the diabolical atrocities we have hinted at, but cannot describe—when outrages the most frightful were being committed by his soldiery, without the slightest interference from his officers, the Lord General wrote in these terms to the Parliament:

"This hath been a very glorious mercy, and as stiff a contest for four or five hours as ever I have seen. Both your old forces and those new raised have behaved themselves with very great courage, and He that made them come out, made them willing to fight for you. The Lord God Almighty frame our hearts to real thankfulness for this, which is alone His doing."

The darkest part of the picture was carefully kept out of sight, and nothing dwelt upon but the "glorious mercy" vouchsafed him and his forces. Yet no mercy was shown by the conquerors, on that dreadful night—the worst they ever had to endure—to the miserable inhabitants of faithful Worcester.

----

## CHAPTER XXXII.

### THE CONSULTATION AT BARBOURNE BRIDGE, AND THE KING'S FLIGHT.

WE left the king at Barbourne Bridge. By this time he had been joined by the Earl of Derby, the Earl of Lauderdale, the Lords Talbot and Wilmot, Colonel Roscarrock, Colonel Blague, Charles Giffard, and many other Cavaliers, and a consultation ——— ' ' ·- ·· ·rhat course should be pursued.　All were of opinion that the day was irretrievably lost, and this opinion was confirmed by the arrival of Careless and the others, who told how they had been worsted in the last desperate struggle at the Guildhall.

"More than half of this brave battalion are gone," exclaimed Careless.　"The rest are dispersed, and will never be got together again. Such frightful havoc has been made among the citizens, who have been slain by hundreds by these ferocious Roundheads, that no more fighting men can be got together.　All is lost!　Your majesty's standard has been torn down everywhere, and replaced by the flag of the Commonwealth.　From this spot you may see their hateful standard floating on the cathedral tower."

Overpowered by this ill news, Charles could make no reply.

"All we can now do for your majesty is to save you from these ravening wolves and regicides," cried the Earl of Derby, "and that, with Heaven's grace, we will do!"

"We will defend your majesty to the last," cried the Lords Talbot and Wilmot, and several others.

"Alas! how many are gone!" exclaimed Charles.　"Brave Sir John Douglas dead—the Duke of Hamilton mortally wounded.　Where is Lord Sinclair?—where are others of my Scottish peers?—where is Sir James Hamilton?—where is Sir Alexander Forbes?"

"Sir James Hamilton is killed, my liege," replied Careless.　"Sir Alexander Forbes is badly hurt—perhaps dead.　Several of the Scottish nobles have been taken prisoners in the city.　But think not of them— think of your own safety.　What will you do?"

"Make all haste to London," replied the king.　"By riding hard I shall arrive there before tidings of the battle can be received."

"A good plan," cried Lord Wilmot.　"Your majesty has many staunch adherents in London."

"I like not the plan," cried the Duke of Buckingham.　"If adopted, it will end in your majesty's destruction.　The moment your defeat is known, your adherents will fall from you, and you will be at the mercy of your enemies."

Almost all the others concurred with the duke in opinion, and were strenuously opposed to the king's plan.

"Nay, then," he exclaimed, "there is nothing for it but Scotland. I will go thither."

"Your majesty has decided right," observed Lesley.

"His approval is enough to make me change my mind," observed Charles, withdrawing to a short distance with the Earl of Derby.

"Go not to London, my liege, I entreat you," said the earl.　"'Tis the most perilous and rash scheme you could adopt.　You will have dangers enough to encounter in whatever direction you proceed, but London is most dangerous of all.　That you will be quickly pursued, and a heavy price set on your head, is certain, for Cromwell's victory will be shorn of half its splendour if you escape him.　In England your chance is lost.　It grieves me to say so, but I cannot hide the truth. You cannot get another army together.　To Scotland, I see, you like not to return.　The sole alternative, therefore, is an escape to France."

"That is what I desire," replied Charles. "But where can I embark?"

"At Bristol, my liege, it may be—but that must be for after consideration. Conceal yourself for a time, and no safer hiding-place can be found than Boscobel, where I myself took refuge."

At this moment Colonel Roscarrock came up.

"How say you, Roscarrock?" asked the king. "Think you I should be safe at Boscobel?"

"I am sure of it, my liege," replied the other. "Strange your majesty should put the question to me, seeing I was just about to counsel you to take refuge there."

"You have already described the house to me," observed Charles. "But can the occupants be trusted?"

"Perfectly," said the Earl of Derby. "Your majesty has no more faithful subjects than the Penderels of Boscobel. Charles Giffard is here. Will your majesty speak with him?"

"Not now," replied Charles. "I would not have it known that I am about to seek a place of concealment, and were I to confer with Charles Giffard just now, my design would be suspected. We have only one traitor here—but I must guard against indiscretion. How far is it to Boscobel?"

"Some six-and-twenty miles, my liege," replied Roscarrock. "Your horse looks fresh, and will take you there in a few hours, if we are not interrupted. We must go by Kidderminster and Stourbridge towards Wolverhampton."

"Lord Talbot is well acquainted with the country, and will serve as guide," observed the Earl of Derby. "He has a servant with him, who knows the whole district, and will be very useful."

The king now signed to Careless, and taking him apart, informed him of his design, but bade him say nothing about it, except to Lord Talbot, Lord Wilmot, Colonel Lane, Charles Giffard, and a few others. Careless entirely approved of the plan, for he was terribly alarmed for the king's safety.

The word being now given that every one must shift for himself, Sir Rowland Berkeley, Captain Hornyold, and several other county gentlemen took leave of the king with such warm expressions of unwavering devotion and loyalty as greatly touched his majesty. Lesley, with his Scottish cavalry, took the direct road northward by Newport.

Escorted by some sixty Cavaliers, all well mounted and well armed, and accompanied by the Duke of Buckingham, the Earl of Derby, the Earl of Lauderdale, Lord Wilmot, Colonels Roscarrock, Lane, Blague, and Charles Giffard, and of course attended by Careless, the king started on his flight.

**END OF BOOK THE FIRST.**

# 𝔅𝔬𝔬𝔨 𝔱𝔥𝔢 𝔖𝔢𝔠𝔬𝔫𝔡.

## WHITE LADIES.

## CHAPTER I.

#### HOW CROMWELL VISITED THE DYING DUKE OF HAMILTON AT THE COMMANDERY; AND WHAT PASSED BETWEEN THEM

ON the morn after the battle, there was weeping and wailing in Worcester, for those lying slaughtered in the houses and streets. Everywhere heart-rending scenes occurred, but they excited no pity in the breasts of the savage foe. Believing they had performed a work of righteous vengeance, the stern sectaries felt no compunction for what they had done. The city had been delivered to them. They had plundered the houses, slain all who opposed them, committed every possible atrocity, and were now searching for the malignants, who had sought refuge in cellars and other secret places. Many prisoners of importance were thus made. Among those placed under the custody of the marshal-general, and subsequently sent to the Tower, were the Earls of Cleveland, Rothes, and Kelly, with the Lords Sinclair and Grandison, General Massey, and the valiant Pitscottie. Some were too severely wounded to be moved. Sir James Hamilton, Sir Alexander Forbes, Sir John Douglas, and General Montgomery were dangerously hurt — while the Duke of Hamilton was lying at the Commandery, mortally wounded. Fanshawe, the king's private secretary, was captured, and treated with especial favour by Cromwell, who was desirous of winning him over, but he rejected the Lord General's overtures. The mayor and the sheriff were committed to custody and ordered to be tried at Chester. A vast number of other prisoners were made, whom it is needless to particularise.

But Cromwell had lost his chief prize. For some hours it was supposed—chiefly on Colonel James's representation—that the king was concealed within the city, and every precaution was taken to prevent his escape. But before morning assured intelligence was brought to the Lord General that Charles Stuart had unquestionably fled towards the north, accompanied by the Duke of Buckingham, the Earls of Derby and Lauderdale, and several others, and that Leslie, with his Scottish cavalry, had taken the same direction.

On receiving these tidings, Cromwell gave immediate orders that Lilburn, Fleetwood, and Harrison, each with a regiment of horse, should start in pursuit of the Royalist leaders. At the same time he especially enjoined Colonel James to follow on Charles Stuart's track, in case the Young Man should separate himself—as was not unlikely—from his attendants.

A Proclamation was likewise issued, promising a reward of One Thousand Pounds to any one who should discover the person of Charles

Stuart—while the penalty of high treason was declared against all those who should harbour or conceal him. Copies of this Proclamation were forthwith despatched by swift messengers to all towns near which it was deemed likely the fugitive monarch would pass.

Colonel James, with a detachment of horse, started at once for Stourport, while the three Republican generals, previously mentioned, prepared to follow the retreating Scottish cavalry. The companies of militia stationed at the various towns were ordered to keep strict watch, and arrest all fugitive soldiers and malignants. Moreover, they were enjoined to search the houses of all declared Royalists.

Several country gentlemen, resident in the neighbourhood of Worcester, and suspected of taking part in the conflict, were arrested on the night of the battle. Sir Rowland Berkeley had a narrow escape. On taking leave of Charles at Barbourne Bridge, as previously related, the brave Royalist turned towards his old mansion, Cotheridge, in a very dejected frame of mind. Not merely was he anxious for the king's safety, but for his own. He felt that his peril was materially increased by the peculiar colour of the steed he had ridden throughout the day.

However, a plan of avoiding the danger occurred to him. Fortunately, he possessed a couple of piebald horses, and on arriving at Cotheridge he sent the steed he had been riding to a distant farm, and had the other piebald horse placed in the stable and covered with body-clothes. This done, he withdrew to his chamber, and prepared to play the part of a sick man.

Two hours later, Colonel Goff, with a detachment of dragoons, arrived at the old mansion and demanded to see its owner. He was told by the butler that Sir Rowland was extremely unwell and confined to his room, but the answer did not satisfy him.

"Lead me to your master instantly," he said.

Attended by half a dozen dragoons, he then followed the butler upstairs, and on entering Sir Rowland's room found him in a loose robe and slippers, and presenting the appearance of an invalid.

"What means this intrusion on my privacy?" demanded the baronet.

"You affect surprise at my appearance, Sir Rowland," rejoined Goff; "but you can feel none. I arrest you as a traitor to the Commonwealth. You took part in the battle to-day, and fought with the malignants."

"You are mistaken, general," was the reply. "I am far too unwell to leave my room, and utterly unable to put on arms or sit a horse."

"Tut!" cried Goff, incredulously. "You were present in the fields near Powick, and, later on, in the fight within the city. I myself beheld you on both occasions—on a piebald horse."

"'Tis true I have a horse of that colour," replied Sir Rowland. "But you will find him in the stable, and his freshness will prove that I could not have ridden him as you state. Satisfy yourself, I pray you, general. If it should appear that I have deceived you, treat me as you list."

"Since you affirm this so roundly I will go see," observed Goff, somewhat staggered. "But you must not stir from this chamber."

"I have not the power to leave it," said Sir Rowland, feigning extreme debility.

Placing a guard at the door of the chamber, Goff then proceeded to the stable, where he found a handsome charger, which, being stripped of its covering, proved to be piebald in colour, and exactly resembled the steed he had seen. The freshness of the horse showed that he could not have been out during the day. Astounded at the sight, Goff made no further inquiries, but returned without his prey. As a declared enemy of the Commonwealth, however, Sir Rowland had subsequently to compound for his estate by the payment of two thousand pounds.

We must now repair to the Commandery, whither, as already related, the Duke of Hamilton was conveyed from the field of battle. His right leg had been shattered by a slug shot, and the injury was so severe that amputation of the limb was deemed absolutely necessary by the king's chirurgeon, Kincaid, who was in attendance upon him; but the duke would not submit to the operation. He had passed a night of almost intolerable agony, and was lying on a couch in the room adjoining the great hall.* His countenance was livid and distorted ; and a cloak was thrown over his lower limbs.

A word as to the dying hero. William, Duke of Hamilton, then in his thirty-fifth year, had succeeded his elder brother, James, who was beheaded for high treason in 1649. Of the large train of distinguished personages who accompanied Charles in his march from Scotland, none was more devoted to the royal cause—none more determinately hostile to the rebellious Parliament—than the Duke of Hamilton. Though despairing of success, the duke adhered firmly to the king to the last, and that he was as brave as loyal was proved by the prodigies of valour he performed on the battle-field at Worcester.

"The torture I endure is almost insupportable, Kincaid," he groaned. " I could not suffer more from the rack."

"No anodyne will assuage the pain, my lord duke," replied the chirurgeon. " As I have already represented to your grace, amputation of the shattered limb is the sole means of saving your life."

" I would rather die than lose the limb," groaned the duke. " 'Tis not pain I dread, but disfigurement."

"The Lord General has signified his intention of sending his own surgeon, Trappam, to attend your grace. You will hear what he has to say."

" I will not suffer him to come near me," said the duke, sternly. " I will accept no favour from the regicide Cromwell."

As he spoke, the door communicating with the great hall was opened, and two persons came in. The foremost was Cromwell, the other was Trappam, the chirurgeon. The Lord General was armed as he had been during the battle, and wore a broad-leaved hat, which he did not remove. Marching direct towards the couch on which the wounded man was stretched, he regarded him fixedly for a few moments, and then said, in not unkindly accents :

" I am sorry to find your grace so grievously hurt. But it may be

---

* The room in which the duke died is still intact. The Commandery is now used as a College for the Blind Sons of Gentlemen, the Rev. Mr. Blair being the Principal. The ancient structure bears evidence of the fray, and contains many relics of the period.

that the Lord will heal your wounds. Such aid as man can render will be afforded by my own surgeon, Master Trappam. He is very skilful, and has wrought many wondrous cures."

"I thank your excellency," rejoined the duke, raising himself, "but the king's surgeon is in attendance upon me, and I lack no other aid."

"Let them consult together," said Cromwell, "I would fain save your life, if I can."

"Wherefore save me?" observed the duke, sternly. "Would you bring me to the block, as you brought the duke, my brother?"

"The duke, your brother, was justly condemned as a traitor to the Commonwealth of England," rejoined Cromwell. "Perchance, your grace may be pardoned. My intercession shall not be wanting if you are disposed to agree to certain conditions."

"I know not what the conditions may be, but I reject them beforehand," rejoined the duke. "I will die as I have lived, a loyal subject of the king, and an enemy of his enemies."

"Charles Stuart is a proscribed fugitive," said Cromwell. "Hitherto he has been king only in name; now he has not even the name of king. My messengers are upon his track, and will assurdly find the lurking-place wherein he hideth."

"They will fail to take him," rejoined the duke. "It is written that he shall escape, and return to triumph."

"Where is it so written?" demanded Cromwell, scornfully.

"In the book of fate."

"You do not read the book aright, my lord duke. Were I to turn over its leaves, I should soon light on one in which his death on the scaffold is recorded,"

"You will find no such record," rejoined the duke. "You have slain the king, his father, but him you shall not slay. His destiny is not in your hands."

"All things are in the Lord's hands," said Cromwell. "But would Heaven have vouchsafed me this crowning mercy if it had not meant——"

"That you should be king!" interrupted the duke. "Not so. Be not deceived. King you shall never be. Hitherto, the third of September has been propitious to you, but another anniversary of that day shall come, and it will prove fatal."

Exhausted by the effort he had made in uttering these words, he sank backwards, and his countenance assumed the pallor of death.

Thinking he was gone, Cromwell called to the surgeons, who had retired to discuss the duke's case.

"While you are conferring together, your patient has expired," he cried.

"'Tis but a momentary faintness, your excellency," said Trappam. "But assuredly his grace will not live long, if he refuses to undergo the operation."

"Then let him die," cried Cromwell, sternly. "He will 'scape the scaffold." And without another word he quitted the room.

Continuing obstinate, the unfortunate Duke of Hamilton died of his wounds. Though he begged to be buried with his ancestors, at

Hamilton, his dying wishes were disregarded, and he was interred before the high altar in Worcester Cathedral.

It was long before the city recovered from the terrible punishment inflicted upon it by the exasperated Republicans. There can be no doubt that Cromwell entertained a strongly vindictive feeling towards Worcester, for the constant attachment it had manifested towards Charles I. and his son. To prevent the possibility of any further rising, he levelled the fortifications with the ground, destroyed the gates, and filled up the dykes. The work was done so effectually, that not a vestige is left of Fort Royal, while only here and there can a few remains of the old walls be discovered. Sidbury-gate is gone; so is the Foregate—so are almost all the memorials of the Battle.

Treated like a conquered city, ravaged, partially destroyed, all its wealthy inhabitants fined, many imprisoned as well as fined, some hanged, it could not be expected that Worcester, elastic as it has ever shown itself, should immediately rise again—nor did it recover until the Restoration.

Then the city became prosperous once more, and it has prospered ever since. If not so picturesque as of yore, it is much better built—at least, we are willing to think so. Most of the old timber houses and ancient edifices have disappeared—but the Commandery is left. The noble cathedral is improved—both externally and internally. A very respectable structure of Queen Anne's time occupies the site of the old Guildhall. In short, it would be difficult to find in the whole realm a city that can vie with Worcester in cheerfulness, prosperity, or beauty of situation. Its inhabitants are as loyal as ever, and ready to fight the old battles o'er again.

FLOREAT SEMPER FIDELIS CIVITAS.

---

## CHAPTER II.

HOW THE FUGITIVE KING AND HIS COMPANIONS RODE FROM BARBOURNE
BRIDGE TO WHITE LADIES.

MORE painful feelings were never experienced by a monarch than were those of Charles as he fled from Worcester on the evening of the battle. All was lost. The crown he hoped to win was gone. His life was in jeopardy, and after a vain attempt to escape, he might be placed in the hands of his enemies.

The cavalcade, as already mentioned, numbered about sixty persons of various ranks, but all devoted to the king, and prepared to defend him to the last. But it was the determination of the leaders of the party to avoid any needless encounter. Having quitted the high road to Kidderminster, they were now speeding along the lanes skirting the left bank of the Severn, under the guidance of Lord Talbot's servant, Yates, and another man named Walker. Charles did not ride at the head of the troop, but with the Duke of Buckingham and the Earl of Derby brought up the rear. None of his attendants attempted to disturb the profound reverie into which the unfortunate king was plunged, and so engrossed was he by painful thoughts, that he scarcely seemed conscious of their presence.

It was a pleasant evening, and though the sun had already set behind the Malvern Hills, the heavens were filled with rosy clouds, which were reflected on the surface of the river. The troop passed by several farm-houses, but the scared occupants only watched them at a distance. Anxious glances were occasionally cast back by the fugitives to ascertain whether they were pursued, but no enemy appeared in sight. By degrees the calmness and beauty of the evening produced a soothing effect on the king's troubled mind. What a contrast was offered between the peaceful lanes through which he was now riding and the city resounding with the din of arms, the roar of artillery, and frightful cries.

Having passed Beveré Green, and dashed through the ford of the Salwarp, at Hawford Mill, but without meeting interruption of any kind, they now pursued the Ombersley-road for some distance, but turned off at the Mitre Oak for Hartlebury, and halted at the Old Talbot Inn, where the king drank a cup of sack, while his attendants refreshed themselves with such liquors as they could procure.

Once more they were in motion, and a narrow by-road brought them to Hartlebury Common, then of great extent and dangerous in places, but as they could still see their way, they rode on without fear.

Nothing can be pleasanter, under certain circumstances, than a gallop across a wild heath at the twilight hour; but when danger lurks on every side, when the riders are flying for life—above all, when a king's safety is at stake, the sensations are not quite so agreeable. Deceived by the gathering gloom, the fugitives are apt to suspect that the foe is lying in ambush for them, and to turn needlessly from their course. This was the case with the flying troop. They avoided Stourport because they fancied there was danger in that quarter, and shaped their rapid course past the dismantled manor-house of Hartlebury, which had been garrisoned by Charles I. during the Civil Wars. The ancient mansion might have afforded them shelter for the night, but they did not dare to stop there.

They were still on Hartlebury Common, and were soon close upon Kidderminster, but did not deem it prudent to enter the town. Skirting the valley in which it lies, and galloping past Hoobrook, they proceeded by Chester-lane and Green Hill to Broadwaters. Thence up Black Hill to Sion Hill. Next traversing the beautiful woody district that now forms Lea Park, they descended a gentle acclivity that brought them to the old bridge across the Stour.

Had there been light enough to distinguish it, a charming scene would have been here presented to the king's gaze. But he crossed Hay Bridge without looking at the beautifully winding river or at the precipitous rocks on its opposite bank, well satisfied that there was no enemy concealed amid the woods to dispute his passage.

By the time the troop reached Kinver Heath it had become quite dark, and the guides declared it was impossible to cross the wild and boggy waste at that hour.

Notwithstanding their representations, the king would have pushed on at all hazards, but the Earl of Derby, Charles Giffard, and Careless, who knew the heath, dissuaded him from his rash design. Lord Derby thought there would be far less danger in passing through Stourbridge, even if it should be occupied by militia, which was doubtful, than in attempting to traverse a morass in which they were almost certain to be engulfed.

" There are so many quagmires in Kinver Heath, that, even in daytime, it is difficult to avoid them," observed the earl. " At night it is impossible."

" I am entirely of his lordship's opinion," said Captain Giffard. " I know Kinver Heath well, and I implore your majesty not to risk your royal person upon it."

" Are you afraid to go with me ?" asked Charles.

" 'Tis my duty to prevent your majesty from rushing on certain destruction."

" Nay, then, if the danger is really so great, we must proceed to Stourbridge, despite the militia."

" The rascals will not be on the look-out for us, so we shall most likely escape them," remarked Careless. " Besides, if we are slain, we shall die like gentlemen. Any death is preferable to being stifled in a quagmire."

" As the hour is late, I do not think the enemy will be on the alert," observed the Earl of Derby. " But no precaution must be neglected. In the event of an attack, all of us who are near your majesty will speak French, so that your presence may not be suspected."

" 'Tis well," replied Charles. " You hear, my lords and gentlemen, we are all to become Frenchmen when we reach Stourbridge."

The party then turned towards Stourton, and once more crossing the Stour by the Stewponey Bridge, galloped on towards Stourbridge. When within a quarter of a mile of the town they came to a halt, and Careless and Captain Giffard were sent on to reconnoitre.

As Stourbridge at that time consisted only of one long street, it was easy to ascertain whether any soldiers were on the watch, but none could be discovered. The street was entirely deserted, all the inhabitants having, apparently, retired to rest.

Perfectly satisfied with their inspection, Careless and Giffard returned to the royal party, and informed his majesty that he might proceed without fear. Charles did not question the information he had received, but judging it safest to speed through the town, placed himself at the head of the troop, and galloped along the street.

Roused by the clatter of the horses' hoofs, several of the inhabitants rushed to the windows, and just caught sight of the flying cavalcade.

The Royalists, however, had not got far when a drum was loudly beaten " to arms," showing that Careless and Giffard had been deceived. It presently appeared that a company of militia was quartered at the further end of the town, and their steeds being ready saddled and bridled, the men mounted and formed as quickly as they could in the street to check the fugitives.

But they did not succeed in their purpose. The king and his companions drew their swords, and dashed upon them with such impetuosity that they cut their way through the phalanx, and in another minute were out of the town. These soldiers of the militia, not being so well-seasoned as Cromwell's Ironclads, were staggered by the fierce and determined assault of the Cavaliers, and did not attempt pursuit. Charles and his party, therefore, galloped on as swiftly as they could for a mile or so, when the king slackened his pace.

"Is there an inn hereabouts?" asked the king. "I am desperately thirsty."

"My liege, there is a solitary hostel between Wordsley and Kings-winford," replied Giffard. "But I know not what can be obtained at it."

"A cup of cider or ale will serve my turn now," replied Charles.

"The White Horse is not so badly provided," remarked Careless. "Nat Coulter, the host, can brew as good a pottle of sack as any man in Staffordshire, but I doubt if he can supply us all—even with ale. However, we shall see."

On reaching the White Horse the fugitive Royalists found much better entertainment than might have been expected. Nat Coulter was in bed, but he was soon roused from his slumbers, and with his wife and his two sons set heartily to work to serve his unexpected guests. He had plenty of ale and cider, with which the Cavaliers were perfectly content, but only a single runlet of canary. However, this amply sufficed for the king and the chief personages with him. As to provisions, they ran rather short, Nat Coulter's larder not being very abundantly supplied, but the hungry Royalists devoured all they could find. Though Nat and his household were known to be loyal, Charles did not discover himself to them, but spoke French, and was addressed in that language by his attendants during his stay at the White Horse. Nat, however, being a shrewd fellow, afterwards declared that he had recognised the king.

A consultation was held in the little parlour of the inn. On quitting Barbourne Bridge, Charles, as we have already stated, had decided upon seeking a refuge in Boscobel. He had not abandoned this design, though during the nocturnal ride his plans had undergone some change. It was now proposed that the king should proceed in the first instance to White Ladies, another secluded house belonging to the Giffards, about a mile distant from Boscobel, where arrangements could be made for his majesty's safety, and where he could separate from his companions. Both the Earl of Derby and Roscarrock agreed that this would be the best and safest course to pursue, and it was decided upon by his majesty.

Again mounting their steeds, which had been as well cared for in the interim as circumstances permitted, they rode on at a quick pace, tracking the woodlands in the neighbourhood of Himley, and obtaining glimpses of the extensive lake. No furnaces at that time bursting from the ground marred the sylvan beauty of the scene.

After passing Wombourn, the troop plunged into Brewood Forest, and were soon buried in its depths. Guided through the intricacies of the wood by Charles Giffard, who was now in his own domain, and knew every roadway, they at last reached a little valley entirely sur-rounded by timber, in the midst of which stood an old-fashioned black and white timber mansion. Closely adjoining this ancient house, and almost appearing to form part of it, were the ivy-clad ruins of a monastery.

Day was just breaking at the time, and the picture presented to the king, and seen by the grey light of dawn, was inexpressibly striking.

"That is White Ladies, sire," said Charles Giffard. "There your majesty will find shelter."

---

## CHAPTER III.

### THE PENDERELS.

IN Brewood Forest, which was situated on the boundaries of Shropshire and Staffordshire, and extended into both counties, two large monasteries had existed—one being a Cistercian priory, and the other Benedictine. It was from the ruined Cistercian priory, which had been founded by Hubert Walter, Archbishop of Canterbury, in the time of Richard Cœur-de-Lion, that the old mansion in which the fugitive king was about to take shelter derived its name. The house dated back to the period when the monastery was suppressed. It has now disappeared, but the ruins of the priory are left, and consist of a massive wall and a few circular-headed windows. A doorway, with a fine Norman arch, leads to what was once the chapel, but is now a small place of sepulture.

Viewed in connexion with the old mansion, the ruins of the monastery produced a singularly beautiful effect—the strangely-secluded situation of the house adding to its charm. It seemed as though it were hidden from a world of strife and care, and as if none of the dire calamities of war, which those now gazing at it had so recently experienced, could disturb it. Fain would the weary Cavaliers who gazed at the peaceful old house have rested there. But rest, as they well knew, was not for them. Their toilsome and perilous journey was not yet over. With some of them the road they were about to take led to the scaffold.

White Ladies and the monastic ruins adjoining it were surrounded by a low wall, in the midst of which was an old gateway of the same date as the house. Around, as we have said, on every side, were woods, and it was these thick groves that gave to the place the peculiar air of seclusion that characterised it.

Praying the king to allow him to go forward, Captain Giffard rode towards the gateway, which was fastened, but he had not reached it, when a tall stalwart individual, clad in a leathern doublet, and having a woodman's knife stuck in his girdle, strode towards the garden wall. Charles watched this sturdy fellow as he advanced, and was very favourably impressed by his manly countenance.

The forester—for such he seemed—was armed with a wood-bill, which he had snatched up on perceiving the troop, but being quickly reassured on finding his young master with them, he flung down his weapon. After exchanging a few words with him Captain Giffard bade the forester open the gate, and returned to the king.

"That's an honest fellow, I'll be sworn," observed Charles, "and as brave as honest. He looked just now as if he would strike down the first man who attempted to enter."

" And so he would, my liege, had we been rebels and Roundheads," replied Giffard.   George Penderel has been a soldier, and served in your royal father's army at Edgehill, where his brother, Tom Penderel, was killed. He is now a woodward, as are all his brothers, except Humphrey, the miller of Boscobel."

" If they are all like George, they must be a gallant set," remarked Charles.   " Are there many of them ?"

" Five living," remarked Giffard.   " And George is a fair sample of the. rest.   They are all true men, stout of heart and strong of limb, as if made of their native oak.   Above all, they are loyal to the core.   It is to their care," he added, lowering his voice, " that I propose to confide your majesty.   Lord Derby and Colonel Roscarrock will give you an assurance of their fidelity."

" They have already done so," replied Charles.   " What ho! George Penderel," he exclaimed.

Hearing himself called, the stalwart forester, who had been standing near the open gate, instantly came forward, but on approaching the king, he stopped and doffed his cap.

" You know me, I perceive, George," said the king.

" I have never set eyes on your majesty before," rejoined the forester, " but I should know that royal countenance among a thousand."

" I hope some others who may chance to see me in these parts may not be gifted with thy discernment, honest George," replied Charles. " You have served the king, my father—now you must serve me."

" In the field, sire ?" cried George, eagerly.

" Alack ! my good fellow, I have no longer an army," remarked the king, sadly.   " These are all the followers left me—and I must, perforce, part with them."

" But I will never leave your majesty unless you bid me," rejoined George.

" You have four brothers, ha ?"

" All as trusty as myself.   Your majesty will be safe with us.   All the wealth of the kingdom should not tempt us to betray you."

" Enough," replied the king, dismounting—his bridle being held by George Penderel.

The principal personages composing the royal retinue dismounted at the same time, and followed his majesty into the house.   By the direction of Captain Giffard all the horses were then taken into the interior of the. ruined monastery, with the exception of the king's steed, which was brought by George Penderel into the hall.

A search was next instituted for provisions, and in this quest Careless· played a conspicuous part.   Repairing to the kitchen, he there found Dame Penderel and a servant-maid, and the fire being fortunately lighted, he soon sent a large dish of fried eggs and bacon to the king, which was greatly enjoyed by his majesty and the nobles with him.   Nor while he provided so well for the wants of others did the thoughtful major neglect his own, but contrived to make a very hearty breakfast in the kitchen.   It must not be supposed that the rest of the troop, who were now in the ruined priory chapel, fared so well.   Bread, biscuits, oat-cakes, and cheese were distributed among them. and they had plenty of sack.

Meanwhile Captain Giffard, who was all anxiety to make arrangements for the king's safety, had sent for Richard Penderel—commonly known as " Trusty Dick "—who dwelt at a cottage in the forest, called Hobbal Grange.    William Penderel, the eldest brother, who resided at Boscobel, which was about a mile distant from White Ladies, had likewise been sent for by the Earl of Derby.

Trusty Dick was first to arrive, and Charles was as well pleased with his looks as he had been with those of the younger brother.    William was powerfully built, and quite as tall as George.

" His majesty has resolved to disguise himself, Dick," said Captain Giffard.    " What sort of attire ought he to put on ?"

" If his majesty will condescend to wear a suit of my clothes," said Richard Penderel, " I'll engage that not a rebel trooper among them all will recognise him.    My best jerkin, leather doublet, and green trunk hose, will just fit you, sire, and I haven't worn them more than once or twice."

" The disguise will suit me exactly," cried Charles.    " I will become a Brewood forester like thyself.    We are about the same height, as I think, though thou hast the advantage of me in respect of bulk."

" Truly, I am somewhat clumsier than your majesty."

" Haste, and fetch the clothes, Dick, for I presume thou hast not got them with thee," said Captain Giffard.

" One thing more is needful to complete the disguise," said Richard Penderel.    " I scarce like to mention it.    Yet if it be neglected, all else will be marred."

" What is the indispensable matter ?" asked Charles.

" Your majesty must consent to part with your long locks," replied Dick.

" Oddsfish ! I had not thought of that," exclaimed the king.    " But I see the necessity.    Better lose my locks than my head.    Go fetch the clothes."

Trusty Dick made a humble reverence and departed.

Not long afterwards, William Penderel of Boscobel made his appearance.    He was the most remarkable of this remarkable brotherhood. All were tall—not one of them being under six feet in height—but William towered above the others by a couple of inches.

Although gigantic in stature, he was well proportioned, and possessed prodigious strength.    His features were cast in a massive mould, and though somewhat heavy, had the same honest expression that characterised the whole family.

On entering the house he found Lord Derby in the hall, and its appearance—filled as it was with Cavaliers, with the king's horse in the midst of them—satisfied him that some great disaster had occurred.

" Your lordship is welcome back," he said, bowing reverently; " though I own I would rather not have seen you again so soon. Rumours of a terrible defeat at Worcester have reached us, I know not how."

" Ill news, they say, travels quickly," replied the earl, surprised ; " but this news must have travelled through the air, if it has reached you before us, for we have ridden here direct from Worcester, and almost without stoppage."

"Oh, my lord, messengers doubtless have galloped from post to post, and so have gotten before you. But tell me, I pray you," he added, anxiously, "is the king safe?"

"The king is here," replied the earl. "Come with me and you shall see him."

So saying he opened the door of a parlour panelled with dark oak, and fitted up with oak furniture. Charles was seated in the room, and Lord Wilmot, Captain Giffard, and Careless were with him.

Without any prompting, the huge forester immediately prostrated himself before the king, who gave him his hand to kiss.

"This is William Penderel, sire," observed the earl.

"I do not need the information," replied Charles. "I am right glad to see thee, William. I have already seen two of thy brothers."

"Then your majesty has seen two of your loyal subjects," replied the forester, rising. "We will defend you to the death."

"William Penderel," said the Earl of Derby, in a voice well calculated to impress his hearer, "I know thy fidelity and worth, and have answered for thee and for thy brothers to the king's majesty. A sacred duty now devolves upon you, and take heed you perform it well. You will have the care of the king. He is surrounded by enemies—cunning as foxes in quest of prey. Beware of their wiles and stratagems. Open foes may be guarded against—secret foes are most to be dreaded."

"I and my brothers will strive to guard his majesty against all foes, open and secret," replied William Penderel; "and with Heaven's help I doubt not we shall accomplish his deliverance."

"Help to conceal me—that is all I ask at present," said the king.

"We have more than one hiding-place at Boscobel," observed Penderel. "I can conceal his lordship as well as your majesty."

"Mistake me not, William," said the Earl of Derby. "I shall not tax thy services—nor will any other. Thou must look to the king alone."

"I understand your lordship," replied William Penderel; "and I promise you that my sole care shall be bestowed upon his majesty. But let me humbly counsel your lordship and those with you not to tarry here too long. A troop of militia under command of Colonel Bloundel is quartered at Codsall, which is not more than three miles off, and as soon as they receive news of the battle, they will assuredly search all the houses hereabouts."

"Thou art right," replied the earl. "We must not remain here long."

At that moment the Duke of Buckingham and Roscarrock entered the room.

"We have news for your majesty," said the duke; "news of Lesley."

"What of the traitor?" cried Charles, frowning.

"He has rallied with the whole of his cavalry on the heath near Tonge Castle," replied Buckingham. "A messenger has just arrived, saying that he waits there to conduct your majesty to Scotland."

"What number of men has he with him?" asked Charles.

"About three thousand, sire, so the messenger affirms," replied Roscarrock.

"Three thousand men might have turned the battle yesterday," said Charles, bitterly. "Let those go with the traitor who list, I will trust him no more. If he would not stand by me when I had an army at my command, of a surety he will not stand by me now that I have none."

The tone in which the king spoke showed that his resolution was taken. No one, therefore, attempted to dissuade him from his purpose.

"We must separate," he continued. "I shall seek safety in flight. Those who have faith in Lesley, can join him. I will not attempt to influence your decision. Retire, I pray you, and consult together."

All then left the room, with the exception of Careless, who remained with the king.

----

## CHAPTER IV.

### HOW CHARLES WAS DISGUISED AS A WOODMAN.

"MUST I, too, quit your majesty?" asked Careless.

"There is no help for it, Will," replied Charles. "My best chance of escape—the sole chance, in fact—lies in being left to myself. I shall be well served by these faithful Penderels."

"Of that you may rest assured, sire," said Careless. "Yet I still think I may be of some service to your majesty. At any rate, I shall not quit the neighbourhood of Brewood Forest, so that I may be readily found, if wanted. I know the country as well as the Penderels themselves. So unimportant a circumstance may easily have slipped from your majesty's memory, and I must therefore remind you that I was born at Bromhall, in Staffordshire, within three miles of White Ladies."

"Ah, I recollect!" cried Charles. "No wonder you are well acquainted with the district."

"I have not seen Bromhall for years," pursued Careless, "and few recollect me. Nevertheless, I can make myself at home there."

"Take my advice, and go not near the place," said Charles. "Of a certainty you will be discovered by the rebel troopers from Codsall. Since you are familiar with the forest, hide yourself within it, and join me at Boscobel. But now for my disguise. No one but yourself shall clip off my locks. Have you procured a pair of scissors from Dame Penderel?"

"Here they are, sire," replied Careless, producing them.

"'Sdeath! they are like shears," exclaimed the king. "However, they will do the work more quickly. Have you aught to throw over my shoulders?"

"A towel borrowed from the good dame."

"That will do," replied Charles. "Now begin, and lose no time."

It required a desperate effort on Careless's part to commence, but in a few minutes he had cut off the long black locks on which the young monarch had justly prided himself.

"Have you done?" asked Charles.

"Be pleased to look at yourself in the glass, sire, and you will find your hair cropped as close as that of a Puritan."

Charles groaned on remarking the frightful change wrought in his personal appearance.

"Zounds! you have disfigured me most horribly," he cried.

"I have reluctantly obeyed your majesty's orders," replied Careless. "Here are love-locks enow for twenty fair dames," he added.

"Unluckily, there is not a single fair dame on whom to bestow them. Bid Dame Penderel burn them."

"Rather let me bid her keep them safely as a memorial for her children," rejoined Careless.

"As you will," said the king. "Now help me to take off my ornaments."

"Little did I think I should ever have this sad duty to perform, sire," observed Careless, as he knelt down to remove the garter from the king's knee.

"These are but badges of royalty, and can be easily replaced," said Charles. "A kingdom is not so easily got back."

With his attendant's aid he then divested himself of the blue riband, the George of diamonds, and all his ornaments.

"My watch has stopped," he remarked. "I have neglected to wind it up."

"It has been struck by a bullet," said Careless, examining it. "Look how deeply the case is dinted, sire. This watch has saved your majesty's life."

"Then I will bestow it on the best friend I have," said the king. "Wear it for my sake, Will."

"I will wear it next my heart," was the fervent reply. "Your majesty could not have bestowed upon me a more precious gift."

Just then Lord Wilmot, Colonel Roscarrock, Colonel Blague, and some others, came in, and almost started back on seeing how strangely the king was metamorphosed.

"You see, gentlemen, to what a state I am reduced," he observed, with a sad smile. "I must commit these ornaments to your custody," he added.

"I hope we shall soon be able to restore them to your majesty," said Lord Wilmot, who received the George.

"What has been decided?" inquired Charles, "Do you all join Lesley?"

"The majority have so determined," replied Lord Wilmot. "But I shall take another course. Perhaps I may attempt to reach London. I shall not be far from your majesty," he added, in a low tone.

"What is to be done with your horse, my liege?" asked Colonel Lane. "Have you any further occasion for him?"

"None whatever," replied Charles. "If the horse should be found here, he might lead to my discovery."

"Then I will gladly take him, for my own steed is dead beaten," rejoined Colonel Lane.

The saddest moment was now at hand. The Duke of Buckingham, the Earl of Derby, and the other nobles came in to take leave of the king.

Charles was profoundly affected, and the nobles were overpowered by emotion.   Very little was said by them, for their grief was too real and too deep to find expression in words.   Ceremony was laid aside, and Charles embraced them all.   With very gloomy forebodings they then left the room—Lord Derby being the last to retire.

"I trust we shall soon meet again, my dear lord," said Charles, as he stood beside him, with his arm upon the earl's shoulder.

"I do not think I shall ever behold your majesty again in this world," replied Lord Derby, in a melancholy tone.   I have a presentiment that I am going to my doom."

"Then stay with me," said the king.   "The hiding-places at Boscobel belong of right to you.   Proceed thither at once."

"Heaven forbid that I should endanger your majesty's safety by any attempt to preserve myself," exclaimed the earl.   "If I fall into the hands of the enemy, I shall be cheered by the firm conviction that your majesty will escape, and in the end will be restored to your kingdom. That I shall live to see that happy day I doubt—nay, I am well assured I shall not—but it will come nevertheless."

"Look forward to it, my lord—look forward to our next meeting!" cried Charles.

"We shall meet in heaven, I trust, sire—not on earth," replied the earl, solemnly.   "I bid your majesty an eternal farewell."

Charles did not attempt to reply, for he was strongly impressed by the earl's manner, and Lord Derby quitted the room.

The chivalrous but ill-fated peer's presentiments were unfortunately realised.   Immediately after taking leave of the king, as described, all the nobles, with the exception of Lord Wilmot, who had engaged the services of John Penderel, the second brother, quitted White Ladies, taking with them the whole troop of Cavaliers, and proceeded, under the guidance of Charles Giffard, to the heath near Tonge Castle, where they expected to find Lesley and his cavalry.   But the Scottish general was gone, and was marching northwards, as they learnt, by way of Newport, so they took the same direction.

They had not, however, ridden many miles when they were overtaken by Lord Leviston and a few of the royal life guards who had fought at Worcester.   Lord Leviston and his handful of men were flying before a strong detachment of horse, commanded by Colonel James, and on seeing his lordship's danger, the Earl of Derby and the other nobles at once faced about, and attacking the Roundheads with great fury, drove them back,   This success greatly raised their spirits, but it was quickly followed by a reverse.   Just beyond Newport, they were encountered by Colonel Lilburn, while Colonel James, having received considerable reinforcement, followed and attacked in the rear.

Lesley's cavalry was completely routed and dispersed.   Lord Derby. Lord Lauderdale, Lord Sinclair, and the faithless Scottish leader, were captured, and conveyed first to Whitchurch, and next to Banbury, in Cheshire.   Subsequently, the ill-fated Earl of Derby was removed to Chester, and imprisoned in the castle, there to await his trial for high treason.   Charles Giffard was likewise taken prisoner at the conflict near Newport, but contrived to escape at Banbury.

But we are anticipating the course of events, and must return to the

ugitive monarch at White Ladies. Careless had witnessed the departure
if the devoted band with feelings akin to self-reproach for not going
with them, when on returning to the house, he found Richard Penderel
with the suit of clothes intended for the king's disguise, and immediately
ook them to his majesty. That nothing should be wanting, Trusty
Dick had brought a coarse shirt and a woodman's cap with the gar-
nents, and in a few minutes Charles had taken off his rich apparel,
ind put on the sturdy forester's habiliments. His buff coat and broad-
sword-belt were replaced by a leathern doublet, and jerkin of green
cloth, while common country hose were drawn above his knees, and
heavy hob-nailed shoes had succeeded his riding-boots.

As soon as the change was effected, William and Richard Penderel
were introduced by Careless, and were astonished by the alteration in the
king's appearance. Both averred that his majesty looked just like one
of themselves, and would impose on the most suspicious rebel.

A clever mimic, Charles tried, and not unsuccessfully, to imitate
Trusty Dick's gait and manner. The elder Penderel could not repress a
smile as he regarded him. The sole objection urged by those who
scrutinised the newly-made forester's appearance was that his hands
were too white, but this was quickly remedied by a little charcoal dust.
His complexion was dark enough, being as brown as that of a gipsy.

" Your majesty must be careful not to answer if you are spoken to by
any of the common folk, since you have not the accent of the country,"
observed William Penderel.

"Fear nothing. I shall easily acquire it," replied Charles. "Is
Lord Wilmot gone ?" he inquired.

" Ay, my liege," was the reply. " He left the house immediately
after the departure of the troop. My brother John went with him, and
intended to take him to Mr. Huntbach's house at Brinsford, where he
will stay till some other hiding-place can be found. Any message your
majesty may desire to send can be readily conveyed to him by John."

"And now, sire, since you are fully disguised," said Careless, " I
counsel you not to remain here a moment longer. 'Tis possible the
house may be surrounded, and then you will be unable to escape."

"Whither do you propose to take me?" asked Charles of the
Penderels.

" It will be best that your majesty should remain in the forest
during the day, in case an immediate search should be made at Boscobel,"
replied William Penderel. " We will hide you in a thick part of the
wood, about half a mile hence, called Spring Coppice, where no one will
be likely to search for you."

"I know Spring Coppice well," said Careless. " If your majesty
should hear a whistle, you will understand it is a signal from me, and
need not be alarmed. Though unseen, I shall not be far off."

He then took leave of the king, and quitted the house.

No sooner was Charles gone than all traces of his visit were removed
by George Penderel and his wife.

His majesty's habiliments were carefully wrapped up and deposited in
an old chest, as were his feathered hat and boots, while his shorn locks
were preserved like relics.

## CHAPTER V.

HOW CHARLES WAS CONCEALED IN SPRING COPPICE, AND HOW IT RAINED THERE,
AND NOWHERE ELSE IN THE NEIGHBOURHOOD.

On quitting the house, Charles and his two stalwart attendants entered
the ruins of the old priory, where Trusty Dick, by the aid of the ivy,
climbed the massive wall, and looked around to satisfy himself that all
was secure. Not perceiving anything to occasion alarm, he soon descended
from his post of observation, and the party left the ruins and entered the
wood at the rear of the house.

Pursuing a roadway among the trees, they marched on at a quick pace.
On either side there was a good deal of fine timber, and several ancient
oaks caught the king's eye as he strode along. Presently they came upon
a broad clearing, where the underwood having been removed, only a few
scattered trees were left, and having crossed it, they penetrated a wilder-
ness of brambles and thorns, through which Charles could never have
made his way unassisted, and this rough barrier passed, they reached a
waste overgrown with short wood, which was cut at certain seasons for
fuel. This was Spring Coppice, and just beyond it were the shady
groves of Boscobel.

Though there were few large trees in Spring Coppice, there was a
good deal of tangled underwood, and a thick covert afforded an excellent
place of concealment. It was towards this spot that his guides now led
the king. While the covert was almost impenetrable to those unacquainted with it, there was an outlet to the Boscobel woods, which
could be easily gained in case of need.

In the very heart of the covert, like the centre of a maze, there was a
small open space, free from underwood, and covered with a carpet of
smooth sward. Here it was proposed that the king should remain, while
his two guides undertook to act as scouts and sentinels, and warn him of
any danger. Having shown his majesty how to hide himself amid the
underwood, and how to gain the outlet into the adjoining thicket, they
left him, promising that one of them would return ere long.

Almost for the first time in his life, Charles was now completely alone.
Yesterday, at the same hour, he was a king, and had an army at his
command. Now he was dependent for his safety upon a few loyal rustics.
Not for a moment did he doubt their fidelity, or believe that threats of
punishment or offers of reward would induce them to betray him. Yet
accident might bring his enemies to his place of concealment. In that
case he was resolved to sell his life dearly, though the only weapon he
possessed was the woodman's knife in his girdle.

He strove to divert his melancholy thoughts and while away the time
by pacing round and round the little circular spot in which he was
enclosed. But he soon got tired of this enforced exercise, and threw
himself at full length on the sward. How he wished that Careless was
with him, or Lord Wilmot! To add to his discomfort, the morning,
which had been dark and dull, became still more gloomy; clouds gathered
overhead, and at length discharged themselves in a steady down-pour.

He sought shelter among the trees, but could not protect himself entirely from the wet.

The rain continued—heavily, heavily.

Several hours passed, which seemed more wearisome, more dismal than any hours the king had ever previously spent.

During the long and dreary interval no one came near him, nor did any sounds reach his ear, except the ceaseless pattering of the rain upon the leaves. Now and then he heard the rustle of a rabbit among the underwood, the cry of a blackbird, or the challenge of a cock pheasant. Nothing else. No whistle from Careless—no signal from the Penderels.

Having now no watch he could not tell how time was passing, but he thought it much later than it really was. At last he heard sounds of some one approaching, and a voice, which he easily recognised as that of Richard Penderel, called out, " A friend!"

Trusty Dick was accompanied by his sister, who was married to a woodman named Yates, and the good wife carried a basket containing some eatables and a bottle of sack, the sight of which greatly rejoiced the king, who had become ravenously hungry. Trusty Dick had brought with him a blanket, which he laid upon the ground beneath a tree, so as to form a dry seat for his majesty, while Elizabeth Yates spread the contents of her basket before him. Charles was so hungry that he thought of nothing at first but satisfying his appetite, but after he had consumed half a dozen hard-boiled eggs, a large piece of cold meat, the best part of a loaf, and had well-nigh emptied the flask of sack, he began to converse with Dame Yates.

Though built on the same large scale as her brothers, Elizabeth had rather a comely countenance, and the good-humoured smile that lighted it up as she watched the king's performances was exceedingly pleasant to behold.

"Saints be praised!" she exclaimed; "it does one good to see your majesty enjoy your humble meal."

" I never enjoyed aught so much," replied the king, "I have got a forester's keen appetite. I thank thee for the blanket thou hast brought me, Dick, but if I remain longer here I shall have rheumatism in all my limbs."

" There is danger abroad," replied Dick. " A body of rebel troopers, under the command of Colonel Bloundel, has been to White Ladies. Colonel Bloundel declared you were concealed somewhere, and not only searched the house, but the ruins of the old priory, and was greatly enraged and disappointed when he failed to discover your majesty. He then ordered a dozen of his men to search the forest and join him at Boscobel, and I make no doubt they are there now. My brother William has gone thither to see what they are about, and will bring your majesty word. It is well you were concealed here."

" The saints have had your majesty in their guard!" exclaimed Elizabeth, who, like all her brothers, was a devout Romanist. "A marvellous thing has happened. Elsewhere it has been fine, but here, at Spring Coppice, it has rained."

" It has rained heavily enough, as I can testify from experience," cried Charles.

"But the rain prevented the rebels from searching this wood," observed Dick. "I followed them unobserved, and undoubtedly they were coming hither, but when they found it so wet they gave up the quest, and proceeded to Boscobel."

"'Tis strange, indeed!" said Charles, gravely.

"I see Heaven's hand in it quite plainly!" ejaculated Elizabeth, crossing herself devoutly; "and so will good Father Huddlestone."

"Father Huddlestone!" exclaimed Charles. "You will have to confess to him."

"Ah! you need not fear him, sire," cried Elizabeth. "The good priest is devoted to your majesty. He has taught us all to fear God and honour the king."

"Father Huddlestone has made us what we are, sire," said Dick. "But we must not tarry here longer. I will come again at nightfall."

"Not till then?" cried Charles. "Have you seen aught of Major Careless?"

"No, sire," replied Dick. "He has kept out of the way of the rebels. And I must again caution your majesty not to stir forth till I return, as some of the enemy may be lurking about."

By this time Elizabeth had packed up her basket, and the pair departed.

It was still raining steadily, but cheered by the hearty meal he had made, the king did not heed the discomfort so much as he had previously done. Wrapped in his blanket he couched beneath the trees, and soon fell fast asleep, nor did he awake till he was roused by a voice, and found Trusty Dick Penderel standing near him.

"What's the hour, Dick?" he demanded, yawning and stretching himself. "It seems growing dusk. I have slept ever since you left me."

"In that case, your majesty must have slept for six or seven hours, for it is now not far from eight o'clock," replied Dick. "I trust you feel refreshed."

"I feel equal to any amount of exertion," cried Charles, springing to his feet. "But what news do you bring me?"

"Not very good, my liege," replied Dick. "You must not go to Boscobel. Colonel Bloundel is still there."

"But I cannot pass the night here," cried Charles.

"I do not mean you should, my liege. I propose to take you to my cottage, Hobbal Grange, where I will try to lodge you, in my humble way."

"Hark ye, Dick, a plan has occurred to me while I have been here. I will try to get into Wales, where I have many subjects of proved loyalty. Once at Swansea, I can easily find means of embarking for France. Can you guide me to any place where I may safely cross the Severn?"

"At Madeley there is a bridge. It is about seven miles distant."

"Only seven miles!" exclaimed Charles. "Then I will go to Madeley to-night after refreshing myself at thy cottage."

"As your majesty pleases. But I am sorry you mean to abandon Boscobel."

"I may go there yet," said Charles.

They then quitted the coppice and issued forth into the more open part of the forest.

The rain had now ceased, and the clouds having entirely dispersed, the night promised to be clear and starlight. They marched along cautiously—halting ever and anon to listen for a sound—but heard nothing to occasion them alarm. Not a trooper was to be seen—indeed, they did not encounter a single individual on the way to Hobbal Grange.

---

## CHAPTER VI.

### HOW CHARLES SUPPED AT HOBBAL GRANGE, AND WHOM HE MET THERE.

HOBBAL GRANGE, the farm-house tenanted by Richard Penderel, was situated on a small green in the midst of the forest on the road between White Ladies and Boscobel. Though described by its owner as a cottage, it was a very comfortable abode. Richard Penderel was married, and his wife, a buxom, good-looking woman, had brought him one son, but he was from home at the time.

On reaching his dwelling, Trusty Dick opened the door, and ushered the king into the house-place, as it was called—a spacious apartment with a huge fireplace at one end, and furnished with a long oak dining-table, a couple of benches, and some half-dozen chairs.

A good fire burning in the grate gave the room a very comfortable look. The ceiling was low and whitewashed, as were the walls, and the rafters were garnished with hams and sides of bacon, while nets contained sundry oat-cakes. Dick's wife and their niece, Frances, the daughter of William Penderel, a good-looking girl, who had just got into her teens, were frying some collops of meat, as the forester entered with his guest.

"Mary," cried Dick, winking at his wife, as he spoke, "this be Will Jackson, whom I told thee I should bring wi' me to supper."

"Glad to see him, I'm sure," replied Mary, dropping a curtsy, which the king returned with an awkward attempt at a clownish bow that provoked a smile from young Frances Penderel.

"Master Jackson is going to Madeley," pursued Dick, "and being unacquainted with the country, might get lost at night, so I have promised to show him the way there after supper."

"Then he ben't going to sleep here?" observed Mary.

"No, my good dame, I thank you," said Charles. "To-night I shall sleep at Madeley, and to-morrow cross the Severn. I want to get to the Welsh coast as quickly as I can."

"Don't ask any more questions, Mary, but get supper ready," interposed Dick.

"'Twill be ready in a trice," she replied. "Lay a clean cloth, Frances."

In a very few minutes a large dish of collops and a great bowl of potatoes were placed on the table, and the king and his host sat down to the meal, and were waited upon by Mary Penderel and her niece.

A jug of strong ale helped to wash down the viands. Charles rather suspected from the good dame's manner that she was aware of his rank, but he didn't trouble himself on the subject, but went on with his supper.

An unexpected interruption, however, was offered to the meal. Some one tried the door, and finding it fastened, knocked against it rather authoritatively. Charles instantly laid down his knife and fork and started to his feet.

"Go see who is there," said Dick to his wife. "But let no one in."

On this Mary went to the door, and in as firm a tone as she could command, for she was a good deal frightened, asked who knocked.

"'Tis I! Don't you know me, Mary?" cried a familiar voice.

"Blessed Virgin!" she exclaimed. "'Tis Father Huddlestone himself!"

"Your majesty may go on quietly with your supper," whispered Dick to the king. "As I have told you, the holy man may be trusted. Open the door, dame."

Mary instantly complied, and a middle-aged and rather stout personage entered the room. His close-fitting cassock of black stuff was covered by a long black gown. His appearance was far from ascetic, his face being round, rosy, and good-humoured in expression, while his scrupulously shaved cheeks showed marks of a very black beard.

Father Huddlestone was priest to Mr. Whitgreave, of Moseley Hall, in the neighbourhood of Wolverhampton, and resided with that gentleman, who was a well-known Royalist.

"Heaven's blessings on this house and on all within it!" exclaimed the priest as he came in. "I do not blame you for keeping your door bolted during these troublous times, good daughter. An enemy might slip in unawares. You have a guest already, I perceive," he continued, glancing at Charles. "I have brought you two more. Nay, do not start, my good woman. No danger need be apprehended from one of your own sex."

"What is this I hear, father," cried Dick, getting up from the table, and stepping towards him. "You have brought some one with you, you say?"

"Here she is," replied Father Huddlestone. "Pray come in, fair mistress."

On this invitation, a young lady in a riding-dress entered the house, followed by a slim, good-looking page.

In the young lady, Charles recognised Jane Lane at a glance. As to her attendant, he almost fancied, from the slightness of the figure, it must be a female in disguise.

"Methought you said there was only a lady, good father?" cried Dick.

"This page counts for nothing," rejoined the priest. "The lady is Mistress Jane Lane, of Bentley Hall. I have promised her an asylum here for the night, and I am sure you will afford it her."

"There may be reasons why I should not remain here," said Jane, perceiving the king. "I will go on with you to Moseley Hall, good father."

"There can be nothing to prevent you from staying here, so far as I am concerned, fair mistress," observed Charles, who had risen from the table, but stood apart. "I am about to proceed on my journey immediately."

"Are you quite sure you had so decided before my arrival?" asked Jane.

"Quite sure," he replied. "Richard Penderel will tell you so."

"Who is this young man, Mary?" asked Father Huddlestone, looking very hard at the king. "He hath the dress of a woodward, but neither the look nor the manner of one."

"I will tell your reverence some other time," she replied, evasively.

"Perhaps your reverence can prevail on Mistress Jane Lane to sit down with us and share our supper," said Charles to Father Huddlestone.

"I shall need no entreaty, for in truth I am very hungry," replied Jane, taking a place at the table, while the priest sat down beside her.

"How are you named, good youth?" asked Charles of the supposed page.

"Jasper," was the reply.

"Then come and sit down by me, Jasper," said the king.

"Shall I, madam?" inquired the page of his mistress, who signified her assent, and the so-called Jasper took a place by the king.

Fortunately, Mary Penderel had made such bountiful provision that there was plenty for the new-comers.

"No accident, I hope, has happened to your mistress, young sir?" observed Charles to the page.

"We were on our way from Wolverhampton to Bentley Hall, when we were attacked by a patrol of rebels in the forest, who were in search for the king," replied Jasper. "They did us no injury, but took our horses."

"How came it that you did not defend your mistress better?" asked Charles.

"How could I defend her against half a dozen armed men?" cried the page. "If I had had a pistol, I would have shot the first Roundhead rascal who came up through the head."

"Rather through the heart, I should say," remarked the king, with a smile.

"Heaven preserve his majesty, and deliver him from his enemies!" exclaimed Father Huddlestone. "May their devices be confounded."

"Amen!" ejaculated Jane Lane, fervently. "Could I communicate with his majesty, I would counsel him to embark for France as speedily as may be."

"Such, I doubt not, is his design," remarked the priest. "But there is danger on every side," he added in a significant tone, and looking at the king as he spoke.

"I have heard no particulars of the battle of Worcester," observed Jasper. "His majesty has escaped, I know, but I would fain learn that his aide-de-camp, Major Careless, is safe."

"Rest easy on that score, Jasper," said the king. "I saw Major Careless this morning."

"Indeed!" exclaimed the page, unable to repress his emotion. "Oh, I am so glad. You have taken a great weight from my breast."

"You appear greatly interested in Major Careless," remarked Charles. "Have you known him long?"

"Only since his majesty arrived in Worcester. I hope I shall see him again."

"Have you any message for him, in case I should meet him?" whispered Charles.

"None," replied the page, in the same tone. "But he will remember the house in Angel-lane."

"Ah! then you are——"

The page imposed silence by a look.

Just then Richard Penderel arose, and glanced significantly at Charles, who at once took the hint, and rose likewise.

"Don't let me disturb the company," said Dick. "But Master Jackson and I have a long walk before us, and must be moving."

"Quite right, my son," replied the priest. "But I should like to say a word to Master Jackson before he sets forth."

Taking Charles aside, he said to him in a low earnest tone: "I will not waste time in professions of loyalty and devotion, nor can I be of any present use to your majesty. Whatever your plans may be, I trust Heaven will prosper them, but should it be necessary for you to seek a place of concealment, you will be safe with my worthy friend and patron, Mr. Whitgreave, of Moseley Hall. Richard Penderel will guide you thither."

"Should occasion require it, I will take refuge in Mr. Whitgreave's house," replied Charles.

"Your majesty will be pleased to learn that Lord Wilmot is now at Moseley," pursued Father Huddlestone.

"I am glad to hear it," replied Charles. "Should he not hear from me in two or three days, he may conclude I have escaped to France. And now give me your blessing, father."

While preferring this request he bowed his head, and the good priest gave him his benediction.

As the king passed her, Jane Lane fixed a meaning look upon him, and said in a low tone: "At Bentley Hall your majesty will find a safe place of refuge, should you require it."

A hasty adieu sufficed for the page, and with a warm expression of thanks to Mary Penderel, Charles quitted the house with her husband.

---

## CHAPTER VII.

HOW CHARLES AND TRUSTY DICK WERE FRIGHTENED BY THE MILLER OF EVELITH.

THE night was so dark, that without a guide it would have been utterly impossible for the king to find his way through the forest. Trusty Dick, however, experienced no difficulty, but marched along through the trees at a quick pace, and Charles kept close beside him. The crackling of sticks and small branches which they crushed beneath their feet as they proceeded, and the rustling of fallen leaves, betrayed their course, but they did not talk much, lest they should be overheard by a patrol of the enemy. Now and then they paused to listen, and on one occasion, fancying he heard the sound of horses' feet in the distance, Dick immediately struck into another path; but he did not stray far from the direct course.

At this hour there was something mysterious in the gloom of the forest, that acted very powerfully on the king's imagination, and led him to fancy that he discerned strange figures among the trees. But Richard Penderel, to whom he communicated his apprehensions, treated them very lightly.

" Your majesty needn't be alarmed," he said. " The forms you behold are merely trunks of old trees, or projecting boughs. They have a weird look at this time, and I myself have been scared by 'em."

At length they emerged from the forest, and got upon a wide common —greatly to the king's relief, for he had begun to feel oppressed by the gloom. The fresh air, so different from the damp atmosphere he had just been inhaling, laden with the scent of decaying leaves and timber, produced an exhilarating effect upon him, and he strode along vigorously.

While crossing the common, they descried a patrol of horse apparently proceeding in the direction of White Ladies or Boscobel, but they easily avoided them, and quitting the common, they soon afterwards mounted a steep hill, on the other side of which was a brook that turned a water-mill. As they drew near the mill, the sound of voices brought them to a halt. The hour being now late, it was singular that any persons should he astir, and Trusty Dick, naturally alarmed by the circumstance, at first thought of turning back. But to do so would have taken him and his companion considerably out of their course, and he therefore hesitated.

" This is Evelith Mill," he observed in a low voice to Charles. " Roger Bushell, the miller, is a cross-grained fellow, and I think a Roundhead, so I shouldn't like to trust him."

" 'Tis safer not," replied the king. " How far are we from Madeley ?"

" About two miles," replied Dick. " But if we were obliged to turn back it will add another mile, at least, to the distance."

" Then let us go on," said the king.

So they waited quietly for a few minutes, when the light disappeared, and the voices became hushed.

" Roger Bushell has gone to bed at last," observed Charles. " We may proceed on our way."

So they marched on without fear. But the king was wrong in his supposition, for as they passed the mill a gruff voice called out, " Who goes there ?"

" 'Tis the miller himself," whispered Dick.

" Well, answer him," said Charles.

Again the challenge was repeated, and more authoritatively than before, " Who are you ? Speak !"

" Friends," replied Dick.

" I know you not," cried the sturdy miller. " If you be friends, stand

and give an account of yourselves, or sure as I'm an honest man, and you are a couple of rogues, I'll knock you down."

And he brandished a stout staff as he spoke.

"What shall we do?" asked Charles.

"Beat a retreat," replied Dick. "It won't do to be stopped here."

And as the miller rushed forth to seize them they hurried off; and ascended another hill, never stopping till they were quite out of breath.

"This is a most disgraceful retreat, I must say, Dick," observed Charles.

"I should like to have knocked the dust out of Roger Bushell's jerkin," rejoined Dick. "But I am certain he has got some rebels with him, or he would not have dared to act thus."

---

## CHAPTER VIII.

### HOW THE KING WAS RECEIVED BY MR. FRANCIS WOOLFE AT MADELEY COURT.

It was past midnight when Charles approached Madeley, an ancient moated mansion, built of stone, and very pleasantly situated on the borders of the Severn. It belonged to Mr. Francis Woolfe, an old Cavalier, and father of the gallant Captain Woolfe, who figured at an earlier period of this history. As the hour was late, Mr. Woolfe and his family, with the whole of his household, had long since retired to rest, but they were disturbed by a loud knocking at the door, which continued with very little intermission until the old gentleman got up, and, accompanied by his butler, went to see what was the matter. On opening the door he found Richard Penderel, who was well known to him, and without giving the forester time to explain his errand, eagerly inquired whether he brought any tidings of Captain Woolfe.

"I know my son was present at the battle of Worcester," cried the old Cavalier; "and I fear he may be wounded, as I have not heard of him since."

"I am sorry I cannot relieve your honour's anxiety respecting your son," replied Dick. "But well knowing how staunch a Royalist you are, I am come to beg you to hide a fugitive Cavalier, who fought, like Captain Woolfe, at Worcester."

"Don't ask me to do it, Dick!—don't ask me!—I dare not harbour a Royalist!" cried Mr. Woolfe. "Willingly—right willingly would I do so, but there is too much hazard in it. I am already suspected by the rebels—there is a company of militia at Madeley, guarding the bridge and the river—and were they to search my house and find a fugitive Royalist concealed within it I should be most heavily fined— perhaps imprisoned—perhaps put to death! No, Dick, I will not run this risk for any one, except the king himself."

"Then what will your honour say when I tell you that he whom I ask you to shelter from his enemies *is* the king? The loyal Mr. Francis Woolfe, I am well assured, will never refuse his sovereign an asylum."

"You are right, my good fellow—you are right," cried the old

Cavalier, trembling. "I never supposed it was the king. Why did you not tell me so at first?"

"Because his majesty forbade me," rejoined Dick, "I have disobeyed his orders."

"But he might have trusted me," cried Mr. Woolfe. "I would lay down my life for him. Where is his majesty?"

"On the other side of the moat standing beneath yon great elm-tree," said Dick.

The old Cavalier required no more, but hastily crossing the bridge, proceeded to the spot indicated, followed by his butler and Richard Penderel.

Seeing him advance Charles came forward, and as they met old Mr. Woolfe threw himself on his knees, while Charles, finding himself discovered, gave him his hand to kiss.

"Sire," cried the old Cavalier, "I never thought to see you at Madeley under such sad circumstances. My house and all within it are yours. Enter, I pray you."

And with as much ceremony as if Charles had been a conqueror instead of a fugitive, he conducted him across the bridge and ushered him into the mansion. For a few minutes he detained his majesty in the hall while the dining-room was lighted up, and when all was ready he led him thither.

To his infinite surprise Charles found an excellent repast awaiting him, and he was served at it by his host and the butler. Seated in the large comfortable room, treated with so much ceremony, and supplied with some of the finest claret he had ever tasted, for a brief space he almost forgot his misfortune.

However, he would not yield to false security, and after emptying his goblet he questioned Mr. Woolfe as to the possibility of crossing the Severn.

The old Cavalier shook his head dolefully. It was utterly impossible; the bridge being guarded by the militia, and all the boats seized. His majesty must be content to stay at Madeley. Mr. Woolfe did not like to make such a suggestion, but as he had no safe hiding-places, and as a search might be made by the rebels at any moment, he would venture to propose that his majesty should sleep——

"I do not require a state-bed," interrupted Charles. "I am so thoroughly tired that I can sleep soundly anywhere."

"Then I have the less hesitation in proposing that your majesty should sleep in the barn," said the ceremonious old Cavalier. "You will be far safer there than in the house."

"And just as comfortable I make no doubt," said the king.

"I can answer for your majesty's safety there, which I cannot do here," said Mr. Woolfe. "It is just possible that some of the officers of the militia rebels might quarter in the house, as they have done before. In the barn your majesty would not be liable to a surprise. I will keep all my people away from it."

"I see—I see," cried the king, rising from the table, and heaving a sigh as he gazed round the old oak room, with its dark wainscots and portraits. "Take me to the barn."

Nothing but the sense that he was performing a great duty could have compelled the formal old Cavalier to act as he did, but he well knew how much was at stake. Doing great voilence, therefore, to his feelings, he took the king to a barn adjoining the mansion, where his majesty found a very comfortable couch in a haymow.

Richard Penderel slept in the barn. Very fortunate was it that the king did not stay in the house, as it was visited by a patrol of horse before daybreak. The soldiers instituted a rigorous search, but finding nothing to excite their suspicion departed.

Charles slept soundly in the haymow, and the day was far advanced before Trusty Dick thought proper to disturb him. As there was no chance of crossing the Severn, and considerable risk even in stirring forth, the king did not leave the barn. Breakfast was brought by Dick, and while the king was discussing it in an out-of-the-way corner, he heard the barn door open, and felt sure from the sounds that followed that more than one person had come in. His alarm, however, was instantly dispelled on hearing Mr. Woolfe's voice, and he immediately left his retreat to meet the old Cavalier. With Mr. Woolfe was a much younger individual, on beholding whom his majesty uttered a joyous exclamation.

"Do my eyes deceive me?" he cried. "Can it be Captain Woolfe?"

"Yes; 'tis my dear son, sire," replied the old Cavalier. "He has only just arrived, but on learning you were here, nothing would content him but I must bring him at once to your majesty."

"I am delighted to see him," said Charles. "I owe my preservation to him. Without Captain Woolfe's aid, I might not have escaped from Worcester."

And as he spoke he extended his hand to the young man, who pressed it fervently to his lips.

"It grieves me to find your majesty here," said Captain Woolfe. "I did not dare to return to Madeley last night, but tarried at Evelith Mill with honest Roger Bushell. Even there we were alarmed about midnight by a couple of Roundhead spies, but the sturdy miller frightened them away."

"Soh! you were at Evelith Mill last night?" cried Charles, laughing.

"I was not the only Royalist there, my liege," replied Captain Woolfe. "With me were Major Careless and Lieutenant Vosper."

"Then learn that the two Roundhead spies whom the miller drove away were myself and Trusty Dick Penderel," said the king, still laughing. "'Tis odd I should be put to flight by my friends. But where is Major Careless? Is he hereabouts?"

"No, my liege, he has gone towards Boscobel, where he fancies your majesty is hiding."

"And where I shall be forced to hide after all, since it appears impossible to escape into Wales," said the king.

"I must again implore your majesty not to make the attempt," cried the old Cavalier. "It would be attended with too much hazard. Your security must be the first consideration, and though I esteem it the highest honour to have the care of your majesty, I feel you will be safer at Boscobel."

"I will go thither to-night," said Charles.

"'Twill be the best course to pursue, my liege," observed Captain Woolfe. "Some plan for your escape can be devised. We shall all be ready to lend you aid."

Soon after this the old Cavalier returned to the house, but his son remained in the barn to bear the king company. Though Captain Woolfe was an agreeable companion, and did his best to amuse the king, Charles was very glad when night came on, so that he could shift his quarters with safety. He supped with the old Cavalier and his son, and passed so pleasant an hour with them that he was quite loth to take his departure.

It was not far from midnight when Charles took leave of Mr. Woolfe and his son. At that moment the old Cavalier almost repented that he allowed the king to depart, and made an effort to detain him till the morrow, but Captain Woolfe thought it best that his majesty should adhere to his plan. Father and son conducted him across the moat, and attended him to the outer gate, and Charles having taken leave of them there, set out on his journey with his faithful guide. Fortunately, their nocturnal walk was unattended by any danger, and the only annoyance they experienced was caused by having to wade across the brook that turned Evelith Mill, but this was a trifling matter, which gave the king no concern whatever.

In less than two hours, as well as they could reckon, for neither of them had a watch, they reached Boscobel Wood; but before entering it Dick deemed it prudent to call at the cottage of his brother John, which was close at hand, and ascertain from him that all was safe.

Accordingly they proceeded thither, and Dick knocked against the door with his staff. An upper window was quickly opened by John Penderel, and seeing who they were, he descended and let them in. His first business was to strike a light, and as he did so the king discovered a Cavalier—for such his attire proclaimed him—fast asleep in a chair.

"A stranger here!" exclaimed Dick, surprised. "Why didn't you tell us so, John?"

"The gentleman is no stranger to his majesty," replied the other.

Just then, the Cavalier, aroused by the light and the voices, sprang to his feet, and the king perceived it was Major Careless. The unexpected meeting was extremely agreeable to both.

"I heard your majesty was gone to Madeley," said Careless, after a cordial greeting had taken place between him and the king; "but I felt sure you would never be able to cross the Severn, and I therefore thought it likely you would come to Boscobel. I myself got as far as Evelith Mill, but returned yester morning."

"Is all safe here?" asked the king.

"No, my liege, very much the reverse I am sorry to say," replied Careless. "Patrols of the enemy are constantly searching the woods and visiting all the habitations around. I had several narrow escapes yesterday, and but for honest John Penderel here should infallibly have been captured."

"I am just as much indebted to Trusty Dick," said Charles. "Without him, I should not be here now."

"There are five of us on whom your majesty can rely," said John, who was just as stalwart and as honest-looking as his brothers. "If we had not been loyal, Father Huddlestone would have made us so. Last night, the good priest went to talk to our brother Humphrey, the miller of Boscobel."

"I will now put your loyalty to the test, John," said the king.

"You majesty cannot please me better," was the reply.

"Go then to Boscobel House, and satisfy yourself that I may safely proceed thither."

"It shall be done, my liege," rejoined John Penderel, evidently well-pleased by the order. "As soon as I have put on my doublet, I will set forth."

"The office is mine, by rights," observed Trusty Dick. "Nevertheless, I willingly resign it to John."

"Judging by myself, thou hast need of rest, my faithful fellow," said Charles, kindly. "I would fain spare thee further trouble."

John Penderel vanished, but in a minute or two reappeared, fully equipped, and grasping a stout staff, sallied forth.

It was now about three o'clock in the morning, and feeling much fatigued with his walk, and uncertain as to the rest he might obtain, Charles threw himself into the arm-chair lately occupied by Major Careless, and almost instantly fell asleep.

Careless found another seat and followed his majesty's example, while Trusty Dick having carefully barred the door, sat down on a settle, and fell into a sort of doze, during which he dreamed he was fighting half a dozen Roundheads.

More than an hour elapsed before John Penderel returned. All the sleepers were aroused by his knock at the door. He had seen a patrol of rebels in the wood, but they were coming from Boscobel—not proceeding thither—and he easily avoided them and went on to the house. There he saw Brother William, who told him they had got rid of all the rebels, so his majesty might come there without fear.

On receiving this satisfactory intelligence, Charles, being most anxious to obtain a secure asylum, set forth at once. He was accompanied by Careless, and guided and guarded by the two stalwart brothers, who would have sold their lives rather than allow him to be captured. They made their way through the depths of the wood by paths only known to the two foresters, and encountered nothing more dangerous than a squirrel or a thrush.

After half an hour's walk through the wood, they came upon a lawn studded by trees, among which were several ancient oaks. Day was just breaking, and now that they had got out of the dense wood, the sun burst upon them. At the further end of the lawn, Charles perceived an old mansion, with walls chequered black and white, gables, bay-windows with lattice-panes, and an immense chimney-stack projecting from the side. He did not require to be told that it was Boscobel House.

How quiet, how sequestered, how beautiful looked the old structure at an early hour! Charles stood still to gaze at it. No place had ever had the like effect upon him.

While he was still gazing at the picturesque old mansion, and noting the huge chimney-stack we have mentioned, a gigantic figure issued from the garden gate.

It was William Penderel, who, having descried the party from an upper window, had come forth to bid his majesty welcome and usher him into Boscobel House.

END OF BOOK THE SECOND.

## Book the Third.

### THE ROYAL OAK.

## CHAPTER I.

SHOWING HOW THE HUNTING-LODGE WAS BUILT BY THE LORD OF CHILLINGTON, AND HOW IT ACQUIRED ITS NAME.

'Towards the latter part of Elizabeth's reign, when those who professed the tenets of the Church of Rome were prevented by heavy penalties from performing the rites of their religion, while such as refused to take the oath of supremacy were held guilty of high treason, John Giffard, eleventh Lord of Chillington, in Staffordshire, himself a strict Roman Catholic, and a great sufferer from the oppressive measures referred to, determined to provide a safe asylum for recusants in a secluded part of his domains; and with this view he built a hunting-lodge in the depths of Brewood Forest, which then belonged to him, and contrived within the lonesome structure several secret hiding-places.

The situation was remarkably well chosen. Buried in a wood, where it was hardly likely to be discovered, the hunting-lodge was placed on the exact boundary line between Shropshire and Staffordshire, so that it was difficult to say in which county it stood. The whole surrounding district was covered with woods and commons—the nearest habitations being the ruined monasteries of White Ladies and Black Ladies. Several large trees had been removed to make way for the lodge and the outbuildings connected with it, but it was screened by majestic oaks, which grew within a few yards of the gates. Through these trees enchanting views could be obtained of the sylvan scenery beyond, of vale and upland, and purple heath, until the vast prospect was terminated by the picturesque Clee Hills and the blue outline of the Wrekin.

Nothing, however, save forest timber could be discerned in the immediate vicinity of the lodge, and from this circumstance it obtained its designation. On the completion of the building, the Squire of Chillington invited some of his friends to the house-warming. Among them was Sir Basil Brooke, then newly returned from Rome.

" How shall I name the place?" asked John Giffard.

" I will give you a charming and appropriate name for it," replied Sir Basil. " Call is Boscobel—from the Italian Bosco bello — Fair Wood."

The suggestion was adopted, and BOSCOBEL it became.

The solitary forest lodge answered its double purpose well. Its real object was not suspected, nor were its hiding-places discovered, though often resorted to by recusants during the reigns of Elizabeth and James I. Hunting and hawking-parties were sometimes assembled at the lodge by the Squire of Chillington to keep up appearances, but on such occasions due precautions were always taken for the security of those hidden within the house. No servants were employed except those on whose fidelity entire reliance could be placed—and who were themselves Romanists. Of the numbers of persecuted priests harboured at Boscobel none were ever betrayed. Nor during the Civil Wars was a fugitive Cavalier ever refused shelter.

A staunch Royalist as well as zealous Romanist, Peter Giffard, grandson of the builder of Boscobel, suffered severely for his adherence to the cause of the unfortunate Charles I. His noble ancestral domains were confiscated, and he himself was imprisoned at Stafford. Not till the Restoration did the loyal family recover their estates.

At the time of our history Chillington was almost entirely abandoned. In this magnificent mansion Queen Elizabeth had been entertained in princely style during one of her progresses by John Giffard ; and the house, from its size and situation, had been once under consideration as a suitable place of confinement for Mary, Queen of Scots. Its hospitalities were now at an end—its halls desolate. When the unfortunate Peter Giffard was deprived of his abode, Chillington was converted into a garrison by Sir William Brereton, and great damage done to it by the Parliamentary soldiers. Luckily, they could not destroy the beautiful avenue and the park, though they despoiled the house and laid waste the splendid old gardens.

Boscobel, though only two miles distant from the hall, escaped injury at this perilous juncture. William Penderel, who had been placed in charge of the lodge by the Squire of Chillington, was not disturbed, and was consequently able to afford shelter to many a Royalist. The rest of the brothers were equally lucky. George was allowed to remain at White Ladies, and the others pursued their quiet avocations in the forest. No doubt they enjoyed this immunity solely because they did not excite Sir William Brereton's suspicions.

William Penderel had now been two-and-twenty years at Boscobel. The office of under-steward was conferred upon him at the time of his marriage, so that he obtained a most comfortable residence for himself and his wife—the only drawback being that the tenure of the post was somewhat insecure, and when the Chillington estates were sequestered, he fully expected to be turned off. However, he was at Boscobel still. William had four children—two sons and two daughters—but they were now from home.

In Dame Joan, his wife, he possessed a capital helpmate. She could not boast of much personal attraction, but she had many excellent qualities. A model of prudence, she could be safely trusted on all emergencies, and she was as good-tempered as discreet. Tall and strong, Dame Joan was not masculine either in look or manner, and her features, though plain and homely, had a kindly expression, that did not belie her nature. She had a thoroughly honest look, and the tidiness of her apparel proclaimed an excellent housewife. Such was the opinion formed by Charles of this worthy woman, as he beheld her for the first time, when crossing the threshold of Boscobel House.

After making him an obeisance, not devoid of a certain rustic grace, Joan drew back respectfully, and ushered his majesty and Careless into a parlour on the ground floor, and then made another obeisance.

"Oddsfish! my good dame," said Charles, smiling. "You understand matters of ceremony so well, that you must e'en come to court —supposing I should ever have a court."

"Boscobel was greatly honoured when the Earl of Derby sought shelter here," replied Joan. "But it is now far more highly honoured since your majesty has set foot within the house. My husband and myself are not fitting persons to receive you majesty, but we will do our best, and you may depend upon it we will watch over you most carefully."

This was the finest speech Joan had ever delivered, but she deemed it necessary to the occasion. Charles thanked her graciously, but said, "Mark me, my good dame. All ceremony must be laid aside. Any observance of it might endanger my safety. When I put on this garb I became one of yourselves. Address me only as Will Jackson."

"I can never bring myself to address your majesty by such a name as that!" said Joan.

"Wife! wife!" cried William Penderel from behind. "You must do whatever his majesty bids you without a word."

"Why, you are committing a similar error, William," laughed the king. "But if you desire to oblige me, my good dame, you will go and prepare breakfast."

"Master William Jackson shall have the best the house can furnish— and quickly," replied Joan, departing.

The apartment into which the king had been shown was tolerably large, though the ceiling was low, and it was lighted by a bay-window at the further end, and by a lattice-window at the side, commanding the entrance to the house, and looking out upon the wood. A very pleasant room, wainscoted with black oak, and furnished with an ample dining-table, and chairs of the same material. In the days of old John Giffard many a festive party had gathered round that board after a day's hunting or hawking in the forest, but it was long, long since there had been revelry of any kind at the lodge. Over the carved oak mantelpiece hung a picture that caught Charles's attention. It was the portrait of a grave-looking personage in a velvet doublet and ruff, with eyes so life-like that they seemed to return the king's glances.

"The old gentleman above the fireplace appears to bid me welcome," observed Charles. "He has a fine face."

"It is the portrait of Squire John Giffard of Chillington, who built this house, my liege," said William Penderel. "It has always been accounted a good likeness. Ah! if the worthy squire could but have

foreseen who would come here for shelter!   Some good saint must ha
inspired him, when he contrived the hiding-places."

"Of a truth, I ought to feel much beholden to him for providing n
with such a place of refuge," remarked Charles.

While examining the room, the king noticed a door on the left, ai
found on investigation that it opened on a small closet, with a lattic
window looking upon a retired part of the garden.  There was i
furniture in the closet except a desk, which might be used for prayer.

" Is this one of the hiding-places ?" asked Charles.

" No, my liege," replied William Penderel, who had followed hii
" This is an oratory.  We are Roman Catholics, as your majesty is awari

" I see no altar," observed Charles.

William Penderel opened a recess in the wall, so contrived that it h
quite escaped the king's attention, and disclosed a small altar, with
cross above it.

" Here we pay our devotions in private," he said.

" And here I will pay mine," rejoined Charles.   " I must return than
to the Great Power that has hitherto preserved me.   Leave me."

Careless and William Penderel at once retired, and closed the door
the oratory.

Left alone, Charles knelt down before the little altar, and was for so
time occupied in fervent prayer.

---

## CHAPTER II.

### HOW TRUSTY DICK BETHOUGHT HIM OF THE OAK.

IN the hasty description of Boscobel House, previously given, it i
remarked that the most singular feature of the edifice was a huge f
jecting chimney-stack.   A very extraordinary chimney it was, for it l
as many as seven small windows, or apertures, within it, placed at vari
heights, the two lowest of the openings being about eight or nine
from the ground.   Viewed at the side it could be seen that the chimr
stack, which rose considerably above the roof, formed part of a project
wing of the house, and that there must be something peculiar in
construction of the funnels.   Altogether it had a strange, myster
look, and suggested the idea that the builder must have been sligl
crazed.   Yet, odd as it was, the huge, heavy, fantastic chimney l
monised with the rest of the structure.   The reader will have alre
surmised that within this chimney-stack a secret hiding-place exist
the entrance to it being from a closet connected with a bedroom on
first floor—as will be more particularly described hereafter—while tl
was an outlet into the garden through a little postern, comple
screened by ivy.

Since the king's arrival at Boscobel, the chimney-stack had acqu
a new interest in Trusty Dick's eyes, and being now left in the gai
to keep watch, he scrutinised it with an anxiety such as he had n
heretofore felt, peering up at the narrow slits of windows, and stool
down to ascertain that the postern was completely hidden by the ivl

Never before had he doubted the security of the hiding-place, misgivings now came over him. What if a careful examination of the chimney, outside and inside, should be made while the king was concealed therein? Discovery would then be inevitable. Pondering upon the matter, Dick quitted the garden, and in another instant was among the noble old trees growing near the house.

An idea had taken possession of him, and he walked on till he reached a giant oak which, standing a little clear of its fellows, was able to spread abroad its mighty arms. This was the tree he sought. Though it mu-t have been centuries old, the oak seemed in full vigour, and had suffered very little from decay. Its trunk was enormous. It had not, however, grown to a great height, but had spread laterally. Dick examined this ancient oak very carefully—walked slowly round it—looked up at the bushy central branches, and seemed perfectly satisfied with his scrutiny.

"This is the tree for the king to hide in!" he mentally ejaculated; "this is the tree!—the best in the whole forest. No one could discover him among those thick branches."

He was still examining the oak when he was roused by Major Careless, who had been searching for him, and having found him, called out, "What ho! Dick—have you deserted your post?"

Dick explained the object that had brought him thither, and when he concluded, Careless said, "You are right, Dick. In that oak our royal master will be safe from his enemies. I will bear him company while he hides within the tree. But I must look at it more closely."

Not content with inspecting the tree, Careless determined to test its efficiency as a place of concealment, and with his companion's aid, he therefore climbed up into it, and concealed himself among the smaller branches.

"Canst see me now, Dick?" he called out.

"See you!—not a bit," rejoined the other. "I should never guess your honour was up there."

The assurance was quite enough for Careless, and he quickly descended.

"Thou hast made a most lucky discovery, Dick," he cried. "'Tis a famous tree to hide in. His majesty will be as comfortable amid its branches as if seated in an arm-chair. I will tell him so."

While returning to the house they caught sight of two persons approaching through the trees, and might have felt some alarm had not Dick instantly recognised his brother Humphrey.

With Humphrey Penderel was a well-clad youth, whose slight figure contrasted strikingly with that of the stalwart miller.

As the pair advanced, Careless's curiosity was much excited by the appearance of this youth, and he questioned Dick concerning him.

"He is named Jasper," was the reply. "He is page to Mistress Jane Lane."

"Mistress Jane Lane's page! Impossible!" cried Careless, whose surprise increased as the youth drew nearer, and his delicately-formed features could be more clearly discerned.

"Nay, 'tis quite certain," remarked Dick. "He came with her the other night to Hobbal Grange. He is a forward youth, and talked much with the king, who sat beside him, and seemed to notice him."

"I marvel his majesty did not tell me of the meeting," cried Careless.

"Doubtless, he had forgotten it," said Dick.

They had waited till the others came up, and as the page approached, he seemed somewhat confused, but quickly regained his composure.

Humphrey Penderel, the miller of Boscobel, was just as big, and as strongly-built as his brothers, but his broad good-humoured countenance did not wear its customary smile. On the contrary, he appeared anxious. After returning the sturdy miller's salutation, Careless addressed the page, who for the moment completely engrossed his attention.

"Good morrow, Jasper!" he said.

"I give your honour good day," replied the page, doffing his cap, and letting fall locks that had evidently not been subjected to Puritan scissors. "I believe I am speaking with Major Careless."

"Right, good youth. If thou hast aught to say to me in private, prithee step aside."

"I have nothing to say to your honour that the others may not hear,' returned Jasper, declining the invitation. "I will only ask you to bring me to his majesty."

"I know not that his majesty will see you," said Careless. "I will take your message to him."

"I am quite sure he will see me," rejoined the page. "Mention my name to him, and 'twill suffice."

"Aha! you think so. His majesty will laugh at me if I tell him that a saucy page desires to be admitted to his presence."

"I pray you make the trial," said Jasper. "You will find that I am right, and you are wrong."

"Do you bring a message from Mistress Jane Lane?"

"Your honour must excuse my answering that question. My business is important—very important—and does not admit of delay. If you decline to take me to his majesty, I will proceed to the house, and endeavour to find him. I will not be thwarted in my purpose."

"You have boldness enough for anything."

"'Tis a duty to be bold when the object is to serve the king."

"How knew you that his majesty is at Boscobel? Tell me that."

"I obtained the information from Humphrey Penderel, who brought me here. But do not question me now—I must and will see the king."

"'Must and will' see him?"

"Ah, and without delay. You will incur his sovereign displeasure if you detain me."

"I will put that to the test," cried Careless. "You must stay here while I go to him."

An end, however, was put to the discussion by the appearance of the royal personage to whom it related.

Charles, having finished his devotions in the oratory, had come forth into the garden, and after lingering there for a short time had passed out into the wood, where he chanced upon an opening that gave him a view of the vast sylvan scene with the Clee Hills and the round Wrekin in the distance.

After gazing at the fair prospect for a few minutes he moved in another direction, and presently came in sight of the party standing neath the trees. Great was his surprise, when the page, who could not be restrained by Careless, ran towards him, and would have bent the knee, if the king had not checked him.

"How is this?" cried Charles. "Have you left your mistress to follow the fortunes of a fugitive Cavalier?"

"I hope soon to rejoin Mistress Jane Lane, my liege," replied Jasper. "I have not come in quest of Major Careless, for sooth to say, I did not know he was here. I have come to warn your majesty that your enemies are on your track, and will search for you here to-day."

"Here!" exclaimed Charles.

"Here—at Boscobel," rejoined Jasper. "They believe they have run you to the ground, and make sure of capturing you. Your majesty will wonder how I obtained this information. You shall hear. Yesterday, Mistress Jane Lane and myself remained at Hobbal Grange, as we did not like to quit our retreat, but in the evening we proceeded to the mill belonging to Humphrey Penderel, being assured that that honest man would convey us to Moseley Hall. We had not long arrived at the mill, when a patrol stopped there, and we had only just time to hide ourselves when the rogues entered the house. I was concealed in a chest standing in the room in which they sat down, and consequently overheard their discourse. It related entirely to your majesty. You have been traced to White Ladies, and they are certain you are somewhere hereabouts. They are equally certain they shall be able to discover your retreat – but I trust you will be able to baffle them. Their orders are to search Boscobel to-day, and they will be accompanied by Colonel James, who is now quartered at Chillington. All this, and a good deal more, I heard while ensconced in the chest. They spoke of the reward offered for your majesty's discovery, and told Humphrey Penderel he should have a thousand pounds, which would make him rich for life, if he delivered you up to them, but that he would be hanged as a traitor if he helped to conceal you. Humphrey made no answer at the time, but afterwards declared he should like to have broken their heads for so insulting him."

"Brave fellow?" exclaimed Charles. "He is as trusty as his brothers."

"No fear of him," said Jasper. "But Colonel James is greatly to be apprehended. He is one of your majesty's most dangerous enemies, and will use his utmost endeavours to find you. I do not think you will be safe at Boscobel."

"Where shall I be safe?" cried Charles. "I have only just arrived here, and now you counsel me to quit my retreat."

"Hide yourself in the forest, sire, and return to the house after it has been searched."

"The advice is good, and I am inclined to follow it," rejoined the king. "Mistress Jane Lane, I trust, is in safety?"

"She is at Moseley Hall, sire. As soon as the rebels were gone, Humphrey Penderel put a pillion on his pad-nag, and took her there."

"And you?"

"I remained to warn your majesty."

"I am infinitely obliged to you—but confess that you had some slight expectation of finding Major Careless with me, and I am glad you have not been disappointed."

"I had no such expectation, sire," replied the page, blushing. "I

understood Major Careless was at Madeley. I neither sought nor desired
a meeting with him."

"Oddsfish! you have changed your mind since we last met."

"Perhaps so, sire. But I would not have my motive misconstrued.
'Tis devotion to you that has induced me to take this step. When I
learnt that Colonel James was at Chillington—in quest of you—and resolved to discover your retreat, I felt that you were in great danger, and
I therefore made up my mind to warn you. Had I not found you here I
should have gone to all the places where you were likely to take refuge.
I have discharged my duty—and unless your majesty has some commands
for me, I shall take my departure for Moseley Hall, where I hope to
find Mistress Jane Lane. If she has gone on to Bentley Hall, I shall
follow her thither."

"Shall I send Major Careless with you ?"

"On no account. Humphrey Penderel has undertaken to take charge
of me. Heaven guard your majesty !"

Making an obeisance to the king, Jasper hastened back to the party
who had been watching the interview with some curiosity, and signing
to Humphrey Penderel, the sturdy miller instantly started off through
the trees, while the page followed him, totally disregarding Major
Careless's entreaties to him to stop.

<hr>

## CHAPTER III.

### HOW THE KING AND CARELESS TOOK REFUGE IN THE OAK.

CARELESS would have followed, but was prevented by the king, who
strode quickly towards the spot where he was standing with Trusty
Dick, and forbade him to stir.

"Spare me a moment, I beseech you, sire," cried Careless. "I must
have a word with this youth."

"Stir not," said Charles, in an authoritative tone. "He has told me
all it is necessary I should know, and you can question him on your own
account at a more convenient season."

"But there seems to be a misunderstanding, sire, which may be
rectified in an instant, if you will only allow me——"

"Not now," interrupted Charles. "No time must be wasted in idle
talk. The youth has come to warn me that this house of Boscobel will
probably be searched to-day by Colonel James, who is quartered at
Chillington."

"Humphrey has just informed me that the rebel troopers were at the
mill last night, sire," observed Dick ; "and they told him they were
sure your majesty was concealed somewhere hereabouts, and they would
never rest till they found you."

"They told him something more," said Charles. "They offered him
a large reward to betray me."

"He didn't tell me that," said Dick. "But Humphrey is no
traitor, sire."

" He is as loyal and faithful as yourself, Dick. I cannot say more. But now—give me your frank opinion. In the event of a rigorous search by this confounded Colonel James, do you think I should be safe in yonder house ?"

" Well, your majesty might be discovered—and you might not," hesitated Dick.

" That's no answer, Dick," said the king. " Speak plainly, man."

" I've already had some misgivings, sire. While these scoundrelly troopers are about, and especially when they've got an active leader, who will peer into every hole and corner, my honest opinion is that your majesty will be safer in the wood than in the house. There are no hiding-places like those of Boscobel—that I'll uphold—but your majesty's safety is too precious to be trifled with."

" Nothing must be left to chance," said Careless. " I am of Trusty Dick's opinion that till this threatened danger has blown over, your majesty will be safest in the wood. We have found a tree in which you can hide."

" I hope it is an oak," cried Charles. " I would rather owe my safety to the king of the forest than to any inferior tree."

" Truly it is an oak—a grand old oak—and hath not its peer in the forest," said Dick.

" Take me to it," said Charles.

In another minute he stood before the tree.

He was gazing at it with admiration, when William Penderel and his brother John were seen at a distance, evidently in quest of his majesty, and no sooner did they descry him than they hurried forward.

" You are looking for me, William ?" said the king.

" Your majesty must be pleased to return at once to the house," replied William Penderel. " Indeed, I must make bold to say it is highly imprudent to stray so far away, when the enemy is lurking about. John, who has been acting as scout, brings word that a small detachment of troopers, with Colonel James at their head, are coming from Chillington, and are almost certain to find their way here."

" I have run so fast to get before them that I have well-nigh lost my breath," gasped John. " But I beseech your majesty to conceal yourself without delay,"

" I mean to do so—in this tree," replied Charles.

" In this tree !" cried William, in a tone of disappointment. " Every thing is prepared in the house."

" His majesty has decided upon taking refuge in this oak," said Careless.

" Nay, then, no more need be said," observed William Penderel. " And perhaps it may be for the best. But you have not breakfasted, sire. And my good dame has got all ready for you."

" I must dispense with breakfast, I fear," observed Charles, with a sigh.

" Oh ! we can breakfast in the tree," cried Careless. " There is every convenience among the branches. Can't you bring a basket of provisions, William, with a flask of wine ?"

" Suppose I am caught by the Roundheads, they will at once conclude the provisions and wine are intended for his majesty.  Most assuredly, the house will be watched."

" You cannot be too cautious, William," observed the king.  " I care not how long I fast."

" But I do," groaned Careless.

"Help me to climb the tree," cried Charles.

" The king, who was remarkably active, scarcely needed the assistance he demanded, and, with very slight aid from William Penderel, was quickly among the branches.

" Your majesty is as nimble as a squirrel," cried the forester, in admiration.

" Are you coming to me, Careless?" said the king, looking down.

" Most certainly, sire," replied the major.

And in another instant he was by the king's side.

" Do not tarry here longer, my good friends," cried Charles to the brothers.  " I feel quite safe, now I am in this oak.  Return to me when you can do so without risk."

In obedience to his commands, the three brothers departed—William Penderel returning to the house, while Trusty Dick and John posted themselves in different parts of the wood, but at no great distance from the oak in which the king was hidden.

---

## CHAPTER IV.

### HOW CARELESS CAPTURED AN OWL IN THE OAK.

Seated upon a large bough, and with his feet upon a lower branch, the king looked down at Careless, and could not help laughing at him.

" This would be an amusing adventure if your majesty's safety were not in question," observed the major.

" I suppose you never spent a day in a tree, Will ?"

" Never, sire.  I don't know what it's like.  I have done a good many strange things in my time, but this is one I never yet did.  We must make ourselves as cheerful as we can under the circumstances."

" You have the happy knack of being always cheerful, Will."

" I am not half so light-hearted as your majesty.  Besides, I have nothing to trouble me.  I have not lost a kingdom.  I have not even lost a mistress."

" I am not so certain of that," laughed Charles.

" At any rate, her loss does not give me much concern.  Women are enigmas, and pass my comprehension."

" Thou art thinking of one in particular."

" The sex are all alike—whimsical, capricious, inconstant."

" But always attractive.  What hath displeased thy mistress with thee ?"

" On my honour, sire, I know not.  Methought she was flying at higher game."

" You need fear no rival in me, Will.  I am proof against all feminine wiles just now. I have something else to think of  But let us examine our quarters."

"Climb a little higher up, my liege, and you will find a most comfortable seat—there!—between the main stem and one of the upper branches."

"I have it," said Charles, seating himself. "Oddsfish! how thick the foliage is! 'Tis a perfect luxury to sit amongst it. Find a place near me if thou canst."

Careless obeyed, and while searching for a convenient place among the branches, suddenly called out:

"Adzooks! We have a companion, sire."

"A companion!" exclaimed the king, in surprise. "What sort of companion?"

"An owl," replied Careless. "A great horned owl. Behold him!—perched on that branch, puffing angrily at me for intruding upon his rest. I wonder he has not taken flight. I'll try and capture him. He may be of use to us."

"In what way useful? We are better without him than with him, methinks."

But the interdiction was too late. Careless had caught the owl by throwing his mantle over him.

"Here he is, sire!" he cried, delighted with his success.

"If thou couldst cook him now he is caught, there would be some gain," laughed Charles.

"He will serve to amuse us if he answers no other purpose," said Careless. "But hark! I hear a sound." And after listening intently for a moment, he added in a low voice to the king, "'Tis the trampling of horse. A patrol is coming this way."

"I hear the voices of the rogues. Are we perfectly concealed?"

"Perfectly, my liege. Keep quite still, I beseech you! The slightest noise may betray us."

From the sounds that reached their ears it was plain that three or four horsemen had halted beneath the tree, and were lamenting the ill success that had attended their search for the royal fugitive.

"'Tis strange Charles Stuart contrives to evade us so long," remarked one of them. "I begin to think he has escaped."

"Had he attempted to escape, we should assuredly have captured him," cried another. "He hath baffled us by keeping quiet. I doubt not he is still in this wood. Ah! if we could only discover his retreat. That Humphrey Penderel could have helped us to it if he would. He is a lying rogue."

"Colonel James thinks that the malignant prince will be found at Boscobel," observed a third. "But I doubt it. He does not enter a house. My belief is that he is hidden in a tree."

"Perchance in a tree like this," observed the first interlocutor. "If such is thy opinion, dismount quickly, and climb the tree—even to the top thereof."

"And be laughed at for my pains. No, I will not climb the tree, but I will discharge my caliver into its branches. If I bring down Charles Stuart with the shot ye will not mock me."

"Of a surety not—we will greatly applaud thy wisdom," cried the others.

Upon this the trooper who had previously spoken, pointed his caliver upwards, and fired into the thick of the branches. A loud rustling sound followed the shot.

"I have hit something!" cried the trooper, exultingly. "Peradventure it is the king.

"If it be the king he has taken the form of a bird," cried the troopers, laughing.

As they spoke the owl dropped down on their heads, and as its wing being broken by the shot, it fluttered along the ground.

Shouting with laughter, the troopers pursued the unlucky bird, but could not catch it.

"I have had a narrow escape," said Careless to the king, as soon as the coast was clear. "That rogue's bullet came confoundedly near me. Your majesty will now admit that an owl may be of some use. It has helped us to get rid of those rascally troopers."

---

## CHAPTER V.

### HOW THEY BREAKFASTED IN THE OAK.

THANKFUL for their escape, the king and Careless remained perfectly quiet for some time, conversing only in whispers, lest an enemy might be lurking near.

More than an hour elapsed without anything occurring to cause them fresh alarm, when a low whistle was heard.

"A signal!" exclaimed Charles.

"It may be a device to induce us to discover ourselves," whispered Careless.

After a pause the whistle was repeated, and somewhat more loudly.

"I will go a little lower down and endeavour to make out who it is," said Careless.

While he was cautiously descending, a voice, which both recognised, called out:

"'Tis I, William Penderel!"

"Heaven grant he has brought us something to eat!" exclaimed the king. "Go down to him quickly, Will."

On emerging from the foliage, Careless beheld William Penderel at the foot of the tree, having a basket in his hand and a cushion under his arm.

"Never wert thou more welcome, friend William," cried Careless, enchanted at the sight. "His majesty is well-nigh famished, and I should have been forced to come to thee for food hadst thou not made thy appearance."

"You must not quit the tree on any consideration," returned William, "Boscobel is surrounded by the enemy. I have been obliged to get hither by a path known only to myself, and even then I ran the greatest risk. Do not come down, I pray your honour," he added, seeing that Careless, who was standing on the lowest bough, was about to descend. " I will hand the basket up to you."

The feat would have been difficult to any man of less gigantic stature than William Penderel, but was easily accomplished by him.

Just as Careless obtained possession of the basket, the king appeared above his head.

" Here is your majesty's breakfast," cried Careless, gleefully.

" And here is a cushion for your majesty to sit upon while breakfasting," said William, handing it up.

" Truly, thou art most thoughtful, William," said the king. " I cannot thank thee sufficiently."

" I must not remain here longer now," said the forester. " I will return when I can do so with safety. Meantime, I counsel your majesty to keep close hidden."

" Answer me one question before you go, William," said Charles. " Has the house been searched?"

" No, sire," he replied. " But it is strictly watched by the rebel soldiers. Apparently, they are waiting for their leader. I must get back before he arrives!"

With this he departed.

The king and Careless then took the basket to the upper part of the tree, and arranged the cushion between the forked branches, so that it formed a very comfortable seat.

Evidently replenished by Dame Joan, the basket contained all that could be desired for a substantial meal—cold meat, a cold pie, bread, butter, and cheese, with wooden platters, wooden spoons, horn cups, and every other requisite, including a couple of white napkins. Nor was a flask of canary omitted.

" Heaven bless that thoughtful Dame Joan! How much we owe her!" cried Charles, as he spread a napkin on his knee. " Give me some of that pie, Will, and take good care you let none fall while cutting it."

" Fear me not, sire," said Careless, performing the office of carver very dexterously, all things considered, and handing a large piece of pigeon-pie to the king.

He then set to work himself, and with such goodwill that in a marvellously short space of time the dish was completely emptied. The horn cups were then filled, and a fresh attack was made on the cold meat, and continued stoutly for some time, till both parties were obliged to give in. Careless, however, held out longer than his royal master.

Everything being replaced in the basket, it was hung upon a branch, to be again applied to in case of need. The pangs of hunger, from which he had been suffering rather sharply for the last few hours, being now appeased, Charles began to feel extremely drowsy, and at length, being quite unable to resist the strong inclination to slumber, he reclined his head on Careless's lap, and almost instantly dropped asleep.

The chief anxiety of the faithful attendant was to prevent his royal master from falling, but there was little chance of such an accident, for the king never moved. The real risk was lest Careless himself should follow his majesty's example, for he was oppressed by drowsiness in an equal degree, but by a great effort he conquered the feeling.

Thus things continued for some time, during which Careless never altered his position for fear of disturbing the slumbering monarch. But Charles was not easily awakened, as will presently appear.

On a sudden, Careless was aroused from the dreamy state of mind in which he was lost by a cry for help, and as he happened to be thinking of Jasper at the moment, he naturally concluded that the cry must proceed from the page.

In another moment he became convinced that his supposition was correct. This was not the first time he had heard that voice in distress, though under far different circumstances from the present. He could not look out from his place of concealment to ascertain the cause of the outcries, but it seemed to him that the luckless page was flying from a patrol, and in imminent danger of being captured. Had it been possible he would have flown to the youth's assistance, but he could not quit his position. His anxiety almost amounted to torture, but he was obliged to bear it.

Charles slept on soundly as ever.

Listening intently, Careless heard the shouts of the troopers as they galloped among the trees, and he again heard Jasper's voice, but faint and far off. Then it ceased altogether. Was the fugitive captured? As Careless could still hear the fierce shouts of the pursuers he hoped not. But he was left in a state of agonising suspense, for very soon the shouts of the troopers ceased also.

Still the king moved not, but continued buried in sleep for some time longer. At last he roused himself, but it took him some minutes to completely shake off his lethargy.

"I have had a strange dream, Will—a kind of nightmare," he said. "Methought that pretty page, Jasper, was calling out for help, and neither of us could stir."

"'Twas no dream, sire," replied Careless. "The circumstance actually occurred. I was awake, and heard the cries. They pierced my heart."

"Why did you not answer them?"

"My duty to your majesty forbade me. I would not even waken you—for I well knew what your chivalrous impulse would have suggested."

"And you allowed him to be captured?—ha!"

"I trust he escaped—but I cannot say. I am now right glad that I did not wake your majesty. 'Twas a hard matter to keep quiet I will frankly confess, but I could not desert my post. Duty before everything."

The king smiled, and patted his shoulder. "Thou art ever faithful," he said.

## CHAPTER VI.

### HOW COLONEL JAMES HALTED BENEATH THE OAK.

NOTHING more passed between them for some time, and Charles seemed to be once more yielding to lethargic feelings, when he was effectually aroused by the trampling of horse. Evidently a small detachment of troopers was coming that way, and a halt took place beneath the oak. No sooner did the voice of their leader reach Careless's ears, than he remarked in a whisper to the king, " 'Tis Colonel James, sire."

"We must not quit this forest empty-handed," said James. " Unless the knave and his wife who have care of Boscobel have deceived me, Charles Stuart is not concealed there. Neither is he at either of those houses of abomination, White Ladies, or Black Ladies. Yet I am well assured he is hereabouts, and have him I will; for what answer shall I give to the Lord General, if the head of the malignants be suffered to escape. Search, then, most carefully. Let men be posted at various points, and if any one be found in the forest—woodman or not—compel him to give an account of himself, and if he fails to do so satisfactorily, arrest him."

"We did discover a youth in the forest, but being exceeding fleet of foot, he escaped us," remarked one of the soldiers.

"How? escaped!" cried Colonel James, angrily. "It might have been Charles Stuart himself. Why did you not shoot him, Madmannah?"

"It was not Charles Stuart, colonel," replied the soldier, " 'Twas a mere stripling. We were close upon his heels when he disappeared suddenly from our sight—nor could we find him again."

" Ye are not half quick enough," said Colonel James, sternly. " In which direction did the youth run?"

"Towards Boscobel House, colonel," replied another of the soldiers. " But he could not have gained the house."

" Ye have done your work negligently," said James, still more sternly.

"The reproof is unmerited, colonel," said Madmannah. " We have shown no lack of zeal."

" Find me Charles Stuart, and I will retract what I have said. But I repeat, ye have done your work imperfectly. I will have every tree in the forest searched wherein a man might be hidden, and I will begin with this oak."

It will be readily supposed that the determination thus expressed by Colonel James caused great alarm to Charles and his companion, but their uneasiness increased when the Republican leader continued in an authoritative voice:

" Thou art active, Ezra. Dismount at once, and climb the tree."

The king and Careless gave themselves up for lost. There seemed to be no possibility of escape. But they were quickly relieved by Ezra's response to the order.

" No use in searching this oak, colonel."

" No, use, sayst thou ?"

" None, colonel. I have already discharged my caliver into the tree."

" That is true," said the other soldiers.

" Nay, if that be so, 'twere a waste of time to climb the tree," said James. " We will look out for another, further on."

" Shall we fire a volley into the tree, colonel, to make sure ?" asked another of the soldiers.

" 'Tis needless," replied James. " March !"

---

## CHAPTER VII.

### HOW THEY PLAYED AT DICE IN THE OAK.

The occupants of the oak breathed again after the departure of Colonel James and his troopers, and though they had been greatly alarmed at the time, they soon recovered their spirits, and laughed at the incident.

" Perhaps the excitement was a little too great," observed Charles; " but it has served to break the monotony of our somewhat dull existence. Time, it must be owned, passes very slowly when one is compelled, like the fowls of the air, to roost in a tree. I hope we shall soon have another visit from our faithful William Penderel."

" Your majesty must not look for him before night."

" I would night were come. How many wearisome hours have we to pass ? Never did I feel so strong a desire for active exercise—just because I must not take it."

" Your majesty had best go to sleep again. Pity we have neither cards nor dice to divert the tedium."

" I have it," cried Charles. " Cards cannot be provided, but the other deficiency may be easily supplied. Acorns will serve for dice, and our horn drinking-cups will make admirable dice-boxes."

" Bravo ! your majesty has a rare wit," exclaimed Careless.

Charmed with the notion, he set to work at once to carry it out, and gathering a few acorns, marked them with the point of his dagger. The horn cups were next produced, and carefully wiped with a napkin, which was then folded and laid on a branch of the tree to serve for a board.

" At what game will your majesty be pleased to play ?" cried Careless, rattling the extempore dice in the cornet.

" Hazard would be most appropriate," replied Charles. " But we have had enough of that of late. I prefer ' passage,' " he added, taking three of the dice. " Plague on't, I have nothing to stake—not a crown."

" Your majesty has already staked a crown——"

" Ay, and lost it," interrupted the king.

" Only temporarily, sire. You will soon have it back again. I have a few pistoles left," he added, producing his purse. " Shall we divide them ?"

"Be it so," replied Charles.

Putting down a couple of the pistoles he had received from Careless, he then threw, calling out "Quatre," as he made the cast, and he continued throwing until stopped by Careless, who exclaimed :

"Doublets above ten.   Your majesty passes and wins."

"I thought I was in luck to-day," cried Charles.

The play went on, without much benefit to Careless.   Ere long, every pistole was swept up by the king, who was put into very good humour by his success.

"Oddsfish!   I have won all thy money, Will," he exclaimed.   "But take back half, and let us begin anew.   Since we have found out this pleasant pastime, I care not how long I am detained here.   Never, sure, was oak so enchanting as this."

"Suppose we try 'in and in,' by way of variety, sire?" said Careless.

Charles assented, and they began to play again, and soon became so excited by the game, that they neglected the dictates of prudence, and talked louder than they ought to have done.   Suddenly a sound from below, like the clapping of hands, brought them to their senses.   They became instantly silent, and regarded each other anxiously.

<hr>

## CHAPTER VIII.

### HOW THEY HAD A VISITOR IN THE OAK, AND IN WHAT MANNER THEY TREATED HIM.

The sound was repeated.   Though believing it to be a signal, they did not dare to respond.

"Do you hear me?" cried a voice which they both recognised. "'Tis I—Jasper.   Come down quickly.   There is danger."

"Danger of what?" demanded Careless.

But no answer was made.   The page was gone.

"We had best attend to the warning, sire," observed Careless.

Charles thought so too, and they were preparing to descend, when they were stopped by hearing other voices—rough and menacing in tone —at the foot of the tree.   It was evident that the speakers were a couple of troopers, who had tied up their horses and come thither on foot.

"If it should turn out as I conjecture, Ezra," said one of them, "and Charles Stuart proves to be hidden in this tree, we shall easily effect his capture, and obtain the reward."

"Without doubt.   But why dost thou think he is here hidden, Madmannah?"

"A revelation seemed made to me, when I came hither an hour or two ago with Colonel James," replied Madmannah.   "But I would not disclose what was then imparted to me—save to thee, Ezra.   "Thou shalt share the reward."

"And the danger," observed Ezra.

"The danger will be mine, seeing that I mean to climb the tree," said Madmannah.   "Thou wilt remain here."

"I am content,' replied Ezra.  "But I have little faith that thou wilt find him thou seekest."

This discourse reached those above.

"There are but two of them, sire," remarked Careless to the king. "Shall we descend and attack them?"

"Not so," replied Charles.  "Let this fellow come up if he will. We can hurl him down on his comrade's head."

It now became evident from the noise that Madmannah was climbing the tree.

"Give me thy dagger," said the king.  "I will deal with him."

Careless obeyed, but held himself in readiness to assist the king.

As Madmannah entered the thick part of the tree, where he was concealed from his comrade's view, he was suddenly seized with an iron grasp by the king, who placed the dagger at his throat.

"Utter a word, and thou art a dead man," said Charles, in a deep whisper.

His looks showed so plainly that he would execute his threat, that Madmannah did not dare to disobey, but prudently held his tongue.

Seeing how matters stood, and fearing lest the trooper might free himself sufficiently from the king's grasp to draw a pistol, Careless quickly descended and disarmed him—depriving him of all weapons he had about him.

"I will slay thee without hesitation unless thou renderest implicit obedience to my commands," said Charles to the trooper.

At this moment Ezra called from below:

"Hast thou found him?"

"Say that thou hast lost thy labour," whispered Charles, holding the poniard more closely to the trooper's throat.  "Speak loudly, so that he may hear thee."

Madmannah did as enjoined.

"I expected as much," cried Ezra, angrily.  "Thou hast brought me here on a fool's errand.  Come down quickly, or I will depart without thee."

"Let thy answer be, 'Go, an' thou wilt,' " said Charles.

And Madmannah repeated what he was told.

"Add, that he may go to the devil if he is so minded," said Careless.

Madmannah made the required addition, and Ezra marched off in high dudgeon.

"Now let me go," implored Madmannah.  "I swear not to betray you."

"We cannot trust him," said Careless.  "These false-hearted knaves regard not an oath.  We can only insure his silence by putting him to death.  Let us hang him to a branch of the tree."

"Spare me!" cried the trooper, horribly frightened.  "By all that is sacred I swear not to betray you!"

"I am for hanging him.  'Tis the safest plan," said Careless.

Though not seriously uttered, the threats produced the desired effect. The trooper begged hard for his life.

"Shall we let him go?" said Charles, somewhat moved.

"Assuredly not," replied Careless.  "Since he has been fool enough to come his head into a noose, he must take the consequences."

"It will greatly inconvenience us to detain him as a prisoner," said Charles. "But there is no alternative."

"Pardon me, there is the alternative of hanging."

"Hark thee, fellow," cried Charles. "Thy life shall be spared, but thou must submit to restraint. Thy hands must be bound, and thine eyes blindfolded."

"Nay, if that be done unto me, I shall fall down from the tree, and break my neck," groaned Madmannah.

"No matter," said Careless.

"Seat thyself between these branches, and move not," said the king.

Aware that resistance would be useless, Madmannah obeyed. Careless then took off the prisoner's belt, and with it fastened his arms tightly behind his back; completing his task by tying his own scarf over the man's eyes.

"Attempt to call out and we will gag thee," he said.

"Nay, I will keep silence," rejoined Madmannah. "Yet tell me how long I am to be detained here?"

"Till this time to-morrow," answered Careless; "for then we shall be far off."

"Then ye mean to leave me here?" said the prisoner.

"We shall leave thee, but the tree will be watched," remarked Charles.

Madmannah asked no further questions. Naturally, his presence was a great annoyance to the king and his companion, and they moved as far from him as they could, and conversed in whispers.

Things went on thus for more than an hour, when the voice of Ezra was heard from below, calling out:

"Art thou still here, Madmannah?"

The prisoner heard the inquiry, but did not dare to make any answer, for he felt the point of the poniard at his throat, and Ezra departed.

No one else—friend or foe—came near the oak.

The day seemed interminable—but night came at last. In expectation of the arrival of William Penderel, they had got all in readiness for departure. But what was to be done with the prisoner? That was rather a perplexing consideration, for the king did not altogether like to leave him in the tree. Charles was still undecided, when a signal was given, and peering out from the screen of foliage he could just distinguish three huge figures standing at the foot of the tree.

"The fellow shall go down with us," he observed in an under tone to Careless. "William Penderel and two of his brothers are below. They will dispose of him. Unloose him quickly."

Careless obeyed the injunction.

"Am I to be set at liberty?" asked the prisoner, joyfully, as his hands were unfastened.

"That depends," replied Careless. "The bandage will not be removed from thine eyes, so it will behove thee to be careful in descending."

Meantime, the king had gone down to explain matters, taking the basket and the cushion with him. As he expected, he found William Penderel with Trusty Dick and John. All three were amazed to hear that a prisoner had been made.  Though the task was by no means agreeable to them, Dick and John did not for a moment dispute his majesty's commands, but agreed to convey the trooper to a distance.

"We will conduct him to the roughest part of the wood and leave him there, to find his way out as he best can," said Dick.

"If he gets drowned in a pool, or stifled in a bog, it won't much matter," added John.

Madmannah reached the lowest branch in safety, but he then slipped down and fell to the ground.  When he arose he was seized on either side by a vigorous grasp, while a stern voice—it was that of Dick—bade him come along, and keep silence.

"We have got thy pistols," added John, "and we will shoot thee through the head shouldst thou attempt to fly, or give the alarm.  So take heed what thou art about."

They then marched off with the prisoner between them.

As soon as they were out of sight and hearing, William Penderel cautiously conducted the king and his companion to Boscobel House.

---

## CHAPTER IX.

HOW CHARLES SLEPT IN THE SECRET CLOSET ; AND HOW CARELESS SLEPT IN A PRIEST'S HOLE IN THE GARRET.

AFTER the long and anxious day he had passed in the oak, it was with a feeling of indescribable satisfaction that Charles found himself once more in Boscobel House—not in the parlour into which he had been shown in the morning, but in the large comfortable hall—a couple of nicely roasted chickens before him, and Dame Joan in attendance. Careless, who was seated at the opposite side of the table, was quite as well pleased as his royal master, and both did justice to the repast provided for them.  Charles, as we have already remarked, possessed a happy temperament, that enabled him to cast off his cares, and with plenty to eat, and a flask of good wine within reach—to say nothing of a black-jack full of strong ale, he desired nothing better—and laughed heartily while recounting the many alarming incidents of the day to Joan.

"What trials your majesty must have gone through!" exclaimed the good dame, lifting up her hands.  "The saints be praised that you are here to describe them."

"I shouldn't mind passing another day in the oak," observed Charles, "if I were certain of having such a supper as this at the end of it.  I trust the noble tree that has given me shelter may 'scape the woodman's axe!"

Just then the door opened, and William Penderel entered, followed by his two brothers.

"William," cried his wife, with irrepressible enthusiasm, "his majesty expects you and your brothers to protect the royal oak!"

"The royal oak!" cried William.

"Thy wife has so named the tree," said the king, "and I approve the designation."

" Then the royal oak it shall be called," cried William, sharing Joan's enthusiasm, as did his brothers.

" Pledge me in this cup of wine that you will protect the good old oak," cried Charles, drinking from the cup which he had just before filled, and handing it to William Penderel, who received it on his knees with the utmost respect.

" I pledge myself to preserve the royal oak, so far as lies in my power," he said, placing the cup to his lips.

When he had finished, each of his brothers knelt down, and drank the pledge solemnly.

" Your majesty may depend that the royal oak will be well protected," cried Joan.

" I doubt it not," said Charles. " Now tell me what you have done with the prisoner ?" he added, to Trusty Dick.

" We took him to Rock Coppice in Chillington Park," replied Dick, " and forced him to descend into a deep dry pit, from which he will find some difficulty in getting out."

" But he may know you again ?" said Charles.

" No fear of that," said John. " We didn't remove the bandage from his eyes, and disguised our voices. Here are his pistols."

" Give them to me," said William. " I may need them. I shall keep watch throughout the night."

" John and I will remain here likewise to relieve guard," said Dick ; " so that his majesty may rest securely."

" No discovery was made when the house was searched by the enemy to-day ? ha !" cried Charles.

" None whatever, sire," replied Joan. " Our lady be praised for misleading them."

" Where am I to be lodged, good dame ?" asked Charles.

" There is a very fine old bed in the squire's room as we call it," replied Joan—" Squire Peter Giffard, and his father, ay, and his grandfather, Squire John Giffard, who built this house, have often slept in it —but I dare not offer it to your majesty."

" Lodge me where you will, good dame," replied the king, with manifest symptoms of fatigue. " I wish you all good night."

" Shall I attend your majesty ?" said Careless.

Charles declined, and preceded by Joan, who carried a light, mounted an oak staircase, which sprang from the further end of the hall.

On arriving at the landing-place, his conductress opened the door of a good-sized apartment, in the midst of which stood a large old-fashioned bed, with rich, though faded curtains. The room, which had a most comfortable look in the eyes of the wearied monarch, was panelled with black oak, and partly hung with tapestry. On the walls were portraits of Sir Thomas Giffard, tenth Lord of Chillington, and his two spouses— Dorothy, daughter of Sir John Montgomery, of Caverswall, and Ursula, daughter of Sir Robert Throckmorton, of Coughton—both extremely handsome women.

Having drawn aside a piece of the arras opposite the foot of the bed, Joan opened a sliding panel in the wainscot, and a dark closet was then revealed.

" Is this the hiding-place ?" asked Charles.

" Your majesty shall see," she replied.

And she then opened another sliding panel at the back of the closet.

The aperture thus discovered admitted them to a small square room, which evidently formed part of the projecting chimney-stack, and had small windows at the front and at either side, looking into the garden. It was evident from its position that the room stood over the porch.

" This cannot be a hiding-place," said Charles.

" Your majesty is right," replied Joan. " But it deceives the searchers."

She then drew back, and signing to the king to follow her, returned to the closet, and taking up a small mat in one corner, raised up a trap-door, so artfully contrived in the floor, that Charles could not detect it, and disclosed a small ladder, leading to a room beneath.

" There is the hiding-place," she said. " The small room below is built in the chimney, whence by a narrow staircase and a small postern covered with ivy, you can gain the garden, and from the garden may reach the wood, where you are safe."

" I understand," said the king, struck with the ingenuity of the contrivance.

" A pallet bed is made up in the lower room. The place is small and uncomfortable, but 'tis safe."

" That is the main point," cried Charles. " I must sacrifice comfort to security."

" The Earl of Derby slept here all the time he stayed at Boscobel," said Joan.

" Then I have no right to complain," cried Charles.

" Should any alarm occur I will run up-stairs instantly and make all secure," said Joan. " Holy Mary and all holy angels watch over your majesty."

Charles then took the light from her, passed through the trap-door, and descended to the lower room.

Having carefully restored the panel to its place, Joan went down-stairs, and telling Careless she would find him a safe resting-place, led him to the upper floor of the house.

There was nothing whatever in the garret they had reached to indicate that it could be used for the purpose of concealment. The roof was so low that Careless could scarcely stand upright beneath it. Beyond it were other small rooms lighted by the gable windows. A straw mat was lying on the floor. This Joan removed and revealed a trap-door, beneath which was a cavity about six or seven feet deep, profoundly dark, and only just large enough to hold a single person. So much did this " priest's hole," as it was called, resemble a cell, that Careless shuddered as he gazed into it. However, he made no complaint, but let himself down into the hole, which he found somewhat more roomy than he expected.

Joan handed him the lamp she had brought with her, and on looking round, he perceived that a pallet was laid at the bottom of the recess, but nothing more than a blanket and a pillow were provided.

" I must perform this act of penance for my sins," cried Careless.

" But I am so sleepy that I do not think I shall pass the night in prayer like the holy men who have previously sought refuge here. I do not require the light, good dame," he added, giving back the lamp to her. " But I pray you not to close the trap-door, for I feel as if I should be suffocated in this hole."

" Colonel Roscarrock slept two or three nights in the priest's hole," replied Joan ; " and he chose to have the trap-door shut, judging it safer. But your honour's instructions shall be carefully attended to, and the lamp shall be left on the table. I wish you good night."

No sooner was she gone than Careless laid himself down upon the pallet, and notwithstanding the confined space, and the general discomfort of the priest's hole, so greatly was he fatigued, that he immediately fell fast asleep.

## CHAPTER X.

### IN WHICH THE KING PROVES HIMSELF A GOOD COOK.

ALL passed quietly that night at Boscobel. Charles slept soundly in the secret closet ; and Careless slept equally soundly in the priest's hole The faithful brothers kept watch, by turns, outside the house, and Joan did not go to bed at all, but took a little repose in an arm-chair in the squire's bed-chamber. Careless awoke at an early hour in the morning, and left the garret as quickly as he could. Finding the king was not astir, he did not choose to disturb him, but went forth into the garden. After strolling about for a few minutes, he proceeded to the little mount we have already described, and entered the arbour on its summit. What was his surprise to find some one asleep there. It was Jasper, who was roused by Careless's approach, and opened his eyes.

" You here !" exclaimed Careless.

" I have not been long here," said the page. " I have been hidden in the forest, and have had several narrow escapes of capture."

" Both his majesty and myself have been most anxious for your safety," said Careless. " You look sadly tired."

" Fasting does not very well agree with me," replied Jasper. " One cannot find much to eat in the forest. I have had nothing for nearly twenty-four hours, and I find myself particularly hungry, I can assure you."

" No wonder," cried Careless, in a sympathising tone. " Come with me into the house, and I will get you some breakfast at once."

" The offer is too welcome to be refused—though I confess I have some scruples. What will his majesty think of me ?"

" His majesty will be delighted to see you—but he has not yet left his couch."

What more passed between them we do not pretend to say, but they remained within the arbour for another minute or so, and then descending from the mount proceeded with very leisurely footsteps towards the porch.

" How strange is this meeting !" murmured Careless. " Never did I dream we should be here together."

" 'Tis a charming old place, I think, and I could be quite happy here for a month, if those Roundhead soldiers wouldn't molest me."

They were now not far from the porch, when a rustling was heard among the ivy that clothed the base of the chimney-stack, and the next moment the king came forth from the secret postern.

Jasper was quite startled by the sudden apparition, for so well concealed was the outlet that it could scarcely be detected, even when the observers were close at hand.

Charles smiled at the page's look of astonishment.

" You are not familiar with the wonders of this enchanted castle," he said.  " But, i'faith, I should not have ventured forth if I had not reconnoitred you through a loophole."

" I hope your majesty has rested well," said the page, with an obeisance.

" Never better," replied Charles.  " I made one long nap of it. Where did you find a couch ?"

" Partly at the foot of a tree, sire, and partly in yonder arbour, where Major Careless found me a few minutes ago."

" Oddsfish ! then you have passed the night in the forest?"

" Precisely so, sire."

" And I fear without supper?"

" Supper would have been superfluous, if I had dined."

" Careless, we must have breakfast instantly," cried Charles.  " Let me know when it is ready."

" Come with me, Jasper, thou may'st be needed."

" No ; Jasper will remain with me.  I want to talk to him."

Careless rather reluctantly departed.

The king then began to question the page as to his adventures in the forest, but had not learnt all particulars, when Careless came back.

" Oddsfish ! thou hast made haste," exclaimed Charles.

" Dame Joan desires to know what it will please your majesty to have for breakfast."

" Didst tell her I have company ?"

" I explained that there is a hungry page with your majesty, and she thought he had best come in and render help."

" Willingly," cried Jasper.

" Nay, we will all go in," said Charles.

Active preparations for the morning meal were being made in the hall as the king entered with his attendants.

A large fire was burning in the grate, at which Dame Joan was roasting a brace of partridges, that emitted a very delectable odour.

" Nothing can be better than those birds, dame, unless it be a broiled mutton-chop ?" he cried.

" There is a neck of mutton in the larder, an' please your majesty, but I fear the meat may prove too fresh," replied Joan.

" Heed not that," cried Charles.  " Mutton-chops are the very thing. I will broil them myself.  Bring me the gridiron, dame."

Very much amused by the order, Joan obeyed, and the chops being duly prepared, were skilfully broiled by the king, who never for a moment quitted his post, but turned them with a fork when requisite.

While he was thus employed, William Penderel came in, and could scarcely believe his eyes when he found the king standing before the fire. But the faithful fellow did not remain long in-doors, for he was now left alone for a time, his brothers having gone to their homes.

Having completed his task to his entire satisfaction, and the infinite amusement of the lookers-on, Charles proceeded to the head of the table, and bidding Careless and the page sit down on either side of him, the chops were served by Joan, and greatly enjoyed. Charles insisted that the good dame should taste his cookery, but she would touch nothing till she had served the partridges. She then discussed the chop at the lower end of the table, and declared, no doubt with truth, that she had never tasted aught so good in her life.

## CHAPTER XI.

### WHAT BROUGHT FATHER HUDDLESTONE TO BOSCOBEL.

After breakfast, Charles, attended by Careless, went out into the garden, and having previously consulted William Penderel, who did not seek to dissuade him from the step, visited the oak, and remained for a long time contemplating it with mingled gratitude and admiration. How majestic looked the tree on that morning! Before quitting it Charles spread his arms round its trunk in a loving embrace.

On returning to the garden, Charles proceeded to the arbour, and sat down within it. So pleasant was the spot that for a short time he surrendered himself to the enjoyment of the moment, and sank into a calm reverie, from which he was rather rudely disturbed by the sound of approaching footsteps, and looking out he saw Father Huddlestone, accompanied by Careless. Greeting the priest with much respect, he met him at the top of the mount, and led him into the harbour, graciously praying him to be seated.

"All good saints bless your majesty!" exclaimed the priest, "and guard you from your enemies. I have just come from Moseley Hall, and am the bearer of a message to your majesty from Lord Wilmot. His lordship is in great anxiety on your majesty's account—very alarming reports having reached him, which I am glad to find are unfounded, and he implores you to come on to Moseley Hall, where he feels sure you will be safe. To his lordship's entreaties I would add those of my patron, Mr. Whitgreave, who places his house at your disposal, and has means, almost better than any other person, of offering you a secure asylum at this dangerous juncture. To these entreaties, my gracious liege," continued the good priest, earnestly, "I will add my own. Do not remain here too long. Your enemies have been temporarily baffled in their quest, but I fear they will renew it, since their obstinacy is great."

The king listened attentively to what was said to him.

"I intended to remain here for a few days, holy father, till the danger should be blown over," he said. "But I perceive there is too much risk in doing so. Loth, therefore, as I am to leave Boscobel, I will come to Moseley Hall to-night."

" Your majesty has determined well," said Father Huddlestone. " But I entreat you to take a sufficient guard with you. The forest is full of rebel troopers. No doubt the trusty Penderels will guard you."

" I can count upon them," replied Charles.

" I will speak with William Penderel myself, before I depart," said the priest.

" Do you depart soon, father ?"

" Almost immediately, sire. I return by Chillington."

" Then come in at once and take some refreshment."

And rising as he spoke, the king led the way to the house.

As the king and Father Huddlestone walked on, they perceived Careless and the page leaning from an open lattice window to the room on the ground floor. Thus seen they formed a very pretty picture. On his majesty's approach they would have drawn back, but he marched up to the window to speak to them.

" A change has taken place in my plans," he said. " Father Huddlestone is returning immediately to Moseley Hall. You must both go with him."

" And leave you here, sire ?" cried Careless. " I do not like the arrangement at all. But, of course, I must obey your majesty's orders."

" If all goes well, I shall rejoin you to-morrow at Moseley," said the king. " I shall travel at night, and with a sufficient escort."

" But why am I not to form one of your majesty's escort ?" asked Careless.

" Because you are wanted elsewhere," replied Charles, smiling.

" Well, since it must be, it must," said Careless. " But your majesty may wish me at your side."

While Charles was thus conversing, the good priest entered the house, and finding Joan and her husband in the hall, paused for a moment at the open door, and bestowed a benediction upon them. They received him with the greatest respect. William placed a chair for him, and Joan quickly brought him some refreshment. While this was going on, the good father briefly explained the purport of his message to the king, and though the faithful pair were grieved to lose their important charge, they raised no objection.

At this juncture Charles came in.

" My good friends," he said, " I perceive from your countenances that Father Huddlestone has told you I must leave you. Never shall I forget your kindness to me, and I desire to express my gratitude in the good father's presence."

" Your feelings do you honour, my liege," said Father Huddlestone, rising. " Your majesty may rest assured that you have not more devoted subjects than the Penderels. As to Dame Joan——"

" Her price is above rubies," interrupted the king. " I know it. Be seated, I pray, your reverence, and heed not my presence. I have more hard work for you, William, and for your trusty brothers. To-night you must all escort me to Moseley Hall."

"We will all be ready, my liege, and shall account it no hardship," replied William. "We will take with us our brother-in-law, Francis Yates. We can trust him as we can trust ourselves."

"The husband of the good woman who visited me in Spring Coppice?" observed Charles.

"The same, sire."

"Then he is well mated," said the king.

"You must all go armed, William," remarked Father Huddlestone, gravely—"armed, and prepared to resist to the death. I warn you there is danger."

"We will go fully prepared for any event," rejoined William Penderel, resolutely. "We cannot do better than die for the king."

"That is a sentiment I have always inculcated," said the father.

"And I have not forgotten it, your reverence." Then turning to the king, he added, "I will bid Humphrey bring his horse for your majesty. Moseley Hall is a long way off, and your majesty looks somewhat footsore."

"Oddsfish! I could not walk half a dozen miles without falling dead lame," cried Charles. "By all means let me have Humphrey's nag."

Soon afterwards, Careless and the page, neither of whom had any preparations to make, came in to bid adieu to Joan and her worthy spouse; and Father Huddlestone, declaring he was sufficiently rested and refreshed, rose to depart.

Before bidding adieu to Careless, the king gave him some instructions in private, saying, as he left him at the garden gate,

"If we do not meet again, you will know what to do."

Charles did not wait for any reply, but as if afraid of betraying the emotion he felt, walked quickly towards the arbour. On gaining the summit of the mount, he looked round and saw that Father Huddlestone and his two companions were gazing anxiously at him from the skirts of the wood. Waving his hand to them, he entered the arbour, and was for some time lost in painful reflection.

**END OF BOOK THE THIRD.**

---

# Book the Fourth.

## MOSELEY OLD HALL.

### CHAPTER I.

#### CHILLINGTON HOUSE.

FATHER HUDDLESTONE being as well acquainted with the paths through the forest as the Penderels themselves, took his companions through the thickest part of it, where they were not likely to encounter a patrol of the enemy, and brought them safely to Chillington Park.

They were now at the lower end of the long and beautiful avenue leading to the ancient mansion, but before proceeding further, the priest deemed it advisable to consult the old gate-keeper, who dwelt in the lodge adjoining the entrance of the park.

Like all the old retainers of the Giffards, John Eccleshall, the gate-keeper, was a Roman Catholic, and consequently devoted to Father Huddlestone. He informed the priest that there was no danger whatever in his entering the park, since Colonel James, with the whole of his troopers, had evacuated the hall.

"Heaven be thanked the rogues are gone to Brewood!" said the old man. "Not one is left behind. I counted them as they passed through the gate."

While Father Huddlestone was talking with the gate-keeper, Jasper's curiosity was excited by an old wooden cross standing in a small green inclosure near the lodge, and in answer to his inquiries as to why it had been placed there, the priest related the following legend:

"That is called Giffard's Cross," said Father Huddlestone, "and it was set up in old times by Sir John Giffard. Sir John, who was excessively fond of the chase, kept a collection of wild beasts, and amongst them a very beautiful, but very fierce panther, which he valued more than all the rest. One day it chanced that this savage animal slipped out of its cage, and escaped into the park. Made aware of what had happened by the cries of his terrified household, Sir John snatched up an arbalist, and rushed out into the park, accompanied by his eldest son. He easily ascertained the direction taken by the panther, for the beast had been seen to skirt the avenue. At that time there were no gates here, and the limits of the park extended far beyond the place where we are now standing. Sir John and his son ran as swiftly as they could, and were still speeding on, when they beheld a young woman and a child coming along the road. At the same moment, they discovered the panther couched amid the fern, evidently waiting for his prey. Sir John and his son had halted, and though the distance was almost too great, the old knight prepared to launch a bolt at the beast. But while he was adjusting his cross-bow, his son remarked that he was out of breath, and fearing he might miss his aim from this cause, called out to him in French, '*Prenez haleine, tirez fort.*' By this time the poor young woman had perceived her peril, and uttering a loud shriek, clasped her child to her breast, and essayed to fly. It may be by the interposition of holy Hubert," continued the priest, reverently, "whose aid Sir John invoked, that she was saved. Just as the panther was about to spring, the bolt flew, and was lodged in the animal's brain. On the spot where the mortally-wounded beast rolled on the ground, this memorial was placed. Thenceforward, also, Sir John Giffard adopted as his motto the words of counsel addressed to him by his son."

Having concluded his legend, with which Jasper was much edified, the good priest bestowed his benediction on the old gate-keeper, and the party entered the park, and proceeded along the avenue.

Viewed at a distance, Chillington House, with its grand façade, its immense oriel windows, its gables, turrets, and noble entrance porch, looked as imposing as ever, but on a nearer approach, the damage done to the mansion could be perfectly distinguished. Built by Sir John Giffard in the early part of the reign of Henry VIII., on the site of a still older edifice, Chillington House had long been kept up in magnificent style by its owners. But the Giffards were gone now, and their ancient residence being in the hands of the Parliamentary commissioners, was allowed to go to ruin. Now and then is afforded quarters to a detachment of soldiers, who took possession of it, without authority, and did an infinitude of mischief.

The old mansion was approached by an extremely picturesque avenue of mingled oaks and hollies, and it was along this beautiful avenue, in 1576, that Queen Elizabeth rode, attended by a splendid cortége, when she visited John Giffard, grandson of the builder of the mansion.

At that time, the park, which was of vast extent, was well stocked with deer, for the old lords of Chillington were great hunters. At the rear of the mansion the park extended to Codsall, and in this part there were several large pools, of which a more particular description will be given hereafter. At a subsequent period these pools were joined together, and now form a large and beautiful lake. Attached to the house were stables that might have befitted a palace, and these were spared by the troopers, who spared nothing else about the place, because they found them convenient.

Placed on a rising ground, Chillington House not only looked down the long avenue we have described, but commanded an extensive prospect over a beautifully wooded country. Familiar with this lovely view, Careless turned round for a few minutes to gaze at it, but it was with very different feelings that he surveyed the ancient mansion. How changed was it since he beheld it last! As his eye ran over the front of the once proud structure, he noted the injuries it had sustained—windows shattered—architectural ornaments mutilated, or thrown down—the smooth lawns trampled over—the terrace grass-grown. Yawning wide, the great entrance door revealed the havoc that had taken place within.

Careless and the priest exchanged mournful glances as they walked towards the house, but not a word passed between them. The great hall which they entered was a complete wreck—its beautifully carved oak screen having been ruthlessly destroyed. The sculptured armorial bearings on the grand oak staircase were likewise irreparably injured. Nothing that hatchet could mutilate was spared.

"Have you seen enough?" inquired the priest.

"No," replied Careless, "I would fain see what these vindictive miscreants can do when they are under no restraint. Come with me, father. Wait for us here, Jasper."

Accompanied by Father Huddlestone he then ascended the great oak staircase, and they proceeded to examine the long gallery and the numerous apartments connected with it, all of which were marked by the hand of the ruthless destroyer.

"What would Peter Giffard say if he could behold his house?" remarked Careless. "It would break his stout heart—if, indeed, his heart is not already broken."

"He bears his misfortunes bravely," said Father Huddlestone. "But the king's defeat at Worcester will be a greater blow to him than the worst of his own losses."

"Ah! if we Royalists had but won that battle, father," cried Careless; "we should soon have enjoyed our own again!   But we must now wait for many a long day."

"I fear so, my son," replied the priest.   " But I trust in the justice of Heaven!"

Meanwhile Jasper, tired by his walk, had sought a seat among the broken furniture scattered about.  Discovering an old arm-chair, he threw himself into it and fell asleep almost immediately.

Having completed their survey of the upper rooms, Careless and the priest were about to descend, but while passing through the gallery they chanced to look out of a window, and, to their infinite dismay, perceived a small party of dragoons, with an officer at their head, riding quickly towards the house.

There was time enough to save themselves by a hasty retreat, but not a moment to lose.  Careless rushed to the head of the great staircase, and called out to Jasper that the enemy was at hand, bidding him fly to the back of the house, and make his way out.

Feeling certain that the page heard him, and would instantly attend to the warning, he gave himself no further concern, but followed Father Huddlestone down a back staircase.  Luckily, there was nothing to prevent their egress—the doors being all unfastened—and they were soon in the court-yard.

Here they waited for a few moments for Jasper, expecting he would join them, but he came not.  Careless now became seriously alarmed and his uneasiness was increased by some sounds that seemed to announce the arrival of the troopers.  Despite Father Huddlestone's entreaties he re-entered the house, but presently came back, and with a look o anguish exclaimed :

"Too late!  The troopers have already entered – he must be captured!"

"Nay, then, we must save ourselves if we can," cried Father Huddlestone.   "Let us make for the wood."

They had scarcely quitted the court-yard when three or four trooper rode into it.

---

## CHAPTER II.

### HOW THE KING WAS WELL-NIGH CAPTURED BY MADMANNAH.

Seated in the arbour, to which he had retired on the departure o Father Huddlestone and his companions, Charles endeavoured to reviev his position calmly.

His great desire had been to remain at Boscobel till the vigilance o his enemies should relax, and an opportunity of reaching the coas might occur to him, but after Father Huddlestone's earnest representa tions of the great risk he would run, he felt the necessity of seeking another hiding-place, and where could a more secure retreat be foun than was offered by Moseley Old Hall ?   Mr. Whitgreave, the owner o the mansion, belonged to the old religion, and the unfortunate monarcl had learnt from recent experience that those who had proved most faithful to him in his hour of peril were Roman Catholics. Besides, Father Huddlestone had given him positive assurance of the fidelity of Mr. Whitgreave's household. There was no risk, therefore, of betrayal. The great danger lay in the journey. If he could only reach Moseley Old Hall in safety all would be well.

Still, he felt reluctant to quit Boscobel. The Penderels had completely won his regard. Their devotion had impressed him deeply, and he well knew that men so honest and trusty, and possessed of such good sound sense, were rarely to be met with. Having been thrown so much into their company—especially into that of Trusty Dick—he knew them more intimately than he had ever done persons in their humble station, and he formed a very high and perfectly just opinion of their worth.

Naturally, the uppermost thought in his mind was how to reach the coast, and procure a vessel to convey him to France, and he was considering how he could best accomplish his object, when the sound of quick footsteps on the gravel-walk leading to the mount caught his ear. He immediately looked forth, and saw it was Trusty Dick, who had come to warn him.

"Your majesty must not stay here any longer," said the faithful fellow. "The enemy is at hand."

On hearing this Charles hurried to the house, where he found William Penderel and his wife in great consternation, for they had just learnt from Dick that Colonel James, being dissatisfied with the result of the first investigation, was about to make another search of the house, and was coming thither with his troopers.

"I will again take refuge in the oak," cried Charles. "I shall be safe amid its branches."

"There is not time to reach the tree," said Dick, who could not conceal his uneasiness. "Besides, that rascally trooper whom your majesty made a prisoner is with them."

"You must hide in the secret closet, my liege, or in the priest's hole," said Joan.

"There are other hiding-places," added William Penderel, "but none so secure as the secret closet in the chimney. Go thither at once, sire, I entreat you. There is not a moment to lose."

"I must not be found here," cried Trusty Dick, "my presence would excite suspicion. But I shall not be far off."

Snatching up a sword that had been left for him by Careless, Charles hurried up-stairs, and opened the door of the secret closet. While he was thus employed, he fancied he heard some one in the adjoining chamber, and at once flew to the trap-door, and let himself down into the lower chamber. In his haste, he had left the sword lying on the floor of the bedroom, and had upset a fauteuil—and, worst of all, he had left the door of the secret closet open—but he felt sure Joan would quickly follow and put all right.

And so she would have done, had she not been prevented. How great was her terror, on entering the bedchamber, to see a trooper standing there, amid all these evidences of the king's hasty retreat.

The trooper she beheld was Madmannah. He had got into the

house through an open window, and had made his way privily up-stairs. Placing his pike at her breast, he ordered her instantly to quit the room. and she did not dare to disobey.

Casting an anxious glance at the accusing sword, but still hoping the trap-door might not be discovered, Joan went down to the hall, where another scene of terror awaited her.

Colonel James was interrogating her husband, who was standing before the stern Republican leader with a trooper on either side of him. Ezra, who was stationed at the foot of the staircase, allowed her to enter the hall, but bade her hold her tongue. Colonel James was seated near the table. His aspect was unusually severe, but William Penderel did not quail before his menacing looks. The forester's gigantic figure dwarfed the troopers who stood on either side of him.

"I know thou art a stubborn knave," said Colonel James; "but I will wrest the truth from thee. I am certain that Charles Stuart is concealed within this house, and I mean not to depart without him. But I will not waste time in the search. Thy life is already forfeited for thy treasonable conduct, and I should be justified in putting thee to death; but I will spare thee, if, without more ado, the malignant prince be delivered up to me. Nay, more, I will reward thee. Dost hear me, sirrah?" he continued, finding that his words produced no visible impression upon the prisoner. "I am not one to be trifled with, as thou wilt find."

As he spoke, he arose, strode towards the prisoner, and drawing a pistol from his belt, placed it at Penderel's head.

"Speak the truth, or thou art a dead man," he said. "Where is the prince?"

This was too much for Joan. She could not stand by and see her husband shot. Rushing forward, she besought the fierce Republican leader to spare him.

"A word from thee will save his life," said Colonel James, lowering the pistol and turning towards her.

"Woman, I forbid you to speak," said William Penderel, sternly.

"Shoot me if you will," cried Joan to the Republican leader, "I have nothing to declare. Charles Stuart is not here."

"That is false," exclaimed Colonel James. "Deliver him to me, or ye shall both die. Your treasonable practices are known to me. I am aware that the fugitive prince and one of his attendants were concealed in an oak hard by this house. Where are they? They cannot have escaped."

"Wherefore not?" rejoined William Penderel. "If, as you assert, they were hidden in an oak, they could not be here. Search the house, and if you find him you seek, then put us to death."

Finding he could not intimidate the resolute forester, Colonel James left him in charge of a couple of troopers, with orders to shoot him if he attempted to escape, and commanded Joan to conduct him over the house.

"If Charles Stuart be found hidden within the house, thou and thy husband shall assuredly die," he said. "But if it be as thou affirmest, I will spare you both."

"Where will you begin the search?" inquired Joan.

"I will leave no room unvisited," replied Colonel James. "But I will first examine the bedchambers."

Joan's heart quaked as the stern officer marched up-stairs and proceeded to the principal bedroom. Colonel James was astonished by finding Madmannah standing in the midst of the room, leaning on his pike, with the door of the secret closet wide open.

"Hast thou found the malignant prince?" he exclaimed.

"Yea, verily, colonel, I have discovered his hiding-place, as you perceive," replied Madmannah. "There is the stool on which he somewhile sat—there is the cup from which he drank—above all, there is his sword. I have waited for you to make further search, that you may have the credit of the capture. But I claim the reward."

"Thou shalt have it," replied Colonel James, stepping into the closet.

He saw at a glance that it was empty, but feeling sure there must be some secret recess, he struck the panels on either side with the pommel of his sword, but discovering nothing, he at last turned to Joan, who was standing by watching his proceedings with ill-disguised anxiety, and remarked:

"There must be a hiding-place here. Disclose it at once, or I will cause my men to break down the panels."

Joan obeyed, drew back the sliding door, and Colonel James instantly sprang through the aperture into the inner room.

Finding no one within it, he vented his disappointment in an angry exclamation.

"Where is the malignant prince, woman?" he demanded, fiercely.

"Gone," she replied. "That is all I will tell you."

"Thou art deceiving me, woman," he exclaimed.

But finding threats useless, he proceeded to make a very careful investigation of the little room in which they stood. Had he searched the outer closet with equal strictness he must infallibly have discovered the trap-door.

Dreadfully frightened, Joan had great difficulty in supporting herself, and it was an inexpressible relief to her when Colonel James strode back into the bedchamber.

"'Tis plain the malignant prince is not here, Madmannah," he said to the trooper, who seemed greatly disappointed by the result of the search.

"I could have sworn I heard him," said Madmannah. "But there are other hiding-places in the house. Answer truthfully, on your life, woman," he added to Joan.

"I will conceal nothing," she replied, anxious to get them away. "There is a priest's hole in the garret."

"A priest's hole!" exclaimed Colonel James. "Show it to me."

Joan took them to the garret, raised the trap-door, and displayed the cavity.

After peering into the hole, Colonel James ordered Madmannah, who had followed him, to descend and examine it. Not without difficulty did the trooper, who was rather stout, obey his leader's injunction. But once in the hole, he found it impossible to get out, and had to take off his breast-plate before he could be extricated from his unpleasant position. He had found nothing, for the pallet on which Careless slept had been removed.

Enraged at his ill-success, Colonel James then went down-stairs, and searched the parlour, the windows of which have been described as looking into the garden. His investigations were rewarded by the discovery of the little altar in the oratory, and offended by the sight of it, he caused it to be destroyed.

After this, he again tried the effect of menaces upon William Penderel, but found the stout forester as stubborn as ever. Nothing could be extorted from him.

At last, after a long and fruitless search, the baffled Republican leader took his departure, and the faithful pair, who had passed an hour of the greatest anxiety, congratulated each other on their escape.

Not till she was quite satisfied that the troopers were gone did Joan venture to release the king from his confinement. He had heard the footsteps of Colonel James in the closet overhead, and thought that the trap-door must be discovered. Had he not feared that a guard must be stationed outside, he would have attempted to escape into the forest.

Now that the danger was passed he laughed at it. But though he made light of his own fears, he did not underrate the risk incurred on his account by stout-hearted William Penderel and his devoted wife.

Later on, Trusty Dick made his appearance. It appeared that the faithful fellow had resolved, if the king had been captured by Colonel James, to rescue him or perish in the attempt; and with this view he had hastily assembled his brothers—John, Humphrey, and George, together with his brother-in-law, Francis Yates.

Armed with pikes and bills, they had laid in wait for the troopers, near the house, but as the men came forth without their prey, and had evidently failed in their design, the devoted little band separated, and each man hurried back to his abode—George to White Ladies, John to his little farm, Humphrey to the mill, and Francis Yates to his cottage —rejoicing that their services had not been required.

"But before parting," said Dick, in conclusion, "we all agreed to meet here to-night to escort your majesty to Moseley Old Hall."

From this simple statement, Charles comprehended how well he was guarded over by these brave and loyal brothers.

---

## CHAPTER III.

HOW THE KING RODE THE MILLER'S HORSE; AND HOW HE WAS ESCORTED
DURING HIS RIDE.

As it was not likely, after the strict search that had just taken place, that another visit would be paid to Boscobel by the troopers, Charles felt quite easy, and passed the remainder of the day in tranquil meditation.

While sitting by himself in the oak parlour, he revolved his plans for the future, should he be happily restored to his kingdom, and formed many noble resolutions which would have greatly elevated his character as a sovereign if they had been carried out.

At this period of his career Charles was unspoiled, and if his higher qualities had been called into play, and his unquestionable military genius fully developed, he might have proved himself worthy of his grandsire, on his mother's side, the great Henry the Fourth of France.

Above all, his heart was uncorrupted and his kindly disposition had not hardened into selfishness. His natural gaiety never deserted him, and his constitutional indifference to danger sustained him under the most trying circumstances. Possible perils were never allowed to weigh upon his mind, and in thus acting he showed true philosophy. His unconcern astonished all who came near him, and Joan and her husband could not sufficiently admire his liveliness of manner. Whether he was quite so free from anxiety as he appeared may be questioned, but at any rate he wore a very pleasant mask.

To such a point did he carry his rashness, that at the risk of being seen by an enemy on the watch, he strolled forth into the garden, and sat for some time in the little arbour.

As soon as it grew dusk, and they could steal through the forest unperceived, the king's promised escort began to appear; each stout fellow being armed with pike or bill, as he had been in the morning, when the brave little band had resolved to effect Charles's rescue.

First to arrive was James Yates, who had married a sister of the Penderels. The king had seen him before, as he had served under Charles Giffard, at Worcester, and had guided the royal fugitive to White Ladies. James Yates was stoutly made, and had a soldier-like bearing, but he was not so largely proportioned as his brothers-in-law. However, he was as loyal as they were, and just as ready to shed his blood in the good cause. We grieve to say that he suffered for his loyalty, being executed at a subsequent date at Chester. Charles was very glad to see him, and possibly the gracious words then addressed to him by the king may have cheered the brave fellow's latest moments.

Ere long the others arrived, and now that they were all assembled, armed and accoutred in the best way they could, Charles thought he had never seen a finer set of men.

" With such a body-guard I shall not fear the enemy," he said.

" Your majesty shall not be taken, while we can defend you," they cried with one voice.

" I hope you have brought your horse for me, Humphrey?" said the king.

" Ay, sire," replied the sturdy miller. " Robin is already in the barn."

" 'Tis well!" cried Charles. " Now sit down to supper, and mind me not."

The king had already supped, and supped very heartily, for his misfortunes had not taken away his appetite, but his majesty ate little in comparison with those who followed him.

It was wonderful to see how quickly the heaped up trenchers were cleared, and how soon the tall tankard of ale was emptied. But the trenchers were filled again, and so was the tall tankard, though only to be emptied once more.   Luckily, there was enough and to spare, for Joan knew the powers of her guests, and had provided accordingly.

When the plain but plentiful repast was ended, and the horn cups were filled for the last time, the stalwart brethren arose, and drank the king's health and confusion to his enemies; after which, William Penderel asked pardon for the freedom they had taken, and declared the impulse was uncontrollable, adding that whenever it pleased his majesty to set forth they were ready to attend him.

Charles sighed, for he was unwilling to depart.

However, there was no help.   So he took leave of Dame Joan, expressing his deep sense of the great services she and her husband had rendered him, and promising to reward them adequately, if he should ever be able to do so.

"I have every belief that a time will come, when I shall be able to prove my gratitude to you, my good dame, and to your worthy husband —indeed, to all my good friends and servants whom I see around me, and then be sure that I will not forget you, one and all.   Trust to my royal word."

"We want no reward, my liege," said William Penderel.   "What we have done has been from pure devotion to your majesty, and from no sordid motive."

"That is quite true," cried the others, "and we entreat your majesty to believe what William says."

"I firmly believe it," said the king.   "Loyal and disinterested you must be, or you would never serve a fugitive king, who can reward you only with promises.   But I shall not forget your services—yours, especially, my good dame.   And now adieu," he added, taking Joan's hand, and preventing her from making the profound obeisance she meditated.   "We shall meet again in happier days."

So saying, he quitted the house by the back door, followed by William Penderel and his sturdy brothers and brother-in-law.

The miller's horse—a short, well set, strong animal, which in these days would be described as a stout cob—was brought out of the barn by his master, who held the bridle while the king mounted.

Meantime, Joan had come forth with a lantern, and its light showed a curious scene—all the stalwart brothers, armed with their bills and pikes, grouped around the king, who was now in the saddle—while William Penderel was arranging the order of march.

With the king's approval, it was settled that Humphrey and John should form the advanced guard, while the rear should be brought up by George Penderel and Francis Yates.   William and Trusty Dick were to march on either side of his majesty, who was well pleased to have their companionship, as they were his favourites.   Till this moment Charles had not formed an exact notion of William Penderel's height, and he was surprised to find that the gigantic forester stood on a level with him, though he himself was seated on the mill-horse.

Before the little band got into the order of march, William Penderel said to his brothers, in deep impressive accents which vibrated through the king's breast, and moved him greatly:

"His majesty needs no assurance of our fidelity. Nevertheless, since he has deigned to choose us as his guards, let us swear by all we hold sacred to defend him to the last, and against all odds."

"We swear it," cried the others. "We will die before harm shall befal him."

Charles thanked them earnestly for their zeal, adding that he well knew their oath would be kept.

The brave little band then quitted the yard in the order prescribed.

Proud of the trust reposed in them, the loyal brothers almost hoped that their fidelity might be proved. Woe to any rebel patrol that might attempt to stop them! In addition to their wood-bills, William and Trusty Dick had each a pistol—taken from Madmannah. But it was not in their weapons, but in their stout hearts, and strong thews and sinews, that Charles had the greatest reliance. Perhaps, no monarch ever had such an escort as he now possessed in those hardy foresters.

Just has Charles rode out of the yard with a guard on either side, he saw Dame Joan standing at the door with the lantern in her hand, straining her eyes through the gloom, and shouted an adieu to her. This was the last he beheld of the faithful creature.

After passing some outbuildings, the party came in front of the house, which presented a long irregular outline. The night was not dark, for the moon, then in its first quarter, had just risen, and its beams illumined the gables and black and white chequer-work of the old hunting-lodge.

Not without emotion did Charles contemplate the huge fantastic chimney-stack, in the recesses of which he had been hidden; while the little arbour, which next caught his eye, excited a different kind of interest. Mentally he bade farewell to a spot which he felt would always have interest for him. Yet strange to say, though he often spoke of Boscobel in after times, he never revisited the house.

"Take me past the oak," he said to Trusty Dick. "I desire to see the tree once more."

Word to this effect was given to those in advance, but they had anticipated his majesty's wishes, and intended to take him past the royal oak.

Shortly afterwards the party halted beside the noble tree. How beautiful it looked at that hour! its summit silvered by the moonlight, while a few beams found their way through openings in the branches, and fell upon the massive stem. Charles was enchanted.

"Truly that is a royal tree!" he thought. "How majestic it looks among the oaks that surround it, though they are all noble trees, and how it lords it over them—like a king among his peers!" He then added aloud to Trusty Dick, "But for you, my good friend, I should not have made acquaintance with this grand old tree, and I should therefore have lost some of the happiest moments of my life, for though in great jeopardy, I was never happier than during my day's sojourn in the oak; and if I am spared I shall ever look back to the time with satisfaction. Farewell, old tree!" he added. "May I spend another happy day amid thy friendly boughs!"

He then moved on, and the party took their way through a thicket, where the moon's radiance being intercepted by the branches overhead, it was so dark that they could not see many yards before them, and they had to proceed with great caution—the advanced guard halting ever and anon. But nothing occurred to cause them alarm.

At length they reached an opening in the wood, and a broad moonlit glade lay before them, but they hesitated to cross it, and kept among the trees; and the prudence of the step was shown a few minutes afterwards, when a patrol, whom they must infallibly have encountered had they gone straight on, appeared on the lawn.

The sight of the enemy aroused the choler of the loyal brothers, and Humphrey expressed a strong desire to give the knaves a drubbing, but, of course, he was not allowed to gratify his inclination.

There were no witnesses of the passage of the king and his companions through the forest—but had there been, the sight would have been worth viewing. Those dark gigantic figures indistinctly seen among the trees looked strange and mysterious. And when the party issued forth into some more open spot not overhung by boughs, so that the moonlight fell upon them and cast their black shadows on the ground, they looked still more unearthly. Despite the peril to which he was exposed, and the many difficulties and hindrances he had to undergo, the king enjoyed the ride. He would have enjoyed it still more if the horse he bestrode had been less rough of motion. But his majesty's seat in the saddle was far from easy.

At last he lost all patience, and exclaimed :

" Plague take thy horse, Humphrey ! Never before was I so jolted."

But his good humour was instantly restored by the miller's ready response.

" Generally, Robin goes well enough," said Humphrey. " But your majesty must consider that he has now got the weight of three kingdoms on his back."

Charles laughed, and made no further complaint.

---

## CHAPTER IV.

### WHERE THE KING FOUND JASPER.

Not long afterwards, they reached Chillington Park, but they did not enter it as Father Huddlestone and his companions had done by the avenue gate, but at the back of the hall where the wood was thickest.

This part of the park was overrun with bushes, and it was here, in Rock's Coppice, as it was called, that the dry pit was situated to which Madmannah had been brought. They forced their way, not without some difficulty, through this broad barrier of brushwood, and then a most charming scene burst upon them for which the king was not at all prepared—having heard no description of it.

At the bottom of a long and deep valley, which constituted the most beautiful feature of the park, were several large pools. In later times these pools have been thrown together so as to form an extensive lake, which has been further embellished with a bridge, boat-houses, and fishing-houses; but at the period of our history the valley was left in its wild natural state, and had an air of seclusion which gave it a charm almost as great as that possessed by the present ornamental lake. The high banks on either side were clothed with magnificent timber, and many trees grew so near the pools as to overshadow them.

Charles first beheld this exquisite scene from an elevation commanding the whole length of the valley, and the numerous sheets of water fringed by trees and glittering in the moonlight produced a truly magical effect, that filled him with rapture.

He halted for a short time to gaze at it, and while his eye wandered over the pool immediately beneath him he fancied he descried a boat stealing along under the shadow of the trees on the further side of the pool, and pointed out the object to Trusty Dick, who was standing beside him.

" Your majesty is right," said Dick. " 'Tis the fishing-boat belonging to the pool. I know it well—having often used it. There is only one person in it now—and that person, unless I am very much mistaken, is no other than the page Jasper. How say'st thou, William?" he added, appealing to his elder brother.

"I am of the same opinion," replied William. " I believe it to be Jasper."

" Oddsfish! this is strange!" exclaimed the king; " give him a signal that we are here."

Upon this, Trusty Dick descended the bank, and approaching the margin of the pool, gave a loud whistle.

The signal did not require to be repeated. In another moment the boat was seen to cross the pool, and now that the bright moonlight fell upon it there could be no doubt that its occupant was Jasper.

A few strokes of the oar brought the page to the spot where Trusty Dick was standing, and with very little delay they mounted the bank together, and came to the king.

" How is it that I find you here?" cried Charles. " Are you alone?"

" Quite alone, sire," replied Jasper. " Major Careless and Father Huddlestone have left me. But your majesty shall hear what has happened. Having been told that Colonel James and his troopers had left Chillington House, we were foolish enough to go thither, and found it in a terrible state, everything knocked to pieces by the rebel soldiers. While Major Careless and the priest went up-stairs to see what further damage had been done, I remained below, and being tired, presently fell asleep on a bench in the hall.

" I was awakened by a great noise in front of the house, and your majesty may conceive my fright when I found that a small detachment of troopers had just arrived. At this moment, I heard Major Careless call me, and not knowing what to do ran up the great staircase, but could find no one. Listening, I heard that the troopers had come in, so I did not dare to go down, but hid myself in a closet, and did not quit it for some time, when finding all quiet, I stole forth, and descended by a back staircase. But this very nearly led to my capture, for some of the troopers were in the kitchen. Fortunately, they were eating and drinking at the time, and did not perceive me, so I hastily retreated and went up-stairs again as quietly as I could.

" After this narrow escape I did not dare to make another attempt at flight, but wandered about among the deserted rooms during the rest of the day. Though I was tired to death of my confinement, I was not troubled by the troopers, for none of them came up-stairs, though I could hear them moving about below.

" At length, to my great delight, it began to grow dark, and I hoped my hour of deliverance was at hand. Taking every precaution, I once more descended the back staircase, and approached the kitchen. No one was there. But the troopers had only just left, for I heard them ride out of the court-yard. On the table were the remains of their repast, and your majesty will not wonder that I picked up all the fragments I could find when you consider that I had eaten nothing since I left Boscobel in the morning."

" I fear you made a very scanty meal," said Charles, compassionately.

" No, indeed, my liege, I got quite enough, and having satisfied my appetite, I quitted the house at the back, and very soon gained the park. Being totally unacquainted with the place I knew not which way to shape my course, and was afraid of losing myself, but I had heard Father Huddlestone say that your majesty and your escort would be sure to pass through this part of the park, so I determined to look out for you.

" When I left Chillington House it was almost dark, but the moon had now risen, and revealed all the beauties of the scene. I wandered on insensibly till I came to this valley, when my further progress was checked by the pool, and I should have turned back had I not discovered a boat moored to the bank. I immediately availed myself of this mode of crossing, but I had only just got into the boat and begun to use the oars, when I heard sounds on the opposite bank that convinced me some persons were there. I hoped it might be your majesty and your attendants, but not feeling quite sure, I thought it best to keep in the shade lest I might be caught in a trap. Your majesty knows the rest, and I have only to beg pardon for my long and tedious narration."

" You have had adventures enough to-day to last you your life," laughed Charles. " But we must not stop here longer. Get up behind me. My horse is somewhat rough, but he is strong enough to carry double."

" He has carried honest Humphrey and Mistress Jane Lane, so I think he will be able to carry me," replied Jasper.

And assisted by Trusty Dick, he sprang up behind the king. Robin's broad back afforded a very comfortable seat, and the page held on securely by the king's girdle.

Once more in motion, the little band, which had now got a slight addition to its numbers, took its way through the woods that hemmed in the long valley. Frequent glimpses were caught of the shining pools as they passed along, and so beautiful was this part of the park, that it was not without regret that Charles quitted it.

The park being enclosed by high pales, they had to make for a gate, and the nearest place of exit being on the Codsall side, they proceeded in that direction, and soon issued forth on a wide heath, which spread out for several miles.

The district that now lay before them was rendered exceedingly picturesque by its undulating surface, and by the patches of gorse that covered it. Here and there arose a knoll crowned with trees. On the right the heath extended to the little village of Codsall, but on this side, there was more wood. Before them, and reaching almost as far as Pendeford, whither they were bound, was a broad uncultivated tract, almost destitute of trees, yet not without a charm of its own.

Viewed, indeed, on a moonlight night like this, when its harsher features were subdued, and its beauties heightened, the heath presented a very lovely picture.

The night, however, was much too bright and fine for the king's escort, who would have preferred a sky covered with heavy black clouds, and not a star visible. They consulted together for a few moments in a low tone, but did not communicate their fears to the king.

" Your attendants do not like crossing this moonlight heath, my liege," whispered the page.

" So I perceive," rejoined Charles. " Hark ye, my friends," he added to his guard ; " we shall be very much exposed methinks, on this heath. Is there no other road ?"

" None, my liege, without going too far about," rejoined William Penderel. " Yon clump of trees is our mark," he added, pointing to a distant eminence. " Those trees are not far from Moseley Old Hall. Heaven grant we may get there in safety !"

They then set off across the heath, and the stalwart brothers marched on as blithely as if they had felt no apprehension. Charles, too, appeared unconcerned, though it may be doubted whether he was not more uneasy than his guards ; but the page gazed timorously around, expecting every instant to behold a party of the enemy start up from the furze bushes.

---

## CHAPTER V.

### BY WHAT DEVICE THE KING ESCAPED BEING CAPTURED BY COLONEL ASHENHURST.

If the king and his escort formed a very striking picture while involved in the forest, the little band looked infinitely more picturesque as they wended their way across the heath. They had begun to dismiss their fears, when, on a sudden, the greatest consternation was caused by the appearance of a detachment of troopers advancing towards them.

The detachment, which seemed to consist of about a dozen men, with an officer at their head, was about half a mile off, and had hitherto been concealed from view by the inequality of the ground. It was now in full sight, and it became clear from the accelerated pace of the enemy that they themselves were perceived.

What was to be done ? Retreat was out of the question, for they were certain to be pursued and captured. They must prove their valour in the defence of the king.

At this anxious moment the ready-witted page called out :

"Fighting is useless against such odds. We must resort to stratagem. Listen to me, loyal foresters. For a short time you must become rascally Roundheads. Pretend you have taken a couple of prisoners— the prisoners to be represented by his majesty and myself. Furthermore, give it out that we are both badly wounded. Do you understand?"

"Ay, we understand well enough," replied Trusty Dick, "and 'tis to be hoped the rogues will believe we are brother rogues, and let us pass. After all, we can but fight it out. But what says your majesty?"

"I like the plan," said the king. "With a little management I doubt not we shall be able to impose upon the rascals. But we must lose no time in preparation. This morning my nose bled profusely. I looked upon it then as a bad omen, but now I regard the matter differently."

And as he spoke, he bound his bloodstained kerchief round his brows, so as to give himself the appearance of a wounded man.

Jasper at the same time tied a kerchief round his left arm, and both put on the appearance of great exhaustion—Charles allowing his head to droop upon his breast.

"Now march on boldly, brothers," said the elder Penderel. "All will depend upon our firmness."

As they went on, William and Trusty Dick kept close to the supposed prisoners.

Presently the detachment came up.

Drawing up his men so as to bar the way, the officer called out in a loud authoritative voice :

"Halt! and give an account of yourselves. Are you good and true men?"

"Good and true men, and friends of the Commonwealth," replied John Penderel, boldly. "Heaven pardon me for the lie," he muttered.

"So far well," said the officer. "But who have you got with you on horseback?"

"A wounded malignant and his servant, who is likewise wounded," replied Humphrey. "The Cavalier is disguised in the garb of a forester, as you see, but he could not 'scape us."

"Where are you conveying the prisoners?" demanded the officer.

"We are taking them to Codsall, and shall deliver them to Colonel Ashenhurst."

"I am Colonel Ashenhurst," replied the officer.

Taken aback by the answer, the sturdy miller did not know what to say. But William Penderel came to his relief.

"Shall we deliver the prisoners to you here, colonel?" he said, "or shall we take them on to Codsall? Since we have come thus far, it matters not if we go a little further. We have been to Chillington House, but did not find Colonel James there."

"Colonel James hath just changed his quarters, and is gone to Brewood," replied Ashenhurst. "Is the chief prisoner badly hurt?"

"He is wounded in the head," rejoined William Penderel. "I do not think he can live long."

"Nay, then, take him and his attendant to Codsall," said Colonel

Ashenhurst. " I have other business on hand, and do not desire to go back. I trust to make an important capture before morn. A couple of my men shall go with you, if you desire it, but I cannot very well spare them."

" I thank your honour—but we do not require them," replied William Penderel.

" You will find a physician at Codsall, who will attend to the wounded malignant," continued Colonel Ashenhurst.

" I don't think any physician will do him much good," said Humphrey, unable to resist the jest. " Your honour is scarcely likely to find him—alive, I mean—on your return."

Colonel Ashenhurst did not hear the remark. He had no suspicion whatever of the trick played him, and ordered his men to ride on, gladdening the hearts of the stalwart brothers by his departure.

" I owe my preservation to you, Jasper," said Charles, as he removed the kerchief from his brow.

" Ay, but for this stratagem your majesty might have been captured," remarked Trusty Dick. " I tremble to think of it."

" You have something more to do, Dick," said Jasper. " You must invent some probable story to account for your not delivering the prisoners at Codsall."

" True," cried Charles. " I fear you may suffer on my account."

" Think not of us," said Trusty Dick. " We must take our chance. 'Tis sufficient that your majesty has escaped."

The road to Codsall lay on the right, but Charles and his companions had no intention of taking it, even as a feint, for Colonel Ashenhurst and his troop were already out of sight. Though anticipating no further danger, they quickened their pace, and soon reached Long Birch.

The portion of the heath they now entered on was wilder than that which they had previously traversed, but there was a tolerably good road across it, and this eventually brought them to the banks of the little river Penk.

About half a mile lower down, this stream turned a mill, and the party now proceeded in that direction, it having been previously arranged that the king should dismount at Pendeford Mill, as it was called, and perform the rest of the journey on foot, and attended only by half his escort, so that his arrival at Moseley Old Hall might not be discovered.

As he was here obliged to part with Jasper, Humphrey Penderel undertook to find the page a secure place of refuge at the mill.

" I know Timothy Croft, the miller, and his wife to be good, honest folks," said Humphrey. " The youth will be perfectly safe with them."

" I will tell Major Careless where he may find thee," said the king to Jasper, " and no doubt thou wilt see him ere long. Thou hast done me good service, and I shall not be unmindful of it. Adieu!"

He then gave him his hand, and the page pressed it devotedly to his lips.

The three persons chosen to attend the king were William, Trusty Dick, and John, and having bidden a kindly farewell to the others, his majesty set off with his guard.

He had not gone far, however, when, turning his head, he saw those he had left standing together, and looking very sad, whereupon he hurried back, and said a few more gracious words to them. His majesty felt that he could not sufficiently thank the brave men who had hazarded their lives for him without fee or reward.

Moseley Old Hall was about two miles from Pendeford Mill, and the heath having been left behind since they had crossed the Penk, the whole aspect of the country had changed, and the road led through narrow green lanes shaded with trees.

Now and then they passed a quiet homestead, surrounded by orchards, or a cottage, and occasionally heard the barking of a dog,. but with these exceptions the whole region seemed buried in slumber.

At length, after a quick walk of rather more than half an hour, they came in sight of an ancient mansion, somewhat resembling Boscobel, but larger and loftier, and far more imposing in appearance.

---

## CHAPTER VI.

HOW THE KING BADE FAREWELL TO THE PENDERELS; AND HOW HIS MAJESTY
WAS RECEIVED BY MR. THOMAS WHITGREAVE OF MOSELEY OLD HALL.

MOSELEY OLD HALL, which we rejoice to say belongs to a direct descendant of the zealous Roman Catholic gentleman who owned it at the period of our story, is one of those charming and picturesque black and white houses that date back to the middle of the sixteenth century; when our old English architecture was in its perfection, and delights the eye with its irregular frontage, its numerous gables, bay windows, projections, and huge stacks of chimneys.

Even now there is an air of seclusion about Moseley Old Hall, but at the period of which we treat, it was almost surrounded by trees, and though there were one or two habitations near it—much nearer than its owner liked—it had a look of extreme privacy.

The house was large, and contained numerous apartments of all sizes. Indeed, it contained some rooms that were never seen by all its inmates, though it was whispered about among the servants that there were closed up passages leading no one knew whither—perhaps to vaults, secret chambers, and secret closets.

These rumours were not altogether unfounded. Like their friends and neighbours the Giffards, the Whitgreaves had adhered firmly to the old religion, and, like them, had found it necessary to contrive hiding-places for priests and recusants. Many such existed at Moseley Old Hall, and some are still extant.

Descended from an ancient Staffordshire family, who had dwelt at Burton, Thomas Whitgreave, owner of Moseley Old Hall, in 1651, had served during the early part of the Civil Wars under Captain Thomas Giffard, and had distinguished himself for his bravery; but having received a severe wound, from which he was some time in recovering, he retired to his old family mansion, and took no further part in the struggle. Still, his zeal for the cause of monarchy was ardent as ever, and his sympathies being entirely for the young king, he was deeply afflicted by the disastrous result of the Battle of Worcester.

Thomas Whitgreave was still young—at all events, he was not more than thirty-five—tall, and handsome, with a grave but kindly expression of countenance. At the time he received the king, he was unmarried, but his mother, a remarkable old lady, resided with him. Mrs. Whitgreave was as staunch a Royalist as her son, and daily invoked Heaven's vengeance upon the regicide Cromwell.

Mr. Whitgreave kept up a good establishment, though not a large retinue of servants. His domestic chaplain was Father Huddlestone, and he behaved with the greatest consideration to the good priest, not only assigning him rooms for study and devotion, but allowing him to take a couple of pupils. Father Huddlestone was very useful in the house, and, without being meddlesome, exercised a beneficial influence over the family. Mrs. Whitgreave was a devotee, and as scrupulous in the performance of her religious duties as if she had belonged to a convent. A chaplain, therefore, was a necessity to her, and no one could have better discharged the sacred office than Father Huddlestone. Not only did the good priest improve the household by his councils, but his society was extremely agreeable to the master of the house.

Such was the constitution of Moseley Old Hall at the time when the fugitive king was received within it.

Among the Roman Catholic gentry of the period, all of whom were Royalists, there was necessarily a good deal of private communication, conducted chiefly through the medium of the priests. Thus secret intelligence was conveyed to Father Huddlestone of the king's arrival at White Ladies, and it was through Father Huddlestone that John Penderel was enabled to secure a place of refuge for Lord Wilmot. It was from the same quarter that the fugitive king's movements were first made known to the good priest and his patron.

Every preparation had been made at Moseley Old Hall so that the king could be got into the house secretly.

It being now past midnight, all the servants had long since retired to rest. Four persons only were on the alert. These were Lord Wilmot, who remained in his bedchamber; Father Huddlestone, who was stationed in a close, called the Moore, adjoining the mansion; Mr. Whitgreave, who had repaired to another close, called Allport's Leasow, and concealed himself in a dry pit, covered with trees; and Major Careless, who was watching for the king and his companions at the entrance of a long lime-tree walk that led to the ancient mansion.

Careless had to wait there more than an hour, but at length was rewarded by the appearance of the party, and satisfied that he could not be mistaken, went forth to meet them.

A cordial greeting passed between Charles and his favourite, and the latter heartily congratulated his majesty on his safe arrival.

"I had begun to feel somewhat uneasy," he said. "But I knew your majesty was well guarded."

"Truly, I have been well guarded," said Charles, looking gratefully at his attendants. "But thou wilt be astonished to hear that we have had an encounter with Colonel Ashenhurst. We owe our escape to a device of that clever little page, Jasper."

"What do I hear?" cried Careless. "Has your majesty seen Jasper?"

"I have only just parted with him," replied Charles. "Nay, do not trouble yourself. He is safe enough. I left him at Pendeford Mill."

"This is good news, indeed!" cried Careless, joyfully.

"I knew it would delight thee," said Charles, smiling. "But let us to the house. Art thou appointed to do the honours?"

"Mr. Whitgreave is at hand," replied Careless. "If your majesty will be pleased to walk on a little further, I will present him to you. You will find him a most excellent host."

They then marched quickly along the lime-tree walk, until they came to the close which we have said was designated Allport's Leasow.

Here Careless gave the signal agreed upon, and Mr. Whitgreave, who had passed a very anxious hour in the dry pit, immediately issued forth from it.

"Do not present him," said the king, in a low voice, as his host approached. "I should like to see whether he will recognise me."

For a moment or two, Mr. Whitgreave was perplexed.

With the exception of Careless all the group were habited alike in foresters' attire, but the stalwart Penderels were not to be mistaken, so after a second survey Mr. Whitgreave no longer hesitated, but threw himself at the feet of the right person, exclaiming:

"This, I am certain, is my royal master."

"You are right, Mr. Whitgreave," rejoined Charles, giving him his hand to kiss. "But oddsfish! I should not have been offended if you had not known me in this garb—though I cannot be ashamed of it, since it is worn by such brave and faithful fellows as these, who have protected me at the hazard of their lives. May I never want such defenders as you and your brothers!" he added, to William Penderel.

"We have simply done our duty, my liege," replied William.

"If others do their duty as well, I shall have reason to be thankful," said Charles, earnestly. "Mr. Whitgreave," he added, "you will excuse me, but since I must now part with these faithful men, I must tell them what I feel in your hearing—and in your hearing too, father," he continued, as the good priest, who having become aware of the king's arrival, had come up. "To all the brothers Penderel I owe much, but to the courage and fidelity of William and Trusty Dick I undoubtedly owe my preservation. Let what I now say be remembered, and repeated to me hereafter, should the great services they have rendered me be inadequately requited when I have the power to requite them. Farewell, my good and faithful friends!" he continued, with an emotion that he did not seek to repress. "Farewell!"

"Must we quit you, my liege?" cried Trusty Dick. "We will quit our homes and all dear to us to follow your majesty's fortunes."

"It cannot be," rejoined Charles. "I am fully sensible of your devotion, but we must part. You would only be a hindrance to me. Farewell! farewell!"

And he stretched out his hand, which the stalwart brothers seized and pressed to their lips.

"Mr. Whitgreave," he added, "you will take care of these brave men."

"They shall have the best the buttery can afford, my liege," replied Whitgreave. "And I will attend to them myself, as I must needs do, seeing that all my servants are abed. Father Huddlestone will conduct your majesty to the house."

Bestowing a last look at the three stalwart brothers, who seemed greatly dejected, Charles, accompanied by Careless, followed Father Huddlestone to the house.

Entering at the rear of the mansion, Father Huddlestone took the king and Careless up a back staircase with cautious steps, and as they neared the summit they perceived a dark figure retreating noiselessly down a passage.

Aware that this was Lord Wilmot, Charles kept silence till he had entered his lordship's room, which was situated at the end of the passage, and he then gave utterance to his satisfaction.

Lord Wilmot, as the reader is aware, was a special favourite of the king, and his majesty had more dependence upon him than upon any one else, save Careless. Lord Wilmot must not be confounded with his son, the dissolute Earl of Rochester, who figured some years afterwards at the court of the Merry Monarch. A brave, chivalrous nobleman, he was able to act as a sort of Mentor to the king.

Lord Wilmot had, in fact, belonged to the court of Charles I., and had acquired the grave manners of that period. Tall and strongly built, he had handsome, expressive features. The Earl of Rochester, as is well known, could successfully counterfeit any part he pleased, but he did not inherit his talent any more than his vices from his father, who could never be prevailed upon to assume a disguise, declaring that, if he did so, he should infallibly be found out.

Seeing that the king looked much fatigued with his journey, Lord Wilmot besought him to postpone all conversation till he had taken some refreshment, and opening a cupboard his lordship produced some cates and a flask of canary.

Charles sat down, and emptying a goblet of generous wine, insisted upon all the others following his example, and while they were doing so a gentle tap was heard at the door, which was opened by Father Huddlestone, and Mr. Whitgreave came in.

"What of my faithful attendants—the Penderels?" cried the king. "Have they been well cared for? Pardon the question, Mr. Whitgreave. I am sure they have."

"They are gone, my liege," replied Whitgreave. "And I must say that I never saw men more grieved to part with a master than these loyal-hearted fellows are to quit your majesty."

"Say you sooth?" cried Charles.

"Your majesty shall judge," replied Whitgreave. "I took them to the buttery, where I have often seen each and all of them make a hearty meal, and where there was plenty of cold meat, and bade them fall to and spare not. They declined. And when I pressed them further, saying they would discredit my house if they went away without supper, they said they had no appetite. 'No appetite!' I exclaimed. 'How is this?' But I soon found out what was the matter. Each honest heart was full, and wanted relief. A single morsel of meat would have choked any one of them. However, they drank a cup of ale to your majesty's health."

"And they are gone?" cried Charles. "I should have liked to see their honest faces once more."

"Your majesty knows where to find them should you again require their services," said Mr. Whitgreave. "And I am sure nothing will delight them more than to have another opportunity of proving their fidelity."

But circumstances, as will be seen as we proceed with our narrative, did not allow Charles to employ any one of the stalwart brothers again. Their part in our story is played. Yet before dismissing them, we would express our genuine admiration of the loyal men we have endeavoured to depict. In describing them we have not gone beyond the truth; nor endowed them with heroic qualities they did not possess. The Penderel brothers were men of unwavering loyalty, brave as faithful, and possessed of such extraordinary strength as rendered them truly formidable antagonists. Fortunately, they were not called upon to display their valour in action. Had they been required to defend the king from an attack during the nocturnal ride from Boscobel to Moseley Old Hall, which we have just described, it is certain they would have done tremendous execution upon his foes, and have delivered him, or died in his defence. That their loyal hearts could not harbour a thought of treason, or quail before peril, we have shown. Their devotion to the fugitive monarch, and the important services they rendered him in his hour of need, have gained them a page in England's history. Very pleasant has it been to chronicle their actions, and we part from them with regret.

---

## CHAPTER VII.

### HOW THE KING WAS PRESENTED TO MRS. WHITGREAVE.

Though the night was now far spent, and he had undergone great fatigue, Charles felt so happy in the society of Lord Wilmot and the others, that he was unwilling to retire to rest, and remained for some time in conversation with the party. Not before three o'clock in the morning, did he ask his host where he was to sleep.

Mr. Whitgreave conducted him to a large chamber panelled with black oak, in which stood an old-fashioned bedstead, with heavy furniture, and a carved canopy almost touching the ceiling.

While looking at this large comfortable bed, Charles feared Mr. Whitgreave would tell him that his safety demanded that he should sleep in some secret closet; but no such suggestion was made.

"I am delighted with my room," said the king to his host; "but where are the hiding-places? I should like to see them, in case an emergency should arise."

"I intended to show them to you to-morrow, my liege," replied Mr. Whitgreave. "But you shall see them at once."

With this he led the king along a narrow passage to another chamber, in which there was a small bed.

"This is my room," said Careless, who accompanied them. "But I am quite ready to give it up to your majesty, should you prefer it to the large oak chamber you have just seen."

"I have no such desire," rejoined Charles.

"Wait till you have seen the arrangements, my liege," said Careless.

"This room has a false floor, my liege," he said, "and beneath is a narrow passage leading to the ground floor by the brewhouse chimney. But this I will more fully explain to your majesty on the morrow."

"Enough," replied Charles. "I am quite content with what I have seen. I shall now sleep soundly."

He then returned to the oak chamber, and his recent privations made him greatly enjoy the luxury of the large and comfortable bed.

Every possible precaution was taken by Mr. Whitgreave and Father Huddlestone to prevent any of the household from obtaining sight of the king. The servants were given to understand that a fugitive Cavalier had arrived at the house during the night, and was lodged in the oak bedchamber, but they believed him to be a relative of their master, and had no suspicion whatever of the truth.

Charles slept very soundly in his large and comfortable bed, and when he awoke he found Careless watching beside him. After the customary morning salutations had passed between them, Careless pointed to a rich velvet suit spread out on a fauteuil, and said:

"I pray your majesty to look at these habiliments. Your worthy host hopes you will deign to wear them during your stay at Moseley Hall."

"Faith! I am infinitely obliged by the attention," replied Charles. "Pray is Mr. Whitgreave married?"

"Not yet, sire," replied Careless. "But his mother resides with him, and Father Huddlestone tells me the old lady is wonderfully anxious to be presented to your majesty."

"Oddsfish! she must be content to see me in my peasant's costume," said Charles. "Had she been young and fair I might have put on that rich suit to please her. I shall only require some clean linen."

"A shirt is already provided for you, sire, as you perceive," replied Careless.

"'Sdeath! I can never wear that fine shirt," cried Charles. "The laced ruffles would betray me at once."

"Well, here is a country noggen shirt, with coarse hosen to match. Do they please you, sire?"

"The noggen shirt and rough hose will suit me exactly," said the king. "As a punishment for tempting me with fine linen, thou shalt help to resume my disguise."

"Willingly, sire. I am here for the purpose of helping you to make your toilette."

Once more habited in his forester's dress, to which he had now become accustomed, Charles was cautiously conducted by Careless to the library, where he found Lord Wilmot, with his host and Father Huddlestone.

His majesty was received with more ceremony than he liked, and he put an end to it by sitting down to the breakfast prepared for him, and begging the others to join him. They excused themselves, alleging that they had already breakfasted, but Careless having no such excuse to offer, obeyed without the slightest hesitation. The king, however, could not prevent his host and Father Huddlestone from serving him.

Charles was in very good spirits, chatted familiarly with every one present, and seemed to make light of all difficulties and dangers. Mr. Whitgreave was quite surprised by his cheerfulness, and could not help expressing admiration at the manner in which his majesty bore his misfortunes.

"I never suffer myself to be cast down," said the king. "And I have hitherto found my courage rise in proportion to the dangers by which I have been surrounded."

"With the spirit you possess, my liege, and with Heaven's support," observed Father Huddlestone, who was standing by, "you cannot fail to overcome all difficulties, and must regain the throne."

"I trust your prediction will be fulfilled, father," replied Charles. "I can afford to wait. After the failure of my great enterprise, nothing more can be done in England at present. Another army cannot be raised. My object, as you are aware, is to reach the coast and embark for France. But I am environed by enemies."

"This reminds me, sire," said Whitgreave, "that my mother has just received a message, brought by a faithful emissary from Bentley House, which it may import you to hear, as I think it concerns your majesty."

"I must chide you for not presenting your mother to me ere this, Mr. Whitgreave," said Charles. "It will delight me to see her."

"The omission shall be repaired at once, sire," replied Whitgreave.

Making an obeisance, he quitted the library, and presently returned with a tall elderly dame, who had still to some extent preserved her good looks.

Mr. Whitgreave led his mother by the hand towards the king, who saluted her very graciously and prevented her from kneeling, telling her with many kind expressions how much he was indebted to her son for receiving him at this perilous juncture.

"Ah, sire," she exclaimed, "my son and myself are only too proud to receive you, and would sacrifice our lives to accomplish your deliverance. Jane Lane, who is devoted to your majesty, and whom I love dearly as a daughter, has just sent a message to me to say that her brother has obtained a pass from Captain Stone, governor of Stafford, for herself and a groom to go into the west."

And she paused.

"Well, madam, what more?" asked Charles.

"I scarcely dare venture to propose that your majesty should perform the part of a groom, yet seeing you in this garb——"

"Hesitate not to make the suggestion, madam," interrupted the king. "So far from regarding it as a degradation, I shall be delighted to act as Jane Lane's groom. The proposal meets my wishes exactly, and seems to offer me the chance I so eagerly desire of reaching the coast. What sort of person is Captain Stone?"

" A fierce Parliamentarian," replied Whitgreave. " I have reason to remember him. At the conclusion of the Civil Wars he came hither in quest of me, and searched the house most rigorously. But I had taken refuge in one of the hiding-places, and escaped his vigilance."

" The circumstance you mention not only illustrates Captain Stone's character, but proves the security of the hiding-place," observed Charles. He then turned to Lord Wilmot, and said, " It strikes me very forcibly, Wilmot, that this pass must have been procured for you."

" Very likely, Colonel Lane obtained it for me," was the reply. " But I gladly resign it to your majesty."

" Nay, I cannot take your place," said the king.

" You will deeply hurt me by a refusal, sire," said Lord Wilmot. " And now a word to you, Mr. Whitgreave, and I beg your particular attention to what I am about to say. Should any search be made by the rebels for the king while I am in your house, I desire that I may be given up, in order to divert them from his majesty."

" I have not been consulted, Mr. Whitgreave," said Charles. " And I peremptorily forbid you to act as directed by Lord Wilmot. Let no more be said on the subject."

Mr. Whitgreave bowed.

At this juncture, Mrs. Whitgreave, fancying she might be in the way, craved permission to retire, and made a profound obeisance to the king, who conducted her to the door.

---

## CHAPTER VIII.

### HOW TWO SPIES CAME BY NIGHT TO MOSELEY OLD HALL.

" I HAVE a suggestion to make, my liege," said Lord Wilmot, as Charles came back. " On consideration, I think it will be best that I should proceed to Bentley House at once. There I can be of use to your majesty, whereas my presence here rather tends to imperil you. Major Careless can accompany me, if he pleases, and return to let you know when Mistress Jane Lane is ready to set forth on her journey."

" Good," replied the king. " Does Lord Wilmot's proposition meet with your approval?" he added to Careless.

" Perfectly," was the reply. " If your majesty can dispense with my personal services during your sojourn here, I think I can be better employed in acting as a messenger. If I should unluckily fall into the enemy's hands, they will get little out of me. Moreover, if the rogues should get on your track, I will engage to mislead them."

" I have every reliance upon thee," said Charles. " But, faith! I shall be sorry to lose thee."

Almost immediately after the conference just described, his majesty repaired with his attendants to the room above the porch, the latticed windows of which commanded the approach to the house, and of course a sharp look out was kept, but the only persons who came near the place were some wounded soldiers, one of whom Charles recognised as belonging to his own guard, and it distressed him exceedingly that he could not speak with the poor fellow. Mr. Whitgreave, however, and Father Huddlestone gave the men relief, but did not dare to invite them into the house.

About this time Careless disappeared, and was not seen again for two or three hours. When an opportunity occurred, the king questioned him as to the cause of his absence, and Careless owned that he had been at Pendeford Mill, but had not seen Jasper. The page was gone. He had departed early in the morning, the miller said, without mentioning whither he was going.

"You need not be uneasy about him," remarked Charles with a laugh. "He is born under a lucky star, and like myself, as I hope and believe, will escape his enemies. Very probably, you will hear of him at Bentley House."

Careless thought so too, and though disappointed, did not allow himself to be cast down.

No troopers were seen that day, but Careless was able to account for their non-appearance, Croft, the miller, having informed him that the patrols had gone in a different direction, and he added a distressing piece of intelligence, to the effect that Colonel Ashenhurst had paid a visit to Boscobel House, and allowed his men to plunder it.

The king, with Lord Wilmot and Careless, dined in the library, where they were less liable to observation than they would have been in any other room. No servants were present, and Mr. Whitgreave and Father Huddlestone again waited on his majesty.

As soon as the household had retired to rest, Lord Wilmot and Careless took leave of the king, and were conducted by Father Huddlestone to the close called Allport's Leasow, where they found Mr. Whitgreave with a couple of steeds, ready saddled and bridled.

Mounting without a moment's loss of time, they bade him and Father Huddlestone good night, and rode off very quietly, till they were far enough from the house, as they judged, to accelerate their pace with safety. They then galloped off in the direction of Bentley House.

After their departure the king remained for some time alone in the room over the porch. Not daring to burn a light, he could not read, and having no inclination for slumber, he was obliged to occupy himself with his own thoughts, and having much to meditate upon, he fell into a deep reverie.

At last he roused himself, and finding that the moon had arisen in the interim, moved towards the lattice window, and gazed at the lovely scene without.

Seen by moonlight, the picturesque old mansion had a most charming effect, but only certain portions of it were visible from the projecting window at which he stood, and he had surveyed with admiration all that came within his ken, when his eye was caught by a glittering steel cap which could just be seen above the garden wall.

A mounted trooper, it appeared, had raised himself in the saddle, and was peering inquisitively at the house.

More careful examination showed the king that the trooper had a comrade with him, the latter being on foot, and armed with a carabine.

Even at that distance, and by that light, Charles recognised the foremost trooper. The man's features were too marked to be mistaken; and, besides, circumstances had fixed them on his memory. It was Madmannah. And Charles did not for a moment doubt that the other was Ezra. Like bloodhounds these two men seemed ever on his track, and the dread that they might hunt him down at last, for a moment shook him.

At this moment the door was softly opened, and Father Huddlestone came in.

"I came to warn your majesty," he said. "But I find you have discovered those two spies."

"Yes, I see them plainly enough," replied the king. "And I can tell you something about them, father, that you would hardly guess. Those are the two rogues who tried to capture me in the oak."

"Is it possible, sire?" exclaimed the priest. "They will fail as they did then. The saints who have your majesty in their guard will thwart their evil designs. Mr. Whitgreave, being somewhat fatigued, has retired to rest. But he bade me call him on the instant if any danger threatened. I will do so now."

"Stay an instant, father," said the king. "I am unwilling to disturb him without cause. I think those two spies are only reconnoitring the house, and do not design to attempt an entrance now."

"Oh! the treacherous villains!" cried Father Huddlestone. "Were I to point them out to my patron, he would fire upon them and destroy them."

"Then do not wake him," said Charles. "I see no cause for apprehension. Look! they are marching off."

"Truly, they are moving, sire, but they have not finished their survey. Having examined the front, they are going to the back of the house."

"You are right, father," replied Charles.

**END OF BOOK THE FOURTH.**

---

# Book the Fifth.

### JANE LANE.

---

## CHAPTER I.

#### BY WHOM THE TWO SPIES WERE PUT TO FLIGHT.

IN order that they might watch the proceedings of the two spies, Father Huddlestone took the king to his own room, the windows of which commanded the rear of the house. For a few minutes nothing could be seen of the troopers, and the watchers began to think they must have departed, when the two men were observed creeping stealthily past the outbuildings on the left.   Both being on foot, it seemed clear that they designed to enter the house.

Becoming seriously alarmed, Father Huddlestone besought the king to retire to his hiding-place, while he himself called up Mr. Whitgreave, when the clatter of horses' hoofs was heard rapidly approaching, and almost immediately afterwards Charles and his companion perceived two horsemen enter the close, known as Allport's Leasow.

As a matter of course, the arrival of the horsemen had been heard by the troopers as well as by the king and his companion, and alarmed by the untoward circumstance, the Roundheads abandoned their design upon the house, and hurriedly made for the spot where Madmannah had tied up his horse.   This was a gate opening upon the close, but before they could reach it, they were confronted by the horsemen, who drew their swords, and prepared to attack them, thus clearly proving themselves to be Royalists.

As an answer to this threat of the Cavaliers, Ezra discharged his carabine at the foremost of them, but evidently without effect, for the individual he had aimed at uttered a fierce exclamation, and would certainly have cut down the trooper, if the gate had not hindered him, and during the time required to force it open, Ezra had made good his retreat.   Nor did Madmannah stand his ground.   When his comrade took to his heels, he fled likewise, and they both sought refuge in the grove that skirted the close.   Here they were quickly pursued by the Cavaliers, who did not rest till they had driven them away from the house, Madmannah's horse being seized upon as lawful spoil by the victors.

Charles and Father Huddlestone were still standing at the window looking out upon the scene, though all those engaged in the conflict had disappeared, when Mr. Whitgreave, who had been roused by the report of the carabine, entered the room, and learnt what had occurred.

"Who can those Cavaliers be?" inquired the king.   "'Tis strange they should have arrived so opportunely."

"Perhaps Major Careless has returned, my liege, and has brought Colonel Lane with him," observed Mr. Whitgreave.   "No other persons would be likely to come here to-night.   I will go forth and see."

Mr. Whitgreave's conjecture proved correct.   By the time he reached the close, Careless and Colonel Lane had returned to it, and they then explained that they had come to conduct the king to Bentley House.

"I do not think his majesty could safely remain here another day, Mr. Whitgreave," said Colonel Lane.   "I have been given to understand that Captain Stone, the governor of Stafford Castle, intends to search this house to-morrow, and to bring Southall, the redoubted priest-catcher, with him.   It seems quite certain that, in some way or other, the king has been tracked to Moseley Hall, and I am therefore of opinion that he ought to change his quarters without delay."

"I do not believe that even Southall will discover the hiding-places in my house," rejoined Whitgreave.   "Still, the king ought not to be exposed to any risk that can be avoided; and if you are prepared to receive him at Bentley House, I think he had best go there to-night.   At all events, after what you tell me of Captain Stone's threatened visit, I should not dare to oppose the plan."

Mr. Whitgreave then returned to the house, and told the king what he had seen and heard.

"Your two faithful adherents are waiting to take you hence, sire," he said. "Colonel Lane affirms," he added, with a sigh, "that my house is no longer a safe place of refuge for your majesty, and though I cannot agree with him, I will not urge you to stay."

"I did not expect this sudden summons, I confess, Mr. Whitgreave," rejoined the king; "and I need not say it is far from agreeable to me. But I have no option. From the appearance of those two spies I am convinced that my retreat has been discovered, and if Colonel Lane had not come for me, I should have deemed it prudent to leave before daybreak. I hope you will not suffer for the devotion you have shown me. But I shall ever remain your debtor." Then, turning to Father Huddlestone, he added, "It might be enough for me to tell you that I shall always think the better of your religion since I have seen how well you practise it, but when I reflect on the many good and faithful subjects you have brought me in these evil times, when almost every hand is raised against me, I feel that I should be ungrateful if I did not say how deeply I am beholden to you. You have made the Penderels what they are, and what I have found them—the truest men living."

"Through Heaven's grace I have made them what they ought to be, my liege," said Father Huddlestone. "I have always striven against those who have sought to overthrow the throne. It is possible that Heaven may have further trials in store for your majesty, to which I earnestly exhort you to submit with patience, but I feel assured that in due season you will be amply rewarded. Place your trust in Heaven, sire, and you will be delivered from your enemies. It may be long ere you regain your kingdom, but the day *will* come—provided you are true to Heaven. Forsake not God, and you shall not be forsaken!"

Charles remained silent for a few moments, and then said in a low tone:

"I will strive to follow your counsel, father."

The king was still pondering on what had been said to him, when Mrs. Whitgreave, bearing a taper, entered the room. Robed in white, and looking excessively pale, she looked like an apparition.

Advancing to meet her, Charles said:

"I should have been sorry to quit Moseley Hall without bidding you adieu, madam, but I trust you have not been disturbed from your slumbers on my account."

"I keep long vigils, sire, and often pass the greater part of the night in prayer," she replied. "When my son tapped at my door just now to inform me that your majesty was about to depart, I was praying for your safety."

"I thank you, madam," replied the king, much moved. "The prayers of so excellent a lady must avail me."

"If I live to see your majesty restored to your kingdom, I shall have lived long enough. Here is a little relic," she said, offering him a small silver box. "I dare say your majesty has no faith in such things—nevertheless, I pray you to wear it."

"I will wear it for your sake, madam," he rejoined, taking the little silver box, "and I shall have no doubt of its efficacy."

Charles would then have taken leave of the loyal-hearted dame, but she besought permission to attend him to the outer door.

Accordingly, the whole party quitted the room, and proceeding as noiselessly as possible, descended the great oak staircase to the hall, where Charles bade adieu to the excellent old lady, and quitted the house, attended by his host and Father Huddlestone.

Left by herself, Mrs. Whitgreave's strength almost forsook her. On regaining her own chamber, she knelt down before a crucifix, placed in a small recess, and again offered up prayers for the king's deliverance from his enemies.

Meanwhile, Charles had proceeded to Allport's Leasow, where he found his faithful adherents waiting for him, and saluted them most cordially.

"I did not expect you quite so soon, Colonel Lane," he said. "But you have arrived in the very nick of time. Without you and Careless we might have had some trouble with those rascally troopers."

"I am only sorry they escaped us," replied Colonel Lane.

"Here is the horse we have taken, my liege," said Careless, who had dismounted, and was holding both steeds by the bridle. "Will you mount him? 'Twill be a good jest to say that I have taken the rogue's horse."

"Oddsfish! the horse is well enough," cried Charles, as he vaulted into the saddle. "These Roundhead knaves have robbed all the best stables."

The party being now ready to set forth, Mr. Whitgreave approached the king, and asked if his majesty had any further commands for him.

"My last injunctions to you are, Mr. Whitgreave, that you come to me at Whitehall, and bring Father Huddlestone with you. I defer all expressions of my thanks till I see you both there. May the good time arrive speedily!"

After receiving the good priest's valedictory benediction, he rode out of the close with his attendants.

At first, the party proceeded at a foot's pace, and they had not gone far, when the king halted for a moment to gaze at the old mansion, which was seen to the greatest advantage on that bright moonlight night. It looked so hushed in repose that no one would have dreamed that its quietude could have been recently disturbed.

But Charles was not allowed to indulge his meditations long. Colonel Lane was impatient to be gone, and after another look at the picturesque old mansion, the king was obliged to bid farewell to Moseley Hall.

---

## CHAPTER II.

### HOW THE KING ARRIVED AT BENTLEY HOUSE.

THE night was so enchanting, that although the king was not without apprehensions of a chance encounter with the enemy, he greatly enjoyed his ride. Moreover, he was very well pleased with the rooper's horse on which he was mounted.

Colonel Lane acted as leader of the party, and took them across a common, now known as Cooke's Gorse, past Essington Mill, and then over another common to Allen's Rough. More heath still lay before them, and having traversed a very wild district, they reached an extensive coppice, which formed part of Colonel Lane's own estate. During the whole ride, they had scarcely seen a habitation, and had not encountered a single individual. Deeming the danger over, Colonel Lane slackened his pace, and began to converse with the king. telling his majesty that he thought his horse had gone remarkably well.

"I think so too, colonel," replied Charles. "What is more, I am of opinion that this is not the first time I have ridden him."

"Indeed, sire!" exclaimed Colonel Lane, in surprise.

"Unless I am greatly mistaken, this is the very horse I rode from Worcester to White Ladies. I know his action. How say you, Careless?"

"It certainly did not occur to me before, my liege," replied Careless. "But now I look at the horse more closely I believe your majesty is right."

"You will be able to settle the question, Colonel Lane," observed Charles. "I gave the Worcester horse to you at White Ladies. What became of him afterwards?"

"I lost him in the fight near Newport, where Lord Derby was worsted by Lilburn and Colonel James. Possibly he may have fallen into the hands of one of the troopers."

"It must be so," exclaimed Charles. "Oddsfish! 'tis a strange circumstance. Now that I have got the horse again, I will not part with him if I can help it."

"Doubtless, he is well worth keeping," observed Careless; "but he may be recognised by the rascally trooper, and the discovery would endanger your majesty."

"The risk is so slight that I shall not heed it," said Charles.

Passing through the coppice they soon afterwards entered a park, in the midst of which stood Bentley House.

This fine old mansion has been since pulled down, and replaced by a modern structure, which, though handsome and commodious, does not of course possess the historic interest of the earlier building. With its ornamented gables, projections, and large windows, Bentley House presented a very imposing front, but it was at the back that the party arrived, and as they rode into the court-yard, a faithful groom, who was waiting for his master's return, came forth from the stables with a lantern and took charge of the horses. Whatever he thought, this trusty fellow manifested no surprise that the colonel and Careless should have a common woodman in their company.

"My man, Lutwyche, thinks you are a fugitive Cavalier, sire," remarked Colonel Lane. "He is thoroughly honest and loyal, but I do not mean to trust him with the great secret. Thank Heaven I have brought your majesty here in safety, and I trust no harm will befal you while you are my guest. You may sleep soundly, for I shall remain on guard during the remainder of the night. It distresses me that I am obliged to offer you such poor accommodation, but if a larger room were assigned you suspicion would be excited.  At any rate, you will be more comfortably lodged than in the secret closet at Boscobel House."

"Pray make no apologies, colonel," said Charles.  "The size of the room is a matter of perfect indifference to me.  Put me where you please."

Entering by the back door, they then proceeded to Colonel Lane's study, where they found Lord Wilmot, who was delighted to see the king, and congratulated him on his safe arrival.  Being much fatigued, Charles begged to be conducted to his room without delay, whereupon Colonel Lane, with a thousand apologies, took him to a small chamber at the top of the house.  Small as it was, the couch appeared extremely comfortable to the wearied monarch, who sank into a deep, unbroken, slumber, from which he was aroused by Careless.  Fain would he have slept a few hours longer ; but that was quite impossible, as Careless informed him.

"It appears to me," said Careless, seating himself at the king's bed-side, "that your majesty does not exactly comprehend what you will have to do, and I think I had better explain matters to you.  In the first place, Mistress Jane Lane sets out early this morning on the pretext of a visit to her relatives the Nortons, of Abbots Leigh, and you will attend her in the capacity of groom."

"But Abbots Leigh is near Bristol," said the king.  "She cannot possibly get there to-day."

"She has no such intention," replied Careless.  "She will proceed first to Packington Hall, where a halt will be made for an hour or so.  Sir Clement Fisher has been apprised of the visit, and will be prepared for your majesty's reception."

"Good," said the king, "I shall be glad to see Sir Clement.  "But where am I to rest for the night ?"

"At Long Marston, near Stratford-on-Avon, the residence of Mr. Tombs, who is a near relative of the Lanes, and a staunch adherent of your majesty."

"Mr. Tombs is a true man—of that I am quite sure," rejoined Charles.  "I shall be quite content to stay at his house."

"Your majesty, I think, understands that Mistress Jane Lane has got a pass for herself and her servant?"

"Yes.  I am to be her groom.  I quite understand it.  Did you imagine I could have any disinclination for the part, after all I have gone through ?  I shall be delighted to act as groom to so charming a person as Jane Lane."

"Then I may as well state, without further preamble, that I have brought your majesty a costume suitable to the part you will have to enact—grey doublet and hose, as you will see.  The garments were made for Colonel Lane's groom, Lutwyche—but I am sure they will fit you.  Here are boots and a hat to complete the disguise.  The arrangement appears to me extremely pleasant, and I should be very happy to take your majesty's place, if I were permitted."

"Are you to be left behind with Lord Wilmot ?" asked the king.

"No, sire," replied Careless.  "His lordship and myself will attend you—but at a respectful distance.  You will be accompanied by Mr. and

Mrs. Petre. Mrs. Petre, I must inform your majesty, is Jane Lane's sister. It is proper you should know that neither Mrs. Petre nor her husband have the slighest idea that they will have the honour of attending upon your majesty."

The king then arose, and assisted by Careless, put on the suit of dark grey cloth provided for him. When he was fully equipped, he said to Careless:

" How think you, Will? Shall I pass muster? Do I look like a groom ?"

" Your appearance is all that can be desired, my liege," replied Careless. " But you must take care not to betray yourself by any inadvertence. Come down to the stables with me, and I will get Lutwyche to give you some instructions in the part you will have to play."

" Oddsfish! I flatter myself I can groom a horse," cried Charles. " 'Tis true I have not had much practice."

" You will be none the worse for a lesson, my liege," said Careless. " This woodman's garb must not be seen," he added, putting the disguise abandoned by Charles into a small valise, which he had brought with him. " I must needs ask your majesty to carry this portmanteau. And please to bear in mind, that you are now Will Jones, the son of one of Colonel Lane's tenants."

He then left the room, but had not taken many steps down the staircase, when he called out in a loud voice,

" Art thou coming, Will? Never was there so lazy a rascal."

" I am quite ready, your honour," replied Charles, following with the pormanteau.

---

## CHAPTER III.

### HOW WILL JONES FOUND A FRIEND IN THE STABLE.

As they passed through the back part of the house on the way to the stables, they met two or three women-servants, who glanced inquisitively at the new groom, and thought him a good-looking young fellow. In the court-yard they found Colonel Lane and Lord Wilmot. The former was talking with his head falconer, Randal Gates, and telling him that he should require the hawks and spaniels after breakfast.

" I mean to give this gentleman, Mr. Harris," he said, glancing at Lord Wilmot, " a little sport. My sister is going to Long Marston, and we will ride with her as far as Packington Hall."

" The hawks and spaniels shall be ready for you, colonel, whenever you require them, and as there are plenty of partridges in the corn-fields, I make no doubt you will be able to show Mr. Harris some good sport."

The falconer then retired, and Colonel Lane turned to bid Careless good morning—glancing significantly at the same time at the king, who stood respectfully aside with his cap in his hand.

" Maybe you don't know me, colonel," said Charles, with an awkward bow.

"Oh! yes, I know thee well enough, Will," replied Colonel Lane. "Thou art David Jones's son, and my sister's new groom. I hope thou wilt serve her well. Put down thy portmanteau and come with me to the stables."

Charles obeyed, and followed Colonel Lane and the others to the stables, which were very large, but there were not many horses in the stalls. Lutwyche came forward as his master entered with the others. He stared when he saw the king in his groom's attire, and a cunning smile lighted up his hard features.

"This is Will Jones, my sister's new groom, Lutwyche," said the colonel. "Explain to him what he will have to do."

"I should guess he has not had much experience, colonel," replied the old groom with a grin. "Mistress Jane, I understand, is going to Bristol, but she has not yet told me which horse she will ride. Her favourite steed has not been right since she returned from Worcester. She can't take him. The horse that came in last night is strong enough to carry double, and I think would do very well."

"Ay, he is a good horse," replied the colonel, in a doubtful tone. "But there are some objections to him."

"I don't see 'em," said the groom. "I wish your honour would just look at him. I fancy he did some hard work yesterday, but he seems quite fresh this morning."

The whole party then went to look at the horse, and he certainly seemed to deserve the groom's praises.

As Charles went into the stall and patted him, the horse turned round and whinnied gently, as if in recognition.

"He knows you, Will Jones," remarked Lutwyche.

"Ay, that's plain enough," replied the king. Then turning to Colonel Lane, he added, "Your honour seems to have some objections to this horse, or I would make bold to recommend him for the journey. Were I allowed the choice, I should prefer him to any other horse in the stable."

"Well, since you like him so much, Will, e'en take him," said the colonel. "My sister ought to have been consulted on the point, but I have no doubt she will be content."

"Here comes the fair lady herself," cried Lord Wilmot, as Jane entered the stable.

While saluting the rest of the party, she looked round for the king, and discovering him, greeted him with a smile.

Charles then came out of the stall, and making a rustic bow, inquired whether she had any commands for him.

"I am glad to find thou hast arrived safely, Will," she said. "But I have no special orders to give thee, except that thou must be ready to start soon after breakfast."

"I shall be ready at any moment you may require me," replied Charles.

"Will this horse suit you, Jane?" asked her brother.

"Perfectly," she replied. "I have been admiring him ever since I came into the stable. Since I cannot have my favourite steed, this will make an excellent substitute. Where did you procure him?"

"Never mind where I got him," replied her brother. "I rode him at Newport, and lost him there, but he has since been captured from a Roundhead trooper, who might recognise him."

After consulting the king by a glance, Jane said, "I will have that horse, and no other."

Colonel Lane shrugged his shoulders and went out of the stables, followed by the others.

As soon as they were gone, Lutwyche said to the king:

"I don't want to know who you are, but I am certain you are not a groom. Go into the house and breakfast comfortably. I will get all ready for the journey."

Charles thanked him heartily, and telling him he placed entire faith in him. quitted the stable, and proceeded to the house.

<hr>

## CHAPTER IV.

### HOW WILL JONES BREAKFASTED WITH THE MEN-SERVANTS IN THE BUTTERY.

ENTERING the buttery hatch, the king found the men-servants assembled at their morning meal. They were breakfasting very substantially on cold roast beef and ale. Concluding that he was the new groom, they asked him to join them, and Mr. March, the butler, who sat at the head of the table, and was treated with much respect by the others, carved him some slices of meat, and bade him fill his cup freely from the big brown jug before him.

"You will find the ale good in this house, young man, I'll warrant you," observed Mr. March, whose stout person showed that he drank plenty of it himself. "We brew no small beer here. You are lucky in getting the place, let me tell you—all the more lucky that our young lady never before had a groom to attend her."

"That's very true, Mr. March," said one of the men. "Mistress Jane would never ride on a pillion with old Lutwyche. This young man may therefore consider himself highly honoured."

"Will Jones I believe is your name," said the butler. "Well, then, Will, you look like an honest young man—a simple young man, I may say—but you may be a very great rogue for all that." Here there was a general laugh, in which Charles himself joined good humouredly. "Nay, I mean no offence," pursued Mr. March. "I repeat, you look like an honest young man, but you may be a Roundhead, and all Roundheads are rogues. Am I not right?" he cried to the others.

General assent to the proposition.

"You see what sort of society you are in, young man, and can draw your own conclusions," pursued the butler. "There may be good fellowship amongst us, or there may not, according as we find you. What are your principles—Royalist or Republican?"

"I am as staunch a Royalist as yourself, Mr. March," rejoined Charles, sturdily.

"Give me your hand. Now that we know your principles, we can trust you, and talk freely. This is a Royalist house. All within it are sworn to the king. Our honoured master, the colonel, fought for his majesty at Worcester, and we should have fought for him had we been there. Our young mistress rendered the king great service."

"Ay, that she did," cried Charles, earnestly—"services he ought never to forget."

"Ay, she's a brave young lady," said March, "and has more spirit in her than many a man. If the king could be saved by a woman, Mistress Jane is the one to do it."

"What has become of the king since Worcester fight?" inquired the supposed groom.

"Thou canst keep a secret, Will Jones?—ha!"

"Ay, marry, can I," was the answer.

"But swear thou wilt not reveal what I shall disclose to thee."

"If an oath be necessary, I swear to keep silence."

"Then learn that his sacred majesty is in this house. He came here yesterday. I recognised him at once, and let him see that I did so."

"Did he admit his high rank?"

"Not exactly—but he didn't deny it. Thou thyself hast seen and conversed with him!"

Will Jones expressed his astonishment.

"Yes, he went with thee to the stables this morning."

"Was that the king?" cried Will Jones. "I should never have thought it."

"Wherefore not? Undoubtedly the person in question is much handsomer than his majesty is reported, for the Roundheads always paint him in black colours—but 'tis the king I will maintain."

At this moment Careless entered the buttery, and looked around as if in quest of some one.

"'Tis he!" exclaimed the butler, rising.

All the other servants rose at the same time, but Will Jones went on quietly with his breakfast.

"Get up," said March, in a low tone. "I tell thee 'tis the king."

"I am not supposed to know him," replied Will Jones.

"Don't disturb yourselves, I beg," said Careless. "When thou hast finished breakfast, Will, I want to speak to thee."

"I shall have done directly," rejoined the disguised groom, regardless of the butler's glances.

"Was there ever such an oaf!" cried March, in a low voice. "Has your majesty any commands that I can execute?" he added, stepping forward and making a profound obeisance to Careless.

"Hush!" exclaimed the other. "You will betray me."

"No fear of Will Jones, my liege," rejoined March. "A dolt, but trusty. Your majesty may take him into your confidence."

"He knows who I am, then?" said Careless.

"He does, my liege. I made the revelation to him under a solemn pledge of secrecy. I hope I have not done wrong."

"If a mistake has been made, 'tis too late now to remedy it," said Careless.

"No harm has been done, I can assure your majesty. I'll answer for

the young man. Will Jones!" he cried authoritatively, "dost not perceive that thou art wanted?"

But the obstinate groom refused to move.

"Let him finish his breakfast, and then send him after me to the
stables," said Careless, quitting the buttery.

"Is this thy respect for the king, sirrah?" cried March, rushing to
the table, and snatching away the plate which the supposed Will Jones
had just filled. "Not another mouthful shalt thou eat. After his
majesty at once, and crave pardon for thy ill manners."

"He has interfered with my breakfast," grumbled Will Jones.

"Interfered with thee! Thou hast eaten too much already. Begone!"

But the imperturbable Will Jones deliberately filled a horn cup with
ale, emptied it, and then marched off, leaving the butler and the other
servants perfectly astounded at his coolness.

---

## CHAPTER V.

### HOW THEY SET OUT ON THE JOURNEY.

About half an hour afterwards, Charles, fully equipped for the
journey, rode round from the stable to the front of the house. He was
mounted on the horse about which there had been so much discussion,
and had a pillion behind him, and a musket at the saddle-bow. He
was accompanied by Lutwyche, who was likewise mounted on a
"double horse," intended for Mr. Petre and his wife.

It may be incidentally remarked that this sociable and agreeable mode
of travelling was customary at the time, and continued to be common
enough in certain parts of the country up to the close of the last century,
and even later.

Having arrived in the middle of the night, Charles had scarcely seen
the old mansion, but while waiting with Lutwyche for the coming
forth of the party, he had an opportunity of examining it, and was much
struck with its aspect. Ordinarily, it must be owned the house had a
somewhat gloomy look, but it was seen to peculiar advantage on that
bright and cheerful September morning, and Charles thought he could
have passed a few days there very pleasantly, if his enemies would have
allowed him.

He was still surveying the house, noting its picturesque outline of
gables, when the front door was thrown open by March, the butler, and
several persons issued forth. Foremost among them was Mr. Petre, a
stout, hearty country gentleman, with nothing very remarkable about
him. Mr. Petre was of a good Buckinghamshire family, and was
married, as we have already intimated, to Jane Lane's elder sister. He
was closely followed by his wife, who possessed considerable personal
attractions, and behind Mrs. Petre came Jane Lane and her mother.
Mrs. Lane was a sister of Sir Hervey Bagot, of Blithfield, and a very
fine old gentlewoman.

The horses were now led to the door, and Mr. and Mrs. Petre having mounted, the king's turn came. He was not very successful in his first essay, and got sharply reprimanded for his awkwardness by Mrs. Lane. Totally unacquainted with the real rank of the supposed groom, the old lady had regarded him curiously, and was quite puzzled by his appearance and manner. She felt sure he did not understand his work, and wondered that Colonel Lane should engage such a man. But when Will Jones in assisting his young mistress to mount her horse, despite all hints given him, offered her the wrong hand, the old lady could no longer contain herself, but called out:

"Why, how now, thou clumsy fellow! Art thou such a blockhead as not to know thy right hand from the left? Thou art not fit for thy place."

"Chide him not, dear mother," said Jane. "He has had but little experience."

"So it would appear," replied the old lady, dryly.

"Excuse me, madam, I hope to do better in time," said Charles, modestly. "I shall use my best endeavours to please my young mistress."

As he spoke he sprang into the saddle with a grace and quickness that surprised the old lady.

"By my troth, now that he has taken his seat on horseback, the fellow looks like a Cavalier," remarked Mr. Petre to his wife.

"Yes; he may not understand the duties of a groom—but he sits a horse well—that's certain," replied Mrs. Petre.

At this juncture, a large party appeared at the other end of the terrace. Colonel Lane came from the stables accompanied by Lord Wilmot and Careless, and followed by Randal, the head falconer, bearing on his wrist a hawk in her hood and bewits. With Randal were two other falconers, one of whom was furnished with a hoop on which two or three hawks were perched, while the other had a hawking-pole and a couple of spaniels in leash.

Of course, Colonel Lane and his friends were on horseback, and the whole party, viewed in connexion with the old mansion, formed a cheerful picture, which the king contemplated with undisguised pleasure.

"Methinks Will Jones would prefer joining that hawking-party to riding on with me," remarked Jane, in a low voice.

Charles sighed, but made no other response.

At this moment Colonel Lane rode up to Mr. Petre, and said:

"Pray don't wait for us. We shall come on slowly, for we may chance on a heron in the park, and we are certain to find plenty of partridges in the corn-fields. We shall always be in your rear as a guard, and if we don't overtake you before, we shall find you at Packington Hall, where you will halt for a couple of hours."

Colonel Lane then rode up to Charles, and said, in a significant tone:

"Should anything happen on the road, Will, turn back and thou wilt find us."

Charles promised obedience, and doffing his cap to Mrs. Lane, who was exchanging adieux with Mr. Petre and his wife, rode on. Colonel Lane and his party did not follow them for some minutes, and by that time those in advance had nearly reached the gates of the park.

On gaining the high road to Darlaston and Wednesbury, the horsemen
proceeded side by side, in order that the ladies might converse together,
and Jane did not seem to feel the king's presence as a restraint, for she
chatted very pleasantly with her sister.   Charles, of course, took no part
in the conversation, and never spoke unless addressed, but he was amused
by what he heard.   Mrs. Petre talked about the events at Worcester,
and wished to have a particular description of the king from her sister.

"I have already described him to you," said Jane.

"Yes, you told me he did not realise the notions you had formed of
him; that his manner was somewhat light and reckless; and that he
wanted the gravity and dignity of his father."

"You must have misunderstood me," observed Jane, uneasily.   "I
said he had many royal and noble qualities."

"But you added that he rarely displayed them."

"If I said so, I did him an injustice.   I never think of his majesty—
never speak of him, save with enthusiasm."

"Colonel Lane is equally enthusiastic," remarked Mr. Petre.   "In
his eyes the king has not a fault."

"He is a brave and chivalrous monarch," cried Jane, "and deserves far
greater success than he has obtained."

"I am sure I should know the king were I to see him," observed Mr.
Petrie.   "Colonel Lane has often described him to me as tall and well-
made, but harsh-featured, and dark as a gipsy."

"Why that description would exactly apply to Will Jones," said Mrs.
Petrie.

"So it would," remarked her husband, laughing heartily.

Having passed through Wednesbury, they were now on the road to
Birmingham, but not desiring to enter the latter town, they soon struck
off into a by-road, which led them through a very beautiful country, where
one large park succeeded another, and the only houses that came in sight
were large and important.   Most of the persons who resided in these old
mansions were friends of the Lanes, but Jane and her sister called upon
none of them, but pursued their journey for nearly three hours without
halt of any kind.

Hitherto they had encountered no obstacle of any kind, and Charles,
though he ran the greatest risk, enjoyed the ride far more than any one
else in the party.   Without addressing him, Jane contrived to give him
such information as she thought would be interesting, and whenever they
skirted a large park, or came in sight of an ancient mansion, she mentioned the name of the owner.

Mrs. Petre was lively and chatty, but her husband was full of secret
anxiety, being apprehensive, as we have said, of an encounter with
Roundhead troopers.   This anxiety was entirely on his own account, for
he had no suspicion of the important charge committed to him.   Had
he been consulted, we fear he would have shrunk from such a heavy
responsibility.

## CHAPTER VI.

### WHAT PASSED BETWEEN WILL JONES AND THE BLACKSMITH.

They were now in the fair county of Warwick, and only a few miles from Packington Hall, the seat of Sir Clement Fisher. Crowning an eminence, said to be as high as any ground in England, this fine old mansion commanded a magnificent prospect over a most lovely country. From its elevated position, the stately pile could be descried afar, and on learning to whom it belonged, Charles regarded the house with great interest, and was well pleased by reflection that Jane might one day become its mistress. The mansion was embosomed in a grove haunted by rooks, and the park contained much noble timber.

Suddenly Mr. Petre called out to the supposed groom:

"Why, Will, thy horse has cast a shoe. Luckily, we are near a village, where thou wilt be sure to find a blacksmith."

Presently they came to a pretty little inn, very pleasantly situated on the outskirts of the village, and having a large tree in front of it, encircled by a bench. Here the party alighted, and Mr. Petre ordered a pottle of sack, while Charles took his horse to the smithy, which was at no great distance from the inn. Bryan Compton, the smith, was a big, burly fellow, with a broad honest face begrimed by smoke. His brawny arms were bared to the shoulder, and a leather apron was tied round his waist. Pleased by his physiognomy, Charles took it into his head that the man must be a Royalist, but in this he was mistaken. The blacksmith proved to be a sturdy, outspoken Republican.

Not happening to be busy at the time, Bryan set to work at once, and having selected an iron plate, was heating it in his forge, when Charles asked him, "What news?"

"Nay, I ought to ask you that question," rejoined Bryan. "We hear but little in this retired village, and I reckon it would be no news to you to learn that that harebrained Charles Stuart has been routed at Worcester. He deserved to be beaten if only for bringing the Scots to England."

"You are right," said Charles, "and I think he must have found out his mistake. It seems the Scots wouldn't stand by him."

"Stand by him : not they! They soon ran away from Old Noll. I hope they're all driven out of the country."

"But I've heard say there were many English nobles and gentlemen with Charles Stuart," remarked the king. "Have any of them been taken?"

"Not that I know of," replied the smith. "There's one person I should like to capture," he added, working away vigorously at the bellows.

"Ah! who's he?" inquired the supposed groom.

"Charles Stuart himself," rejoined the smith, placing the red-hot iron on the anvil and making the sparks fly about, as he hammered it into shape. "I wish I had the chance of taking him—ha! ha! But he's not likely to come this way." Then resting for a moment, he asked, "Where do you come from, friend—and where may you be going ?"

"I come from Bentley House with my young mistress, and am taking her to Packington Hall," replied Charles, readily.

"Why, then, you must be Mistress Jane Lane's groom," observed the smith. "The gossip hereabouts is that Sir Clement Fisher is betrothed to her. But I don't think the marriage will take place just yet."

"Wherefore not ?" inquired the king.

"Because Sir Clement has got himself into trouble by his foolish adherence to Charles Stuart. He is sure to be heavily fined, if not imprisoned. Why, you look confounded young man. Hold up your horse's foot while I clap on the shoe."

Charles complied, and nothing more passed between them until the smith had completed his job, when he remarked :

"This is a good horse of yours, friend. He would go a long way without tiring."

"Yes I have ridden him a good many miles at a stretch," rejoined Charles.

"Perchance from Worcester to Bentley House ?" remarked the smith, with a knowing look.

"Not quite so far as that," replied the king.

"Nay, I don't wish to appear inquisitive," said the smith. "I've heard that Colonel Lane was at Worcester, and I thought you might have been there with him."

"I am Mistress Jane Lane's servant, as I have already told you," said Charles.

"Mistress Jane was at Worcester as well as her brother, unless I have been misinformed," rejoined the smith.

Charles made no answer, but paid for the shoe, and departed.

"There's something odd about that young man," mused the smith, looking after him. "I should like to have questioned him a little more. However, I shan't forget him or his horse."

---

## CHAPTER VII.

### HOW THEY WERE RECEIVED AT PACKINGTON HALL.

MEANWHILE, Colonel Lane and his two companions had come up, and when Charles got back to the little inn, he found them seated on the bench beneath the tree. After enjoying half an hour's good sport, they had sent back the falconers with a few brace of partridges. Colonel Lane filled a cup of sack for the king, who took it with a grateful bow as beseemed the character he represented. Before they set off again, Careless contrived to exchange a few words in private with his majesty.

On quitting the village, the party entered the extensive and beautiful domains belonging to Packington Hall. The park contained a great deal of fine timber, and several large sheets of water could be descried through the trees, contributing greatly to its beauty.  The charm of the prospect was also heightened by the picturesque inequalities of the ground—the uplands being crowned by trees.   From all these heights enchanting prospects could be obtained.  The old mansion towards which they were riding was frequently lost to view, owing to the intervention of the trees, but reappeared with additional effect.

The party were within half a mile of the house, which was then in full view, when they were met by Sir Clement Fisher, who had been anxiously expecting their arrival.

Sir Clement looked somewhat depressed, but gave a warm welcome to his friends, and conducted them to the house.

With a special view to the king's convenience, the party alighted in the court-yard, and Sir Clement contrived that his majesty should be relieved from any duties in the stable, and taken at once to the buttery. It was excessively annoying to the loyal young baronet that he could not attend to the king in person—but that was impossible.  Even with his other guests great caution was observed—Major Careless's name was never mentioned, and Lord Wilmot's real rank was concealed from the servants.

Dinner was served in the great hall immediately after the arrival of the party.  Circumstances seeming to necessitate a slight alteration in the plans, it was now arranged that Colonel Lane, with Lord Wilmot and Careless, should stay where they were, while the others proceeded, as before settled, to Long Marston, in order to pass the night there.

Before Jane's departure an interview took place between her and her suitor.   They had walked to a retired part of the garden, but for some minutes each remained silent.  At length Sir Clement, looking at her earnestly, said, " I know the courage of your nature, Jane, and I will not, therefore, attempt to disguise from you the perilous position in which I am placed.   Had all gone well, I hoped to have made you mistress of this house ; but now you may never be mine."

"Do you say this to try me, Sir Clement?" she exclaimed, turning very pale.

" Alas, there is no exaggeration in what I am saying to you," he rejoined.   " Before you return I may be a prisoner in Warwick Castle."

" If you deem yourself in such great danger, why do you not fly?" she cried.

" No, I will stand my ground," he rejoined.   " Those who come to arrest me shall find me here.   I am prepared to die for the cause I have espoused."

" Oh ! do not talk thus, dear Sir Clement," she exclaimed.   " You give me credit for far more fortitude than I really possess.   Again, I entreat you to fly."

" My resolution is taken," he rejoined firmly, but sadly.   " But I wished to acquaint you with it, that you may judge me rightly.   Our union may be deferred for years, or it may never take place ; but I regard you as my wife."

" And if I wed not you, Sir Clement, be sure I will wed no other," she rejoined.   " I will not break my plighted troth.   We must bear these heavy trials with resignation, and perhaps we may be the better for them in the end. Our affection will be severely tested, but my feelings will undergo no change."

"Nor will mine," he added, taking her hand, and pressing it affectionately to his lips. "Jane," he added, in accents that bespoke his sincerity, "you are a noble girl. I always thought you. so; but now more than ever. Some men, incapable of estimating your character, might be jealous of the devotion you display to the king, but I have no such feeling. On the contrary, it excites my highest admiration. Nay, I think I should not love you so well, were you less loyal."

"Hear, also, the truth from me, Sir Clement," cried Jane, in a tone of exaltation; "I could but have loved you as I do, had you not been true to the king. That you would approve my conduct I never doubted, because you know my feelings, and can appreciate them; but I have also the approval of my own heart, for I am sure I am acting rightly. This firm conviction will sustain me through any trials that may be reserved for me. I am vowed to one object—the king's deliverance from his enemies. If I can accomplish it, I shall be content. Devoted loyalty like mine is perfectly compatible with love, for, though I am engrossed by it at present, it does not exclude the deeper feeling. Do you understand me?"

"Perfectly," he replied, clasping her to his breast. "You are my own Jane. Go on with your task. You are destined to be the king's preserver."

"I firmly believe so," cried a well-known voice that somewhat startled them at first, for they had not heard the approach of the speaker. It was the king, who had come to seek Jane, and had overheard the latter part of their discourse.

"I firmly believe you are destined to be my preserver, Jane," he said, stepping forward.

"I am not sorry that your majesty has heard the expression of my opinions," said Sir Clement. "Jane is free to act as she will, and I have no control over her; but had she been my wife, I should have charged her to act as she is doing."

"You will not repent your confidence in her, nor your reliance on me, Sir Clement," said Charles, with dignity. "All our difficulties will be overcome in time, and then you will have the best wife in England. Nay, be not cast down. 'Tis written that you shall be Jane Lane's husband. 'Tis written, also, that Jane shall be mistress of Packington Hall; for should you be deprived of it, you shall have the house back again if I come to the throne."

"Sire, after your gracious promise to me, I can no longer feel uneasiness," cried Sir Clement, shaking off the gloom that had hitherto oppressed him.

"As your groom," said Charles, bowing to Jane, "I come to inform you that Mr. and Mrs. Petre are already mounted, and waiting for you in the court-yard. Your own steed is ready."

Having delivered this message, he again bowed, and left the lovers together.

They followed him almost immediately to the court yard, where the rest of .

After some consultation with his friends, the king had determined to prosecute that day's journey without any additional attendance. Careless would fain have gone on to Stratford-on-Avon, but his royal master would not permit him, deeming it safer to proceed in this quiet manner than with an attendance liable to attract attention, and that might cause them to be stopped. It was therefore agreed that Lord Wilmot and Careless should follow their royal master next day. This could easily be done, as they knew the precise route he intended to take. Colonel Lane, not being required, was to remain at Packington Hall.

A tender parting between the lovers took place at the park-gates, which Charles from his proximity was obliged to witness.

The party, comprehending the same persons as heretofore, rode on in silence, and Charles fancied he saw tears stealing down Jane's cheeks; but she chased them away, and soon afterwards recovered her composure, and forced herself to enter into conversation with her sister and Mr. Petre.

Their road led them through beautiful country, and the contemplation of this charming scenery tended to tranquilise her mind. Sometimes they mounted a gentle hill which gave them an extensive view over wide-spread open fields, through which a river took its course, fertilising the district, and adding greatly to its beauty. Several mansions came within their ken; but the most picturesque feature of the scene was an old castle standing on the banks of the river. The view was so delightful that the party stopped for a few minutes to admire it.

As a scene that could not be beheld elsewhere than in England, it had a special charm for the king, who gazed at it with undisguised rapture. Chancing to look at him at the moment, Mr. Petre was struck by the singular expression of his countenance.

" You seem to be greatly pleased by the prospect, Will," he cried. " Have you never beheld it before ?"

Charles made no reply, and Jane touched his arm to recal him to his senses.

" Mr. Petre asks if you have ever beheld this view before," she said.

The supposed groom begged pardon, and said :

" I was looking at yon old castle, and thinking I should like to have it, with a few guns and a dozen artillerymen."

" Why, what wouldst thou do with the castle, Will ?"

" Hold it against Cromwell and the rebels," was the reply.

" Heaven help thee for a fool, Will !" cried Mr. Petre, laughing. " Thou wouldst fare no better than the king fared at Worcester."

----

## CHAPTER VIII.

HOW THEY WERE STOPPED BY THE TROOPERS AT WOOTTON WAWEN.

ONCE more the party were in motion, and they now proceeded along a road skirted by high hedges, that for a time shut out the view of the broad well-cultivated meadows on either side. For the most part, the persons they encountered on their way were husbandmen and common folk. Carts were frequently to be seen, and now and then a waggon with its team of strong horses. Occasionally they met a farmer and his wife on a "double horse," but none of the gentry of the neighbourhood. The latter evidently deemed it prudent to keep at home. Mr. Petre often pulled up to have a word with the husbandmen, and their talk was generally concerning the battle of Worcester. Many sympathised with the king for his misfortunes, and expressed concern at his defeat; but all blamed him for bringing the Scots to England.

Thus they journeyed on through a rich agricultural district, past farms and homesteads well stocked with cattle, till they came to a woody tract that had once formed part of the Forest of Arden, some vestiges of which could yet be discerned. These woodlands offered a pleasant contrast to the richly cultivated district just left behind, and having skirted a park, they reached the picturesque old town of Henley-in-Arden.

Here they halted, and while Charles, in his quality of groom, attended to the horses, Jane and the others went to view the old cross which then stood in the market-place. To support his character, Charles thought it necessary to drink a pot of ale with the ostler; and the man's tongue being loosened by the good liquor, he informed the king that about two hours previously a troop of horse had passed through the town on their way to Stratford-on-Avon.

"That doesn't matter to us, friend," said Charles. "We are on the right side, and belong to the Parliament."

"An that be so, you'll be glad to hear that the malignant prince has been captured," observed the ostler. "We shall have no further trouble with him."

"That's too good news to be true I fear, friend," rejoined Charles. "Where did you learn it?"

"From the troopers I've just mentioned. They couldn't be misinformed. Charles Stuart was caught in a woodcutter's hut in Brewood Forest. He fought so hard that it took ten men to secure him, and the reward will be divided among 'em, consequently, they'll only have a hundred apiece. Well, here's Old Noll's health, and hoping he may soon reign over us."

"Reign over us!" cried Charles.

"Ay, reign," said the ostler. "When he has cut off Charles Stuart's head he'll be King of England. He has got the army with him, and can do as he likes."

"He aims at the crown, I make no doubt," said Charles. "But here comes my young mistress. She'll be greatly surprised to learn that Charles Stuart is taken."

Having mounted their horses, the party quitted the little town and took the road to Stratford-on-Avon.

Mr. Petre was a good deal alarmed on hearing that a troop of soldiers had preceded them, but Jane sought to reassure him by saying that they should be able to pass through the town without being noticed by the men, and he made no more remarks till they drew near Wootton Wawen, a small town about [illegible] and Stratford.

He then discovered that some of the Roundheads must have halted in this little town, as a dozen troopers, at least, were refreshing themselves at the inn.   It was impossible to avoid them, except by making a considerable détour, and this the timorous gentleman declared he would do : and after some discussion he actually turned back with his wife, while Jane and the king rode boldly on towards Wootton.

As they approached the village, two mounted troopers barred the road, and ordered the supposed groom to halt and give an account of himself.

Before Charles could answer. an officer, fully accoutred. came forth from the inn with the evident intent of interrogating the travellers. But Jane anticipated his design, and holding out a piece of paper. exclaimed :

"I have a pass for myself and my man from Captain Stone, governor of Stafford.   Here it is."

The officer took the paper, and glancing at it, said, in a respectful tone :

"You are the lady herein described, I presume?"

"I am Jane Lane, of Bentley House," she rejoined, haughtily.  "This is my servant, Will Jones."

"Has he been long in your service?" pursued the officer, fixing a keen glance on Charles, who bore his scrutiny well.

"Not long," she replied.   "He is a tenant of my brother's."

"Whither are you going?" he demanded.   "I require a precise answer."

"I am going to Long Marston, the residence of my relative, Mr. Tombs, and shall pass the night there," she rejoined.   "Long Marston is four miles beyond Stratford-on-Avon."

"I know the house," rejoined the officer.   "Mr. Tombs is a notorious malignant, but your pass is sufficient.  You may proceed on your journey."

Charles did not neglect the hint, but moved on instantly.

As soon as they were gone the officer said to the mounted troopers :

"Follow them, but at such a distance as not to cause alarm.   Enter the house where they stop, aad examine the groom.   I suspect him."

The troopers promised strict obedience to the command, and set off cautiously after the travellers.

---

## CHAPTER IX.

### HOW THEY ARRIVED AT LONG MARSTON.

APART from being the birthplace and the burial-place of Shakspeare, Stratford-on-Avon had a special interest to Charles from the circumstance that it had been the temporary residence of his mother, Queen Henrietta Maria, who, in 1643—some eight years anterior to the period of our story—entered the old town at the head of a large force, and was subsequently joined there by Prince Rupert.   Charles remembered also that

Stratford had been the scene of more than one sharp conflict between the Royalists and the rebels, and that an arch of the old stone bridge had been broken down by the latter to prevent the attacks of their opponents. These reflections occurred to the king as he and his fair companion halted within a quarter of a mile of the charming old town.

Before them, on the opposite bank of the Avon, stood the ancient church, in the vaults of which rest Shakspeare's hallowed bones. But the bridge was guarded by a party of cavalry drawn up in front of it. Nothing had been seen of Mr. Petre and his wife, since they had gone off in another direction at Wootton, and Jane waited for them for some time before entering Stratford; but as they did not make their appearance she at last agreed to go on without them, and Charles rode on towards the bridge.

Never in the conflicts that had taken place on that bridge during the Civil War did Cavalier ride up to the enemy with bolder front than the king now displayed. He was sharply examined by the troopers as he advanced, but Jane, again producing her pass, answered the questions of the officer in command so satisfactorily, that they were at once allowed to pass. Moreover, she accomplished the liberation of her brother-in-law and his wife, who had been detained till her arrival.

All difficulties being thus surmounted the party crossed the bridge—noting that the broken arch had only been partially repaired—and entered the old town in triumph. Under pleasanter circumstances they might have been disposed to halt for a short time at Stratford, and Jane, casting a longing look at the avenue of lime-trees leading to the church, suggested a visit to the beautiful old fabric, but Mr. Petre would not hear of it. Not to excite suspicion they rode at a very deliberate pace through the town, being regarded with some curiosity by the townsfolk, and frowned at by a few troopers collected in the market-place; but as they had passed the ordeal of the bridge it was presumed by those who watched them that they must be well affected towards the Parliament.

Mr. Petre felt much easier in his mind when he got out of Stratford, but chancing to cast a look behind him he saw a couple of troopers pursuing the same course, and fancying they must be following him his fears returned. He mentioned his apprehensions to his wife and Jane, but they treated them very lightly.

For some little time the road pursued by the party lay along the banks of the Avon, and offered delightful views of the town they had just quitted, with its picturesque old church and bridge; but aftey they had proceeded about a mile they quitted the gently-flowing river, and struck across a wild district that presented but few attractions. However, they were now not far from their destination, but before they reached it the aspect of the country had materially improved.

A large, substantially-built farm-house of the better class, Long Marston looked like what it was, the abode of an unostentatious country gentleman. The transomed windows and arched doorway showed the antiquity of the house. In front was a large pond bordered by trees, and at the back there was an old-fashioned garden, and beyond that an extensive orchard.

Evening was coming on as our travellers approached the house, and coloured by the warm sunset the grey old structure appeared to great advantage.

Of good family, and living upon his own estate, Mr. Tombs, the owner of Long Marston, was blessed with a very amiable, affectionate partner, so that we may venture to say that he was a happy man. He did not keep a large establishment, but lived in a quiet, comfortable style, and was thoroughly hospitable. With his rosy, handsome countenance, beaming with health and good humour, and his stout figure, he looked the personification of a country gentleman. Mrs. Tombs, who was some years younger than her husband, was likewise rather stout, but well-proportioned and comely.

Such was the well-assorted and kindly couple that greeted the party on their arrival at Long Marston. They were very glad to see Mr. and Mrs. Petre, but their warmest greeting was for Jane Lane, who was an especial favourite with both of them. Of course, Mr. Petre had a good deal to tell of the difficulties experienced at Wootton and Stratford, and was congratulated on getting through them so well; but Jane made no remarks, and indeed she was occupied at the moment in giving private instructions to Charles, who was waiting for her orders.

"Don't neglect your horse, Will," she said, in a significant tone. "Groom him well and feed him well. Don't gossip with the men at the stables, but as soon as you have finished your work go to the kitchen."

Charles promised obedience, and took his horse to the stables, which adjoined the house.

"That's a new groom, Jane," observed Mr. Tombs. "I don't recollect seeing him before."

"You never saw me travel in this fashion before," replied Jane; "and I shouldn't do so now if I could help it. But it is dangerous to go alone."

"It's not safe to travel in any way in my opinion," observed Mr. Tombs. "But you are a courageous girl, Jane. After your exploits at Worcester, I shan't be surprised at anything you do—not even if you turn soldier."

"Nothing daunts her," cried Mr. Petre. "She would ride through the rebel pack at Wootton."

"Though you didn't like to face them," laughed Mr. Tombs. "Well, I should have acted in the same way myself. I don't mean to go near Stratford, while it is occupied by the enemy."

"Nothing surprises me that Jane does," remarked Mrs. Tombs to Mrs. Petre; "but I wonder you like to travel when you are constantly liable to be stopped and maltreated by these Roundhead troopers."

"I don't like it, I assure you," replied Mrs. Petre. "But we want to get back to our house in Buckinghamshire. If I could have anticipated the annoyances I have met with I would never have left it."

"But you are going to Bristol, I understand, Jane?" said Mr. Tombs, turning to her.

"I am going to the Nortons of Abbots Leigh," replied Jane. "Their place is about three miles from Bristol. I would have postponed my visit to a more convenient season—but I have something important to do."

" But I hope you mean to spend a day or two with us ?"

"Quite impossible," rejoined Jane. "On my return I shall be delighted to stay with you. But not now. I must start early in the morning."

" But you can't reach Abbots Leigh to-morrow."

" No, I shall pass the night at Cirencester."

" You can't do better," remarked Mr. Tombs. "There is a good inn there, kept by a very worthy woman, Widow Meynell, who will take every care of you."

" I know Widow Meynell very well," replied Jane, "and shall feel as much at home with her as I do here."

" Well, let us go in-doors," said Mrs. Tombs, leading the way.

They then entered the house, which was larger and more commodious than its exterior seemed to promise.

" You know your own room, Jane, so I needn't show you to it," said Mrs. Tombs.

Jane tripped up the oak staircase, while her sister and Mrs. Tombs followed more leisurely.

---

## CHAPTER X.

### HOW CHARLES INCURRED THE COOK'S DISPLEASURE.

Having finished his work in the stable, the supposed Will Jones proceeded to the kitchen, where he found Bridget the cook preparing supper. Bridget was fat, and not ill-looking, but something must have gone wrong, for she did not accord the new-comer a very gracious reception. The kitchen was large, occupying the entire ground floor of one wing of the house, and was lighted on either side by deep mullioned windows, filled with lattice panes. From the huge rafter supporting the low ceiling hung a goodly collection of hams. At the further end was an immense fireplace, before which, dangling from a jack, slowly revolved a large joint of beef.

Charles saluted Bridget very respectfully, but she only just nodded her head, and said:

" You're Will Jones, Mistress Jane Lane's groom, I suppose ?" And receiving an answer in the affirmative, she went on. " Well, then, make yourself useful, Will Jones, and see that the meat is properly roasted. I've plenty to do without attending to the jack."

Deeming it necessary to conciliate her, Charles marched at once to the fireplace. All went well for a few minutes, when the jack stopped. The king tried to put it in motion again but could not turn it. After several attempts to set matters right, he gave up the task in despair, when Bridget, who had been absent from the kitchen for a short time, returned, and at once made aware that the meat was burning, she rushed up, exclaiming furiously:

" Why, where have you been bred up, you lazy varlet, that you don't know how to wind up a jack ? I'll teach you to attend to my orders in future."

So saying she snatched up the ladle from the dripping-pan, and threatened to belabour him with it.

"Come, come! my good woman," cried Charles, seizing her arm, "this is carrying the joke a little too far."

"I'm not a good woman, and I won't be called one," exclaimed Bridget. "And it's not a joke to spoil the meat, as my master will let you know."

And she struggled to get free, but the king held her fast.

At this juncture an interruption was offered by loud roars of laughter proceeding from a couple of troopers standing at the kitchen door. Having approached unawares, they had witnessed the occurrence, and were highly diverted by it. On beholding them Bridget instantly calmed down, and the king released her. The troopers then stepped into the kitchen, and the cook having set the jack going again, asked them what they wanted.

"We have come in search of this young man," said one of them, designating Charles. "We thought he might be a malignant, or, as you would say, a Cavalier in disguise, but we now think we must be mistaken."

"He a Cavalier!" exclaimed Bridget, scornfully, "no more a Cavalier than I am. Go about your business directly, or I'll spoil your red coats."

And she flourished the greasy ladle menacingly.

"Nay, nay, good Bridget," said Charles, trying to appease her. "Treat them civilly; they have found out their mistake. Draw them a jug of ale. They may give us trouble," he added, in a whisper.

This consideration brought the cook to reason, and she left the kitchen, and presently returned with a foaming jug of ale. During her absence the troopers had seated themselves at a table, and as it was clear they would not depart without some refreshment, Bridget went back for some cold meat and bread, while Charles poured out the ale. By the time they had finished the cold meat the hot joint was ready, and they insisted on having a few slices. Bridget did not dare to refuse, and was also obliged to draw them another jug of ale. Charles waited upon them and pleased them so much by his attention, that they went away at last declaring he was a very honest young man, and had nothing of a malignant about him.

Shortly afterwards, Mr. Tombs entered the kitchen, accompanied by Jane Lane. Great consternation had been caused by the visit of the troopers, but as the men conducted themselves so quietly and made no disturbance, Mr. Tombs hoped they might be got rid of without any interference on his part. At last he yielded to Jane's entreaties, and they went to the kitchen together, and were greatly relieved by finding that the enemy had departed.

"Look here, sir," cried Bridget, "here's a joint to send to table! But it's not my fault. The rogues forced me to carve it for them."

"Never mind, Bridget," cried Mr. Tombs, laughing at her distress. "I'm thankful they're gone. But what brought them here?"

"Most likely they only wanted a supper, sir," replied Bridget; "but they pretended they came in search of that young man, declaring he was a Cavalier in disguise."

" Ridiculous !" cried Jane. " Evidently a mere excuse to obtain a supper. What did they say to thee, Will ?"

"They put a few questions to me," replied the king. " But I soon convinced them of their mistake."

" They were not very good judges," remarked Mr. Tombs, in a low tone to Jane. " Now I look more narrowly at him, your groom has the air of a gentlemen. Besides, it is fair to tell you that my suspicions were excited by the glance he threw at you as we came into the kitchen. Nay, you need have no disguise with me."

The king's eyes were fixed upon them, and before making a reply Jane consulted him by a look. She then took Mr. Tombs aside, so as to be quite out of Bridget's hearing, and said in a whisper :

" You are right. Will Jones is not what he appears."

" I felt sure of it," rejoined Mr. Tombs in the same tone. " He must be a person of the highest importance, for I know you would not run this great risk for any one of inferior degree. I have my suspicions, but I scarcely dare breathe them."

" Give them utterance," said Jane.

" Is it the king ?" he asked.

" It is," she replied. " But be careful not to betray the secret by word or gesture. You must not even take your wife into your confidence. My sister and her husband are entirely in the dark, and must be kept so, for Mr. Petre is not a fit depositary for a secret of this vast importance."

" I feel the prudence of your counsel, Jane, and will follow it strictly," said Mr. Tombs ; " yet I can hardly refrain from throwing myself at his majesty's feet. Had I known who is here, how alarmed I should have felt at the visit of these troopers ! Never should I forgive myself if aught were to happen to the king while he is under my roof. But I must see that he is attended to. Hark ye, Bridget, this young man must have a good supper. Do you hear that ?"

" Yes, I hear it, sir," she replied. " But he must wait till his betters have been served. Begging Mistress Jane Lane's pardon, I must say that a more ignorant fellow than her groom never came into a kitchen. He can't even wind up a jack ! Ah ! if I had him under my care for a month I'd work a change, I warrant him."

" Hold your peace, Bridget. Take good care of the young man, or you'll displease me," said Mr. Tombs. " If thou art neglected, Will, complain to me."

And fearing he might excite the cook's suspicions if he said more, he quitted the kitchen with Jane.

But in spite of the worthy gentleman's injunctions, Charles obtained nothing till the dishes were brought from the dining-room, when he was allowed to sit down with the servants, and eat as much as he pleased.

A small couch in a small room served his turn that night, but he slept very soundly, and waking early, hied to the stables to prepare for the day's journey.

Charles was grooming his horse, when Mr. Tombs came into the stable, and making an excuse to send his men away, expressed his profound regret that he had not been able to pay his majesty more attention.

"I have not done more," he said, "because I fear to trust my household."

"I quite understand your motives, Mr. Tombs, and appreciate them," said Charles. "And pray understand that it was from no want of faith in your loyalty, which was vouched for by Jane, that you were not trusted with the secret from the first. It was simply to spare you trouble and anxiety; and believe me, I am just as much obliged as if you had made preparations for my security. For this reason I counselled Jane to keep silence; but I am not sorry the disclosure has been made, since it affords me an opportunity of speaking to you freely. My object, as you will have conjectured, is to quit the country as speedily as I can, and take refuge in France, and for this purpose I am going to Bristol under the care of this devoted girl, who is hazarding her life for me. You have been an involuntary agent in the scheme, Mr. Tombs, and I hope you will have no reason to regret taking part in it."

"Whatever betides, it will always be a matter of proud satisfaction to me that your majesty has found shelter at my house during your flight. That you have not been received in a more worthy manner is not my fault, but the fault of circumstances."

"You have done all that I could desire, Mr. Tombs," said Charles; "and I pray you to pursue the same course to the moment of my departure. Treat me as Jane Lane's groom, and nothing more. Do not stay here longer, or you may excite suspicion."

"Your majesty shall be obeyed," replied Mr. Tombs.

And with a profound obeisance he withdrew.

When he had finished dressing his horse, Charles quitted the stables and found his way to the kitchen, where he met with a better welcome from Bridget than he had experienced overnight. He had found his way to her good graces at supper, and she now gave him an excellent breakfast.

Anxious, for many reasons, to start at an early hour, Jane made a hasty breakfast in her own room, and without waiting to take leave of Mrs. Tombs or the Petres, who had not yet made their appearance, went in quest of Mr. Tombs, whom she found in the garden. He told her what had passed between him and the king, and how distressed he felt that he could not render his majesty any real service.

"If you think I can be of any use I will accompany you on your journey to Bristol," he said. "I did not propose this to his majesty, but I am ready to set out at once if you deem my attendance desirable."

"I need not consult the king on the subject, because I know what his decision would be," she rejoined. "His plans are settled, and he would not care to change them. Besides, your sudden departure would occasion remark among the household, and might draw suspicion upon us. Your wife would think it strange, for you could not explain your motives to her. No, believe me, you are far better at home at this critical juncture. Some unforeseen difficulty may occur after the king's may be required to check indiscretion on the part of the servants. Were the Roundhead rogues to learn that you had gone on with us they would inevitably follow, and then there is no telling what the consequences might be. You can best serve the king by remaining at home. I will acquaint his majesty with your proposal, as well as with my reasons for declining it."

No more was said, for noticing that Charles had brought the horse from the stables, they proceeded towards him. In another minute Jane was seated on the pillion behind the king. As some of the other servants were standing by, Mr. Tombs was exceedingly cautious in his observations.

"I wish you a safe and pleasant journey, Jane," he said; adding to the supposed groom, "be sure to take good care of your young lady, Will."

"Fear nothing, sir," replied the king, doffing his cap respectfully. And as Mr. Tombs drew somewhat nearer, he added, in a low tone, "when you next hear of me I trust it will be from France."

Bidding her relative adieu, Jane ordered Will Jones to go on, and accompanied by many fervent prayers for the king's safety, murmured in secret by Mr. Tombs, they soon gained the road to Chipping-Campden.

END OF BOOK THE FIFTH.

# Book the Sixth.

## ABBOTS LEIGH.

## CHAPTER I.

### HOW THE TWO GROOMS CHANGED HORSES AT STOKE-ON-THE-WOLD.

A FINE, fresh, autumnal morning gladdened Charles and his fair companion as they set out from Long Marston. The king was in excellent spirits, and laughed at his adventures on the previous night. After passing Church Honeybourne and Weston Subedge, they ascended Dover's Hill, on which the renowned Cotswold Games, sung by Ben Jonson and Drayton, were celebrated in the time of the king's grandsire, but were discontinued on the outbreak of the Civil Wars. While crossing this hill, which had been the scene of so many pleasant gatherings in former days, Charles promised himself that if he ever ruled the land those manly sports should be revived. From this eminence they looked down upon the fair and fertile valley in which Chipping-Campden is situated, and after enjoying the delightful prospect for a short time, they descended from the uplands and rode towards the pleasant old town.

Chipping-Campden, at the period of our story, was a great mart for wool; and it chanced that on this very day a large sheep fair was held in the vicinity of the town. Numerous flocks of sheep driven by shepherds and attended by farmers, mounted on horses as rough-looking as themselves, beset the road.

As Charles rode on, hoping to pass through the throng unmolested, the sheep-breeders pressed around him, each vaunting the excellence of his fleeces, and affirming that he had the best sheep on the Cotswolds. Jane took upon herself to answer, and explained that they were merely travellers, and did not desire to purchase wool. The explanation did not prove altogether satisfactory, and the churlish farmers began to eye the supposed groom suspiciously.

"Thee warn't bred on the Wowlds," remarked one of them. "Where dost come from?"

"Why, thou'rt as fierce as a Cotswold lion, and that's a sheep," rejoined Charles. "What be it to thee where I come from?"

"Thou look'st as sharp as if thou lived on Tewkesbury mustard," cried the farmer.

"And I should take thee to be a man of Dursley," responded Charles, who was acquainted with some of the local proverbs.

"Why, there he has hit thee, Guy Naunton," cried another of the farmers. "I never knowed thee keep a promise."

"I never broke my word to thee, Mat Mickleton, or to any one else," rejoined Naunton, angrily.

"Did any of you ever join the sports on Dover's Hill?" cried Charles.

"Why dost ask?" cried Mickleton.

"Because I would challenge one and all of you to run, leap, wrestle, or use the quarter-staff," rejoined Charles.

"There be no more Cotswowld Gaames now—more's the pity," cried Mickleton. "But I be ready and willing to try a bowt with thee at quaarter-staff."

"No, no, Will Jones," interposed Jane. "Pass on thy way. Thou wilt get into a brawl with these men."

"Thy groom be a saucy knave, and shall give an account of himself to the town bailiff," said Naunton.

"Keep thy hands off my bridle, or I will lay my whip on thy shoulders," cried Charles, sharply.

"Contain yourself, or we shall have a quarrel," whispered Jane, beginning to feel alarmed at the menacing looks thrown at the king. "Let me go, I beg of you," she added aloud to the others. "I have a pass for myself and my servant."

"Show it to the bailiff," rejoined Naunton. "We'll take you to him."

Chipping-Campden consisted of a single street of some length, in the centre of which stood the Court-house and the Market-house. Owing to the fair the little town was very full, and the concourse collected in the market-place stared hard at the strange cavalcade as it approached, the general impression being that a fugitive Cavalier had been captured.

Informed that an arrest had been made, the bailiff, as the chief magistrate of the place was styled, came forth from the Court-house, to ascertain particulars, and when an explanation had been given him, and

Jane's pass produced for his inspection, he directed that the lady should be allowed to proceed on her journey without further hindrance.

"As you have thought fit to stop her without authority," he said to the farmers, "my order is that you make amends by conducting her to the further end of the town."

This was done, and Charles and his fair companion got safely out of Chipping-Campden.

Skirting Northwick Park, and passing over the bleak downs beyond Blockley, they reached Bourton-on-the-Hill, where they halted for a short time. Being now among the wolds, they had nothing before them but a succession of low, rolling downs, which afforded excellent pasture for sheep, but were entirely uncultivated, and covered with great patches of furze. Not a village was to be seen for miles—only, here and there, a solitary farm-house or a shepherd's cot.

On mounting the lofty hill on which Stow-on-the-Wold is situated, the travellers obtained an extensive view of the wild district they had just traversed. Stow-on-the-Wold is said to want three of the elements —fire, earth, and water. How this may be we know not, but air it can never lack, seeing that it is exposed to all the winds of heaven. Bleaker place cannot be found. What the old town might be like in winter, when the hill on the summit of which it was perched was covered with snow, and when the bitter north wind howled round the corners of the houses, and found its way through every window and door, Charles did not care to consider. It looked pleasant and cheerful now, with the sun shining brightly on the quaint old buildings, and upon the pinnacles of the lofty church tower.

Riding up to the hostel, which bore the sign of the Three Choughs, our travellers alighted, and while Charles took the horses to the stables, Jane put herself under the care of the landlady—a decent middle-aged dame—and was conducted by her to a private room, where refreshments were soon afterwards set before her.

As Charles was returning from the stable, another arrival took place, that brought forth host and hostess. A second groom, with a young dame seated behind him on a pillion, had ridden up to the inn door.

Great was the king's astonishment on discovering that the new-comers were no other than Careless and Dame Gives, the latter having resumed the habits of her sex, while the former had put on a disguise similar to his own. On beholding the king, Dame Gives called out:

"Ah, Will Jones, I am glad to see thee. My man, Tom Elton, has ridden hard to overtake thee and thy young mistress, and at last he has succeeded."

"I did not know you were following us, madam, or I would have stopped," replied Charles. "My young lady is in the house."

"She is partaking of a slight repast within, madam," remarked the hostess. "Shall I take you to her?"

Dame Gives then alighted and entered the house, while Charles and Careless marched off together to the stable. As soon as he could find an opportunity Careless explained the cause of his unexpected appearance, as well as the object of his disguise.

"Those confounded troopers, Ezra and Madmannah, are following your majesty," he said; "and I have adopted this disguise to baffle them. Evidently, the object of the rogues is to secure to themselves the whole of the reward offered for your apprehension, and they will not, therefore, let any of their comrades into their plan. Had they done so you must have been captured. That Worcester horse has been the main cause of their getting on your track. The blacksmith at the little village near Packington Park described the horse you had brought to his smithy, and Madmannah at once knew it to be his own. Having obtained this information, they came to Packington Hall, and owing to that piece of imprudence I discovered their plans, and immediately started after them. They went on to Henley-in-Arden, to Wootton, and Stratford-on-Avon, where they passed the night. At Stratford I was fortunate enough to meet with Dame Gives, and she suggested the plan to me, which, as you see, I have put into execution. Everything necessary to carry it out was procured at Stratford, the groom's dress I now wear, and the pillion for Dame Gives, who readily agreed to accompany me. All that now remains to be done is that your majesty and myself should change horses, and then I will undertake to put the rogues on a false scent."

"Oddsfish! 'tis an excellent plan!" cried Charles, laughing heartily. "No wit like a woman's wit, and Dame Gives is as sharp-witted as any of her sex."

Careless then proceeded to inform the king that he had left Stratford-on-Avon before sunrise, so that as far as he could judge they must be considerably in advance of the troopers.

"I give your majesty half an hour here—not longer," said Careless.

"Half an hour will suffice," said the king. "But let us in at once. I feel outrageously hungry."

Entering the house, they called out lustily for something to eat, whereupon a cold meat pie and the remains of a ham were set before them. On these they set to work, and in less time than had been allowed by Careless had entirely demolished the pie and emptied a jug of ale. They had just finished their repast when the hostess informed them that the ladies were ready to start, whereupon they proceeded to the stable and changed horses, as agreed upon.

Meanwhile, Dame Gives had fully explained matters to Jane, who quite approved of the plan. On coming forth she made no remark, but unhesitatingly took her seat behind the king, who was now mounted on the horse previously ridden by Careless. Dame Gives was equally expeditious in her movements, and the two grooms setting off at once, the change of steeds was unnoticed by the host and hostess.

Before descending the hill Careless surveyed the country round, but could descry nothing of the pursuers.

Leaving the old mansion of Maugersbury on the left, they entered a pleasant valley, watered by a clear trout-stream, and proceeded along the old Roman Foss Way. After crossing Stow Bridge, they passed a charming little village, through the midst of which ran the trout-stream before mentioned, and shaped their course towards Bourton-on-the-Water.

Nothing could be pleasanter than this part of the ride, and enlivened by the cheerful companionship of Careless and Dame Gives, Charles for a time gave vent to his natural gaiety, and seemed quite to forget that the enemy was on his track.

Though apparently quite as unconcerned as his royal master, Careless kept a sharp look-out. Nothing, however, had occurred to cause them alarm. After passing through the pretty town of Bourton-on-the-Water, the houses of which are built on either side of the river Windrush, they returned to the Foss Way, which they had temporarily quitted.

---

## CHAPTER II.

HOW CHARLES TOOK SHELTER DURING A STORM IN RATS ABBEY BARN; AND HOW HE DELIVERED CARELESS AND DAME GIVES FROM THE TROOPERS.

ONCE more they were in the midst of bleak and barren wolds, and were pressing on towards Northleach, when they perceived a small detachment of cavalry coming along from that town.

As they were in sight of the enemy, to quit the road or turn back would only be to invite pursuit, so they went boldly on, hoping they might not be stopped.

The officer in command of the troop ordered them to halt, and interrogated them very sharply. With Jane's pass he was satisfied, and after a brief parley permitted her and her groom to proceed on their way. Reluctant to abandon his friends, Charles rode slowly on, but he soon found it necessary to accelerate his pace. The two troopers, Ezra and Madmannah, who were on his track, had now appeared in sight, and judging that nothing but instant flight could save him, he quitted the Foss Way, and rode off into the wolds.

Meantime, the officer in command of the detachment had come to the determination of arresting Dame Gives and her supposed servant, and he was about to send a guard with them to Northleach, when the two troopers came up. At once recognising the horse, they felt sure the disguised groom must be the king, and fearful of losing their prize they made no remark, but immediately offered to take charge of the prisoners and conduct them to Northleach. Greatly to the satisfaction of the cunning troopers, their proposal was accepted.

Committing the prisoners to their charge, the officer rode off with his men, while the two troopers, secretly exulting in their good fortune, and feeling now secure of their prize, placed the supposed royal captive between them, resolved to take him to Bristol, and there deliver him up to the commander of the garrison, and claim the rich reward.

Meanwhile Charles, finding he was not pursued, made his way across the wolds in the direction of Northleach, and passing on the right of that town, which was then an important mart for cloth and wool, returned to the Foss Way. Unable to ascertain what had become of Careless and Dame Gives, the king was greatly concerned that he could render them no assistance.

The morning, as we have already intimated, had been extremely fine, but within the last hour a change had taken place, and the blackness of the heavens portending a heavy thunder-storm, Charles looked about anxiously for a place of shelter.

They were again on the Foss Way, with nothing but the bare wolds spread around them, like the billows of a tempestuous sea.

Jane pointed out a solitary barn about a quarter of a mile off on the left, and as soon as he could descend from the elevated road which he was tracking, Charles rode quickly in that direction.

Just as they reached the barn the storm came on with great violence. The flashes of lightning were almost incessant, the peals of thunder awfully loud, and the rain came down in torrents.

It was now so dark that except for the lightning they could not see many yards before them, and as Charles rode into the barn through the open door, he called out to ascertain whether any one was within, but no answer being returned he dismounted, and after assisting Jane to alight, led his horse to a stall at the further end of the barn, and fastened him up. This done, he returned to Jane.

Almost deafened by the peals of thunder, they were looking out through the open door upon the wolds, and watching the progress of the storm, when a brighter flash than any that had gone before revealed a startling spectacle.

"Gracious heavens!" ejaculated Charles. "either my eyes deceived me, or I saw Careless and Dame Gives guarded by a couple of troopers."

"You were not deceived, sire," replied Jane, "I saw them distinctly. Their captors are evidently coming to seek shelter here."

As she spoke, another brilliant flash revealed the party.

"You are right, they are about to take shelter in this barn," said Charles. "The rogues must not find us. It shall go hard if I do not contrive to liberate the prisoners."

In another minute the party arrived at the door of the barn. Ezra rode in first, and was followed by the captives, while Madmannah brought up the rear, and posted himself at the entrance to prevent any attempt at escape. However, he did not remain there long, but jumped from his horse, declaring that the lightning had well-nigh blinded him.

Meanwhile the others had dismounted, but Ezra kept strict guard over the prisoners.

"If thy life is of value to thee thou wilt keep quiet," he said to Careless.

"Are we alone here?" cried Madmannah, in a loud voice. "What ho! is there any one in the barn?"

"Ay," replied a voice that sounded like that of a countryman, "I be here, Sam Cubberly, of Scrubditch Farm. Who may you be, and what are you doing in Rats Abbey Barn?"

Struck by the oddity of the response, Careless began to think that a friend was at hand.

"Methinks thou art mocking us, Sam Cubberly," cried Ezra. "Come forth, and show thyself, or I will prick thee with my pike."

A derisive laugh was the only response to this threat, and his choler being roused, he marched towards the back of the barn in search of the audacious rustic. But he had not got far, when an athletic young man suddenly sprang upon him, seized him by the throat, and disarmed him.

Hearing the disturbance, and at once comprehending what was taking place, Careless made an instant attack on Madmannah, and not only succeeded in depriving him of his weapons, but forced him to the ground. Material assistance was given by Dame Gives, who prevented the trooper from using his carabine, and now held it at his head.

"Shall I shoot him?" she asked, in a tone that showed she was in earnest.

"Ay, shoot him through the head if he stirs," rejoined Careless.
He then flew to the spot where the king was engaged with Ezra, and between them they dragged the trooper back to his comrade.

"Our safety demands that both these villains be instantly despatched," said Careless. "They have justly forfeited their lives."

"Truly, they deserve death, yet I am inclined to spare them," said Charles. "Hark ye, rogues," he continued; "will you swear to desist from this pursuit if your lives be given you?"

Both readily responded in the affirmative.

"Trust them not," said Careless; "they have broken half a dozen oaths already."

"But we will not break this," said Ezra. "We will hold our peace as to all that we have seen and heard, and go back to Colonel James."

By this time the fury of the storm had abated. The thunder had rolled off to a distance, and though the lightning still flashed, the rain had entirely ceased.

"The storm has cleared off," observed Jane Lane, in a low tone to the king. "There is nothing to prevent our departure."

"Then we will not remain here a moment longer," he rejoined. "We must deprive these rascals of the means of following us," he added to Careless; "we will take their horses."

"Take their lives as well as their horses. You are dealing far too leniently with them," said Careless.

Fancying all was over with them, the two wretches besought mercy in piteous terms.

"Stand back, then," cried Charles, fiercely; "and do not stir till we are gone, or you will rush upon your death."

The troopers moved back as enjoined, but Careless did not like their looks, and called out to them:

"Further back, or we will shoot you!"

The order was quickly obeyed.

At a sign from Charles, Jane Lane and Dame Gives then quitted the barn, and were immediately followed by the king and Careless, each leading a couple of horses.

As soon as the party had mounted, they returned to the old Roman road, crossed the Foss Bridge over the Coln, and then proceeding for a couple of miles further, turned the troopers' horses loose on Barnsley Wold.

## CHAPTER III.

### WHAT PASSED IN THE BARBER'S SHOP AT CIRENCESTER.

THE storm having now entirely passed away, the sun came forth again. Though the district through which they were travelling was exceedingly wild, it was solitary, and that gave it a special charm in the eyes of the fugitive monarch and his attendants. Occasionally a large flock of sheep could be seen among the wolds, with a shepherd tending them, but nothing more formidable.

As they approached Cirencester, which was to be the term of their day's journey, the aspect of the country improved, and they passed two or three large mansions surrounded by parks.

Far more important, and infinitely more picturesque in appearance, was this ancient town in the middle of the seventeenth century, than at the present time. The castle, celebrated for many historical events, had been demolished, but the walls surrounding the town were still standing and the streets were full of old timber houses, most of which, we regret to say, have since disappeared. Even the old inn, where Charles and his companions rested for the night, has vanished. Notwithstanding these changes, which some may deem improvements, though we cannot regard them in that light, Cirencester *(vulgo,* Ciceter*)* is a quiet, clean-looking country town, possessing a half-antique, half-modern air, and boasts the finest parochial church, with the most elaborately ornamented porch, in Gloucestershire. Let us mention that the interior of this stately fabric has been admirably restored of late years.

Passing through the gate without hindrance of any kind, our travellers rode along a narrow street to the market-place. The king was struck by the dull and deserted appearance of the town, but its quietude pleased him.

On reaching the market-place, he halted for a moment to gaze at the richly-decorated church porch we have just mentioned. Not far from the church stood the Chequers—the inn at which they intended to put up—and proceeding thither, the party alighted, and were warmly welcomed by the hostess, Dame Meynell, who was delighted to see Jane, and conducted her and Dame Gives into the house, where every attention was shown them.

After partaking of a light repast they retired to rest. Charles and Careless were of course treated according to their supposed condition but no guest, whatever might be his degree, fared badly at the Chequers and they were supplied with some marrow-puddings and fried eels and pottle of excellent sack. Not caring to sit among the other guests, the went out, after supper, to take a stroll through the town.

Night having now come on, they could not see much, so aft. rambling about for half an hour they returned to the market-place, an entered a barber's shop which Charles had noticed near the inn.

Not expecting any more customers at that hour, the barber, a sharp looking middle-aged man, was about to shut up his shop, but he deferre his purpose when the two grooms came in, and one of them—it was th king—seated himself in the chair ordinarily assigned to customers, and desired to be shaved.

" 'Tis gettiug late," observed the barber ; "cannot you come in the morning ?"

" No," replied Charles, " my young mistress starts early. I must be shaved now."

Trimming a lamp that hung overhead, the barber made all necessary preparations for the task.

While he was thus occupied, Careless, who was seated on a bench, observed the man look inquisitively at his customer, and began to regret that they had entered the shop.

" You have been accustomed to wear moustaches and a pointed beard, I perceive, friend," remarked the barber, as he covered the king's cheeks and chin with lather ; " and I am of opinion that the fashion must have suited you."   And as Charles made no reply, he went on : " Yours is a face that requires a beard—a pointed beard, I mean, such as the Cavaliers wear——"

" But Will Jones is not a Cavalier any more than I am," interrupted Careless.

" 'Tis not an ill compliment, methinks, to say that both of you— despite your attire—might pass for Cavaliers," said the barber.

" We do not desire to be taken for other than we are—simple grooms," said Careless.   " Prithee, hold thy peace, unless thou canst talk more to the purpose, and proceed with thy task."

" Nay, I meant no offence," said the barber.   " I only wish you to understand that you need make no mystery with me.   I am a true man, and not a Roundhead."

He then plied his razor so expeditiously that in a trice he had finished shaving the king.

As he handed Charles a napkin and ewer, he said, in a tone of profound respect :

" I ought to know that face."

" Where canst thou have seen me, master ?" rejoined the king.   " I have never been in thy shop before."

" 'Tis not in Ciceter that I have seen you," said the barber, still in the same profoundly respectful tone ; " but in a far different spot, and under far different circumstances.   Little did I think that I should be thus honoured.

" No great honour in shaving a groom," cried Charles.

The barber shook his head.

" No groom has entered my shop this night," he said, " and no groom will leave it.   Whatever opinion may be formed of me, let it be under- -tood that I am no traitor."

" Nay, thou art an honest fellow, I am sure of that," observed Charles.

" I am a loyal subject of the king," said the barber, " and were his majesty to come hither I would aid him to the best of my power."

" Were thy suspicions correct, friend," said Charles, " thou must feel that I could not satisfy them.   Think what thou wilt, but keep silence."

He was about to place a pistole on the table, but the poor man looked so pained that he stretched out his hand to him. The barber sprang forward, and pressed the king's hand to his lips.

At a very early hour next morning all the party quitted Cirencester, and again tracked the old Roman road across the plain.

They had a long day's journey before them, Bristol being thirty-one miles distant from Cirencester, while Abbots Leigh was four miles beyond Bristol. The morning was delightfully fresh, and the woody district they were traversing offered charming views.

After awhile they left the Roman way, and pursued a road at the foot of a range of low hills, and in less than two hours arrived at Tetbury, where they halted. As they had been unable to breakfast at Cirencester, owing to the early hour at which they started, they were now very glad to repair the omission. Jane and Dame Gives, of course, breakfasted in private, but the two grooms, after seeing to the horses, repaired to the kitchen, where they astonished the host by their prowess as trencher-men.

After an hour's halt at Tetbury, the party set forth again. Passing High Grove and Doughton, and then riding on to Westonbirt Bottom, they skirted Silk Wood, and continued their course till they reached Didmarton.

During this part of the journey they had met with no interruption. Indeed, there seemed no troopers on the road. On quitting Didmarton they passed Badminton Park, in which, at a subsequent period, the magnificent mansion belonging to the Duke of Beaufort has been erected, and rode on through the woods and past the fine old manor-house of Little Sodbury to Chipping-Sodbury, where they again halted to refresh themselves and rest their steeds.

Their road now lead them past Yate, and through Wapley Bushes to Westerleigh. Thence they proceeded by Hanborow and Stapleton, and crossing an old stone bridge over the river Frome, rode on to Bristol.

---

## CHAPTER IV.

### BRISTOL IN THE SEVENTEENTH CENTURY.

SURROUNDED by walls, above which rose its picturesque timber habitations and numerous fine churches, Bristol, at the period of our history, presented a very striking appearance. So closely packed together were the houses, that viewed from the neighbouring heights they seemed to form a solid mass, and indeed the majority of the streets were so narrow that they were little better than lanes. Through the midst of the city ran the Avon, the river being crossed by an ancient stone bridge, with houses on either side like old London Bridge. On the north-west the city was bounded by the river Frome, and it was here that the chief quay had been formed, ships of very large burden being able to come up the Avon with the tide. On the east the city was protected by the castle, a very large pile, surrounded by a broad, deep moat, and approached by a drawbridge. Near the castle was a strong fort of modern construction, in which there was a large garrison. Four years later both castle and fort were demolished by the Parliament. On the west the fortifications were in tolerably good repair. But between the western walls and the Avon there was a wide marsh, which extended to the left bank of the Frome, near its junction with the larger river. In recent times, this marshy ground has been converted into large docks and basins, and surrounded by warehouses. The south side of the city was likewise protected by strong walls, extending to either bank of the Avon, which here made a wide curve. Both St. Augustine's and St. Mary Redcliffe, justly esteemed the most beautiful church in the kingdom, were outside the walls. From its elevated position, St. Augustine's, as the cathedral was then called, formed a conspicuous object from the north and west. The city was approached by four gates: on the north by Frome-gate, and on the south by Temple-gate, New-gate, and Redcliffe-gate, the latter leading to the grand old fane before mentioned. What with its many beautiful churches, incomparable St. Mary Redcliffe, the castle, the old walls, the ancient houses, and the two rivers, Bristol, in the olden time, was a most striking and picturesque city, and its inhabitants were justly proud of it.

During the Civil Wars, Bristol had played a conspicuous part, and was justly accounted the chief Royalist stronghold in the West, and though it was frequently in the hands of the Parliamentarians, it still preserved a character for loyalty. Charles was well acquainted with the city, having been taken there by his royal father in August, 1643, when it capitulated to Prince Rupert, who had besieged it with twenty thousand men. Though but a boy at the time, Charles had been greatly impressed by the loyalty of the men of Bristol, and entertaining the belief that a large portion of them must still be faithful to his cause, though they did not dare to manifest their zeal, he approached the city without much misgiving.

Our travellers were stopped and questioned by the guard stationed at Frome-gate, but Jane Lane's pass sufficed, and they were soon mounting a steep narrow street bordered by tall timber houses, with overhanging stories, leading to the centre of the city.

It had been arranged that the party should separate at Bristol. Dame Gives had some relatives dwelling in Wine-street, with whom she could take up her abode, while Careless meant to fix his quarters at the Lamb Inn in West-street till he should receive a summons from the king. Charles and his fair companion did not intend to remain at Bristol, but to proceed at once to Abbots Leigh, which, as already mentioned, was distant about four miles from the city.

In accordance with this plan they now separated, and Careless, having consigned Dame Gives to her friends, proceeded to the Lamb Inn.

Having crossed the old bridge, and tracked the long, narrow street to which it led, Charles and his fair companion passed out at Redcliffe-gate, and after halting for a short time to gaze at the superb old church, shaped their course along the left bank of the Avon.

How changed is now the scene! Where a vast floating harbour has been formed, constantly filled with ships from all parts of the world, and surrounded by busy wharves and enormous warehouses, only the river flowed through its deep channel, with very few buildings near it.

After a long ascent, the travellers reached the uplands on the left bank of the Avon—then, as now, covered with magnificent timber. Half an hour's ride through these romantic woods brought them to Abbots Leigh.

The fine old family mansion of the Nortons no longer exists, having been pulled down in 1814, in order to make way for a yet more stately structure, that now forms the residence of Sir William Miles, and is celebrated for its magnificent gallery of pictures. Abbots Leigh was approached by an avenue of trees, terminated by an antique gate-tower. Passing through the wide archway of this tower, the king and his fair companion came in front of the old mansion, which, with its numerous gable and large mullioned windows, presented a very imposing appearance.

Situated on an elevated plateau, and facing the west, Abbots Leigh commanded a most extensive and varied prospect, embracing Durdham Downs on the further side of the Avon, a vast tract of well-wooded country, the broad estuary of the Severn, and the Welsh hills beyond it.

Jane's arrival having been announced by a bell rung at the gate by the porter, Mr. Norton who was playing at bowls with his chaplain, Doctor Gorges, on the smooth lawn in front of the mansion, hastened to meet her, and, after greeting her very cordially, assisted her to alight.

The lord of Abbots Leigh was a tall, distinguished-looking personage, attired in black velvet. His wife, who presently made her appearance, was somewhat younger, and extremely handsome.

A most affectionate meeting took place between Jane and Mrs. Norton, who embraced her young relative very tenderly, and expressed great delight at seeing her.

" I rejoice that you have got here safely," she said. " We hear of so many disagreeable occurrences, that I can assure you we have felt quite uneasy about you. Your looks don't betray fatigue, but I dare say you are greatly tired by your long journey."

" No, indeed, I am not," replied Jane. " I think I could ride thirty or forty miles a day for a month, and not feel the worse for it. But I have been troubled about my poor groom, Will Jones, who is very weak from the effects of a quartan ague."

" Give yourself no further concern about him, Jane," said Mrs. Norton. Then calling to the butler, who was standing near, she added, " Pope, this young man, Will Jones, is suffering from ague. Bid Margaret Rider prepare for him an infusion of aromatic herbs."

" A hot posset cannot fail to do him good," said Jane. " But, above all, he must avoid a damp bed."

" There are no damp beds, I trust, at Abbots Leigh," replied Mrs. Norton. " But Pope shall see that he is well lodged."

Pope, a tall, strongly-built man, who looked more like a soldier than a butler, promised attention to his mistress's orders, and stepping towards Charles, said a few words to him in a low tone, after which the king, bowing gratefully to Mrs. Norton, took his horse to the stable

Jane had next to answer Mr. Norton's inquiries relative to her brother and Sir Clement Fisher.

"They must be full of anxiety for the king," he remarked. "All sorts of reports reach us, and we know not what to believe. Can you give us the assurance that his majesty is safe?"

"I wish I could," replied Jane. "But he is so environed by his enemies that he cannot escape."

"Not immediately perhaps," said Mrs. Norton. "But an opportunity must occur. No one will be base enough to betray him."

"Betray him! I should think not," cried Mr. Norton. "If chance brought him here, I would place my house at his disposal."

"I am delighted to hear you give utterance to such sentiments," said Jane.

"Did you doubt my loyalty?" he rejoined.

"No," she returned. "But I am glad to find that the king has so true a friend."

They then entered the house.

---

## CHAPTER V.

### HOW CHARLES FOUND A FAITHFUL ADHERENT AT ABBOTS LEIGH.

JANE was in her room—a large old-fashioned bedchamber, with a transom-window looking upon the lawn, and commanding a splendid view of the Severn's mouth and the distant Welsh hills—when a tap was heard at the door, and a maid-servant came in.

"You have something to say to me, I perceive, Margaret?" observed Jane.

"Yes, madam," was the reply. "My mistress has ordered me to attend upon your groom, Will Jones, and to be very careful of him. So I prepared a nice carduus posset, knowing it to be good for the ague, but when I took it to him, he wouldn't drink it, but said he should prefer some mulled sack."

"Well, Margaret, you had better indulge him in his whim. Let him have some mulled sack, since he fancies the brewage."

"But that's not all," pursued Margaret Rider. "Mulled sack won't content him. He declares he is very hungry, and must have a good supper."

"Poor young man!" exclaimed Jane, in a commiserating tone. "He has had a long day's journey. Let him have some supper."

"It strikes me, madam, that he is not so ill as he pretends to be. I don't see why he shouldn't sup in the servants' hall."

"Indulge him, Margaret—pray indulge him. He is worse than he looks. Ague is very obstinate."

"In my opinion, madam, the young man himself is very obstinate. Nothing seems good enough for him. I am sure he is very well lodged, yet he is not satisfied with his room."

"Well, let him have a better room, Margaret."

"I think you show him too much indulgence, madam.  But I will attend to your orders."

And Margaret departed.

On going down-stairs, Jane repaired to the butler's pantry, where she found Pope, and was about to give him some further directions, when he said to her, in a very grave tone :

"I do not know, madam, whether you are aware that I had the honour of serving Mr. Thomas Jermyn, when he was groom of the bed-chamber to the Prince of Wales at Richmond.  His royal highness was a boy at the time, but I recollect him perfectly."

He paused and looked at Jane, but as she made no remark, he went on :

"Subsequently, I served in the late king's army under Colonel Bagot, and constantly saw the prince at that time, so that his features are graven upon my memory."

"Why do you mention this to me, Pope ?" inquired Jane, uneasily, for she suspected what was coming.

"Can you not guess, madam ?" he rejoined.  "Well, then, since I must needs speak plainly—in your groom, Will Jones, I recognise the king."

"You are mistaken, Pope," she cried.

"No, madam," he rejoined, gravely, "I am too well acquainted with the king's face to be mistaken.  But you need not be alarmed.  His majesty may rely on my silence."

Just as the words were uttered, the object of their conversation came in.  A look from Jane told the king that the secret had been discovered.

"Soh, Pope has found me out !" he exclaimed  "I thought he would.  But I can trust him, for I know him to be an honest fellow, who would scorn to betray his sovereign."

"I have sworn allegiance to you, sire," replied Pope, "and I will never break my oath."

And as he spoke he knelt down and kissed the hand which Charles graciously extended to him.

"Do not let your zeal lead you into any indiscretion, Pope," said the king.  "Show me no marks of respect when any one is present, except Mistress Jane Lane, but continue to treat me as Will Jones."

"I will carefully attend to your majesty's injunctions," said Pope.

Feeling now quite sure that the king would be well attended to, Jane left the room.

But the loyal butler had his own duties to fulfil, and could not neglect them without exciting suspicion.  Praying the king, therefore, to excuse him, he proceeded to serve supper, and while he was thus occupied, Margaret Rider, by his directions, brought a jug of metheglin for the king.

For more than an hour Charles was left alone in the butler's pantry, but at the end of that time Pope reappeared.

"I am now entirely at your majesty's service," he said,

"Sit down, and take a cup of metheglin," said Charles.  "I want to have a chat with you."

"To prove that I place entire confidence in you, Pope," observed the king, "I will tell you what I desire to do, and possibly you can aid me. My object is to obtain a passage for France. Do you think I shall be able to find a vessel at Bristol to take me to Bordeaux?"

"Very few vessels sail from Bristol to France, my liege. You had better hire a schooner for Cardiff or Swansea."

"But I have no money," said Charles.

"Mistress Jane Lane can procure any sum your majesty may require from Mr. Norton," replied Pope. "But of course she will be obliged to enter into explanations with him."

"I should not feel uneasy on that score, because I know your master can be trusted," observed the king.

"That is quite certain," rejoined Pope. "But with your majesty's leave, the first thing to be done is to ascertain that a vessel can be hired. There are plenty of ship-masters, plenty of ships, and plenty of seamen to be found at Bristol, but one doesn't know whom to trust. Or rather, I should say, one can't trust any of the skippers, since most of them are Roundheads. But if you desire it I will go with your majesty to Bristol to-morrow night. At the Dolphin, a tavern near the quay, frequented by seafaring men, we may be able to pick up some information."

"But will it be safe for me to go to a tavern like the Dolphin?"

"If I thought there was the slightest risk I would not offer to take your majesty there," replied Pope. "I am well known to David Price, the keeper of the tavern, and he will not question any one I may take to his house. Possibly we may obtain from him all the information we require. If I succeed in obtaining your majesty a passage to Bordeaux —or even to Swansea—I shall esteem myself the happiest of men."

Shortly afterwards Pope conducted the king to the pretty little chamber prepared for him. Needless to say that his majesty slept soundly.

<hr>

## CHAPTER VI.

CARELESS BRINGS THE KING GOOD NEWS.

Next morning Charles was alone in the butler's pantry, when Mr. Norton, accompanied by Doctor Gorges, who had been the late king's chaplain, and now filled the same office at Abbots Leigh, came into the room to inquire after him. The appearance of the latter, with whom he was well acquainted, rather confused Charles, as he feared that the chaplain must recognise him. However, the divine suspected no deception, and Charles acted his part so well that he completely imposed upon the worthy man. The interview did not last many minutes, and was interrupted by Jane Lane, who came to the king's assistance.

"I hope I have not over-acted my part," observed the king to Jane, as soon as Mr. Norton and the chaplain were gone. "But it occurred to me that my recovery was too rapid, and that I ought to have a relapse."

"You acted the part so naturally, my liege, that you would certainly have imposed upon me, had I not been a confederate. It will be sure to be spread about among the household that you have had another attack, and as the servants may have thought your conduct strange in keeping aloof from them, their suspicions will now be removed."

"I shall go forth presently," said the king. "I think it likely that Careless may venture here in the course of the day."

He then informed Jane of his intention to visit Bristol at night with Pope, for the purpose of hiring a vessel to convey him to France.

"If I succeed in my object I shall not return here," he said; "and in that case I shall not require your further services. You will then be at full liberty to inform Mr. Norton who has been his guest."

"I must be quite sure your majesty is safe before I make any such communication to him," she replied.

"If Pope returns alone, you will know that I am gone," said Charles.

"Heaven grant that your majesty may find means of escape!" said Jane. "But I own I am not very sanguine, and I implore you not to run any heedless risk. I think there is great hazard in visiting Bristol."

She then quitted the room, and Charles, who found his confinement rather irksome, went to the stables, where he remained for some time. He did not return to the house, but passing through a retired part of the garden gained the long avenue leading to the mansion.

While wending his way slowly beneath the over-arching trees, he perceived a horseman at a distance riding towards the house. As the person drew nearer, he felt almost certain it must be Careless—but if so, Careless had abandoned his disguise as a groom, and attired himself in a costume more befitting his condition. Careless it proved to be, and no sooner did he discern his royal master, than he quickened his pace and rode up.

"Well met, my liege," he exclaimed, springing from his steed and saluting the king. "I have come in quest of your majesty."

"I hope you bring me good news," replied Charles. "I see you have thrown off your disguise."

"I found it necessary to do so," said Careless. "Habited as a groom I should never have been able to make any arrangements for your majesty. Luckily, at the Lamb, where I put up, I met with Tom Hornyold of Worcester, who not only supplied me with a good sum of money, but with a change of attire. Thus provided, I lost not a moment in endeavouring to carry out your majesty's plans. By Tom Hornyold's advice, I repaired to the Dolphin, a tavern frequented by ship-masters and seafaring men in the neighbourhood of the quay——"

"And kept by David Price," interposed the king.

"Your majesty knows the tavern?" exclaimed Careless, in surprise.

"I have heard of it," replied Charles. "But proceed. Did you see the tavern-keeper?"

"I did, my liege, and found him exactly the man described by Tom Hornyold. I had a long conference with him in private, and told him I wanted to hire a vessel to convey me to France, and if that could not be managed, to Swansea. I said that I meant to take with me a young dame, to whom I was about to be wedded—but whose parents objected to the match——"

" Dame Gives, I suppose ?" observed the king.

" Exactly, my liege. I had previously obtained her consent to the scheme. But your majesty has not heard me out. I thought it necessary to acquaint David Price that I should be accompanied by a friend — a fugitive Royalist who had fought at Worcester—but I took care not to lead him to suspect that my friend was a person of rank."

" Well, what followed ?"

" He listened to all I said, and after some reflection, replied that he knew the master of a small lugger, who he thought might be induced by a good round sum to convey me, my intended bride, and my friend to Swansea. ' I think the man is in the house now,' he added. ' If you desire it, I will call him in here, and you can speak to him yourself?' I said this was exactly what I wished, so he went out, and shortly afterwards returned with a sturdy, broad-shouldered man, whom he introduced as Captain Rooker. The skipper had an honest look that prepossessed me in his favour. In order to give a friendly character to the interview, David Price placed a flask of Nantz on the table, and filled a glass for each of us. My object having been explained to Captain Rooker, he entered upon the matter at once. He said it was a hazardous job, and might get him into trouble, but as he sympathised strongly with the Royalist party he would undertake to assist me, provided he was well paid. After some talk he agreed to take me and my companions to Swansea for fifty pounds—but he required twenty pounds down, which by David Price's advice I paid him. I hope your majesty will think I have done well in making the arrangement."

"You have done admirably," cried Charles, joyfully. " But when will Captain Rooker sail ?"

"To-night," replied Careless, " To-morrow, I hope your majesty will be at Swansea. Once there, you cannot fail to secure a passage to France."

" Yes, I shall feel perfectly safe at Swansea. But where am I to embark ?"

" I am unable to inform your majesty at this moment. All I know is, that Captain Rooker means to send his lugger down the Avon to-day, and the vessel will wait for us at some point where we can safely go on board. Come to Bristol to-night, and then I shall be able to give you exact information."

" You have forestalled my plans," said Charles. " I had arranged with Pope, the butler at Abbots Leigh, who turns out to be a trusty fellow, to go to Bristol to-night, and we meant to visit the Dolphin."

" Then let that tavern be our place of rendezvous," rejoined Careless. " We will meet there at nine o'clock to-night. And now, unless your majesty has some further commands for me, I will take my departure."

" I have nothing more to say," said the king. " At nine o'clock expect me at the Dolphin."

Thereupon, Careless mounted his steed, and bowing profoundly to the king, rode down the avenue.

When he had disappeared, Charles turned and walked slowly towards the house. On arriving there, he repaired at once to the butler's pantry where he found Pope, and acquainted him with the arrangements made by Careless.   The butler approved of the plan, and thought it could be safely carried out.

Later on in the day the king had an  opportunity of conferring with Jane Lane, who did  not seek  to disguise  her uneasiness when she was informed of the scheme.

"I pray that  your majesty may not be drawn into some snare," she said.   "I have great fears that the captain of  the lugger may prove treacherous,"

"Why  should  you  distrust  him?"  cried  Charles.   "Careless has perfect faith in his honesty."

"I can give  no reason for  my suspicions," she replied, "and I hope they may prove groundless.   Zeal for your majesty makes me  anxious. Pray allow me to consult with  Mr. Norton."

"No," replied the king, in a decided tone "'Tis needless to do so."

"Your majesty, I am  sure, has not  a  more devoted  follower  than Major Careless.   But he may be deceived."

"Tut!  these are  idle fears," exclaimed Charles.   "I never knew you so timorous before.   Ordinarily, you are full of courage."

"I cannot conquer  my apprehensions, sire.   I have a presentiment of ill, and I beseech you to listen to me."

"I can scarcely think that it is the high-spirited Jane Lane who speaks to me thus," said the king.

"Think of  me as you  please, my liege, but follow  my counsel," she rejoined.   "Again, I entreat you to let me consult with Mr. Norton."

"No—no—no," cried Charles.   "Not till I am gone will I allow you to tell him who has been his guest."

Nothing more passed between them.

The prospect of immediate escape, now held out to the king, threw him into such a state of excitement, that he felt it almost impossible to continue to play the sick man, and in order to avoid observation, he withdrew to his chamber, and remained there till evening, all his time being occupied in watching the sails on the broad estuary of the Severn.

---

## CHAPTER VII.

### THE TAVERN-KEEPER AND THE SKIPPER.

In the good old  times supper was generally served  at an hour which would not  now be deemed particularly late for dinner, and after  he had finished his  attendance at  the evening meal, Pope, who had obtained leave from his master to go to Bristol, set out with the king.

Charles had no opportunity of bidding Jane farewell, but she sent him a message by the  butler, expressing her heartfelt wishes  for his success. Though it was nearly dark at the time that he and Pope started on their expedition, and the gloom was greatly increased by the thickness of  the woods into which they had plunged, the butler was well acquainted with the road, so that they were in no danger of taking a wrong course.

gained the open ground, known as Stokeleigh Camp. As they reached the verge of the steep upland, the valley, deeply ploughed by the Avon, lay before them, while the lights of the city were distinguishable in the distance. Descending from this eminence, they pursued their course along the bank of the river, and met with no interruption.

"The tide is flowing," observed Pope. "Two hours hence the channel will be full. The moon will have risen by that time, and then there will be light enough for your majesty's business."

"It is quite light enough now, methinks," said Charles.

"It is pitch dark at this moment in the gorge of the Avon," rejoined Pope.

Presently, they drew dear St. Mary Redcliffe's pile, the outline o. which noble fabric could only be discerned through the gloom.

They then entered a narrow street skirted on either side by old timber houses, and leading towards one of the city gates, which took its name from the church they had just passed. Pope readily satisfied the guard at Redcliffe-gate, and entering the city they proceeded towards the bridge.

At that hour there were few people in the streets, which were almost dark owing to the overhanging stories of the old houses. Just after they had crossed the bridge and entered High-street, they encountered the city watch, which had begun to make its rounds, and were challenged by the captain, but allowed to pass on.

Shortly after this encounter, Pope turned into a narrow street on the left, and descending it, they had nearly reached the quay, when Pope stopped, and pointed to a tavern on the right, above the open door of which hung a lamp that cast a feeble glimmer on the footway.

"That is the Dolphin, my liege," he said.

Charles looked at the house for a few moments, as if debating with himself what he should do, and then said :

"Go in first. I will follow."

Pope obeyed, and went into the tavern, Charles keeping close behind him. On crossing the threshold they found themselves in a large, low roofed, old-fashioned room, in which a number of seafaring men were seated at small tables drinking and smoking. The room was so dimly lighted, besides being filled with tobacco-smoke, that the whole of the guests could not be clearly distinguished, but amongst them were three or four individuals, whose puritanical garb and tall steeple-crowned hat showed that they were sectaries.

Besides these there were a couple of troopers.

On making this discovery, Charles felt inclined to beat a hasty retreat, and would have done so, if the tavern-keeper, David Price, who had been watching them, had not come forward, and beckoning them to follow him, ushered them into a small inner room, where they found Careless and a stout-built personage, whose appearance answered to the description Charles had received of Captain Rooker.

Tall glasses and a big bowl of sack and sugar, or "Bristol Milk" as was termed, were set on the table, and light was afforded by a lamp. Careless saluted the new-comers on their entrance, and begged them be seated, but nothing passed till David Price had quitted the room.

" This is Captain Rooker," said Careless. " He has engaged to give us a passage to Swansea."

" Ay, it's all right," cried the captain, in rough but cheery accents. " My lugger has already gone down the river, and we shall follow her as soon as the tide suits, and that will be in about two hours. The current will then be running down quickly. If so be you don't like to embark on the quay, I can take you up somewhere lower down — say at the Gorge of the Avon."

" That's a long way off," observed Charles. " What's your reason for wishing us to embark at that place, captain ?"

" Because it's the safest spot I know of," returned Rooker. " You need have no fear of any one lying in wait for you there."

" No, we'll make sure of that," observed the king, glancing significantly at Careless.

" Hark ye, captain," said the latter, " you and I must not part company till we reach Swansea."

" Why, you don't doubt me ?" cried the skipper, gruffly.

" No, I don't doubt you, but I won't let you out of my sight. We will arrange it in this way. You and I will start from the quay, and we will take up the others as proposed."

" Well, I'm agreeable," said the skipper. " But I understood that a young lady was going with you. Is she to be left behind ?"

" No," replied Careless. " My friend will bring her with him. You will find her near the high cross on St. Augustine's Green," he added to Charles. " I would go there myself, but——"

" You don't want to leave me," supplied the skipper, with a laugh.

" Ay, that's just it," said Careless. " It won't make much difference to you," he continued, again addressing the king. " You need not come back. You can embark on the right bank of the river."

" Just as easily as on the left," remarked Captain Rooker, " if you can only get down the cliffs without breaking your neck."

" I will guide him," said Pope. " I know the path down the rocks."

" Well, the place will suit me," said Charles. " So you may look out for us at the entrance of the gorge, captain." Then bending towards Careless, he added, in a low tone. " Don't lose sight of this man."

" Depend on me," replied Careless, in the same tone.

No one but Captain Rooker was aware that all that had passed had been overheard by David Price, who, on going forth, had left the door slightly ajar. The cunning rascal had now heard quite enough, and, fearful of being detected, crept cautiously away.

He was only just in time, for almost immediately afterwards Charles and Pope quitted the room. David Price attended them to the door, and after watching them for a moment or two, as they proceeded towards the quay, he beckoned to the troopers, whom we have mentioned as being among the guests. They were expecting the summons, and instantly joined him.

Meanwhile, the king and Pope had crossed the quay, and calling for a boat, were taken to the other side of the Frome.

As soon as the boat returned from this job, the two troopers, each of whom was armed with a carabine, and had a brace of pistols in his belt, jumped into it, and ordered the waterman to take them across.

The man prepared to obey, but by some accident got foul of another boat, causing a slight delay, which exasperated the troopers. They rated him soundly, but their anger did not mend matters, for he moved with the greatest deliberation.

---

## CHAPTER VIII.

### ST. AUGUSTINE'S GREEN.

WHOLLY unconscious that they were followed, the king and his attendant mounted the eminence on which stood St. Augustine's Church. By this time the moon had risen, and its beams silvered the tower and roof of the majestic edifice. Before entering St. Augustine's Green—now known as College Green—a large quadrangular piece of ground bordered by trees, spread out in front of the cathedral, Charles cast a glance at the city, which, viewed from this elevation, with its walls, ancient habitations, and church towers, illumined by the moon's radiance, presented a striking picture. While gazing in this direction he noticed two troopers at the foot of the hill, who had evidently just crossed over from the quay, but they did not excite his apprehension.

The moon being at the back of the collegiate church, the broad black shadow of the venerable pile was thrown upon the green, reaching almost as far as the high cross which stood in the centre of the enclosure. As Charles walked towards the cross he saw a female figure hurry away, and enter the alley of trees that bordered the geeen on the west. He instantly followed, and found Dame Gives.

"Why did you fly from me?" he asked.

"I was not certain that it was your majesty," she rejoined. "The person with you is a stranger to me."

"He is a faithful adherent whom I have found at Abbots Leigh," replied Charles. "I could not bring Major Careless with me, for he is otherwise occupied, but you will see him anon."

And he then proceeded to explain that Careless had been left to look after the master of the lugger.

"Heaven grant that all may go well!" she exclaimed. "How rejoiced I shall be when your majesty is safe at Swansea!"

"You will be still more pleased when we are all safe in France," said Charles.

"I do not think I shall ever arrive there, sire," she rejoined, sadly. "I am not usually down-hearted, as you know. But I am so low-spirited to-night that I think you will be better without me."

"No, no," cried Charles. "Go you must. Major Careless will be miserable if you are left behind."

"Nay, I don't desire to make him miserable," she rejoined, forcing a laugh. "Whatever may happen I will go. But I will tell your majesty why I feel so uneasy. While I was standing under the shadow of the church a dark figure approached me, and at first I thought it was Major Careless, whom I expected.  A strange terror seized me.  The figure slowly and noiselessly advanced, and as it drew near the blood froze in my veins, and my heart ceased to beat, for I saw that it was Urso.  Yes, it was Urso, come from the grave to torment me!  His face was the face of a corpse, but his eyes gleamed with preternatural brightness.  I tried to fly, but I continued chained to the spot.  The phantom approached— and oh, horror! it stood close beside me, and these words, uttered in a sepulchral tone, reached my ear: 'I have come to summon you.'  For a moment my senses seemed to desert me.  When I recovered, the phantom was gone."

" 'Twas the delusion of an over-excited imagination," observed Charles, who nevertheless was powerfully impressed by the relation.

" No, sire," she replied, shuddering.  " I could not be deceived.  I saw Urso too plainly.  Nothing could equal the horror with which he inspired me.  Death would be dreadful indeed if I must rejoin him."

There was a pause, during which Charles made no remark, for, in spite of himself, he felt a sense of terror creeping over him.

At length Dame Gives broke the silence:

" As soon as I regained the use of my limbs," she said, " I went to yonder chapel," pointing to a small sacred structure on the eastern side of the green, " and finding the door open I went in, and kneeling down, prayed fervently.  Since then I have felt greatly relieved, and prepared for whatever may ensue."

" 'Tis a mere trick of fancy," cried Charles.  " But, despite the fancied summons, you must go with me.  If we remain here longer, I shall think I see Urso's ghost myself."

He then called to Pope, who was standing near at hand, and bade him lead the way to the downs.  Marching in advance, the butler took them to the further end of the green, and then commenced another steep ascent. Dame Gives still felt rather faint, and required the aid of the king's arm in mounting the hill.  Not one of the party was aware that they were cautiously followed by the two troopers.

<hr>

## CHAPTER IX.

### THE GORGE OF THE AVON.

They had now gained an eminence, at that time nothing more than a bare down, but now covered with streets, squares, and terraces, and forming the charming suburb of Clifton.  From this lofty point the whole of the city could be descried, bathed in moonlight, and presenting a very striking picture.

After a few minutes' rest, Dame Gives seemed to have recovered from the fatigue of the steep ascent, and walked on briskly over the elastic turf.  Though they were on a very lofty elevation, they had not as yet reached the crown of the hill, which was then surmounted by a watch-tower, but they walked to this point, and avoiding the watch-tower, entered a wide open space, partly surrounded by earthworks, which had once formed a Roman camp.

A most remarkable scene now lay before them, the picturesque effect of which was heightened by the moonlight. From the giddy height they had attained they looked down upon the Avon, flowing in its deep channel between two walls of rocks, evidently riven asunder, ages ago, by some convulsion of nature. This marvellous chasm, than which nothing can be grander, is known as the Gorge of the Avon. Bushes and small trees springing from the interstices of the lofty and shelving rocks added materially to its beauty. In appearance the uplands on either side of the gorge were totally different. The heights on which the king and his companions stood were wild, and only covered with patches of gorse, while those on the opposite side were crowned with the thickets in the midst of which Abbots Leigh was situated. Divided for long centuries, as we have said, these towering cliffs have been once more united by a light and beautiful bridge suspended over the abyss at such a height that the tallest ship can pass beneath it.

From the lofty point on which Charles stood the course of the Avon from Bristol to the rocky gorge could be distinctly traced in the moonlight, except in places where the river was obscured by a slight haze that gathered over it. The upper part of the cliffs was illumined by the moon, but her beams could not penetrate their mysterious and gloomy depths. Lower down, where the chasm widened, and the cliffs were further apart, the river could be seen rushing on to join the Severn. A strange and fascinating picture, which the king contemplated with great interest.

Meanwhile, the troopers had gained the summit of the hill, and concealed themselves behind the watch-tower.

"There is the boat!" exclaimed Pope, pointing to a dark object distinguishable in the river about three hundred yards from the entrance of the gorge.

Charles listened intently, and, in the deep stillness that prevailed, felt sure he heard the plash of oars.

"'Tis the boat, no doubt," he cried.

"Shall we go down to meet it?" inquired Pope.

Charles signified his assent.

"Your majesty will please to be careful," continued Pope. "The descent is somewhat perilous."

"You hear what he says, fair mistress," remarked Charles to Dame Gives.

Struck by her extreme paleness, he added :

"Let me help you to descend."

But she thankfully declined the gracious offer.

Pope then led them along the edge of the precipitous cliffs, till he arrived at a spot where the bank was not quite so steep, and was fringed with bushes.

"Here is the path, my liege," he exclaimed. "Follow me, and proceed cautiously, I beseech you. A false step might prove fatal."

He then plunged amid the bushes, and was followed by Charles. Close behind the king came Dame Gives.

Their movements had been watched by the troopers, who carefully marked the spot where they commenced the descent, and in another minute were cautiously following them.

The path taken by Pope brought those whom he conducted among the rocks lower down, and here Charles gave a helping hand to Dame Gives, and saved her from the consequences of more than one unlucky slip; but nothing worse occurred, and they all reached the bottom of the cliff in safety.

They were now at the entrance of the gorge, and the river, confined by the rocks, was sweeping rapidly past them through its narrow deep channel.

Charles was gazing at the darkling current and at the towering cliffs, that filled him with a sense of awe, when Pope called out that the boat was at hand.

Next moment it came up, and Captain Rooker, who had been rowing, leaped ashore and made it fast to the stump of a tree. Careless did not land, but helped Dame Gives into the boat, and Charles was about to follow, when shouts were heard, and the two troopers rushed towards them.

Jumping into the boat, Charles ordered Rooker to set her free. But the skipper paid no attention to the command.

"'Thou art taken in the toils, Charles Stuart," he cried. "As an instrument in accomplishing thy capture, I shall receive my reward."

"Be this the reward of thy treachery, villain," cried Careless.

And drawing a pistol from his belt, he shot him through the head.

As the traitor fell to the ground, Pope unloosed the rope, and set the boat free, jumping into it, as he pushed it from the bank. At the same moment, Charles seized the oars, and propelling the boat into the middle of the stream it was swept down by the rapid current.

Unluckily, it had to pass near the troopers, and they shouted to the king, who was now plying the oars, to stop; but as he disregarded the order, they both discharged their carabines at him, and he must have been killed, if Dame Gives had not suddenly risen, and placing herself before him, received the shots. The devoted young woman fell back mortally wounded into the arms of Careless, who was seated near her.

"Are you much hurt?" he cried, in accents of despair.

"Hurt to death!" she rejoined, faintly. "I have not many moments left of life. I knew this would be, and am prepared for it. Farewell for ever!"

"Uttering these words, she breathed her last sigh, and her head declined upon Careless's shoulder.

"She has died for me!" exclaimed Charles. "'Tis a sad and sudden ending, but she anticipated her doom."

"Anticipated it, sire! How mean you?" cried Careless.

"I will explain hereafter, if we escape," said Charles.

Several more shots were fired by the troopers, but no one was hurt. The current swept the boat down so rapidly that those within it were soon out of reach of harm.

"What will you do?" said Charles to Careless.

"I know not," rejoined the other, distractedly. "But I will never rest till I have avenged her. But think not of me, my liege. Save yourself. If you go further down the river, you will most assuredly fall into some new danger."

"If I might venture to advise your majesty," said Pope, "I would recommend you to land as soon as possible, and return at once to Abbots Leigh."

"Thy advice is good," rejoined Charles. "But what is to be done with the unfortunate victim of this treacherous design? How is she to be disposed of?"

"Leave her to me, sire," replied Careless. "Again, I implore you to save yourself. Return to Abbots Leigh, as Pope suggests. If she could speak," he added, solemnly, looking at the lifeless figure, which he still held in his arms, "she would urge you to take this course!"

"If you will consent to keep Pope with you, to assist you in your mournful task, I will go—not otherwise," said Charles.

"Be it so, my liege," replied Careless.

During this colloquy, the boat was carried rapidly through the gorge, and had now reached the point where the chasm grew wider and the cliffs were further apart.

Looking out for a favourable point to land, Charles drew near the left bank of the river, and Pope, jumping ashore, quickly fastened the boat to a tree.

Charles followed, but for some time could not make up his mind to depart.

At last, however, he yielded to the entreaties of Careless, who besought him earnestly to go, urging that his stay would only endanger himself, and ascending the cliffs, he made his way alone through the woods to Abbots Leigh.

END OF BOOK THE SIXTH.

---

# Book the Seventh.

### TRENT.

---

## CHAPTER I.

### ON THE VENGEANCE TAKEN BY CARELESS ON THE TROOPERS.

NOT without great difficulty did Charles succeed in reaching Abbots Leigh after his perilous adventure in the gorge of the Avon. More than once he got lost in the wood, and had just resolved to lie down at the foot of a tree and wait for dawn, when he caught a glimpse of the mansion. Before they parted Pope had advised him to take refuge for a few hours in the stable, explaining how he could obtain admittance to that building even if the door should be locked; and acting upon this counsel the king proceeded thither at once, and having got inside as directed, threw himself upon a heap of clean straw, and presently fell fast asleep. About five o'clock in the morning he was roused from his slumbers by some one who shook him gently, and when he opened his eyes he beheld Pope and Careless standing near him. The latter looked haggard and worn in the grey light of morning.

Half stupefied by the profound slumber in which his faculties had been wrapped, Charles could not for a few moments recal the events of the preceding night, but as soon as he did so he started up and fixing an inquiring look on Careless, asked what had happened since he left him.

" She is avenged, and your majesty is freed from two unrelenting enemies," replied Careless, in a sombre tone.

" I understand," said Charles. " I will ask no further questions now. When you have had some repose, of which you must be greatly in need, you shall give me the details."

" There is no time for converse now, my liege," interposed Pope. " I must take you to your chamber at once. Half an hour hence the household will be astir, and then your absence will be discovered. Your honour must be good enough to remain here till I return," he added to Careless, " unless you choose to mount to the loft, where you will be perfectly safe and undisturbed."

" The loft will suit me as well as the richest chamber," rejoined Careless. " I am so desperately fatigued that I can sleep anywhere."

And as Pope and the king quitted the stable, Careless climbed the wooden steps that led to the loft.

Proceeding to the rear of the mansion, Pope opened a small door that had been purposely left unbolted, and entering with the king, they mounted a back staircase with the utmost caution, and gained Charles's bedchamber, which was in the upper part of the house.

" Your majesty may take your full rest," said Pope; " all the servants believe you have had a relapse of ague."

He then departed, and Charles threw himself on his couch, and soon forgot his dangers and disappointment.

The day had made a considerable advance before the butler reappeared.

The king was awake and thoroughly rested. While assisting his majesty to dress Pope told him that he had seen Mistress Jane Lane, and informed her of the failure of the enterprise.

" She did not appear surprised," continued the butler, " because she had been full of misgivings, but she was rejoiced that your majesty had been preserved from the treacherous skipper's plots. I did not acquaint her with the sad catastrophe that occurred, as I felt sure it would greatly distress her. No doubt strict inquiries will be made into the affair, but they will lead to nothing, since a clue cannot be obtained to your majesty's retreat."

" I thought you were known to David Price, the tavern-keeper?" observed the king.

" The rascal only knows my name, and has no idea that I am Mr. Norton's servant. On the contrary, he believes that I dwell in Bristol.

Captain Rooker, who planned your majesty's capture with the perfidious tavern-keeper, is gone, and the two troopers who aided them in their scheme are likewise disposed of, as Major Careless will explain to you anon. I only wish David Price had shared their fate. But your majesty need have no fear of him. You are quite safe at Abbots Leigh."

"I cannot remain here longer," said Charles. "I must seek assist-ance from other trusty friends. You are an old soldier, Pope, and have served in the late wars. Do you know Colonel Francis Wyndham, the late knight marshal's brother, and somewhile governor of Dunster Castle ?"

"I know him very well, sire," replied the butler, "and I do not know a better or a braver man, nor a more loyal subject of your majesty. About two years ago Colonel Wyndham married Mistress Anne Gerard, daughter and heiress of Squire Thomas Gerard, of Trent, in Somersetshire. Since then he has gone with his wife to live at Trent. His mother, Lady Wyndham, widow of Sir Thomas Wyndham, likewise resides with him. As your majesty may not be acquainted with Trent, I will describe its position. 'Tis a small secluded village, charmingly situated, about midway between Sherborne and Yeovil, and consists of a few scattered habitations—cottages, I ought perhaps to call them—in the midst of which, surrounded by fine old elm-trees, stands the ancient mansion. Close to the yard gate—within a bow-shot of the house—is the church, a fine old pile. I know the manor-house well, for I have often been there, and, unless I am greatly mistaken, it contains hiding-places, in which your majesty could be securely concealed should any search be made. The position of Trent is extremely favourable to your plans. Not only is it out of the main road, and extremely retired, but it is within a few hours' ride of the coast, and I have no doubt whatever that Colonel Wyndham will be able to procure you a vessel at Lyme Regis to transport you to France."

"Was not the colonel taken prisoner when he surrendered Dunster Castle ?"

"He was taken to Weymouth, my liege, but released on his parole, so that he can move about without fear of arrest. Formerly he resided at Sherborne, and was there jealously watched by the Parliamentarians, but since his removal to Trent he has not been subjected to so much annoyance. Your majesty may wonder that I know so much about him, but I am well acquainted with the colonel's man, Harry Peters."

"You have decided me," cried Charles. "I will go to Trent. Major Careless shall serve as my avant courier to apprise Colonel Wyndham that I am coming to him."

Shortly afterwards Charles repaired to the butler's pantry, where he breakfasted, taking care when any of the servants came in to feign great debility.

After breakfast he proceeded to the stables, and watching his oppor-tunity, mounted to the loft in which he had learnt from Pope that Careless was concealed.

A slight signal brought out his faithful follower, whose altered looks and manner could not fail to grieve the king. Careless's natural gaiety seemed to have entirely deserted him, and had given place to a gloomy, almost stern, expression.

"I am at your majesty's orders," he said, saluting the king respectfully.  "Is there aught I can do?"

"You look so ill," rejoined Charles, in accents of deep concern, "that I hesitate to put your devotion to further test.  You need repose.  Take it, and we will talk further."

"Action will cure me sooner than rest," rejoined Careless, with a ghastly smile.  "Sleep seems to shun me, or if I close my weary eyelids for a moment, I start up again in horror."

"Ease your breast, and tell me what has happened, said the king, in tones that bespoke his profound sympathy.

After a powerful struggle, Careless conquered his emotion sufficiently to enable him to speak coherently, and said :

"You know what anguish I endured when she whom I loved so dearly expired in my arms.  I swore to avenge her, and I have kept my oath.  No sooner was your majesty gone than I prepared to execute my purpose, and I found Pope, whose blood was up, well-disposed to second me.  From the sounds we heard, we felt sure that the two murderous caitiffs were still on the opposite bank of the Avon.  While I laid down the body tenderly, Pope pushed the boat to the other side of the river, and enabled me to leap ashore.  The villains were hurrying towards the spot, and as soon as they descried me through the gloom, they both discharged their pistols at me, but the bullets whistled past me harmlessly. I returned the fire with better effect, for I brought down one of them. Sword in hand, I then rushed upon the other, and a sharp conflict took place between us.  Infuriated as I was, he was no match for me, and I drove him to the edge of the precipitous bank.  He made a desperate effort to avoid his fate, but I still pressed fiercely on, smote him, and with a wild cry he fell backwards, and was instantly swept away by the rapid current.  Having thus executed my vengeful task, I returned to the boat, and was quickly transported to the opposite bank by Pope.

"But now arose the painful question—how were her loved remains to be disposed of?  I was almost distracted by the thought of leaving her.  Yet what else could be done?  At last, however, the difficulty was unexpectedly solved.  Pope had fastened the boat to a tree, and had come ashore to confer with me.  We were anxiously deliberating together, when the boat, containing her loved remains, suddenly disappeared ; it was swept away in an instant—gone beyond the possibility of recovery.  Doubtless, as Pope suggested, the rope with which he endeavoured to secure the bark, had become loose, and so the disaster occurred.  But I looked upon it then—as I regard it now—as a cruel stroke of fate, by which I was deprived of the sad consolation of seeing her decently interred."

There was a pause, during which Charles showed by his looks how profoundly he sympathised with his attendant.

"Fear not, she will find a grave," he said, at length.

"It may be so," rejoined Careless.  "But I shall never know where she lies."

"Banish the painful thought from your mind," said Charles  "You cannot do more than you have done. My firm conviction is that she will find a resting-place in some quiet churchyard, and not at the bottom of the deep as you seem to dread."

"I will strive to think so," rejoined Careless.

Again forcibly repressing his emotion, he added in a firm voice, " Your majesty has some commands for me ?"

" You know Colonel Francis Wyndham, I think ? He now resides at Trent, in Somersetshire, and I intend to seek an asylum in his house. Do you approve of the plan ?"

" Perfectly, my liege. Frank Wyndham is a staunch Royalist. You will be quite secure with him."

"I am glad to hear you say so, though I did not doubt his loyalty. You must ride on to Trent, and advise him of my coming."

" Give me till to-morrow, my liege, and I shall be ready to set out. Were I to start to-day, I might break down on the road."

## CHAPTER II.

### HOW JANE LANE AGREED TO ATTEND THE KING TO TRENT.

Quitting the stable, Charles repaired to the butler's pantry, where he found Pope. When the latter was informed of the arrangements made he undertook to provide Major Careless with a horse for his journey to Trent.

" It will be merely necessary to inform Mr. Norton," said the butler, " that a fugitive Cavalier has taken refuge here, and requires to be passed on to the coast. The worthy gentleman will afford him every assistance, and ask no questions."

While they were still conversing, Jane Lane entered the room, and expressed her sincere delight at seeing his majesty safe back again.

" You have proved a true prophetess," Charles said. " You foretold that the attempt would fail, and it has failed. Henceforth, I will be guided by you."

" Then since your majesty permits me to speak, I will venture to say that the plan which Pope tells me you have decided upon is the best that could be adopted. No doubt you will be able to reach Trent without greater difficulties than you have hitherto encountered, and which you have so successfully overcome, and I trust, through Colonel Wyndham's agency, you may procure a vessel to transport you to France."

" To insure me a safe journey to Trent you must accompany me, Jane. Once there I will not tax your services further. Why this hesitation ? Surely, you will not fail me at this important juncture ?"

" I am bound to obey your commands in all things———"

" But you do not like to go with me to Trent. 'Tis but a two days' journey from this place."

" 'Tis not the distance, sire. I would willingly attend your majesty to the furthest point of your kingdom, if you desired me to do so, but———"

" What means this hesitation, Jane ? 'Tis scarcely consistent with your previous noble conduct, which led me to suppose that I might rely upon you to the last. Well, I will put no constraint upon you. I will go alone."

"Forgive me, sire," she cried, with a look of great distress. "I will explain myself. A special messenger has just brought me a letter from Sir Clement Fisher."

"Does he forbid your further attendance upon me?" observed Charles, coldly. "Is his authority paramount to mine?"

"I have just said that I will obey you in all things, my liege," she rejoined, in tones that bespoke her trouble. "And do not, I beseech you, blame Sir Clement. He is as deeply devoted to your majesty as I am myself."

"Till now, I thought so."

"Think so still, sire. Sir Clement is a loyal gentleman, and will sacrifice his life for you; but even for his king he will not sacrifice his honour."

"His honour!" exclaimed Charles, startled. "I demand no such sacrifice. Ha! I understand," he added, as a light suddenly broke upon him. "He is fearful that evil and calumnious tongues may seek to blemish your spotless reputation."

"Your majesty has divined the truth," she replied, casting down her eyes.

"I might have guessed it before. But I judged Sir Clement differently. I deemed him superior to the ordinary run of men. Aware as he is of the feelings by which you have been actuated—confident as he must be of your rectitude of principles—how could a single doubt cross his mind?"

"You do him an injustice, my liege. Sir Clement's confidence in me is unshaken. But he fears that others may not view my conduct in the same light."

"There is a spice of jealousy in this," thought the king.

"In the letter which I have just received from him," pursued Jane, "Sir Clement informs me that he is about to start for Abbots Leigh forthwith, and begs me to await his coming."

"I would not have you do otherwise," rejoined Charles. "I am glad he has so decided. His presence will silence all scandal. When do you expect him?"

"To-morrow, sire. I am sure he will be delighted to escort you to Trent."

"His satisfaction will not be diminished by your companionship," remarked Charles, smiling. "No doubt you will have a great many things to say to each other, and that I may not interfere with the conversation, a slight change shall be made in our arrangements. If another horse can be procured, you shall no longer ride behind me."

"Mr. Norton has plenty of horses in his stable, and will lend me one, I am quite sure," she rejoined. "But it is not necessary to make any change on my account."

"Nay, let it be so," said Charles. "You will enjoy much greater freedom. I shall still continue to act as your groom."

"The disguise has hitherto served your majesty so well that I should be sorry if you abandoned it."

" 'Twould be highly imprudent to do so," rejoined Charles. "If I reach Trent in safety, I may be compelled to play some new part. Till then I shall continue to be Will Jones. In the expectation of Sir Clement's early arrival, I will send off Major Careless to-morrow to announce my coming to Colonel Wyndham. The rest I leave to you."

"And your majesty may rely upon my making all needful arrangements with Mr. Norton. When do you desire to set out for Trent?"

"Nay, you must consult Sir Clement," observed the king, with a smile. "But should it suit him, we will start on the day after his arrival."

"Your majesty's wishes will be his law," replied Jane.

---

## CHAPTER III.

### COLONEL FRANCIS WYNDHAM, OF TRENT.

UNDERSTANDING from Pope that a fugitive Cavalier had sought shelter at Abbots Leigh, Mr. Norton had a private interview with his guest, and on learning his name, offered him all the assistance in his power.

Thanking him most heartily, Careless said if he would provide him with a horse he would esteem it a very great favour.

"What is more, Mr. Norton," he added, "you will materially serve the king."

"Since it is for his majesty's service," replied Mr. Norton, "you shall have the best horse in my stable. Return him or not, as may suit your convenience."

"I shall not fail to acquaint his majesty with your zeal on his behalf, sir," said Careless. "He is well aware of your attachment to him."

"I only wish I had a better opportunity of proving my loyalty, sir. I pray you say as much to the king. I will not ask questions which you may be unwilling to answer, but I shall unfeignedly rejoice to hear that his majesty has escaped."

"I trust it will not be long before you receive that satisfactory intelligence, sir," said Careless. "And I am sure it will gratify you to reflect that you have contributed to so desirable a result. When next we meet I hope I may salute you as Sir George Norton."

"I hope so, too, sir," rejoined the other; "for in that case his majesty will have been restored to the throne."

After this interview Careless was not allowed to return to his place of concealment in the stable, but was lodged in a chamber in the upper part of the house, not far from the room occupied by the king, so that they had an opportunity of conferring together.

At a very early hour on the following morning Careless started on his mission. He was well mounted, for Mr. Norton had strictly fulfilled his promise, and given him his best horse. In his present distracted frame of mind, nothing could have suited the king's faithful adherent better than the task he had undertaken, as he had hoped that hard exercise would enable him to shake off the painful idea by which he was haunted.

He rode on throughout the day, halting only when it was necessary to refresh his steed. Fortunately, he met with no hindrance, though once or twice he was compelled to quit the direct course. His last halt was at Sherborne, and he was then nearly at the end of his journey.

A pleasant ride of a few miles from this charming old town brought him to a secluded little village, consisting only of a few scattered cottages, in the midst of which stood an antique church.

This was Trent. It was growing dusk as he approached the village, and the place was so surrounded by trees that he could only just discern the spire of the church. But he knew that in the midst of those lofty elms stood the old manor-house, of which he was in quest, so he rode on without making any inquiries from the few rustics he encountered.

Pursuing his course along a narrow winding lane, overhung by trees, and skirted here and there by a cottage, having whitewashed walls and a grey thatched roof, he came to the church, close to which stood the old manor-house—a large, low building, solidly constructed of stone, with shingled roof, mullioned windows, and an entrance covered by a penthouse. This was the rear of the mansion, but the front looked upon a smooth lawn, bordered, as we have said, by lofty elm-trees, inhabited by a colony of rooks.

Trent House was not approached by an avenue, and this circumstance it chiefly owed its extreme privacy. The entrance being at the rear was reached from a large yard, differing very little, except in size, from the enclosure ordinarily attached to a substantial farm-house. On the right of the yard were the stables and other outbuildings.

Careless had pulled up at the gate, and was contemplating the old house, and thinking how well adapted it was as a place of refuge for the king, when a serving-man, who was crossing the yard from the stables, noticed him, and at once came up to ascertain his business. As the man drew near he recognised Major Careless, and saluting him respectfully, addressed him by name.

"Your honour has forgotten me, I make no doubt," he said, taking off his cap as he spoke. "I am Harry Peters, and was once your groom."

"Nay, I have not forgotten thee, Harry," replied Careless. "I am glad to find thee here, for I know thee to be a trusty fellow, and thou may'st be of use to me, and to another beside me. Is Colonel Wyndham at home?" And as Peters responded in the affirmative, he added, "that's well; open the gate, and let me in. Now go tell thy master that Mr. Norton desires to speak with him."

"Had I not better announce your honour correctly?"

"Do as I bid thee," said Careless.

And Peters departed.

Left alone Careless dismounted, awaiting Colonel Wyndham's appearance. In a minute or two afterwards the colonel came out of the house and marched towards him.

The former governor of Dunster Castle was a remarkably fine-looking man, in the prime of life, and, though plainly attired, had a very distinguished air, and looked like one accustomed to command.

When within a few yards of the stranger he suddenly stopped, and exclaimed :

"Why, how is this?   My man said that Mr. Norton, of whom I know nothing, and never heard of before, desired to see me, but I find it is my old friend Will Careless."

"Yes, 'tis I, in good truth, Frank," replied the other, laughing. "But I had reasons for the disguise, as I will explain anon."

"You are welcome to Trent, Will—right welcome—under whatever name you come," said Colonel Wyndham, heartily.   "Take Mr. Norton's horse to the stable," he added to Peters.   "Now come in with me, and I will present you to my wife and mother."

"Hold a moment, Frank," cried Careless.   "I must have a word with you.   When you have heard what I have to say, you will judge what is best to be done.   I come from the king."

Colonel Wyndham started back, and uttered an exclamation of joy and surprise.

"You amaze me!" he cried.   "We heard that his majesty was slain at Worcester."

"'Twas a false report, invented by the enemy," replied Careless. "Not only is the king alive and well, but he is coming to take refuge with you here at Trent."

"By Heaven, I am glad to hear it!" cried the colonel.   "No news could please me better—nay, not half so well.   As the bearer of such joyful tidings thou art doubly welcome, Will.   And think not there is need of secresy.   I will answer for my womankind as I would for myself.   Of my mother, Lady Wyndham, I need not speak, for you know her."

"And know her to be loyal," remarked Careless.

"My wife is just as loyal," pursued the colonel.   "And my fair cousin, Juliana Coningsby, is as loyal as my wife.   They have been profoundly grieved by the rumour I have just alluded to of the king's death ; but Juliana refused to credit it, and maintained her confident belief that he is still living, and will be restored to the throne."

"'Tis clear from what you say, Frank, that there will be no risk in communicating the secret to your ladies."

"Fear nothing.   Women can keep a secret as well as we men can— better, perhaps.   My household consists of some twenty persons, and I firmly believe there is not a traitor among them."

"That is much to say.   Yet 'twill be best not to try their fidelity. There is one honest fellow, I'll be sworn—Harry Peters."

"Peters is not an exception—they are all honest.   But come in.   I am anxious to acquaint the ladies with the good news respecting the king."

He then took Careless into the house, and led him to a parlour, which was lighted by a lamp placed on the table.   In this room three ladies were assembled, two of them being young, and engaged on some feminine occupation, while the third and oldest of the party was reading a devotional work.

The elderly dame, as will be surmised, was the colonel's mother. Lady Wyndham had a stately figure and a dignified deportment, and though her finely formed features bore the impress of age, they were still regular in outline.  Her costume belonged to an earlier period, and suited her well.  Her daughter-in-law, Mrs. Wyndham, the heiress to whom the colonel owed Trent, possessed considerable personal attractions —magnificent black eyes and luxuriant black tresses.

A striking contrast to Mrs. Wyndham was Juliana Coningsby—a charming blonde, with summer blue eyes, delicately formed features, snow-white skin, and light locks.  When she smiled—and she smiled very frequently—two rows of exquisite pearls were displayed.  Juliana was just nineteen, and our description would be incomplete if we did not add that her figure was slight and exceedingly graceful.

Careless's appearance caused some excitement among the company.  As we have intimated, he was known to Lady Wyndham, who received him very cordially, and after he had said a few words to her he was presented in due form to the other ladies.

When the presentation had taken place, Colonel Wyndham remarked:

"Major Careless brings us very good news.  The rumour we have heard of the king's death at Worcester is utterly unfounded.  His majesty is safe and well."

"I can vouch for that, since I only left him this morning," added Careless.

Joyful exclamations arose from all.  Juliana clapped her hands together, and called out:

"I knew it!  I knew the king was safe,  Nothing would persuade me to the contrary.  And I am just as sure now that he will escape his enemies, and regain the throne."

His majesty will be delighted to find he has such a zealous partisan," observed Careless, smiling at her vivacity.  "You must give him the assurance from your own lips."

"I should like to have an opportunity of doing so," she rejoined.

"Then your wish will be speedily gratified, Juliana," said Colonel Wyndham.  "You will very soon have an opportunity of conversing with the king."

His wife and Lady Wyndham were greatly surprised by the announcement, and questioned him as to its meaning by their looks; but Juliana called out:

"You are jesting with me, Frank."

"Not so," he rejoined.  "But I won't keep you longer in suspense.  Learn then that the king is coming here."

"His majesty coming to Trent!" exclaimed Juliana, again clapping her hands.  "Oh! that is delightful.  I have longed so much to see him."

"Moderate yourself, my love," said Mrs. Wyndham, who looked scarcely less pleased.

"You are his majesty's harbinger, I suppose?" said Lady Wyndham to Careless.

"Your ladyship is right," he replied.  "I have attended the king ever since the great disaster at Worcester.  Several attempts which he has made to escape to France, have been frustrated, and he has therefore resolved to abide a time when the vigilance of his enemies shall relax.  With this design he has fixed upon Trent House as a retreat, feeling well assured that he has not a more devoted adherent than Colonel Francis Wyndham."

"His majesty has formed a just opinion of my son," said Lady Wyndham. "He will be quite safe under his roof."

"Women are not generally trusted with important secrets," observed Mrs. Wyndham. "But his majesty need fear no indiscretion on our part. Juliana is sometimes rather thoughtless, but she will now see the necessity of keeping strict guard upon her tongue."

"I have never yet had a secret confided to me," said the young lady in question; "but if everybody is as careful as I shall be his majesty won't be in much danger."

"I have already assured Major Careless that the servants can be relied upon," said Colonel Wyndham.

"Yes, they are all perfectly faithful and honest," said his wife. "But of course every precaution shall be observed."

"His majesty shall have my room," said Lady Wyndham. "I will describe it to you, Major Careless, and then you will judge of its fitness for the purpose. It is not in this part of the house, but is situated above the kitchen. It is reasonably large, and loftier than you would expect, because the ceiling is raised into the roof, and supported by oaken rafters. On either side are lattice windows which look into the garden and command the yard, so that his majesty would be made immediately aware of the arrival of any dangerous visitor. The room is wainscoted with old oak, and at one end is a secret closet in which the king could take refuge. But this is not all. A movable board within the closet affords access to a short, narrow staircase contrived in the wall, by means of which an outbuilding can be gained, and thus any search may be eluded. I must not omit to mention that in the principal room there is a small cupboard, concealed by a sliding panel, and in this cupboard wine and provisions may be stored. But you must see the room yourself. No other apartment in the house offers such facilities for concealment and flight."

"Your ladyship's description is so clear," said Careless, "that I need not see the room to decide that it is exactly suitable to the king's present requirements. My only concern is that you should be obliged to relinquish it."

"Poh! that is a mere trifle," exclaimed the loyal old dame. "I would give up all I possess to benefit his majesty. I shall easily find another room."

"You shall have mine, dear aunt," cried Juliana, eagerly.

"When is his majesty's arrival to be expected?" inquired Colonel Wyndham.

"He is staying at Abbots Leigh, near Bristol," replied Careless. "In all probability he will leave there to-morrow morning, attended by Mistress Jane Lane and Sir Clement Fisher, but he will not proceed beyond Castle Cary. Early on the following day he may be looked for here."

"All shall be ready for him," said Colonel Wyndham.

A long conversation then ensued, which it is not needful to report. The ladies had a number of questions to ask respecting the fatal fight at Worcester and the king's subsequent adventures, and while Careless gratified their natural curiosity, Colonel Wyndham left the room to give directions for the accommodation of his unexpected, though most welcome guest. Careless's auditors listened with the deepest interest to his vivid description of the king's hair-breadth 'scapes, but no one was so excited by the relation as Juliana Coningsby.

From the first moment when she beheld the king's faithful messenger, Juliana had been struck by his appearance, but when he recounted some stirring incident in which he himself, as well as his royal master, had taken part—when his eyes flashed, and the gloom that had hitherto hung upon his brow was dispersed—she thought him the handsomest man she had ever beheld, and began to feel an interest in him, such as she had never before experienced. She was still watching his animated countenance—still drinking in his accents—when Colonel Wyndham broke the charm—very unpleasantly to her—by coming in, and announcing that supper was ready. The party then adjourned to the dining-room, where a substantial repast awaited them.

---

## CHAPTER IV.

### JULIANA CONINGSBY.

Comfortably lodged, and fatigued by his long journey, Careless slept very soundly, and awoke in better spirits than he had felt since the sad catastrophe in the gorge of the Avon.

On descending from his room he went forth upon the lawn in front of the house, and was admiring the range of magnificent elms by which it was surrounded, when Juliana Coningsby came out of the garden with a little basket of flowers in her hand, and tripped towards him with a light footstep across the smooth greensward.

If Careless had been struck by her beauty overnight, he was far more impressed by it now. Her figure, we have said, was exceedingly light and graceful, and in her very becoming morning costume, with her blonde tresses hanging over her shoulders, and her fair complexion slightly heightened, she looked really charming.

He had persuaded himself that he could never love again, but now that this exquisite creature stood before him, and greeted him with the sweetest smile imaginable, and in accents that sounded melodiously in his ear, he began to think it possible he might do so.

Formal salutations having passed between them, she said :

" Do you know, Major Careless, I have been dreaming all night of the king's romantic adventures, which you related to us. I quite envy Jane Lane the part she took in them. I should consider it the greatest privilege to attend upon his majesty."

" Jane Lane is a person of the highest courage, full of ardour and zeal for the royal cause," replied Careless. " You must excuse my saying that very few of your sex would have gone through what she has done."

And a slight shade crossed his features as he spoke.

" It is plain you think I could not do as much," said Juliana, in a slight tone of pique. " But I am certain I could. To ride on a pillion behind the king would be an event to remember all one's life. Lady Lane must feel very proud. Is she good-looking ?"

" Remarkably so," rejoined Careless. " I have seen very few persons who can compare with her. She is not only beautiful but full of spirit. But you will see her, for she is coming here with the king. Sir Clement Fisher, to whom she is betrothed, will form one of the party. Should she succeed in bringing his majesty safe to Trent, her duties will be at an end, and you can then, if you think proper, assume her post. The king, I am sure, will be enchanted to have so fair a companion. But the service is not without great risk."

" There would be no excitement in it—no honour to be won—if there were no risk," she rejoined. " I hope some circumstance may occur to prove that I am not inferior to Jane Lane."

While thus conversing, they had moved to a part of the lawn from which the church was visible. It has been already stated that the beautiful old structure was quite close to the mansion, and indeed a narrow road only divided the churchyard from the garden.

" Though the church is so near to us, and contains the family pew," said Juliana, " we are prevented from offering our devotions within it." The worthy rector, the Reverend Richard Langton, has been deprived of his benefice, and has been succeeded by an Independent minister, and though the Reverend Lift-up-Hand Meldrum, for so he is named, may be a very good man, we none of us care to listen to his discourses. We have prayers at home, and Mr. Langton, who, though driven from the rectory, still resides in the village, officiates as Colonel Wyndham's domestic chaplain."

As Careless expressed a desire to inspect the sacred edifice, with which he was much struck, they passed out at a small gate at the bottom of the garden. A few steps brought them to the entrance to the churchyard—a quiet spot, full of graves of rounded turf. On the left of the churchyard stood the old rectory, now occupied by the Independent minister,

On approaching the church they found the door open and walked in. The interior of the old fabric was as beautiful as the exterior, and not much damage had been done to its monuments, though the painted glass in the windows had been destroyed. A hasty survey of the chancel sufficed for Careless. As they returned through the churchyard, a tall, sallow-complexioned personage, in a black gown and Geneva bands, could be seen standing at the door of the rectory.

" The Reverend Lift-up-Hand Meldrum is watching us," said Juliana. " Perhaps it would have been more prudent in you not to come here."

" It matters little, I think," said Careless. " If he is inquisitive, he must have learnt that a stranger has arrived at the manor-house."

" Very true ; but he will now discover from your attire that you are a Cavalier."

They did not return by the garden, but entered the yard, which we have described as contiguous to the church.

Here they found Colonel Wyndham, who was giving some orders to Peters and another groom, and after a hearty greeting had passed between Careless and his host, they proceeded to the stables to look at the horses. On their return from this inspection, which occupied only a few minutes, the colonel stopped Careless in the middle of the yard, and bade him notice the upper windows in the projecting wing of the house.

"Those windows belong to the room which my mother proposes to relinquish to his majesty," he said. "Below is the kitchen, which we will visit anon, in order that you may see how the house is arranged. Notice the little outbuilding on the left, attached to the main structure. 'Tis a brewhouse, but it is important because the projecting chimney which you see beyond the gable contains the secret closet and staircase. On the other side there is an outlet to the garden, perfectly concealed by shrubs. Now notice the penthouse in the angle of the building. It has two arches as you will observe, and behind each is a door, one of which affords an exit and the other an entrance. The room which his majesty will occupy possesses the means of exit. Now come and look at the kitchen."

So saying, he led his guest to a deeply-arched doorway near the brewhouse, which at once admitted them to a goodly room, occupying the entire ground floor of this part of the building. The roof was somewhat low, but it was festooned with hams, and the kitchen contained an enormous fireplace, at which a baron of beef or a whole sheep might be roasted. The cook was now busily at work for breakfast, roasting a brace of partridges, and frying eggs and bacon. Colonel Wyndham did not disturb her in her occupation, but took Careless into the outbuilding, and showed him how secret access might be gained to the room above.

"I see exactly what could be done," remarked Careless. "If the house should be searched, his majesty might come down from the room above, and, mingling with the servants, would not be observed."

"Precisely," replied Colonel Wyndham.

They then repaired to the dining-room, where they found all the ladies assembled. With them was the deprived rector of Trent, who dwelt in a small cottage hard by, but generally took his meals in the house.

The Reverend Mr. Langton's manner was grave, and not devoid of dignity, and his venerable appearance was heightened by his silver locks. That the good man bore his losses with resignation was shown by the placid expression of his countenance. Colonel Wyndham had already explained to Careless that Mr. Langton must be considered as one of the family, and that no secrets need be kept from him, adding that the king had not a more devoted subject than the reverend gentleman.

As will be readily conceived, the king's expected visit engrossed the thoughts of all concerned in the scheme, and preparations for his majesty's reception were immediately commenced, though with all due caution. Lady Wyndham removed to another room; and when Careless was shown the antique and curious chamber she had just quitted, he pronounced it admirably adapted to the purpose desired.

Having most successfully accomplished his mission, Careless prepared to set out to Castle Cary, where he had appointed to meet the king, and inform him how he had prospered. So charmed were the ladies of Trent with the very agreeable manners of the king's handsome messenger, that his departure would have caused them great regret if he had not promised to return next day, in company with his royal master.

Colonel Wyndham, attended by Harry Peters, rode with his friend as far as Sherborne. Here they separated, and Careless pursued his journey alone, proceeding to Milborne Port, and Wincaunton, where he halted for a short time.

On arriving at the prettily situated little town of Castle Cary, he put up at an inn where he thought that the king and his companions would alight. They were not there, but he learnt that a party answering to their description had gone to the manor-house, then belonging to Mr. Kirton, who, it subsequently appeared, was well known to Sir Clement Fisher.

The manor-house was situated on the further side of a hill, on which the castle had once stood, and thither Careless proceeded on foot. He did not make himself known at the house, as he was fortunate enough to find the king in the stable. During the short interview he had with his majesty, he acquainted him with the entire success of his mission, and Charles was delighted with the description given him of Trent. In return, the king informed his attendant that he had left Abbots Leigh early in the morning, accompanied by Sir Clement Fisher and Jane Lane, and had encountered no difficulty or interruption during the whole day's journey.

"Feeling that Jane must be tired of the pillion," he said, "I induced her to discard it. Like a discreet groom I lagged behind, and left the lovers to enjoy their conversation unmolested, only joining them when they seemed tired of each other's society. It would appear that Sir Clement has been slightly jealous, though he has no reason on earth to be so: but he is quite cured now, and I am glad of it, for he is a most excellent fellow."

"All is well, then," said Careless, laughing. "It would have been a sad thing if the match had been broken off. Has your majesty any further commands for me?"

"None. We shall start betimes in the morning, You can join us a mile or two out of the town. Good night!"

Careless then returned to the inn.

---

## CHAPTER V.

### HOW CHARLES ARRIVED AT TRENT.

NEXT day, about an hour before noon, Colonel Wyndham and his lovely cousin mounted their steeds and rode towards Sherborne to meet the king. They had not got beyond the colonel's domain when he went into a field to speak to some of his men, leaving Juliana beneath a tree, which threw its branches across the road. She had been alone for a few minutes, when a solitary horseman was seen coming from the direction of Sherborne.

For a moment her expectations were raised, but as the horseman drew nearer she judged from his garb and general appearance that he could only be a farmer's son. Presently the young man rode up, and doffed his cap respectfully. He was excessively swarthy, and his hair was clipped very close to his head. With a certain freedom of manner, which Juliana did not at all like, he inquired whether Colonel Wyndham dwelt thereabouts.

"The colonel is in yonder field," she replied. "You can go to him. if you think proper."

"No; I will wait for him here," said the young man. "If I am not mistaken, you are his cousin, Mistress Juliana Coningsby."

The young lady regarded him haughtily, as much as to say, "What can it matter to you who I am?"

"Nay, I meant no offence," he said, construing the look correctly. "If you are Mistress Juliana Coningsby, as I shrewdly suspect, report has done you scant justice."

Juliana's proud lip slightly curled.

You are reported to be very handsome, but more might be said, methinks," continued the young man, scarcely repressing his admiration.

"Thou art a bold fellow to tell me this to my face," cried Juliana.

"I may be bold, but I am not a flatterer," rejoined the young man. "Truth ought not to be disagreeable, and I have spoken nothing but truth."

"But were I to say thou art singularly ill-favoured, it would be truth, yet thou wouldst not like it," remarked Juliana.

"It would certainly be a poor return for my civil speech." rejoined the young man, laughing. "But if you knew me better you might change your opinion. I have not always been thought ill-favoured."

"They who thought thee otherwise must have been bad judges. with whom thy impertinence might pass for wit," said Juliana. "But I will tolerate no more of it. Stand back, and do not presume to address me again, or I will acquaint the colonel, and he will punish thy presumption."

"I am not aware that I have presumed, fair mistress." replied the other. "But if you deem so, I humbly ask your pardon."

"Ah! here comes the colonel," cried Juliana. "He will read thee a wholesome lesson for thy freedom of speech."

Colonel Wyndham's approach produced a sudden change in the young man's demeanour that astonished Juliana.

Pushing forward to the gate, he called out lustily:

"Frank, Frank! how art thou?"

At the sound of this well-known voice the colonel quickened his pace. exclaiming joyously

"Welcome, my liege!—welcome! I am rejoiced to see you."

"And I am equally rejoiced to see thee, Frank," cried Charles. heartily.

"'Tis the king!" exclaimed Juliana. in mingled surprise and consternation. "Oh, sire! pardon my excessive stupidity! I ought to have recognised your majesty in any disguise. What appears impertinence in a groom is only condescension in a monarch."

"Oddsfish! I have nothing to pardon," rejoined Charles, laughing. "You have told me some home truths, that's all. I am very glad I rode on, or I should have lost this diverting scene. Ah! here they come," he cried, as Jane Lane and the others appeared in sight.

Next moment the new-comers rode up, and were introduced to Colonel Wyndham and his fair cousin by Careless. The two young ladies seemed mutually pleased with each other.

"I must explain that during your stay at Trent you are to be treated as a near relative of the family," observed Juliana to Jane. "I shall address you as cousin."

"An excellent arrangement," said Jane. "But my stay must of necessity be very brief. Having brought his majesty in safety here, my duty is fulfilled, and I shall return with Sir Clement to-morrow."

"I am sorry to hear that," said Colonel Wyndham. "I hope you and Sir Clement would have remained with us for a few days, but I will not attempt to persuade you to act against your inclinations. Do exactly as you please."

They then proceeded towards the house, and as they passed through the village the cottagers rushed to their doors to look at the strangers, and Charles had to enact his part carefully while he was under their observation. The Reverend Lift-up-Hand Meldrum likewise came forth from the rectory, and carefully scrutinised the party, but he paid little attention to the disguised monarch.

Naturally there was a great deal of bustle in the yard while the party was dismounting, and Colonel Wyndham seized the opportunity of saying a few words in private to the king, but some little time elapsed before his majesty could be taken to the room prepared for him.

In a very few minutes after he had taken possession of the apartment it was as full of visitors as if he had held a levée.

As a matter of course, the ladies of the house were first presented to him, and were most graciously received, Charles expressing his warm obligations to Lady Wyndham for the kindness she had shown him. Mrs. Wyndham had some pleasant observations made to her, and Juliana was so charmed with the king's manner that she wondered how she could ever have been mistaken in regard to him. Mr. Langton was likewise presented to his majesty, and congratulated him on his escapes.

In this agreeable and sympathetic society Charles passed the pleasantest hour he had enjoyed for some time. Not one of the persons present, as he well knew, but was devoted to his cause, and several of them had given abundant proofs of their devotion. No wonder, then, that he felt unusually cheerful; and while listening to his lively sallies, several of those who were present could scarcely believe that they were uttered by a fugitive king, upon whose head a price was set.

## CHAPTER VI.

### OF THE PARTING BETWEEN THE KING AND JANE LANE.

NEXT day, however, Charles's cheerfulness for awhile deserted him. He had to part with Jane Lane; and though he was fully prepared for the event, it caused him a much greater pang than he had anticipated. They had been thrown together so much of late, and she had shown such deep and disinterested devotion to him, that he had began to regard her almost as a sister. Throughout their intimate association she had displayed so many high and noble qualities, such good judgment and discretion, such untiring zeal and intrepidity, that the king must have been insensible indeed if he had not rightly estimated her. Jane's character was so pure, so simple, so irreproachable, that it could not be misrepresented. Charles looked upon her as a superior being, and when speaking of her in after years, and alluding to the important services she had rendered him, always admitted that he had never met with her like.

He was seated near a small table when she entered the room, followed by Sir Clement Fisher, who remained near the door, while she advanced towards him. Her mournful looks announced her purpose. Charles immediately rose, and prevented her from kneeling to him.

"I am come to take leave of your majesty," she said, in a voice that that betrayed her deep emotion.

"I need not say how grieved I am to part with you, Jane," replied the king, sadly. "In losing you I lose my guardian angel, and I tremble lest my good fortune should desert me. To you—under Heaven!—I am mainly indebted for my preservation."

"If I thought I could render your majesty further assistance nothing would induce me to quit you," said Jane. "But my task is fulfilled. Others, equally devoted, and better able to serve you, will perform the rest. That your speedy deliverance from your foes is at hand I nothing doubt; and it is that firm conviction which strengthens me at this moment. My prayers will go with your majesty."

"I thank you from my heart," replied Charles. "I know that I am with those who are devoted to me, yet somehow I cannot reconcile myself to parting with you. But I will not be thus selfish," he cried. "I will not impose needless duties upon you. Others must be considered——"

"Jane has my free consent to remain, if she can be of any further service to your majesty," said Sir Clement.

"No—no," cried Charles. "She has done too much already. My chief regret in parting with you, Jane, is that I cannot requite your services, but a time, I trust, will come when I shall be able to do so. Of all who have served me, you have the strongest claim to my gratitude, and the debt shall not remain undischarged. And now, since the word must be spoken, I will no longer hesitate to pronounce it—farewell to both! I need not wish you happiness, Sir Clement, since you will possess a treasure, such as few men have been fortunate enough to obtain."

"I know it, my liege," replied Sir Clement, earnestly.

Making a profound reverence to the king, Jane then retired, exclaiming in fervent tones, as she quitted the room :

"Heaven preserve you majesty!"

Charles was much affected by her departure, and remained for some minutes engrossed by painful reflections.

Roused from his reverie by a noise in the yard, he stepped to the window, and saw that Jane and Sir Clement had mounted their steeds, and were bidding adieu to Colonel Wyndham and Juliana. She raised her eyes for a moment towards the window at which the king was stationed, but he could not tell whether she perceived him or not. The gate was thrown open by Peters, hands were waved as they passed through it—and she and Sir Clement were gone.

---

## CHAPTER VII.

### OF THE INTERVIEW BETWEEN THE KING AND SIR JOHN STRANGWAYS IN MELBURY PARK.

LATER on in the day Colonel Wyndham came into learn the king's commands, and finding him much depressed, said :

"Your majesty seems cast down by Mistress Jane Lane's departure, and I do not wonder at it ; but I trust you believe that you have friends here who will serve you as faithfully as she has done."

"I do not doubt it, Frank," sighed Charles. "I have every reliance on your fidelity."

"It will interest your majesty, I am sure, to be made acquainted with a prophetic speech uttered by my honoured sire, Sir Thomas Wyndham, not long before his death, in 1636, now some fifteen years ago. Sir Thomas at the time being dangerously ill, and not likely to recover, called together his five sons, and spoke to us of the peace and prosperity which the kingdom had enjoyed during the three last glorious reigns ; but he added, that if the puritanical faction was not controlled it would inevitably obtain the mastery, and the pillars of government be undermind. 'My sons,' he added, with a sorrowful expression of countenance, 'we have hitherto known serene and happy times, but the sky is growing dark. Clouds and troubles are at hand. But come what may, I command you to honour and obey the king. Adhere to the crown, and though it should hang upon a bush I charge you not to forsake it.' My father's prophetic words made an ineffaceable impression on us all. Since then three of his sons and a grandson have died while fighting for the good cause. But the dark and troublous times, to which he prophetically referred, have arrived. Fanatics and regicides prevail. The crown itself hangs on a bush."

"Truly it does," remarked Charles.

"But it will not fall. It will rest there till placed on your majesty's head. Heaven, as I firmly believe, has reserved me for a great work— has brought me safely through many and great dangers, in order that I may prove myself a dutiful son and a loyal subject, by faithfully serving your majesty in your hour of greatest need. It has occurred to me, that my neighbour, Sir John Strangways, of Melbury Park, may be useful to your majesty. Sir John, I need scarcely say, is a staunch Royalist, and has given abundant proofs of his loyalty. His two sons were colonels in the army of your late royal father. He has friends at Weymouth, and I think he can procure you a vessel there. With your permission I will ride over to Melbury to-day, and see him."

"I will ride with you, if it can be managed," cried Charles.

"It can be easily managed, my liege, if you will deign to take Juliana Coningsby on a pillion behind you."

"Nothing could please me better," cried Charles. "I shall greatly enjoy the ride."

"And Melbury is a very fine park, and contains some noble oaks," said the colonel. "We will set out at once."

Descending the back staircase, they then proceeded to the stable, where they found Peters, to whom the colonel gave all necessary instructions, after which, he returned to the house to inform Juliana of the arrangement. Greatly delighted she flew to her room to make some needful change in her toilet, while Careless, who desired to be included in the party, and felt certain the king would be glad of his company, marched off to the stable. Shortly afterwards the horses were brought out. Juliana looked charming in her riding-dress, and her cheeks glowed and her eyes sparkled as she took her seat on the pillion behind the king. No doubt it was a great event in her life, and she did not attempt to conceal her delight. Careless rather envied the king his fair companion.

The road to Melbury Park, which was about eight or nine miles distant from Trent, led them through Over Compton and past the commanding eminence known as Babylon Hill. Proceeding thence through the beautiful valley of the Yeo, after halting for a short time to examine the noble old church of Bradford Abbas, the party rode on past Bradford Mill, and along the banks of the river to Yetminster. The pretty little village of Melbury Osmund, which adjoined the park, was next reached.

As the day was extremely fine, and the scenery enchanting, Charles greatly enjoyed the ride. Moreover, he had a very lively companion, who exerted herself to amuse him, and succeeded perfectly.

Melbury Park, which they shortly afterwards entered, was exceedingly picturesque and beautiful, and, as Colonel Wyndham had stated, contained some noble old oaks. Among them was a huge patriarch of the forest, the trunk of which was enormous. The tree has been well described as a "curly, surly, knotty old monster."

"That old tree is called Billy Wilkins, my liege—wherefore I know not," remarked Colonel Wyndham.

"It deserves a better appellation," replied Charles, laughing. "But you will find us near it when you return. Off with you to the house."

"Shall I bring Sir John to your majesty?"

"As you please."

Colonel Wyndham then rode off at a rapid pace towards the ancient mansion.

Nothing could be more charming than the situation of Melbury House. At the rear was a noble grove of trees, while the green lawn in front sloped down to a beautiful lake. With its lofty tower and numerous gables, the old edifice presented a most picturesque appearance, and this effect was heightened by the pinnacles of an ancient church which could just be seen above the trees.

Charles did not long remain stationary beneath the rugged old oak, but rode to such points as commanded the best view of the house. Familiar with the park, Juliana pointed out its chief beauties to him.

Having finished his survey, he returned to the place of rendezvous. They were examining the gnarled trunk of Billy Wilkins, and wondering what the age of the old monster could be, when the colonel was seen coming back from the house.

Riding by his side was an elderly personage, whom Juliana at once proclaimed to be Sir John Strangways. Charles regarded him with great interest, for he was a perfect specimen of an old Cavalier—his attire, hat, doublet, hose, and boots belonging to the days of his majesty's grandsire, James I.

Turning his horse's head towards them, Charles awaited the approach of the pair, while Careless placed himself on his majesty's left.

On being presented to the king by Colonel Wyndham, Sir John Strangways uncovered his white flowing locks, and bowed reverently.

" I am glad to see you, Sir John," cried Charles. " Had it been safe for me to do so, I would have ridden up to your house."

" I should have been greatly honoured by the visit, my liege," replied the old Cavalier. " But I would not have you incur any risk on my account. I render thanks to Heaven that you are in safety, and I pray that you may speedily be delivered from your enemies. Colonel Wyndham has explained your majesty's wishes, and it deeply grieves me that I am unable to procure a vessel to convey you to France. All the shipmasters whom I knew at Weymouth and Poole have been banished for their loyalty. Those left are rebels and Roundheads. Some trustworthy man may possibly be found at Lyme, but I have no acquaintance there, and might do your majesty more harm than good by making inquiries. Colonel Wyndham can serve you far better than I can."

" It would seem so, Sir John," rejoined Charles, coldly ; " and I shall therefore rely upon him."

" I pray your majesty not to attribute my non-compliance with your wishes to want of zeal," said Sir John. " I dare not promise more than I may be able to perform, but I am quite ready to obey your behests."

" I have no commands to give, Sir John," said Charles, still more coldly. " Colonel Wyndham led me to believe you had the power to assist me, but I find he was in error."

" I have the will, but not the power, my liege. I can offer you a secure asylum at Melbury."

" I am already provided with a secure asylum," said the king.

" Possibly your majesty may require funds. I have brought with me three hundred broad pieces—all I have in my coffers."

And as he spoke he took a leather bag from his saddle-bow.

" Put back the bag, Sir John," said Charles.  " I do not require the money."

And he made a movement as if about to depart.

" For Heaven's sake stay, my gracious liege, and say something kind to him," whispered Juliana to the king.  " You will break the old man's heart if you depart thus.  I will answer for it that he is devoted to your majesty."

" Well, perhaps, I have been too easily moved," replied Charles in the same low tone.  " I have bethought me, Sir John," he added to him.  " I may need this money, and I will therefore borrow it from you.  Take the bag, Careless.  That you are sincere in your professions of zeal I nothing doubt, but I now want energetic action."

" Were my sons at home, my liege," said Sir John, whose accents showed that he was much distressed, " they would procure you a vessel, I am certain.  But I am too old——"

" Enough!" cried the king.  " I have been too hasty in my judgment.  I perceive that I was wrong,"

And as he spoke he extended his hand towards the old Cavalier, which the other pressed gratefully to his lips."

This gracious action operated like balm upon Sir John's wounded feelings.  He attended the king to the park gate, and as they rode thither, Charles conversed with him in the most affable manner, and completely effaced all painful impressions.

---

## CHAPTER VIII.

HOW THE KING HEARD THE PARTICULARS OF HIS OWN DEATH AND BURIAL.

THE party rode back as cheerfully as they came.  Though disappointed by the result of the interview with Sir John Strangways, Colonel Wyndham did not seem discouraged, but said he had another plan to propose to his majesty.  However, an unlooked for occurrence had taken place during their absence.

When about a mile from Trent, they were greatly surprised by hearing the church bells ring out a loud and joyous peal.  Mingled with these sounds was the occasional discharge of a musket.  What could have happened to call forth such manifestations?  Not even Colonel Wyndham could conjecture.  But as they drew near the village, they learnt that a small troop of Cromwell's horse that had fought at Worcester had just arrived, and had proclaimed the utter rout of the royal army—adding the important, and as they declared authentic intelligence, that the Malignant Prince himself had been slain, and buried among a heap of his misguided followers.

News then reached a retired village like Trent so slowly, that only vague rumours of the decisive battle had been hitherto received.  But here were men who, having fought at the great fight, could not be discredited.

The inhabitants of Trent, most of whom were fanatics, were greatly elated by the news, and desired to have the bells rung, and to this their minister willingly assented. They were also preparing to feast the victorious troopers, and at night there were to be bonfires and other rejoicings.

Charles laughed when he learnt these particulars of his own death and burial, and not unreasonably thought that further search for him was not likely to be made in this quarter.

As they went on, they found that the churchyard was filled by the villagers, while a score or more red-coats had tied up their horses in the yard of the mansion, and were now regaling themselves on the cold viands and ale with which they had compelled Mrs. Wyndham to supply them.

His house being thus in the hands of the enemy, it behoved Colonel Wyndham to be careful how he approached it, but Peters met him before he reached the gate, and hastily explaining what had happened, told him the red-coats had behaved quietly enough as yet, and would no doubt depart peaceably if they were not thwarted.

Acting on this advice, the colonel, on entering the yard, addressed a few words to the soldiers, telling them he was glad to see them, and adding that they should have as much ale as they liked. The prudence of this course was soon shown. The men thanked him, and allowed him and Careless to pass on unquestioned, but Charles was not quite so lucky. A stalwart trooper laid hold of his bridle, and declared he must give an account himself.

"I will answer for him," cried Juliana. "He is my groom, and as true a man as ever breathed."

"True to whom?" demanded the trooper, gruffly.

"To the Parliament, to be sure," said Charles. "I am ready to drink Old Noll's health."

"Coupled with the wish that he may soon be king?" said the trooper.

"I forbid him to drink that toast," cried Juliana.

"Why so, fair mistress?" demanded the trooper, knitting his brows.

"Because it would be treason to the state," she rejoined.

"Nay, friend, I have no such scruples," remarked Charles, in an undertone to the trooper. "I will bring you a stoop of good liquor anon, and then we will drink any toast you please."

"Verily, thou art a true man," rejoined the trooper. "Thou shalt learn to whom thou speakest. I am Fetch-him-out-of-the-Pulpit Strongitharm, by whose hand the young man Charles Stuart was slain."

"Was Charles Stuart slain by thee?" exclaimed the king.

"Yea, verily by me," rejoined Strongitharm, exultingly. "The buff coat which I now wear forms part of the spoils taken from the body of the Malignant Prince. Pass on."

As may well be imagined, old Lady Wyndham and her daughter-in-law were in great consternation at this visit, but owing to the prudent and conciliatory measures adopted by Harry Peters, the annoyance was very slight. Some of the troopers certainly entered the house, but they

did not get beyond the kitchen, where they were very well entertained.

Charles, however, was obliged to remain in the stables, and to mingle
with the red-coats, but he comported himself so well that no suspicion
whatever attached to him. How could it, indeed, when after listening
to a further account from Strongitharm of his own death and burial, he
emphatically declared that England had had a great deliverance!

Later on in the day, the troopers marched off for Yeovil, where they
meant to pass the night. The inmates of Trent House were thus
relieved from anxiety, and Charles was able to return to his room.

At dusk, bonfires were lighted by the sectarian villagers to celebrate
Cromwell's great victory at Worcester. The flames could be seen from
the king's windows, and the shouts reached his ears.

" 'Tis Cromwell's turn now—it may be mine to-morrow," remarked
Charles to Mr. Langton, who was with him at the time.

"Heaven grant it!" exclaimed the divine. "This poor misguided
folk will shout quite as loudly as they do now—ay, and light just as
large bonfires, when your majesty is happily restored to the throne."

The next day passed very tranquilly at Trent House. After an
agreeable walk in the garden with the fair Juliana, whose lively talk
helped to chase away the gloom which, despite all his efforts, began to
steal upon him, Charles had returned to his room, and was conferring
with Careless as to what ought to be done, when Colonel Wyndham
came in, with a letter in his hand, and having a very joyful expression
of countenance.

"I have just received a piece of information that promises to make
amends for our disappointment of yesterday," he said. "My brother-
in-law, and your majesty's most loyal subject, Colonel Bullen Reymes,
of Wadden, in Dorsetshire, writes me word that he has succeeded in
obtaining for Sir John Berkeley a passage to France through Captain
William Ellesdon, of Lyme Regis. I am not personally acquainted
with Captain Ellesdon, but I know him to be a man of strict honour
and a staunch Royalist—as indeed this action proves him. What he
has done for Sir John Berkeley he can do for your majesty."

"Oddsfish! this Captain Ellesdon seems to be the very man we
require," cried Charles. "But how comes it you never thought of him
before?"

"He did occur to me, my liege," replied the colonel. "But though
I felt sure of his desire to serve your majesty, I doubted his ability.
Now I entertain a very different opinion. With your majesty's approval,
I will ride over to Lyme to-morrow and see him."

"Do so, by all means," cried Charles, eagerly. "Careless shall go
with you. The plan holds out every prospect of success. Captain
Ellesdon, I conclude, can be told for whom the vessel is to be hired?"

"You may entirely confide in him, sire," replied the colonel. "He is
loyalty itself, and will feel honoured by being thus employed."

"Then see him without delay," cried Charles, rising from his seat,
and pacing the room with manifest signs of impatience. "I am eager
to be off. Can you not set out this evening? Nay, I am taxing your
loyalty too strongly."

"Not a whit, my liege," replied the colonel.  "I will obey you in everything.  Major Careless and myself will start this evening.  We will sleep at Axminster, and ride thence betimes to-morrow to Lyme."

"You are a zealous friend, indeed, Frank," cried Charles, looking well pleased.

"With this important matter on my mind, sire, I shall not be able to rest till I have seen Captain Ellesdon," said the colonel.  "Are you prepared to start so soon ?" he added to Careless.

"I need only five minutes to saddle my horse," replied the other.

"Should a satisfactory arrangement be made, your majesty shall be immediately apprised of it," said Colonel Wyndham.  "I shall take Harry Peters with me."

Thereupon the conference ended, and Colonel Wyndham quitted the king to give such instructions to his wife as he deemed necessary before his departure.

---

## CHAPTER IX.

### CAPTAIN ELLESDON, OF LYME REGIS.

Evening was coming on when Colonel Wyndham and Careless, attended by Peters—all three being well mounted and well armed—quitted Trent on the important mission.

At Yeovil they learnt that the troopers who had troubled them on the previous day had marched on to Crewkerne, and fearing some interruption, they made a slight détour, in order to avoid the latter place.

Their road led through a very charming country, but its heauties were lost to them owing to the darkness, and they were not sorry to arrive, after a two hours' ride, at the picturesque old town of Axminster, where they put up at a very comfortable hostel.

Next morning, after an early breakfast, they quitted the inn, and took the road to Lyme Regis.

On this side of Axminster the environs of the old town were extremely beautiful.  Grey-thatched, white-walled cottages skirted the road, and attached to most of these pretty little habitations were apple-orchards, while green slopes in their vicinity, shaded by trees, lent a peculiar charm to the scene.

Very soon the cottages and orchards were left behind, and the horsemen began to mount a lofty hill, from the brow of which a magnificent prospect was obtained—comprehending extensive views into the two fair counties of Dorset and Devon, long ranges of hills, varied in form—some crowned with woods, others wild and bare, or covered only with becoming heather and gorse—and wide deep valleys, through each of which a small river took its way towards the sea.

After halting for a few minutes to breathe their steeds and enjoy this splendid panorama, the horsemen descended the further side of the hill, and on reaching the valley, found a charming little village, nestled among trees, consisting of a few habitations and an ancient church.

Nothing can be finer than the ride between Axminster and Lyme

Regis. Two lofty hills have to be crossed, each commanding splendid views, though totally differing in character. Cultivated almost to the summit, and divided into small patches by innumerable hedge-rows, the hills have a most pleasing effect. But the prospect is ever varying, and as the point of view is continually shifted, new beauties are displayed.

Our horsemen had now mounted the second hill, and were approaching Uplyme, when a glorious view burst upon them. A vast expanse of ocean, smooth as a mirror, and glittering in sunshine, lay before them; while on the left stretched out a bay, girded by bold and precipitous cliffs. The hills to which these cliffs belonged rose to a great height, the loftiest among them being known as the Golden Cap, on the summit of which a signal was placed, distinguishable far out on the main. The long sweeping line of coast was terminated by the Isle of Portland, which, as the morning was remarkably clear, could be distinctly descried.

Again the horsemen halted for a few minutes to gaze at this splendid view. Careless gave utterance to his admiration, and Colonel Wyndham showed him where Charmouth and Bridport were situated, and pointed out the Golden Cap, of which mention has just been made.

Hitherto Lyme itself had almost been hidden by intervening woods, but after they had passed through Uplyme, they could look down upon the collection of straggling and picturesque houses, built on the steep side of the hill on which the spectators were stationed.

Desirous that his companion should have a more complete view of the place than could be obtained from the road, Colonel Wyndham turned into a field on the right, and conducted him to the edge of a lofty cliff that overlooked the port and the buildings adjoining it.

"That is Lyme Cobb, as it is termed," said the colonel. "There are a few vessels in the port, as you perceive. Heaven grant we may be able to secure one of them for the king!"

When Careless had sufficiently examined the Cobb from the lofty point of observation they had chosen, they returned to the road, and soon gained the narrow and straggling street that climbed the hill-side.

Captain Ellesdon's residence was easily discovered, and the colonel and Careless proceeded thither on foot, while Peters took their horses to the George Inn. A narrow lane on the right led them to a commodious habitation, very pleasantly situated on a natural terrace facing the sea.

On inquiring at the house they learnt to their great satisfaction that Captain Ellesdon was at home, and were shown into a comfortable and well-furnished parlour, where the captain shortly afterwards joined them.

Captain Ellesdon was a man of middle age, with nothing very striking in his appearance, but his features were good, and his manner frank and prepossessing. The captain stood upon no ceremony with his visitors. Though not personally acquainted with Colonel Wyndham, he knew him, and shook hands with him very cordially. By the colonel he was introduced to Careless, and shook hands with him as well.

"Pray sit down, gentlemen," he said, "and tell me how I can serve you."

"You can serve us most materially, Captain Ellesdon," returned the colonel; "and I will explain how. I have just heard from my brother-in-law, Colonel Bullen Reymes, that you have enabled Sir John Berkeley to escape from his pursuers by procuring him a passage from this port to France. Can you do as much for a far more exalted personage than Sir John, and who is in yet greater peril from his enemies?"

"Do I misunderstand you, Colonel Wyndham?" demanded Ellesdon, almost breathless with astonishment. "Do you allude to the king?"

"I ought to bind you to secrecy, sir, before answering the question," said the colonel. "But I know I am dealing with a loyal gentleman."

"You may trust me implicitly, colonel," rejoined the captain. "But if an oath be requisite, I swear solemnly not to reveal whatever you may disclose to me."

"After this, I will not hesitate to ask you plainly if you can procure a vessel to transport his majesty to France?"

"Do not let the hire of the vessel be a consideration, captain," said Careless. "I am charged by his majesty to offer any terms that may be required."

"Too large a sum must not be offered, or it would excite suspicion," rejoined Captain Ellesdon. "The skipper we engage must be led to believe that his passengers are only fugitive Cavaliers from Worcester— nothing higher. I know a shipmaster who is an honest fellow, and a perfect Royalist, but for all that, I would not trust him with this great secret."

"Is the shipmaster you refer to in Lyme now, captain?" inquired Careless, eagerly.

"His vessel is in the Cobb, but he himself is at Charmouth. He is a tenant of mine, by name Stephen Limbry. Yesterday I chanced to enter the Custom House, and I found that Limbry had just entered his bark, intending a speedy voyage to St. Malo."

"To St. Malo!" exclaimed Careless, joyfully. "The very port to which his majesty desires to sail. Nothing could be more fortunate."

"A most fortunate circumstance indeed," said Colonel Wyndham. "It would seem as if Providence designed that the king should be thus delivered from his foes. You must see Stephen Limbry without delay, captain."

"We will all ride over to Charmouth together," said Ellesdon. "'Tis but a mile hence. Your horses, I suppose, are at the inn? I will follow you there as soon as I can get my own horse saddled."

Colonel Wyndham and Careless then proceeded to the George, which was in the lower part of the town, aud they had only just got out their horses when Captain Ellesdon made his appearance, mounted on a stout hackney.

"We will ride by the coast, if you please, gentlemen," he said. "The tide is low, and the sands are firm and good."

## CHAPTER X.

### STEPHEN LIMBRY, OF CHARMOUTH, SHIPMASTER.

A WIDE opening on the right, at the bottom of the street, led to the seaside, and turning off in this direction, the party crossed the shingles and soon gained the hard sand, which was very pleasant to ride upon. But before proceeding, they stopped for a moment to look around. On the right, about a quarter of a mile off, was the Cobb, in which, as we have already intimated, a few vessels were moored, while somewhat nearer a dozen fishing-boats were lying at anchor, waiting for a favourable breeze. Some little bustle seemed going on at the Cobb, but otherwise the place was perfectly quiet. The huge wooden pier then in existence did not last out the century, and was succeeded by three or four other structures that shared the same fate; but Lyme is now provided with a handsome stone pier strong enough to resist any storms, and large enough to shelter any number of ships. Between the Cobb and the spot where Captain Ellesdon and those with him were stationed rose high banks, covered with trees, amidst which an occasional habitation might be descried. Now there are numberless charming villas in the same quarter.

Having contemplated this scene for a few minutes, the party set off for Charmouth. Harry Peters's services not being required, he was left at the George. Exhilarated by the sea air, Colonel Wyndham and Careless greatly enjoyed their ride over the hard, dry sands—now glancing at the tall, black, shelving cliffs as they passed them—now allowing their gaze to wander on as far as the distant Isle of Portland. But their pleasant ride soon came to an end, and in less than a quarter of an hour they had reached the spot where the little river Char loses itself in the sea. Three or four boats were drawn upon the beach, but there was not even a solitary fisherman's hut on the sand-hills. Now-a-days, this is a bathing-place.

" I have brought you to this spot for a particular reason," observed Captain Ellesdon to the others. "Here Sir John Berkeley took boat on the night when he effected his escape to France, and if we arrange matters satisfactorily, I propose that his majesty shall join Limbry's bark from the same place. No safer spot can be found, I am certain. There is not a habitation within a quarter of a mile."

" 'Tis as private as could he desired," said Colonel Wyndham. " And I am sure his majesty will approve of the arrangement."

" It has other advantages which I need not enter into now," said Ellesdon.

" No; the perfect privacy of the spot is sufficient recommendation," said Careless. "If we can secure the vessel all will be well."

They then quitted the beach, and rode singly along a narrow lane which led them over an eminence to Charmouth.

This pretty and pleasantly situated little town is much changed since those days. Most of the old houses are gone, and have given place to modern habitations far less picturesque, but the general features of the place are the same, and the old inn at which the Royalists put up, as we shall proceed to relate, is still in existence.

As they entered the village, Captain Ellesdon pointed out a pretty little house with a garden in front, and said :

" That is Limbry's dwelling,  I will see whether he is at home."

He then rode towards the house, and calling out lustily, the summons was immediately answered by a buxom woman and her daughter, a good-looking damsel of some sixteen or seventeen.

In answer to the captain's inquiries, Dame Limbry informed him that her husband had just gone out, but would return presently.

" He has not gone to Lyme, I hope ?" said the captain.

" No ; he is somewhere in the village," replied the dame.

" That's right," cried Ellesdon.  " I am going to the inn with these gentlemen.  Send him there.  I want to speak to him on business—on important business, mind."

Dame Limbry promised compliance, and the captain rode off.  Not being devoid of curiosity, both mother and daughter watched the party alight at the inn, which was close at hand.

" I wonder what Captain Ellesdon's important business can be," remarked Dame Limbry.  " I shall make your father tell me."

" Such fine gentlemen as those can't be traders," said her daughter. " They look like Cavaliers."

" And Cavaliers they are, Dorcas, or I'm no judge," said the dame.

Meanwhile Captain Ellesdon and his companions, having sent their horses to the stable, entered the little inn, and being shown into the parlour by Dame Swan, the hostess, ordered a flask of sack.

Just as the wine was brought, Stephen Limbry made his appearance, and was heartily welcomed.  The shipmaster was stoutly built, and his bronzed complexion showed that he had undergone a good deal of exposure to the elements.  His features were rather coarse, but he had a bluff, good-humoured expression, and looked perfectly honest and trustworthy.

Saluting the company after his nautical fashion, Limbry sat down, and emptied the cup of sack filled for him by Captain Ellesdon.

" My good dame tells me as how you have got some business for me, captain.  What may it be ?"

" Take another glass of sack, Stephen, and you shall hear," rejoined Ellesdon.  " I have assured my friends here, Mr. Manly and Mr. Massey," nodding to each, as he spoke, " that you are a right honest fellow and a staunch Royalist."

" You are pleased to give me a good character, captain," said Limbry, laughing.  " But I hope I merit it.  At any rate, I serve my employers faithfully, and I hate a Roundhead woundily."

" I am quite aware of it, Limbry.  And now, without further parley, I'll explain my business to you.  These gentlemen are Royalists."

" I guessed as much," replied Limbry, with a knowing wink. "They don't look like Roundheads."

" One of them, Mr. Massey," pursued the captain, glancing at Careless, " was at Worcester."

" I hope he killed a lot of rebels.  I shouldn't be sorry if he had killed Old Noll himself," observed Limbry.

" Had that been the case things would have taken a different turn, and loyal men would not have been forced to fly from their country," said Captain Ellesdon. "We want you to transport two or three distressed Cavaliers to France. You will do it, I am sure."

Limbry shook his head.

"You don't like the job," cried Colonel Wyndham. "Say so frankly.

"Understand that you will be well paid—very well paid," added Careless.

"I've no disinclination whatsomdever to the job," said the burly shipmaster. "On the contrary, I should be glad to serve any loyal gentlemen; and I don't care so much for the payment, though I don't mean to say as how I should object to it—but——"

"But what?" cried Ellesdon.

"The risk is too great. If I were found out, I should be hanged as a traitor."

"These fears are idle," rejoined Ellesdon. "Such precautions will be taken that you cannot be found out. Take another glass of wine, and pluck up your courage. I'll tell you what has just occurred. Sir John Berkeley was taken over to France from this very port of Lyme, only a few days ago, and I have not heard that any skipper has been hanged for taking him."

"Be that true, captain?" asked Limbry.

"True as gospel. Do you think I'd deceive you, man?"

"Then I'll do it!" cried Limbry, striking the table as he spoke with his heavy fist, "I'll do it!"

"Well resolved," exclaimed Colonel Wyndham. "You're a brave fellow, Limbry."

"You shall have sixty pounds for the job," added Careless. "To be paid on your return."

"I don't ask the Cavaliers' names," said Limbry. "And I don't desire to know their rank and station—but I'll take them to St. Malo."

"Now you show yourself the man I always thought you, Stephen," said Captain Ellesdon. "When will you sail?"

"On Monday next—that's three days hence," replied Limbry. "I cannot get ready afore,—seeing as how I have to take in ballast, and victual the ship, besides I must feign to have some lading; but on Monday, as I have said, I'll hale the *Eider Duck*—that's the name of my bark—out of the Cobb's mouth, for fear of being beneaped, as the tides will be at the lowest at the time, and about midnight I'll bring her into Charmouth road, and send the long-boat with Tom Chidiock, of Bridport, and George Cranage, of Beaminster, two of my best mariners, to any spot that may be appointed to fetch the Cavaliers, and put them on board; and if the wind proves favourable, we'll set sail at once for France."

"Heaven grant the wind may prove favourable!" ejaculated Ellesdon. "Send the long-boat to the mouth of the Char."

"A good spot," replied Limbry. "It shall be done."

"Then all is settled?" said Colonel Wyndham.

"All settled. Rely on me. Stephen Limbry is a man of few words, but he'll stick by what he says. On Monday next, at midnight, my men shall bring the long-boat to the mouth of the Char."

"I shall see you again before that, Limbry," said Captain Ellesdon.

"As you please, captain," replied the skipper. "The *Eider Duck* will be ready. "I wish you good day, gentlemen."

Thereupon he went out, leaving the others overjoyed at the result of the negotiation.

---

## CHAPTER XI.

### OF THE ARRANGEMENTS MADE BY HARRY PETERS WITH DAME SWAN.

Our three Royalists did not make any stay at the little inn at Charmouth, after their negotiation with Limbry had been so satisfactorily concluded, but ordered their horses, paid their reckoning, and departed. They did not return by the beach, Captain Ellesdon being desirous to show his companions a secluded farm-house belonging to his father, about a mile and a half off among the downs, where he thought the king should halt on the appointed day, before proceeding to Charmouth.

"Lonesome the place is called," said Captain Ellesdon, pointing out the solitary house, "and it well deserves its name, since there is not another habitation within a mile of it. The farm is let, but the tenant is an honest fellow, on whom I can rely. I will come there early on Monday, and wait his majesty's arrival. I have likewise just bethought me that Lyme fair occurs on Monday. Consequently, the town will be thronged, and so will Charmouth. Rooms must, therefore, be engaged beforehand at our little inn. Another point requires consideration. His majesty and those with him will have to sit up till midnight, and if they quit the house at that late hour, suspicion may be excited. Some pretext, therefore, must be found to satisfy Dame Swan and her servants."

"Very true," replied Colonel Wyndham, "I will send my servant, Harry Peters, to Charmouth. He will invent some plausible tale that will impose upon the hostess."

Their business at Lonesome being accomplished, the party rode across the downs to Lyme Regis, and repaired to the George. Harry Peters was at once despatched on his mission, and during the absence of the trusty groom, Colonel Wyndham and Careless dined with Captain Ellesdon, at the residence of the latter.

Concocting his scheme as he rode along, Harry Peters arrived at Charmouth full of confidence, and alighting at the little inn, sent his horse to the stable, and ordering a flask of sack, begged the pleasure of Dame Swan's company for a few minutes in the parlour.

After a few preliminary observations, and the offer of a glass of wine, which was graciously accepted by the hostess, he delicately approached the business.

"I have a very great favour to ask of you, madam," he said, "but I am inclined to think you will readily grant it, since the happiness of two young persons depends upon your willingness to assist them.

When I tell you it is a love affair, I shall have said enough, I am convinced, to awaken your tender sympathies. I must not mention names, but my master has gained the affections of a very beautiful young gentlewoman. Unluckily, her father refuses him her hand. Prayers have been in vain. Cruel father, you will say! Such fathers, however, reap their own reward, and are deceived like jealous husbands."

"Generally," observed the hostess, sipping her wine.

"You will not be surprised, therefore, madam, that the young gentlewoman in question, justly provoked by such harsh treatment, has yielded to her lover's prayers, and agreed to run away with him."

"In good sooth, I am not surprised at it, sir," remarked Dame Swan. "I should have done just the same myself at her age, and under similar circumstances."

"Say you so, madam! Then I have no hesitation in claiming your assistance. On Monday next the elopement will take place. Promised refuge with you, the young couple will come here. That they may not be interfered with, I am directed by my master to engage all the rooms in the house."

"Stay! Lyme Fair is held on Monday, and we are always full on that day. I dare not promise the rooms."

"But I will pay double for them, and make you a handsome present into the bargain. It must be Monday. No other day will suit the young gentlewoman."

"Well, I would not disappoint her for the world. You shall have the rooms, and I will put off my other guests."

"I expected nothing less from you, madam. But you will not lose by your good nature. You will make friends of the young people for life. Another danger has to be guarded against. The lovers may be pursued, and chance may bring the angry father here."

"Mercy on us! I hope not," exclaimed the hostess

"Do not alarm yourself, madam. Such an untoward event is not likely to occur; but every precaution ought to be taken. The young pair must sit up during the night, and their horses be kept ready saddled and bridled, so that they can be off at a moment's notice. You must be pleased to give directions to your servants accordingly."

"You may depend upon me, sir," said Dame Swan. "All preparations shall be made for the young couple. I take a particular interest in them, and to insure their being properly attended to, I will sit up myself."

"I do not think that will be necessary, madam; but as you please. My master begs your acceptance of half a dozen pistoles." And he slipped them into her hand as he spoke.

"He acts like a gentleman—that is quite certain," said Dame Swan.

"And now for the rooms. Shall we say half a dozen pistoles more?"

"That will be most handsome payment."

"On an occasion of this kind one must behave handsomely," said Peters, putting down the money. "My master is rich—at any rate, he will be so."

"I hope he has got an heiress," observed the hostess.

Peters said nothing, but winked significantly.

This concluded the arrangement.

Everything being settled in a manner entirely satisfactory to both parties, the adroit emissary took leave of Dame Swan, and rode back as quickly as he could to Lyme, being anxious to communicate the good news to his master and the others.

On hearing his account of the affair, they laughed very heartily, and complimented him on the skill he had displayed.

The party then went down to the Cobb to look at the *Eider Duck*, and were very well satisfied with her appearance. At Captain Ellesdon's earnest request our two Royalists agreed to pass the evening with him, and did not return till next day to Trent.

---

## CHAPTER XII.

### HOW THE KING PLAYED AT HIDE-AND-SEEK AT TRENT.

WHILE these preparations for his escape were so successfully made, Charles had run considerable risk of capture.

On the evening of the second day he was alone in his chamber, occupied with reflections, and wondering what Colonel Wyndham and Careless were about, when Juliana entered suddenly, and with anxiety depicted on her charming countenance informed him that the Reverend Hold-up-Hand Meldrum had been questioning the women-servants about the new groom who had lately arrived at the house.

"The inquisitive minister came to the kitchen door," she said, "and stating that he knew the young man was in the house, desired to speak with him. Both Eleanor Withers and Joan Halsenoth declared that the groom was gone, but Mr. Meldrum affirmed the contrary, adding that he suspected the young man was a malignant Cavalier in disguise, and was certain he was hidden in the house, and as he would not come forth, he would bring those who would find him. As the two women made no answer, Mr. Meldrum departed, but they think he will make good his threat. I believe so too, and I therefore advise your majesty to conceal yourself, for of course you will not see him."

"Humph! I don't know that," observed Charles. "I am sure I could baffle him."

But he changed his tone when, shortly afterwards, Joan Halsenoth burst into the room, with a terrified look, exclaiming:

"Mr. Meldrum is in the yard, and has got two troopers with him."

"Troopers! that looks serious!" cried the king. "Clearly, a strict search will be made."

"Not a moment must be lost. Conceal yourself, I entreat you," cried Juliana.

And as the king opened the secret door and disappeared, she and Joan removed every article likely to betray his presence.

"Carry these to my chamber quickly, and hide them," continued Juliana. "That done, bring down everything from my dressing-table, and we will arrange them here, as if the room were mine."

Joan obeyed, and in another minute returned with hair-brushes, combs, and other articles of the toilette, which were quickly placed as Juliana had directed.

"Now go down-stairs and do thy best to dupe them," cried Juliana. "I will remain here."

Left by herself, the young damsel stepped to one of the lattice windows that looked upon the yard, and being partially open, it enabled her to hear what was passing outside. She could not see the Reverend Mr. Meldrum, but she heard his voice, and perceived the troopers, who stood behind him.

The servants, it appeared, had locked the kitchen door, which was of strong oak, studded with nails, and positively refused to unfasten it. They were talking to him through a smalled barred window.

While Juliana was listening to what was going on, the secret door was cautiously opened, and Charles peeped out.

"Are they gone?" he called out in a low voice, perceiving she was alone.

"No. no," she replied in the same tone. "Do not quit your hiding-place. They are below, but the servants won't let them into the kitchen."

"That's a pity," cried Charles. "Most likely they would have stopped there. Those rogues are fond of the kitchen."

"They have got in," said Juliana. "Mrs. Wyndham has unfastened the door. She will give them plenty of ale."

For a few minutes all remained quiet, and Charles ventured out of his hiding-place.

"I don't think they will disturb me," he said.

Just at the moment, however, Joan Halsenoth cautiously entered the room.

"Mr. Meldrum and his companions are coming up-stairs presently," she said. "They have poked their noses into every hole and corner below, and mean to search every room in the house. So you must prepare for them."

And she disappeared.

Charles again retreated to his hiding-place, but paused before closing the door.

"Can you not give me a signal," he said, "in case it should be necessary for me to descend the secret staircase?"

"I can tap against the panel," she rejoined. "But you had better remove the plank at once."

"I am not sure that I can find the plank," he rejoined.

"I will show you where it is," she cried, flying towards him. But she stopped on hearing footsteps on the staircase.

"They are coming!" she exclaimed.

The secret door was instantly shut.

Next moment, the room door was thrown open, and Mrs. Wyndham entered, accompanied by the Independent minister, and followed by the two troopers.

"When I tell you that this is Mistress Juliana Coningsby's room, perhaps a very slight inspection of it will satisfy you," said Mrs. Wyndham to the minister.

"I am not so sure of that," he replied. "'Tis likely enough that the malignant whom we seek may be concealed here."

"You have just been told that it is my room," cried Juliana, suddenly turning round and facing him.

"That does not make it more unlikely," observed one of the troopers. "Fair damsels have concealed their lovers before now."

"Hold thy peace, Hilkiah," said the minister, gravely. "Thou art come hither to search for a malignant, and not to jest. Do thine office."

Thus rebuked, Hilkiah and his comrade examined the room most carefully, their proceedings being anxiously watched by the two ladies, though they strove to assume an air of indifference. Finding from the manner in which the men were sounding the panels that the discovery of the closet was inevitable, Mrs. Wyndham thought it better to anticipate it, and, stepping forward, she opened the secret door.

It was an anxious moment for Juliana, but she perceived at a glance that the king had found the moveable plank, and used it. The secret closet was empty. The minister gazed into it with a blank expression of countenance.

"Pray examine the place carefully!" cried Mrs. Wyndham, in a taunting tone. "Sound the walls, try the roof and floor—you will find nothing. 'Tis not a hiding-place, but a small room attached to the larger chamber. A moment's inspection will convince you it has not been occupied."

The closet was scarcely large enough to hold the minister and the troopers, but they squeezed themselves into it nevertheless, and being thus crowded they could not possibly examine the floor. But, indeed, they had to think of their own deliverance. The secret door closed with a spring, and unable to resist the impulse that prompted her to shut them in, Juliana closed it. A loud laugh from the giddy girl told them they were made prisoners. Mr. Meldrum did not relish the jest, but Mrs. Wyndham and Juliana derided his anger.

The troopers tried to force open the door, but the bolt resisted their efforts. Juliana positively refused to let them out unless they engaged to leave the house at once, and to these conditions they were eventually compelled to submit. On being liberated they all went away looking extremely crestfallen.

Not till it was quite certain that the coast was clear did Juliana venture to intimate to the king that he might come forth from his hiding-place. He did not appear much discomposed, but treated the matter very lightly.

"I have played so often at hide-and-seek of late," he said, "that I feel certain of coming off the winner. But the game was never better played than it has been just now."

"I am glad to hear your majesty say so," observed Juliana.

Careful watch was kept that night at Trent, and the king did not retire to rest for fear of a surprise. However, nothing occurred, and in the morning it was ascertained that the troopers had departed.

In the afternoon, Colonel Wyndham and Careless returned from their expedition, and at once repaired to the king's chamber.

"All has been most satisfactorily arranged, sire," said the colonel. "I will give you the details anon. The sum is this. A vessel has been hired by Captain Ellesdon from a trusty shipmaster at Lyme, named Limbry, and your majesty will embark for St. Malo on Monday next at midnight. We have seen the vessel in Lyme port in which you are to sail, and find her all that could be desired. It will be an additional gratification, I am sure, to your majesty to learn that, on our way back, we encountered Lord Wilmot. I invited him to Trent, but he did not deem it prudent to accept the invitation, though he greatly desires to see your majesty."

"Where is he?" cried Charles. "I will take him with me to St. Malo."

"I have ventured to anticipate your majesty's wishes in that respect," said Careless. "Feeling certain you would desire his company, I promised him a passage, and appointed a place of meeting near Charmouth, on Monday."

"You have done well," cried the king. "I shall be glad to have Wilmot with me. Fortune, at length, seems disposed to favour me. In a few days—nay, in a few hours—I shall be out of the reach of my enemies."

Colonel Wyndham then gave the king full details of the negotiation with Limbry, and his majesty was very much amused by the relation. He was, also, well pleased with the colonel's description of Captain Ellesdon.

The short interval between the king's departure was passed very pleasantly by his majesty, and when the day arrived he could not help feeling regret at leaving a place where he had been so happy. As regards female society he could not have been better circumstanced. Three more charming women, each in her way, than those with whom it had been his good fortune to be associated, could scarcely have been found. For Lady Wyndham, whose interest in him seemed quite maternal, he had begun to feel an almost filial regard. The loyal old dame often spoke to him of her three valiant sons who had fallen in his royal father's cause, and said she accounted their deaths her highest honour.

"I can only replace one of them," said the king. "But you must look upon me as a son."

Sunday was the last day on which it was supposed that his majesty would stay at Trent, and it was spent very decorously. Religious service was performed in the king's room by the Reverend Mr. Langton, and all the company in the house, including Harry Peters and two of the women-servants, were assembled at it. The circumstances gave a special interest to the meeting, and those present on the occasion often called it to mind. The good divine preached an eloquent and stirring discourse that roused the feelings of all who listened to him. His text was taken from Samuel : "*And Saul sought David every day ; but God delivered him not into his hands.*" He spoke of the king's miraculous escapes from the many and great dangers to which he had been exposed, and showed that he could not thus have been preserved, if he had not been under the care of a watchful Providence. "While the flood of rebellion has covered the face of his kingdom," he said, " in this ark he has been safely shut up, and here he will remain till his faithful servants have time to work his deliverance. But that day is near at hand. The malicious designs of his adversaries will be frustrated, and he will be restored to his father's throne. Then shall we all say with the Prophet: " My Lord, the king is come again in peace to his own house."

Charles was much moved by the good man's discourse, and thanked him for it when the service was over.

" As I have just declared, sire," said Mr. Langton, " the hand of Providence has been clearly manifested in your preservation hitherto, and it will not desert you. Take comfort from the words of the Prophet, for they are very applicable to you: ' Fear not, for the hand of Saul shall not find thee, and thou shall be king over Israel,' "

---

## CHAPTER XIII.

### HOW CHARLES SET OUT FOR CHARMOUTH.

THE day had arrived when it was hoped that his majesty's deliverance would be accomplished.

After taking leave of Lady Wyndham and her daughter-in-law, Charles mounted his horse, and Juliana, half-crazed with delight, seated herself on the pillion behind him. Colonel Wyndham and Careless were already in the saddle, and attended by the prayers of Mr. Langton, and by the good wishes of all who witnessed their departure, the party set out on their journey. Harry Peters had been sent off beforehand privately, in the hope that the king might be mistaken for him by Mr. Meldrum, should the minister be on the look-out; but the faithful groom joined the party about a mile from the village, and subsequently acted as guide, as they intended to take some cross roads.

Brilliant sunshine cheered them on their way, and brought out the best features of the richly-wooded district through which they journeyed —giving new splendour to the glorious autumnal tints of the foliage, and revealing scenes of rare sylvan beauty. Nothing could have been pleasanter than the ride. Sometimes involved in a thick wood—sometimes pursuing their course on the banks of a clear and beautiful stream —sometimes passing a village remarkable for a noble old church—anon tracking a long valley, hemmed in by lofty hills—now called upon to admire a fine old mansion, situated in the midst of an extensive park— now skirting a lovely lake—anon compelled to quit the valley, and climb a hill which seemed to bar further progress, but which, when its summit was gained, offered a magnificent prospect—through such varied scenes they proceeded pleasantly on their way.

At first, they pursued the same road they had taken on the occasion of the king's visit to Melbury Park, passing by the foot of Babylon Hill, and tracking the valley of the Yeo; but they then struck off on the right, and proceeded towards Berwick and Sutton Bingham. Avoiding the latter village, they entered a thick wood, through which they

were guided by Harry Peters, and on emerging from it skirted Abbots
Hill, and crossing two other eminences, came upon a very picturesque
district, having a beautiful woody knoll on the right, and a succession
of wild holts on the left.

Leaving these woodlands, they passed through a gap in the hills, and
shortly afterwards descended into a richly-cultivated and well-watered vale
—their road leading them past numerous farm-houses, each possessing a
large orchard.  Before them the two bold eminences, Lewesdon Hill
and Pillesdon Pen, reared their lofty heads, and seemed to bar their further progress.  Distinguishable far out at sea, and forming excellent
landmarks, these twin heights, from their resemblance to each other, are
called by sailors  " the Cow and the Calf."  Further on the right was
a third remarkable eminence, equally striking in character, and known
as Blackdown Hill.

The road taken by the party led them over Pillesdon Pen, and the
view from its summit of the towering hill was superb, comprehending
the rich vale they had just traversed, with its meadows, orchards, and
farms, and the beautiful combes and downs on either side.  They then
descended into the valley, in which stood Pillesdon, the residence of Sir
Hugh Wyndham, the colonel's uncle, but they did not go near the
mansion.

Shortly afterwards they mounted another lofty eminence, on the
summit of which was a large and very perfect British encampment,
known as Lambert's Castle.  Hence a magnificent view of the sea was
commanded.

Aware of what he might expect, Charles rode on in advance of his
companions, and when he had reached Lambert's Castle, and the grand
view burst upon him, he looked neither to the right nor to the left, but
at the sea.

Yes, there it was at last!  There was the sea!  Deliverance was at
hand!  A few hours more, and he should be wafted across that broad
expanse to the friendly shore.

So enchanted was he by the sight that he gave vent to his rapture in
a joyous shout.  Juliana was almost equally excited.

"By this time to-morrow your majesty will be safe in France," she cried.

"I must not be too confident.  The wind is fair now—but it may
change.  I have had so many disappointments, that I cannot feel quite
secure."

" Nothing is certain, sire—at least, wise people say so.  But it seems
to me that the chances are a thousand to one in favour of your majesty's
safe embarkation to-night, and therefore you may calculate on arriving
at St. Malo to-morrow.  The sea itself seems to smile upon you, and
promise you a fair passage."

" Smiles are somtimes treacherous, and promises are often broken,"
said Charles.  " But I will gladly trust myself to those bright waves."

At this moment Colonel Wyndham and the others rode up.

" There is a sight to gladden your heart, sire," exclaimed the colonel.

" Ay, it is the pleasantest prospect I have beheld for many a day,
Frank.  Yet my satisfaction at the hope of immediate escape is not un-
alloyed.  I go into exile.  I leave my friends behind me."

" Your exile will not be long, sire," rejoined the colonel. " Your friends will soon have you back again."

" Heaven alone can tell when I shall return—and how I shall return," rejoined the king. " But return I will."

" You will return to ascend the throne," said Juliana.

" I accept the prediction," said Charles. " Coming from such fair lips it cannot be falsified."

Riding down the south side of the hill, they shaped their course towards the solitary farm-house, appointed as a place of rendezvous by Captain Ellesdon.

Being now on the open downs, they could no doubt be seen from a distance, for a horseman was descried galloping towards them. At first, the king thought it must be Captain Ellesdon, but as the horseman drew nearer, his majesty easily recognised Lord Wilmot, who had appointed to meet him at this place, and had been waiting for him for some time.

A very affectionate greeting took place between the king and his friend, and the latter, after briefly recounting his adventures since they separated, gave his majesty many particulars respecting his devoted partisans. The intelligence that most deeply interested Charles related to the Earl of Derby, who, it appeared, was now a prisoner in Chester Castle, and had been condemned to lose his head. Lord Wilmot himself had been in great danger, but had contrived to escape capture.

This conference lasted for some time, and the king had been so deeply engrossed by Lord Wilmot's narration, that he quite forgot the presence of Juliana, who had listened to the recital in terror.

When Lord Wilmot had finished his sad tidings, Charles remained for some minutes lost in painful reflection, and during this time no one ventured to disturb him. At length a slight movement on the part of Juliana recalled him to himself. Starting as if aroused from a painful dream, he rode on towards the farm-house, which was only a mile distant.

Captain Ellesdon had been for some hours at the place of rendezvous, and, made aware of the approach of the royal party, stationed himself at the gate to receive the king.

---

## CHAPTER XIV

### HOW THE KING AND JULIANA WERE RECEIVED BY DAME SWAN.

LONESOME was a substantial farm-house, with whitewashed walls and a thatched roof, and being a dairy-farm, at which the best double Dorset blue-mould cheeses were made, it had large cowsheds and other out-buildings attached to it, and its comfortable appearance was heightened by a very extensive orchard, the trees of which were still heavily laden with fruit.

Captain Ellesdon did not dare to make a reverence to his majesty on his arrival, lest he should be noticed by the farming men, who naturally came forward to look at the party, and take charge of the horses, but while assisting Juliana to alight, he had an opportunity of saying a few words to the king, and later on he had a private conference with his majesty.   Charles thanked him most warmly for the important service he had rendered him—a service, he declared, that could not adequately be rewarded—and to these gracious observations Captain Ellesdon made a fitting response ; adding, that he was most happy to inform his majesty that everything was going on well.   Not an hour ago, he had seen Limbry, and had learnt that the *Eider Duck* was already victualled, and out of the Cobb, and would he quite ready to set sail at midnight, as soon as the passengers were on board.

"The seamen have been given to understand," pursued Captain Ellesdon, "that the reason why the passengers embark at Charmouth at such an unseasonable hour, and not at Lyme, is, that they fear an arrest, their factor at St. Malo having detained their goods, which they trust to recover by appearing in person against him.   With this explanation the seamen are perfectly satisfied, and a few gold pieces on your majesty's arrival at St. Malo will effectually seal their lips.   As the wind is fair, I think your majesty may calculate on a prosperous voyage. You have no doubt been informed that a large fair is held in Lyme to-day.   Advantage has been taken of the meeting by the mayor of the town to publicly read the Proclamation made by the Men of Westminster, offering a reward of a Thousand Pounds for the discovery of your majesty, with the penalty of death against all who shall conceal you.   I am rejoiced to think that the *Eider Duck* is out of port, so that the seamen will not be likely to hear of the notice ; and I am still better pleased to find that our staunch shipmaster appears to care little about it.   Your majesty will be off before any mischief can be done. As it turns out, it would have been quite impossible for you to embark at Lyme, since Captain Macy has just arrived there with a regiment of horse, and his men are spread about the town, and the inns and ale-houses are full of them.   I must also put your majesty on your guard against Reuben Rufford, the ostler at the little inn at Charmouth.   He is a Roundhead, and a notorious knave, as I have discovered."

"I will observe all due caution in regard to the rascal," said the king. "But as my stay at Charmouth will be so short, I do not think there is much to fear from him."

Some further conversation then took place, at the close of which the king reiterated his thanks to Captain Ellesdon, and presented him with a piece of gold, through which a hole had been drilled, so that it could he worn, bidding him keep it as an earnest of what he would do for him hereafter, should better days arrive.

"Most assuredly those days will arrive, sire," said the captain , "but I desire no greater reward for my services than that which I have now received.   I shall always wear this medal next my heart."

There being nothing to detain him longer at the farm-house, the king now gave the word for departure, and all his attendants mounted their horses.   Captain Ellesdon rode by his majesty's side, and conducted him to the summit of the steep hill that rises between Charmouth and Lyme ; pointing out the *Eider Duck*, lying off the mouth of the Cobb, as well as the exact spot where it had been arranged that the long-boat should fetch his majesty and his companions at midnight.

From this elevated point Lyme seemed immediately beneath them, and the king could clearly perceive the crowd in the principal street, as well as hear the shouts and other noises that arose from the fair. Amid the throng he noticed that many red-coats were mingled. From the church tower floated the flag of the Commonwealth.

Satisfied at last with the survey, Charles bade farewell to Captain Ellesdon, and with his attendants rode down the left side of the declivity to Charmouth, while the captain took his way on the right to Lyme.

As they approached the little town, Charles asked Juliana if she was quite prepared for the part she had to play, and received a laughing response in the affirmative.

Harry Peters had ridden on beforehand, so that when the party arrived at the little inn, the hostess, with the ostler and all the servants, were at the door ready to receive them.

Luckily, most of the villagers were at Lyme fair, or there would have been a little crowd collected to gaze at the strangers. So dazzled was Dame Swan by Juliana's beauty, as she assisted the young lady to alight, that she could look at no one else, but when she did bestow a glance on the king she did not think him half handsome enough to be the husband of such a charming creature.

Leading Juliana into a parlour, where a cold collation was laid out, the good dame kissed her and wished her all happiness. They were followed by Charles, who laughingly inquired if the hostess meant to rob him of his intended bride.

" I won't rob you of her, sir," replied Dame Swan ; "and I'll do my best to prevent any one else from taking her from you. Ah ' sir, you ought to esteem yourself the luckiest man on earth to have obtained such a treasure."

" Why, so I do, dame. But is she not the luckiest woman ?"

" I'm sure I think myself so," said Juliana.

" I'm a very bad judge," remarked the hostess. " I often say to myself, ' It's very well we are not all of one mind. What suits one person wouldn't suit another.' "

" It's very clear I don't suit your fancy, good dame," cried Charles, laughing.

Here they were interrupted by the entrance of the rest of the party, and they all on the king's invitation sat down to the repast—Juliana, of course, being seated beside his majesty, and receiving particular attentions from him.

Careless sat on the other side of the young damsel, who did not seem displeased to have him near her, but chatted with him very gaily. And the hostess subsequently remarked to Harry Peters, who had assisted her to wait on the company ·

" I shouldn't have been surprised if that lovely creature had run away with the gallant-looking Cavalier on her right, and I almost think she prefers him to the accepted suitor. It's not too late yet for her to change her mind."

" Oh ! yes, it is a great deal too late," rejoined Harry Peters. " Take care yon don't put such whims into her head."

" Not I, i'faith !" she rejoined.   " But I'm pretty sure I'm right."

Later in the evening, the hostess was confirmed in her opinion when Careless and Juliana walked out into the little garden at the back of the house.   She could not help listening to their conversation, and heard the Cavalier say, in very tender accents. as it seemed to her :

" I must now bid you farewell !   Fate seems resolved to separate us— but I hope we shall meet again.   I will not ask you to be constant to me."

" I should think not," mentally ejaculated Dame Swan, " seeing that she is just about to be wedded to another."

" But I vow that I will be so," cried Juliana.   " If a certain person, whom we both detest, and who interferes with our happiness, should only be removed, you will return at once, will you not ?"

" There is very little chance of his removal, I fear," said Careless, with a profound sigh.   " His success has been too complete of late."

" But something unexpected may occur," said Juliana.   " He may not be long in our way."

" I hope not," said Careless.   " But his present position appears secure."

" Still, I do not think he can long maintain it," said Juliana.   " He must fall soon."

" The announcement of his death will be my summons to return," said Careless.   " If some sure hand would only strike the blow."

" At a crisis like the present, when such great interests are at stake, that hand is not likely to be wanting," said Juliana.

" Great Heavens !   She is planning the poor young man's destruction, before she has married him," thought Dame Swan.   " 'Tis fortunate I have overheard the dreadful design, and can therefore prevent it.   Hist ! hist !" she cried.

Alarmed by the sound, Juliana came instantly into the house.

" I want to speak to you," said the hostess, taking her hand, and drawing her into a small room which she called her own.

After closing the door, she said in a tone of great sympathy, " I find you are very unhappily circumstanced."

" I do not understand you," interrupted Juliana.

" I have accidentally overheard what has passed between you and the handsome young Cavalier in the garden, and I find that you greatly prefer him to the swarthy-complexioned gentleman, to whom you have promised your hand.   You are very young, and feeling for you like a mother, I cannot see you rush to destruction, without trying to prevent it.   Break off this foolish engagement at once — at once, I say—and return to your father.   Nay, if you hesitate, I will take you to him my-self.   You must not—shall not — marry this man !"

" I do not mean to marry him," said Juliana.

" What is it you mean to do, in Heaven's name ?" cried Dame Swan, with an energy that alarmed the young damsel.

" I find I must trust you," she said.   " I am sure you are perfectly loyal."

"Loyal! yes! I should like to see the king on the throne, and his enemies confounded. But what has my loyalty got to do with your engagement?"

"Everything," replied Juliana, reassured by the good woman's words. "The king is now beneath your roof. He is the person whom you have been led to believe would be my husband; but the wretch of whom you heard us speak in the garden is the accursed regicide Cromwell. Now you understand it all?"

"I do, I do," cried Dame Swan.

"I won't trust you by halves," said Juliana. "The king is about to embark at midnight for France. Major Careless, with whom I was conversing in the garden, will sail with him."

"Oh! I hope they will soon return!" cried the hostess. "I hope you will soon be wedded to the major! He is worthy of you. I am glad you have told me this, though the information is so astounding, that it has quite upset me. But I shall be right in a few minutes."

Now that this explanation had taken place with the hostess, Juliana felt quite at ease with the good dame, and was very glad to spend the rest of the evening with her in her room.

To Charles the hours seemed to pass very slowly, and he longed for midnight, but he was in extremely good spirits, and all his attendants exerted themselves to amuse him.

Every half-hour—indeed, more frequently—some one went out to ascertain the state of the weather. The night was fine and starlight, and a light breeze from the north-west was just what was desired. Charmouth, as the reader is aware, is about half a mile from the shore, but as an eminence intervenes the sea is not visible from the little town.

These constant reports of the favourable state of the weather helped to keep up the king's spirits. Missing Juliana, and deeming it necessary to maintain his part as her intended husband, he went in search of her and found her in the hostess's room. Dame Swan was with her at the time, and the extreme deference now paid him by the hostess soon showed him that she had been let into the secret.

Feeling, therefore, that further disguise was useless, he addressed her in his own proper character, and quite enchanted her with his affability.

"I was not aware of the great honour intended me, my liege," she said, "or I would have made more fitting preparations for your reception."

"You have done quite enough, my good dame," said Charles. "In strict fulfilment of your promise, you have kept your house free from guests at a busy time, so that I have been perfectly private, and if I had departed without making any disclosure to you, I should have desired others to thank you in my name."

Quite overwhelmed by his majesty's condescension, the hostess could make no reply.

"I must, also, compliment you on your discernment," pursued the king, smiling. "You quickly perceived that I wanted some necessary qualifications for the part I attempted to play, and that I was not exactly the person with whom this charming young gentlewoman would have made a runaway match. A great liberty has been taken with her—

excusable only under the circumstances—but you will understand that her loyalty alone induced her to consent to the scheme."

"Yes, but I played my part so indifferently, that I do not deserve your majesty's thanks," said Juliana.

"Nay, the fault was mine," rejoined the king.   And he added in a low voice, "I ought to have changed parts with Major Careless."

---

## CHAPTER XV

### THE WATCHERS BY THE SEA.

By this time, most of the inhabitants of the little town who had been at Lyme fair had returned, and a great number of them flocked to the inn, and made so much disturbance that the hostess was fain to serve them, but she would not let them into the parlour, and after they had emptied a few pots of cider—that being the liquor for which Charmouth was renowned—they quietly departed.

Half an hour later, every house in the village—except the little inn, was closed—and its inmates had apparently retired to rest, since not a light could be seen in any of the windows.

To avoid any chance of danger to his majesty, it had been arranged that Colonel Wyndham, attended by Harry Peters, should ride to the mouth of the Char about an hour before midnight, and there await the long-boat.   On its arrival, Peters was to gallop back and give information to the king, who would be prepared to start on the instant with his companions to the place of rendezvous.   The horses would be ready saddled, so that no delay could occur.

Soon after eleven o'clock, the colonel, having received his majesty's last commands, prepared to set out.   Reuben Rufford, the ostler, brought out the horses, and both the colonel and Harry Peters noticed that the fellow appeared very inquisitive, and held up his lantern, so as to throw its light on their faces.   When they were gone, Reuben observed to his mistress that he thought they could be about no good, but she rebuked him sharply, and he went back to the stable.

Riding singly along the narrow green lane, already described as leading to the sea-shore, Colonel Wyndham and Peters presently arrived at the mouth of the Char.

The place was perfectly solitary.   They had encountered no one in the lane, and no one was to be seen on the beach.   The only sound that could be heard was that of the waves breaking on the sandy shore.   It was within half an hour of high water, and the tide was flowing rapidly.

The night was dark, but clear, and they looked out for the *Eider Duck*, and fancied they could distinguish her in the offing about a mile out. A light could be seen at the head of Lyme Cobb, which looked like a huge black ship moored to the shore.   The dark sloping cliffs were wrapped in gloom, but nothing was to be feared in that direction, for the road along the beach was impassable in this state of the tide.

For some time the watchers remained with their gaze fixed upon the sea, hoping to descry the boat, anxiously listening for the sound of oars. They heard nothing except the wearisome and monotonous sound of the waves.

Hitherto scarcely a word had passed between them, but now the colonel could not help expressing astonishment that the boat did not make its appearance.

"Have a little patience, sir," said Peters. "It will soon he here, I'll warrant you. Stephen Limbry will not prove false."

"I think not," said the colonel. "Hark! 'tis the hour!"

As he spoke a distant bell struck twelve, so slowly that in the deep stillness the strokes could be counted.

The appointed hour had come, but no boat came with it.

In vain the colonel and his servant strained their gaze towards the spot where they supposed the boat was lying. No boat could be seen.

Sometimes they fancied they could descry it, but the delusive object, whatever it might be, quickly vanished.

Another hour passed by, and found them at their post, still gazing at the sea, still hoping the boat would come, vainly hoping, as it proved.

The tide had turned, but had not yet perceptibly receded.

Though staggered and uneasy, Colonel Wyndham had not lost faith in the shipmaster.

"Should Limbry turn out a traitor, I will never trust man again," he said.

"Perhaps the seamen have gone ashore to the fair, colonel, and he has not been able to get them back again," rejoined Peters.

"The delay is unaccountable," cried the colonel. "His majesty will be distracted."

"Shall I ride back, and inform him that no boat has yet come ashore?" said Peters.

"That would make matters worse," rejoined the colonel. "Stay till you can take him good news."

They waited for another hour, and for an hour after that, patiently—striving to persuade themselves that the boat would still come.

The tide having now retreated to a considerable distance, the colonel rode upon the sand, and dashed into the water in his anxiety to discern the object he so fruitlessly sought.

No boat met his gaze; and the sky having become clouded, the sea looked dark and sullen. His own breast was full of sombre thoughts. The hopes that had animated him a few hours ago were gone, and had given place to bitter disappointment.

Still, though his hopes were crushed, he clung despairingly to his post, nor would he quit it, or allow Peters to depart, till day broke.

When the first streaks of dawn fell upon the sea, he looked out for the treacherous bark, and beheld her lying within half a mile of the Cobb. She had not quitted her position since yesterday.

However, it was useless to tarry longer. Even if the boat were sent now it would be impossible to embark in it at low water. Bidding Peters follow him, and in a state of mind bordering on distraction, he rode along the lane to Charmouth.

But how could he face the king?

## CHAPTER XVI.

### HOW THE GREY MARE PROVED THE BETTER HORSE.

LIMBRY was not altogether in fault, though appearances were against him.

Like many other men, he was under the governance of his spouse. And, as we shall now proceed to show, it was owing to Dame Limbry that the king's well-planned escape to France was frustrated. It may be remembered that she had expressed to her daughter a resolution to ascertain the nature of the important business on which Captain Ellesdon and the two Cavaliers desired to see Limbry at the inn. But she did not succeed. Strange to say, the shipmaster for once kept his own counsel, and this unwonted reticence on his part only served to inflame his wife's curiosity the more. Feeling his inequality in a contest with such a determined woman, Limbry showed his discretion by keeping out of her way as much as possible, and did not even acquaint her with his intention to go to sea; but desirous to propitiate her, he urged her to take her daughter to Lyme fair. As it turned out, he could not have acted more injudiciously. While at the fair, Dame Limbry heard the terrible Proclamation, and a suspicion immediately crossed her that the two gentlemen she had seen were fugitive Cavaliers from Worcester. The suspicion was converted into certainty, when about nine o'clock at night, just after she and her daughter had returned from Lyme, Limbry, who had been absent from home all day, came in, and instead of sitting down like a good husband and father to chat with them, went up-stairs at once to his own room, in order to pack up some linen.

While he was thus employed, his wife, who had followed him, entered the room, closed the door, and putting on an injured expression of countenance, which she knew so well how to assume, asked him, in a tone that made him quake, what he was about.

"Surely, you are not going to sea to-night?"

"Yes I am," he replied, finding further concealment impossible. "My landlord, Captain Ellesdon, has provided me with a freight which will be worth infinitely more to me than if the *Eider Duck* were laden with goods. Distrusting your power of keeping a secret, I have hitherto kept the matter from you, but now that there is no risk of your blabbing, I may tell you that I am about to transport some passengers to St. Malo, and on my return I shall receive a very handsome sum from Captain Ellesdon for my pains."

But instead of appearing pleased, and congratulating him as he expected on his good fortune, with a countenance inflamed with anger, his wife screamed out:

"I knew it. I felt quite certain you were about to transport some Royalists to France—perhaps the Malignant Prince himself. Foolish man! do you know that the penalty is death? Do you know that you are liable to be hanged for aiding the escape of traitors? This very morning I heard the Proclamation published at Lyme by the mayor, offering a reward of a thousand pounds for the capture of Charles Stuart, and threatening, with the heaviest penalties—even death—those who may aid the escape of his partisans. Now, I know that the men you have engaged to carry over to France are Royalists, and, as a dutiful and loving wife, I am bound to save you from the consequences of your folly. You shall not throw away a life which, if not valuable to yourself, is valuable to me and to my child. You shall NOT sail to France to-night!"

"How will you prevent me?" inquired her husband, contemptuously. "Tell me that."

"By locking you up in this chamber," she replied.

And before he could stop her, she slipped out of the room, and locked the door on the outside.

"Now, get out if you can," she cried, derisively.

"Ten thousand furies!" cried Limbry, vainly trying to force open the door. "Let me out at once, or you will rue it."

"'Tis you who will rue it, not me," she rejoined. "Unless you are quiet, I will go at once to Lyme, and give information to Captain Macy against both you and Captain Ellesdon."

"Zounds! woman!" he cried. "You don't mean to say you will commit such folly?" Assuming a coaxing tone, he then added, "Hear me, sweetheart! Open the door, and I'll bring you the handsomest present from St. Malo—I swear I'll do it."

"I'm not to be cajoled," she replied, in accents that left him no doubt of her fixed determination. "Keep quiet, or I will at once set off for Lyme, and see Captain Macy, and then you know full well what will follow."

"Was ever fair plan so absurdly defeated!" groaned the shipmaster. "If I could only give information to the gentlemen ; but that's impossible, with this infernal woman at the door. Since there's no help for it, I must submit."

And throwing himself, dressed as he was, on the bed, he gave utterance to a few more groans, and fell asleep.

When he awoke, about five o'clock in the morning, the events of the previous night rushed forcibly upon him, and his self-reproaches were so keen, that he started from his bed, and rushed to the door.

Finding it still locked, he called out lustily for his wife. The summons was quickly answered, for Dame Limbry had sat up all night, and in reply to his demand to be released, she refused, unless he solemnly promised to give up his intended voyage.

After some little demur, and another attempt at coaxing, which proved unsuccessful, he assented, and gave the required promise, but he added that he must go down to the sea-side and inform the gentlemen who were waiting for him, that he was unable to fulfil his engagement. Thereupon, the door was opened, and Limbry prepared to set out at once.

Rather doubting his design, notwithstanding the solemn promise he had just given, his vigilant spouse would not allow him to go alone, but followed him closely with her daughter, and they were proceeding along the narrow lane leading to the sea, when they met Colonel Wyndham and his servant. The colonel could not fail to be struck by Limbry's downcast looks, and he was also surprised to see him attended by the two women. But he was too exasperated to heed their presence.

"Treacherous rascal!" he vociferated. "Art thou not ashamed to look me in the face after breaking thy engagement to Captain Ellesdon and myself? I have been waiting for the boat since midnight. How dost thou attempt to justify thy scandalous conduct? ha!"

"I cannot justify it, sir," said Limbry. "I have been made a prisoner in my own house."

"An idle story!" exclaimed Colonel Wyndham, incredulously.

"'Tis the truth," cried Dame Limbry, stepping forward. "I know my foolish husband was running his neck into a noose, so I locked him up to save him. Don't tempt him to sail, or as sure as I'm a living woman, I'll inform against you all."

"Be not afraid, woman, I've done with him," rejoined the colonel. "Take care thy termagant spouse doesn't get thee into mischief," he added to Limbry.

So saying he rode past them, and made his way towards the inn.

Arrived there, he despatched Peters to Lyme Regis to acquaint Captain Ellesdon with the failure of the scheme, and ask his advice.

<hr>

## CHAPTER XVII.

### THE REVEREND BARTHOLOMEW WESLEY.

On entering the house the colonel found Charles and his attendants in a state of the greatest anxiety. His looks announced the ill-tidings he brought; and it was scarcely necessary for him to relate what had happened. The king bore the grievous disappointment better than might have been expected, but he could not wholly repress his feelings of vexation.

"If I had had to do with a man of mettle, master in his own house, as well as master of his ship, I should have been half-way across the English Channel by this time," he cried. "Fate thwarts me at every turn; but I will not be cast down. We shall hear what Captain Ellesdon says. Perhaps he may be able to find me another vessel."

"After what has occurred, I do not think it will be safe for your majesty to remain here," said Colonel Wyndham. "Limbry's wife will probably publish all she knows. Besides, I do not like the looks of the ostler. The knave eyed me suspiciously as I gave him my horse just now, and muttered something about my being out all night."

"Where would you have me go? What would you have me do?" cried Charles.

"Perhaps Captain Ellesdon may suggest some plan," said the colonel. "We shall hear when Peters returns; but my notion is that your majesty should ride on to Bridport. You may have better luck there than here."

"My horse has cast a shoe," said Lord Wilmot, rising to quit the room. "If we are going to start immediately, I must send him to a smith."

So saying, he went out, and proceeding to the stable, gave the ostler the necessary instructions. Like Colonel Wyndham, he was struck with the man's inquisitive manner, and declined to have any conversation with him.

"I can't make these folks out," thought Reuben. "There's the strangest goings on with them I ever knew. 'Tis my belief they're a pack of malignants trying to escape; but I'll soon find it out."

Thus ruminating, and considering what reward he should obtain for giving information against his mistress's guests, he took Lord Wilmot's horse to a blacksmith, named Seth Hammet, whose smithy was in the lower part of the village. Bidding the smith good morrow, he told him he had brought him a job.

Seth Hammet, who was a sharp-looking young man, thanked him, but being of an inquisitive turn, he added, "You've got some gentle-folks at the inn, I think?"

"Ay, ay," replied Reuben, not desiring to take him into his confidence. "This horse belongs to one of them."

"A fine horse," observed Hammet, looking at him admiringly. "But they all seem well mounted. Where do they come from?"

"I don't happen to know," replied Reuben, in a tone meant to signify that he did not feel inclined to tell. "Somewhere in Devonshire, I believe."

"Well, I can easily find out," observed Hammet, with a knowing look.

"I should like to know how?" rejoined Reuben, surprised.

"I'll show you presently," said the smith.

"If there's witchcraft in it, I won't have anything to do with it," said Reuben.

"Bless you! there's no witchcraft in it. 'Tis the simplest thing possible, as you'll see. Two of your guests have been out all night."

"How do you know that?" asked Reuben.

"Because I saw them return, not half an hour ago. The servant rode on to Lyme. I'm sure of it, for I heard his master tell him to go on to Captain Ellesdon's house."

"Ah, indeed!" exclaimed the ostler, surprised.

"Yes, you didn't know that, Reuben," said the smith. "Now let us proceed to business."

Thereupon, he took up the horse's feet, and examined the shoes, twice over, very deliberately.

After the second examination, he said, with a grin:

"Now, Reuben, I can tell you something that will surprise you. This horse has only three shoes on, as you know. Each shoe has been put on in a different county—Somerset, Stafford, Worcester."

"Did you say Worcester?" cried Reuben.

"Look here," replied Hammet, lifting up one of the horse's fore-feet. "That shoe came from Worcester. Now, don't you think I'm a conjuror?"

"I don't know what to think," replied Reuben.

But it seemed as if something had suddenly struck him, for he said rather hastily:

"I can't stay any longer. I want to see our minister, Mr. Wesley; I'll come back for the horse presently."

So saying, he ran off to Mr. Wesley's dwelling, which was at no great distance, but he found that the minister was at prayers with his family, and knowing from experience that the reverend gentleman's discourses were rather lengthy, he would not wait, but went on to the inn.

During his absence Harry Peters, who had galloped there and back, had returned from Lyme, and was now with the king. Peters had seen Captain Ellesdon, who was quite confounded to hear of the failure of the plan, having persuaded himself that his majesty was then on the way to St. Malo.

"Never in my life have I seen a man so greatly troubled as the captain appeared," said Peters. "He humbly tenders his advice to your majesty not to make any longer stay in Charmouth. He would have ridden over to offer his counsel in person, and urge your immediate departure, had it been safe to do so. Rumours, he says, are sure to be bruited abroad, which will infallibly lead to strict search and pursuit by Captain Macy."

Captain Ellesdon's counsel so completely coincided with the opinion previously expressed by Colonel Wyndham and his other adherents, that the king determined to act upon it, and preparations were made for his immediate departure. Juliana had retired to rest in a chamber provided for her by Dame Swan, but she had been astir for some time, and was now in the hostess's room, quite ready to start.

Dame Swan was with her, when a maid-servant entered and informed her mistress that Reuben, the ostler, desired to speak with her, and she went out to him.

Displeased by his manner and looks, Dame Swan said to him, very sharply :

"Why are you not in the stable, Reuben, helping the young man to get ready the horses? If you have aught to say to me, it can be said at a more convenient opportunity, when the guests are gone."

"No, it cannot," replied the ostler. "No opportunity like the present. Hear what I have to say, and be warned. I will not saddle or bridle the horses—neither will I suffer your guests to depart. They are malignants. I have proof of it."

"Fie upon you, Reuben!" cried his mistress. "You have been drinking strong waters on an empty stomach, and your brain is confused."

"I have only drunk my customary pot of cider," he rejoined; "and my brain is clear enough to convince me that Charles Stuart is now in this house."

"What do I hear?" cried Dame Swan, putting the best face she could on the matter. "Out on thee, for a false knave! Dost want to injure my house by thy lies? There are none but gentlefolks here—men true to the Commonwealth. Go to the stable at once, and bring round the horses, or thou shalt quit my service."

"I do not design to remain in your service, misguided woman," he rejoined; "and I warn you not to let these malignants depart. I am now going to the Reverend Bartholomew Wesley, and will bring him back with me."

"A fig for thy minister!" she rejoined.

But as soon as he was gone she flew to the parlour in which Charles and the others were assembled, and informed them of the danger. On this, the whole party hastened to the stable.

Fortunately, Harry Peters had got the horses ready, so that in another minute they were all mounted—all, except Lord Wilmot, whose horse had not been brought back. Careless accompanied his lordship to the smithy.

As Dame Swan assisted Juliana to take her seat on the pillion behind, the king bade her adieu, and putting his arm round her neck, kissed her heartily.

He then rode off with his attendants towards Bridport, Lord Wilmot and Careless being left behind.

They had not been gone long, when a short, stout personage entered the inn, and greeted the hostess, though in rather a singular manner. He was arrayed in a black gown with Geneva bands, and a close-fitting black velvet skull-cap, that set off his ruddy visage. This was the Reverend Bartholomew Wesley, an ancestor we may remark of the renowned John Wesley. His countenance had a strange sarcastic expression, though he put on an air of mock respect.

"I scarce know how to approach you, Margaret, you are grown such a mighty grand dame," he said, with an affected reverence.

"Eh day! what's the meaning of this foolery?" she cried.

"You must be a maid of honour, at least," pursued the minister. "Nay, nay, you can't gainsay me. Charles Stuart slept at your house last night, and kissed you when he went away. 'Twas a great honour, no doubt—a very great honour—and you may well be proud."

"I should be proud, if I thought it was the king who had kissed me," she rejoined, sharply. "But the guests who slept in my house last night were plain country gentlemen, and it's no business of yours to meddle with them."

"Slept, quotha!" cried Wesley, lifting up his hands. "Why, not one of the party has been a-bed except the young damsel, and two of them have been out all night. You see I'm well informed, Margaret!"

"I know who has told you these shameful falsehoods—'tis that false, mischief-making knave, Reuben Ruflord."

"Reuben is an honest man, and of the right leaven. You will have to render an account of your guests, dame."

"I tell you my guests were all strangers to me. How can I give an account of them? They paid their lawful reckoning, and that's more than everybody does. All you desire is to get me into trouble—but I'm not afraid. Out of my house with you!"

"Woman! woman! listen to me!"

"No, I won't listen to you any longer. Out of my house, I say; or I'll find some one to kick you out."

Not knowing to what extremities the indignant dame might resort, the minister deemed it prudent to retreat, but he shook his clenched hand at her as he went out.

On coming forth he was joined by Reuben, and they went down to the smithy together. Seth Hammet told them that the gentleman had taken away his horse not many minutes ago, whereupon they both upbraided him for his want of zeal.

"Dolt! we should have captured the malignant, had you deprived him of the means of flight," said Wesley.

"I did resist," rejoined Hammet: "but he had a friend with him, and they forced me to deliver up the horse. However, I was right well paid for the job, for one of them flung me a pistole."

"Which way did they go? To Bridport?" demanded the minister.

"I think so," replied Hammet. "They rode up Stonebarrow Hill, and seemed to be making for Moorcomblake."

"They have fled, but they shall not escape," said Wesley. "We will hie unto Mr. Butler of Commer. He is the nearest justice of peace, and when he has heard our statement, he will despatch his warrants to raise the country for the apprehension of the Malignant Prince, and those traitors to the Commonwealth who were with him last night at Dame Swan's hostelry."

Thereupon, they all set off for Mr. Butler's residence, which was at no great distance from Charmouth, and on arriving there they were quickly admitted to the presence of the justice.

Now Mr. Butler was secretly a Royalist, though he prudently concealed his opinions, and on hearing Reuben Rufford's statement, he assumed a very severe countenance, and said:

"I know your mistress, Dame Swan, to be a very honest woman, and I also know you to be an arrant knave, having had several complaints made against you. I attach not the slightest credence to your statement. I do not believe that Charles Stuart is in this part of the country, and I therefore refuse to issue a warrant for his apprehension."

Mr. Wesley made an effort to move him, but the justice continued inflexible, and the applicants, who had made certain of success, left in high dudgeon.

But they were determined not to be baffled, and at the minister's instance, Reuben and Hammet set off at once for Lyme Regis, for the purpose of laying the matter before Captain Macy.

"I shall be greatly surprised," said Wesley, "if the captain, who is keen and clear-sighted, very different from this dull-witted, prejudiced justice, does not immediately discern the truth."

They were not long in getting to Lyme Regis, and very soon found Captain Macy—a fierce and zealous Republican soldier—who listened to all they had to narrate with the utmost interest and attention.

As Mr. Wesley anticipated, he took a very different view of the case from Justice Butler.

"You have done well in coming hither," he said; "and if the young man, Charles Stuart, be captured, as with Heaven's grace he will be, ye shall both be amply rewarded. I will start in pursuit of him at once. Ye say that he and his attendants are gone towards Bridport."

"The person, whom I believe to be Charles Stuart, is gone in that direction," said Reuben. "You will know him, inasmuch as he hath a fair young damsel seated on a pillion behind him."

"Two of his companions took a different course," remarked Hammet. "But no doubt they will rejoin him."

"Charles Stuart is the prize I aim at," cried Captain Macy. "Him will I follow."

"Him will you assuredly capture, provided you loiter not by the way, captain," said Reuben.

"'Tis not my custom to loiter," rejoined Captain Macy. "Thou shalt go with me. I may need thee."

Not five minutes afterwards, he was riding at a rapid trot, at the head of a dozen men, across the hard sands to Charmouth. Mounted on a stout trooper's horse, Reuben rode beside him, and it was a great satisfaction to the spiteful ostler, when the detachment was drawn up before the little inn, and Dame Swan was summoned forth to speak to Captain Macy.

The interrogation did not last many minutes, the captain stating that he would question her further on his return. He was detained a little longer by Mr. Wesley, who wished to have a few words with him, and declared it to be his firm conviction that Charles Stuart had passed the night at Dame Swan's hostel.

After this, Captain Macy gave the word, and the troop trotted off, in the same order as before, on the road to Bridport.

"Heaven grant the king may escape them!" ejaculated the hostess as she returned to her room. "I wonder I didn't sink to the ground when that stern officer spoke to me. I trembled in every limb. This is all that wicked Reuben's doing. I saw the villain with the troopers. May Heaven requite him!"

<hr>

## CHAPTER XVIII.

### HOW THE KING FLED FROM BRIDPORT HARBOUR.

Unconscious of the danger by which he was threatened, and not fearing pursuit, Charles soon slackened his pace, and rode slowly up the side of Stonebarrow Hill towards Moorcomblake. From this elevated point an extensive view over the Vale of Marshwood was obtained, while on the right rose the beacon-crowned summit of the Golden Cap. Charles halted for a short time to contemplate this fine prospect, still hoping that his friends would overtake him ; but they came not, and he went on. By this time, he had shaken off his disappointment, and completely recovered his spirits ; conversing as gaily as usual with Juliana, and seeming greatly to enjoy the ride.

A little beyond Moorcomblake they met a small band of travellers, and among them was a person whom both his majesty and Colonel Wyndham recognised as having been a servant of the late king. The sight of this man caused them both considerable uneasiness, but he passed on, apparently without noticing them.

After a long descent they reached Chidiock, and crossing the valley, mounted another hill, which offered charming prospects—a conspicuous object being the singular cone-shaped eminence, known as Colmer's Hill.

Passing several farm-houses, with large orchards attached to them, they approached the pleasant old town of Bridport, delightfully situated among the hills; Colonel Wyndham rode on in advance, and entering the town, to his infinite surprise and vexation, found it full of soldiers. On inquiry, he ascertained that Colonel Haynes, an active Republican commander, was marching troops from several garrisons to Weymouth and other places, in order to embark them for Jersey and Guernsey, as those loyal islands still continued to hold out against the Parliamentarians. The troops now in the town were to be shipped in a few days from Bridport harbour.

Charged with this unsatisfactory intelligence, he rode back to the king, and besought him not to enter the town, which was swarming with his enemies, but Charles refused to turn aside, saying he had promised to wait for Colonel Wilmot amd Careless at Bridport, and whatever the consequences might be, he would keep his word. However, he at last consented to proceed to the harbour, but ordered Peters to remain in the town to look after the others. He then rode boldly on, closely attended by Colonel Wyndham.

Round the town-hall was collected a large body of men in steel caps, buff coats, and funnel-topped boots, armed with calivers, pistols, and long basket-hilted swords. Most of them were smoking their pipes. They scrutinised the travellers as they went by, but did not attempt to molest them.

The sight of so many of his foes, who could have captured him in an instant, did not appear to intimidate the king. Juliana's fair cheek was blanched, but she showed no other signs of fear.

Thus they passed through the town without hindrance, and rode on to the port, which was about a mile and a half distant. The little quay was unusually bustling, there being two or three ships in the harbour waiting to convey the troops to Jersey. The pier was a huge, clumsy wooden structure, somewhat resembling Lyme Cobb. Not far from it was the George Inn, and thither the travellers repaired, but they found it full of soldiers; and when Juliana had alighted, and Charles was taking his horse to the stable, he found himself completely environed by troopers. Nothing daunted, however, he pushed his way through the throng, calling out lustily "By your leave," and caring little if he trod on their feet. Colonel Wyndham followed his example, and they both found that with such men rough usage answered better than civility.

Some time elapsed before the slight repast they had ordered in a private room was served, and they had just finished it, when Juliana, who was looking from the window at the quay, perceived Harry Peters. He promptly obeyed the sign she gave him, and coming up-stairs, informed the king that he had been sent by Lord Wilmot to warn his majesty to depart instantly.

"Captain Macy, with a troop of horse from Lyme Regis, is in pursuit of you, my liege," said Peters. "They are now in Bridport, and are searching all the inns, and are certain to come here."

"What is to be done?" cried Charles. "I am caught in a trap. My retreat is cut off."

"Not so, my liege," replied Peters, confidently. "I will engage to deliver you. Get out the horses without delay, and ride towards Bridport."

"But by so doing I shall rush upon destruction," cried Charles.

"You will meet me before you meet the enemy, my liege," replied Peters.

"Well, I will follow thy advice, though it seems strangely hazardous," said Charles.

Peters then left the room and rode off. Hurrying to the stable, Charles and Colonel Wyndham got out their steeds, and in less than ten minutes, the king, with Juliana seated behind him on the pillion, and attended by the colonel, was proceeding at a rapid pace towards Bridport.

When they were within half a mile of the town, they came to a road that turned off on the right, and were debating whether to pursue it or go on, when they heard the clatter of a horse's feet, and the next moment beheld Peters galloping towards them. The faithful fellow signed to them to turn off, and with such energy of action that they instantly obeyed, but were surprised to find he did not follow them, but went on at the same swift pace towards the harbour. His object, however, was soon apparent. The heavy trampling of a troop of horse was heard mingled with the clank of swords, and the next moment a detachment of cavalry dashed past, evidently in pursuit of the fugitive, who had thus contrived to draw them on, putting his own life in jeopardy to preserve the king. Though Charles himself was concealed by a turn of the road, he clearly distinguished the troopers, and felt sure that their leader was Captain Macy.

Scarcely knowing which way to proceed, but fearing to pass through Bridport, lest they should be stopped, they rode on to a pretty little village called Bothenhampton, and there inquired the road to Dorchester. The person to whom the king addressed this inquiry, stared, and told him he must go back through Bridport, but Charles declined, and they rode on to Shipton Gorge, above which was a remarkable hill shaped like a ship turned keel upwards, with a beacon on the summit, and were directed to proceed to Hammerdon Hill, and this course they took.

Having crossed a high range of furze-covered downs, and traversed a broad common, they were approaching Winterborne Abbas, when they descried their pursuers coming down the hill they had just descended. Captain Macy, no doubt, had heard of the inquiries made by the king as to the road to Dorchester, and had followed in that direction.

Fortunately, a coppice was at hand, and the fugitives managed to conceal themselves within it, till their pursuers had passed. So near were the troopers that the king could hear their shouts, announcing that they felt certain of finding him at Dorchester. After this, Charles required little persuasion to induce him to take a different course, though he could not make up his mind altogether to quit the coast.

Having gained the Roman road which once led to Dorchester, they proceeded along it in the opposite direction, towards a fine down known as Eggardon Hill, the summit of which was crowned by an ancient camp, with very remarkable intrenchments. Thence they proceeded through the downs and along the beautiful valley of the Birt towards Beaminster.

Some seven years previously, Beaminster was a flourishing and cheerful little town, but it now looked like a collection of ruins, having nearly been burnt down in 1644, during the Civil War. and it had only been partially rebuilt. Charles was so struck by the melancholy aspect of the place that he would not halt there as he intended, but proceeded to Broad Windsor, which was about three miles distant.

On the road thither, they descried three persons on horseback on the summit of a high conical hill, called Chartknolle. Evidently, these persons had stationed themselves on this conspicuous position in order to survey the country round. Juliana declared they were friends, but the king and Colonel Wyndham scarcely dared indulge the hope.

The question, however, was speedily set at rest. Dashing down the side of the hill at a headlong pace came Harry Peters, and he was followed, somewhat more leisurely, by Lord Wilmot and Careless.

It was a joyous meeting, and a few minutes were occupied in mutual congratulations and explanations. Harry Peters, it appeared, had escaped by swimming his horse across the Brit, his pursuers not daring to follow him. He then made his way to Eype, where he encountered Lord Wilmot and Careless, who had galloped thither from Bridport.

At this point Lord Wilmot took up the story:

"Feeling it would be impossible to render your majesty any service at the time," said his lordship, "after a brief consultation, we determined to proceed to Trent, as we could not doubt that you would soon find your way thither. So we rode on to Netherbury and Stoke Abbots. By Careless's advice, we then mounted this hill in order to survey the country, and right glad I am that we did so."

"No post could have been better chosen," said Charles. "Had you been long on the hill top?"

"More than an hour." replied Wilmot. "I confess I thought it useless to remain so long, but Careless judged better, and was loth to depart."

"I had a firm conviction that I should discover your majesty," said Careless. "I saw you when you left Beaminster, and I felt certain it was your majesty from the fair damsel who rides behind you."

"The fair damsel has as quick eyes as you have, and instantly detected you," said the king. "I am right glad we have met. That I myself have escaped is entirely owing to thee, my faithful fellow," he added to Harry Peters. "Hadst thou fallen into the hands of the enemy I should have been truly grieved."

"Heaven be thanked I am still able and ready to serve your majesty," rejoined Peters.

----

## CHAPTER XIX.

### BROAD WINDSOR.

THE king and his companions then rode on to Broad Windsor, and proceeded to the George, the only inn the place contained. Rice Jones was the name of the host, and he and his wife were well known to

Colonel Wyndham, having been servants to his uncle, Sir Hugh Wyndham, of Pillesden. Charles was so well pleased with their manner, and with the comfortable appearance of the inn, that he resolved to pass the night there, and bade the colonel secure all the best rooms in the house, which was done. All the party, indeed, were so wearied that they were enchanted at the prospect of a good night's rest, but they did not obtain it, for late in the evening a troop of horse, which was marching to Lyme Regis, arrived in the town, and demanded quarters at the George. Poor Rice Jones humbly represented to them that all the rooms were engaged, but this did not satisfy the troopers. They insisted on being accommodated, and when Jones protested it was quite out of his power to oblige them, they took complete possession of the lower part of the house, and made such a disturbance that the occupants of the rooms above could not obtain a wink of slumber. The noise was bad enough, but Charles and the others were not without apprehensions that the officer in command of the troop might compel them to appear before him. This danger, however, they escaped, owing to the management of Rice Jones and his wife, who answered for them.

At daybreak, however, the reveillé was sounded, the troopers got upon their horses, and rode out of the town, and the inn was left quiet. Before his departure, however, the officer made some further inquiries of Rice Jones as to his guests, and wished to know whither they were going, but this the host could not inform him.

As it was quite certain that when the troopers arrived at Lyme Regis, they must learn that Macy had been in pursuit of the fugitive king, it would have been in the highest degree imprudent for his majesty and those with him to remain longer at Broad Windsor, and preparations were therefore made for immediate departure.

During breakfast, a consultation took place as to the best course to be pursued in the present state of affairs. Colonel Wyndham was clearly of opinion that it would be extremely hazardous for his majesty to attempt to embark from any part in Dorsetshire, so many forces being now drawn to the coast for the expedition to Jersey, and he besought him to return to Trent, and to remain there till some other plan could be devised for his escape.

"Pillesden, the residence of my uncle, Sir Hugh Wyndham, is close at hand," continued the colonel; "and I would propose to your majesty to retreat there for a time, but I feel certain, after the recent occurrences, that the house will be strictly searched, and you might unhappily be discovered."

"No, I will not go to Pillesden," said Charles. "I do not doubt the security of Sir Hugh Wyndham's house, but I would rather be with thee, Frank. I will return to Trent, and Careless shall attend me as before."

"I am glad your majesty has so decided," said the colonel. "If I may further advise I would propose that Harry Peters shall conduct Lord Wilmot to the house of my friend, John Coventry, in Salisbury. He resides in the Cathedral Close; and Dr. Hinchman, one of the former prebends, lives with him. No man in the kingdom is more devoted to the royal cause than John Coventry, and he will not only be well able to advise how to procure a vessel for France, but will furnish any moneys that may be required."

"I like the plan," said Lord Wilmot. "When I have seen Mr. Coventry and consulted with him, I will send back Peters to Trent with all particulars. If I am obliged to write, my letter shall be rolled up like a bullet, so that the messenger may swallow it, in case of need."

Here the conference ended. Soon afterwards the horses were brought round, and they set off—Rice Jones promising, if Captain Macy should come to the inn, that he would give him a wrong direction.

The whole party rode together to within a few miles of Yeovil, where they separated—Lord Wilmot, attended by Harry Peters, proceeding to Sherborne, on the way to Salisbury; while the king and his companions went on to Trent, and arrived there in perfect safety.

---

## CHAPTER XX.

### COLONEL ROBIN PHILIPS, OF MONTACUTE HOUSE.

Nothing could be more agreeable to Charles, after the great fatigue he had undergone, than the repose he was able to enjoy for the next few days. But he then began to find his confinement irksome, despite the attentions shown him by Lady Wyndham and her daughter-in-law, and the agreeable companionship of the fair Juliana Coningsby. Harry Peters had not yet returned from Salisbury, and the king could not help fearing that Lord Wilmot had failed in obtaining Mr. Coventry's assistance. Action, even attended by risk, suited Charles infinitely better than quietude, and he longed for something to do. Mr. Langton sat with him for several hours in each day, but he found the worthy man's discourses intolerably tedious, and declared to Careless that he was becoming moped to death.

Careless, on the contrary, found his stay at Trent far from disagreeable, and had no particular desire to incur fresh perils. Quite content to wait till a good chance of escape to France should offer, he saw difficulties in every plan that was suggested. He was so happy in the society of Juliana Coningsby, that he quite dreaded a separation from her.

One day, when the young pair were strolling together in the garden, Mrs. Wyndham came forth to inform them that Harry Peters had just returned from Salisbury, accompanied by Colonel Robin Philips. Upon this Careless hastened to the yard, and found Colonel Wyndham conversing with a tall, strongly-built man of soldier-like aspect and bearing. This was Colonel Robin Philips, of Montacute House, grandson of Sir Edward Philips, formerly Master of the Rolls. Though not handsome the colonel had a manly, expressive countenance. Harry Peters was leading the horses to the stable, but stopped for a moment to salute Careless, who was then introduced to Colonel Philips, with whom he shook hands heartily.

At this juncture, a lattice window, looking upon the yard, was opened, and a voice called out:

"Robin! Robin! come up to me instantly."

"'Tis the king!" cried Colonel Philips.

And he instantly doffed his broad-leaved feathered hat, and respectfully saluted Charles, whom he perceived at the window.

"Come up to me instantly, Robin," vociferated the king. "I am all impatience to talk to thee. Come with him!" he added to the others.

Thus summoned they all repaired to the king's chamber. Charles embraced Colonel Philips as he entered, and clapped him warmly on the shoulder.

"I am the better pleased to see thee, Robin, because I did not expect thee," he said. "How didst thou learn I was here?"

"From John Coventry, my liege," replied Colonel Philips. "I have of late been in Salisbury, and on Lord Wilmot's arrival Mr. Coventry sent for me, knowing my anxious desire to serve your majesty, and after conferring with him, I immediately proceeded to Southampton, and succeeded in hiring a ship."

"Indeed!" exclaimed Charles joyfully.

"Pardon me, sire, I have raised your expectations too highly. Soon after I had concluded an arrangement with the skipper, the vessel I had hired was pressed to transport troops to Jersey."

"Then you have failed?" cried Charles.

"So far, my liege. But I do not regret the failure, for I have since discovered that all vessels from Southampton are now stopped at Calshot Castle, and again at Hurst Castle, and the passengers strictly examined, so that the risk to your majesty would have been very great."

"Discovery would have been almost certain," observed Colonel Wyndham. "'Twill be best that your majesty should embark from some small port on the Sussex coast, where the vessels are not watched."

"Exactly my opinion," said Colonel Philips. "With the assistance of my friend Colonel George Gunter, of Rackton, near Chichester, I feel confident I shall be able to hire a vessel at Little Hampton or Shoreham. Before taking this step, however, I deemed it necessary to consult your majesty, and have come hither for that purpose."

"Colonel Gunter, of course, can be relied upon, or you would not propose him," observed Charles.

"He is thoroughly loyal, exceedingly active, and will spare no pains," said Colonel Philips.

"From my own personal knowledge, my liege, I can confirm this description of George Gunter," added Careless. "Your majesty may depend upon his fidelity."

"Then I place myself in his hands. Make any arrangement with him you please."

"Since your majesty approves the plan, I will set out for Rackton forthwith."

"Nay, thou shalt not depart to-day, Robin," cried the king. "To-morrow will be quite time enough. I must have some further talk with thee. The sight of thy honest face cheers me. Thou shalt lodge in my room."

"Nay, your majesty shall not be put to inconvenience. I can find him a room," remarked Colonel Wyndham.

It was then arranged that Colonel Philips should remain at Trent till the following day. His company was a great pleasure to the king, and helped to dissipate the ennui under which his majesty had been labouring of late. They had some further discussion as to the proposed embarkation from the Sussex coast, and the more he considered the plan the better the king liked it.

That night, Charles supped with the family party in the dining-room, Colonel Philips, of course, being present, and the improvement in his majesty's spirits was noticed by all the ladies. Supper was just over when Harry Peters rushed into the room, with a very anxious countenance, and said that Mr. Meldrum and some of the villagers—notorious fanatics—were coming to search the house immediately. They had witnessed Colonel Philips's arrival, and felt certain he was the king—the report of his majesty's death at Worcester having been authoritatively contradicted.

On this alarming intelligence, Charles immediately hurried up-stairs to conceal himself in the secret closet, while Colonel Philips and Careless followed more leisurely, and sat down in the king's room. The searchers were not long in making their appearance, and Mr. Meldrum demanded that Charles Stuart should be delivered up to them.

Colonel Wyndham answered them courteously.

" You shall see the gentleman who arrived here to-day, and judge for yourselves whether he is Charles Stuart."

With this, he conducted them to the room up-stairs. It was illumined by a lamp, which showed them the two gentlemen seated near a table. Both arose on the entrance of the party, and saluted Mr. Meldrum.

" You have seen me before, I doubt not, reverend sir," observed Careless, respectfully ; " because I regularly attend your church, and have profited much by your discourses."

" Truly I have seen you, sir," replied the minister, " and have been much pleased by your devout manner and attention. I have, also, been well pleased to find that Mistress Juliana Coningsby has become a convert—peradventure, on your persuasion. I begin to think we are mistaken," he added to those with him. " This is a person of middle age, whereas Charles Stuart, as ye wot, is designated the Young Man."

" This gentleman is Captain Copthorne," said Careless, " a staunch Republican and a Puritan."

" That is how I should describe myself, if called upon," said the so-called Captain Copthorne, with a courteous bow. " I am neither a fugitive prince, nor a malignant."

" The assurance is sufficient, captain," rejoined the minister. " We have been labouring under a grievous error," he added to the zealots with him, " and have no further business here."

As he turned to depart, he perceived Juliana standing at the back, and said to her in a low tone :

" Ere long, I hope I may have the happy privilege of uniting you to one who deserves you."

Juliana blushed deeply. Without waiting for a reply, Mr. Meldrum

ind his company went down-stairs, and were shown out of the house by
Harry Peters. When the details of the incident were related to the
king, they caused him a good deal of amusement.

Promising to return to Trent as soon as any arrangement had been
made, through the instrumentality of Colonel Gunter, for the hire of a
vessel, Colonel Philips, next morning, took leave of his majesty, and
set out for Chichester, attended by the faithful Harry Peters.

## CHAPTER XXI.

### HOW THE KING LEFT TRENT.

A week elapsed, and Colonel Philips had not returned, nor had any
tidings been received from him. The king's life differed very little from
that of a prisoner who enjoyed certain privileges, and whose friends
were permitted to visit him. However, he no longer felt impatient,
because he knew that every effort was being made for his deliverance.
He did not read much, though Colonel Wyndham possessed a good
library, which might have proved a great resource to him, had he been
of a studious turn, but he occupied himself in various ways, and not
infrequently cooked his own dinner. In this self-imposed task he was
assisted by Careless, and they flattered themselves they achieved great
success in their little dinners. It is quite certain, however, that these
repasts would not have been half so good as they were, if the chief
part of the work had not been done in the kitchen. Mr. Langton
used generally to dine with them, and thought the repast inimitable;
but then, perhaps, he was no judge. No more troopers appeared, for
ever since Juliana's conversion, Mr. Meldrum had thrown a protecting
wing over the house. The inmates were no more disturbed by
fanatical and inquisitive villagers.

Such was pretty nearly the daily routine at Trent during Charles's
enforced sojourn there. That it was enforced will account for his not
being entirely happy.

At length the welcome summons came. Altogether, Charles had
been a fortnight at Trent, when late in the evening of the 5th of
October, Colonel Philips, accompanied by Harry Peters, returned from
his mission. He had been at Rackton, and had consulted with Colonel
Gunter, who expressed the most earnest desire to serve his majesty, and
had used his best endeavours to hire a vessel at Little Hampton, but
had failed, after spending some days in fruitless negotiation. He and
Colonel Philips had since proceeded to Shoreham, and had seen a
certain Captain Nicholas Tattersall—a very honest fellow, and an
undoubted Royalist, though passing for a Roundhead—with whom
there seemed every prospect of coming to terms.

"I left Colonel Gunter at Brightelmstone, in Sussex, my liege,"
pursued Philips, "which is only a few miles from Shoreham, and he
will remain there till he has concluded an arrangement with Tattersall.
When the affair is settled as satisfactorily as I believe it will be, he will

come to Heale House, near Salisbury, and I have ventured to promise that he will find your majesty and Lord Wilmot there. Heale House, which is a very retired place, is the residence of Mrs. Hyde, a widow gentlewoman, and as faithful to the royal cause as loyalty can make her. The house is large, and the widow keeps up a good establishment, so that she can accommodate any number of guests. I have known Mrs. Hyde intimately for many years, and do not know a better or kinder-hearted woman — or one more hospitable. She will consider it a duty, as it will be her pride and pleasure, to place her house at your majesty's disposal—so you need have no hesitation in going thither."

"I shall put Mrs. Hyde's hospitality pretty severely to the test, for we shall form a large party," observed Charles.

"She will be delighted to receive your majesty and all your retinue," said Colonel Philips.

Arrangements were then made that Charles should set out for Heale on the following morning, accompanied by all those who had attended him on his expedition to Charmouth. Before his departure he took a kindly leave of Mrs. Wyndham and Lady Wyndham, thanking them warmly for their attention to him, and showing the utmost respect to the old lady. From Mr. Langton he received a blessing. Nor did he neglect to thank the servants who had contributed so materially to his comfort.

Having bidden a grateful farewell to all, he mounted his horse, and Juliana, who was delighted with the idea of another expedition, took her accustomed seat on the pillion behind him. Besides the king and his fair companion, the party included Colonel Wyndham and Careless, and their new ally, Colonel Philips, and they were followed by the faithful Harry Peters. While passing through the gate Charles looked back, and saw old Lady Wyndham, with her daughter-in-law and Mr. Langton, standing at the door gazing after him, and waved his hand to them. He also noticed a group of women-servants collected near the entrance to the kitchen.

By starting at an early hour, Colonel Wyndham hoped to escape observation, but he was disappointed. Mr. Meldrum was watching them from the churchyard, and seemed astonished at the number of the party. Thinking to remove his suspicions, Careless stopped to say a few words to him, and told him they were going to Weymouth. But the minister had some doubts, and being struck by Charles's appearance, he got some of the villagers to follow the party.

Meantime, the king and his retinue proceeded slowly through the village, as if they had no desire for concealment. In another minute the house was hidden from view by the tall elm-trees, and Charles saw no more of it.

Their road led over the heights of Rowbarrow to Sandford Orcas. They then climbed a steep hill, and were crossing Horethorne Down, when they heard shouts behind them, and saw that they were followed by a band of peasants mounted on ragged steeds.

Among this troop Colonel Wyndham at once recognised certain fanatical villagers from Trent, who had made themselves prominent on recent occasions, and his first impulse was to wait for their coming up, and chastise them, but on second thoughts he deemed it prudent to send Harry Peters to confer with them, while he and the others rode on.

This was done, and the party had not reached the little village of Charleton Horethorne, when Harry Peters galloped back, and told them, with a laugh, that he had managed to get rid of the enemy. By what device he accomplished this he did not explain, nor did the colonel inquire.

It was a fine bright October day, and the autumnal tints of the foliage were glorious. Skirting Charleton Hill, they passed North Cheriton, and proceeded through a wide and fertile valley on the picturesque banks of the little river Cale, to Wincanton, but they did not halt at this picturesque old town, their purpose being to dine at the George, at Mere, in Wiltshire—Dick Cheverel, the landlord of that excellent hostel, being well known to Colonel Philips as a perfectly honest fellow and a Royalist. There they knew they would be well entertained and run no risk.

---

## CHAPTER XXII.

HOW THEY DINED AT THE GEORGE AT MERE ; AND HOW THE HOST RELATED
HIS DREAM.

On arriving at Mere, they alighted at the George, which turned out quite as comfortable as it had been represented. Dick Cheverel, the host, a stout, good-humoured personage, sat at the head of the table, chatting with them very cheerfully.

The king took a place near the bottom of the table, but Juliana sat beside the host, who was very attentive to her. During a pause, Colonel Wyndham inquired of Cheverel if he had any news?

"Little that I care to relate," replied Dick. "Since the disaster at Worcester, I have heard nothing that gives me satisfaction. Fifteen hundred men have been shipped to Jersey and Guernsey to subjugate those faithful islands. But I am told that the Men of Westminster are in great perplexity, for they cannot conceive what has become of the king."

"Most likely his majesty is in London and in disguise," remarked Colonel Philips.

"That is the general opinion, but it is not mine," said Dick. "Several houses, I understand, have been searched ; but the searchers were not likely to find him."

"Why do you feel so confident on the point?" asked Juliana.

"Because I firmly believe he is in France," replied Dick. "At the very moment we are now talking of him, I am persuaded he is at the great palace of the Louvre, seated between his mother, Henrietta Maria, Queen of England, and his royal brother the Duke of York."

"Would to heaven it were true!" exclaimed Juliana.

"It must be true, for I have dreamed it thrice," said Dick.

"Is that all your authority?" cried Juliana, smiling.

"What better authority would you have, fair mistress ?" he rejoined " I'll tell you a singular thing. A rebel officer who fought at Worcester came to the George the day before yesterday, and said to me, 'I've had a remarkable dream, landlord, and it quite haunts me. I've dreamt that Charles Stuart is concealed in a house at Trent, in Somerset. I should know the house,' he continued, ' for it has a great patch of trees near it.'"

"That was very odd !" exclaimed Juliana.

" So I told him, and the idiot might have gone to Trent, if I had not recounted my thrice-repeated dream to him. When he had heard my relation he gave up all intention of searching for the king."

Everybody laughed, but the host maintained a grave face.

" You are a sly fellow, Dick," exclaimed Colonel Wyndham.

When his services were no longer required at the upper end of the table, the host came and sat down by the king. Filling a couple of glasses to the brim with sack, he said :

" Are you a friend to Cæsar ?"

" Ay, that I am," replied Charles. " As much Cæsar's friend as thou art."

" Then here's a health to King Charles !" cried the loyal host, rising as he spoke. " If his majesty is not on the other side of the water, and safe from his enemies, let us hope he soon will be !"

The toast was enthusiastically drunk by all the gentlemen present, who rose at the bidding of the host.

Shortly afterwards the party again rose, but this time it was to take their departure, for though the wine was very good they could not make a long sitting.

After assisting Juliana to her seat on the pillion, Dick said to the king, in a low voice :

" Forgive me, sire, if I have presumed too much. I knew you from the first, and could not repress my feelings. May my dream soon become a reality !"

While riding out of Mere, they gazed at the fine old church with its lofty tower, at the ancient market-house, and at the lofty mound on which were some vestiges of a castle, built in the reign of Henry III. When they had quitted the little town, the most striking object was a precipitous hill, about two miles distant, known as Whitesheet Camp.

After crossing a wild and bleak waste full of earthworks, they reached Hindon, and then passed over downs, guarded by hills crowned by camps through Chilmark and Great Teffont, and through the old forest of Grovely, to Wishford.

From Grovely Hill, on which are the remains of an ancient British town, they obtained a fine view of Salisbury Plain, with the lofty spire of the cathedral in the distance. Evening was coming on as they took their way across part of the plain, and the numerous barrows near which they rode, tinged by the radiance of the declining sun, had a very striking effect. But as soon as the sun had set, the picture became cold and grey, awakening a train of melancholy thoughts. The air, likewise, began to feel cold, so they quickened their pace, and soon afterwards arrived at their destination.

# CHAPTER XXIII.

### HEALE HOUSE.

HEALE HOUSE was a large stone structure, with square turrets at the corners, pleasantly situated on the banks of the Avon.

Colonel Philips had ridden on from Wishford to announce the approach of the party, so that when they arrived Mrs. Hyde came forth with her brother-in-law, Mr. Frederick Hyde, to give them welcome.

Though Mrs. Hyde cannot he described as young, she was still very handsome, and being rich, it is somewhat surprising that she still remained a widow. In the presence of her servants, who were drawn up at the door, she took care that not a look or gesture should betray her knowledge of the king, though she recognised him the moment she beheld him. Her chief attentions were bestowed upon Juliana, to whom she seemed to take a great fancy.

All the guests were quickly conducted to their rooms by the chamberlain, but that discriminating personage, not having received special orders from his mistress, and judging merely from personal appearance, assigned a very small room to his majesty.

About two hours later the whole party was assembled at supper in a large room panelled with oak, and adorned with portraits of the Hyde family. The season was now sufficiently advanced to make a fire desirable, and the logs blazing on the hearth gave the room a very cheerful look. The repast was excellent and abundant, and the guests, whose appetites had been sharpened by the keen air of Salisbury Plain, did ample justice to it. Hitherto, as we have said, Mrs. Hyde had acted with the greatest discretion, but she was now so transported with delight by seeing the king seated at her board that she could scarcely contain herself. Some excellent trout from the Avon were served, and she took care he had one of them. A roast bustard happened to be among the dishes—for that almost extinct bird then abounded on Salisbury Plain and the adjoining downs—and observing that the king seemed pleased with the dish, she ordered the carver to take him some more slices from the breast, with plenty of sauce. Subsequently, she sent him a couple of larks, though the others had only one each, and she quite surprised the butler by drinking to her humble guest in a glass of malvoisie, and sending him a silver flagon full of the same wine. After supper, Mr. Frederick Hyde, a lawyer, who eventually rose to be Chief Justice of the King's Bench, had a long discourse with the king, not in the slightest degree suspecting who he was, and was astonished at the young man's quickness and wit. Among the guests was Dr. Henchman, a prebend of Salisbury, who had come over to Heale on that day, but without acquainting the widow with the real object of his visit, which was to deliver a message to the king from Lord Wilmot. Observing the utmost caution, Dr. Henchman waited till Charles retired to his own room, and then had a private conference with him there. Let us state that after the Restoration Dr. Henchman was created Bishop of Salisbury, and in 1663, was translated to the see of London.

Next morning Mrs. Hyde found an opportunity of saying a few words in private to the king during a stroll which they took together in the garden.

"I find I was very indiscreet last night," she said. "I allowed my loyalty to carry me too far, and have awakened the suspicions of my servants. To prevent any ill consequences, your majesty must apparently take leave this morning, but you can return privately at night, when I will have a safe hiding-place prepared for you. Then there will be no risk, for the servants will not be aware that you are in the house."

Charles entirely approved of the plan, but hoped he should not have to trouble her long, as he expected to receive an early communication from Colonel Gunter.

"I will go to Stonehenge this morning," he said. "If Colonel Gunter should arrive, send him on to me there. In that case, I shall not return. If he comes not, you will see me again."

"And the hiding-place shall be ready; but I sincerely trust your majesty may not require it."

"I hope so too," rejoined Charles. "But there is no certainty of my departure."

They then proceeded towards the house, but had not gone far when they met Dr. Henchman coming towards them.

"I am about to return to Salisbury immediately," he said. "Has your majesty any message for Lord Wilmot? I am sure to find him with Mr. John Coventry."

"Tell him to meet me at Stonehenge," replied Charles. "He must come prepared for a ride to the Sussex coast."

"I will tell him exactly what you say, my liege," rejoined Dr. Henchman.

"Perhaps he may bring me news," said the king. "Perhaps I may have news to give him. In any case, let him be prepared."

"Heaven protect your majesty!" exclaimed Dr. Henchman. "I trust your deliverance is at hand?"

With a profound obeisance he departed, and Charles and Mrs. Hyde returned to the house.

The king found his attendants in the hall, and at once communicated his intentions to them. After breakfast the whole party took leave of Mrs. Hyde and her brother-in-law, mounted their horses, and set off apparently for Salisbury.

---

## CHAPTER XXIV

### HOW CHARLES ENCOUNTERED DESBOROUGH ON SALISBURY PLAIN.

AFTER riding for a short distance along the banks of the Avon, the party separated, Colonel Philips and Colonel Wyndham proceeding towards Salisbury in the expectation of meeting Lord Wilmot, and perhaps Colonel Gunter; and the king and his fair companion, attended by Careless, shaping their course in the direction of Stonehenge, which was fixed as the general place of rendezvous.

Salisbury Plain has a charm of its own, which those who rode across it on that fine October morning fully experienced. Juliana was enchanted with the strange novelty of the scene, and allowed her gaze to wander over the apparently boundless expanse of turf. Not a tree could be seen—not a solitary cottage—not a shed—the undulating surface of the plain being only broken by the numerous barrows, that seemed to have been heaved up from the sod like gigantic mole-hills. Here and there a shepherd, looking grey as the turf itself, and tending a flock of sheep, could be distinguished. A singular cluster of sepulchral tumuli attracted them, and they spent some little time in examining the group. On coming forth from among the barrows they aroused a flock of bustards, and watched them scud swiftly over the plain, hallooing after them, and almost tempted to give them chase.

So occupied were they with the bustards that they did not perceive till they turned that a strong regiment of horse was advancing across the plain. Deeming a bold course the safest, Charles rode straight on, and Careless kept by his side. To ride through the ranks of the enemy was certainly a daring thing to do, but the perfect confidence with which the action was performed insured its success. The men looked sternly at them, but discovering nothing suspicious in their manner, allowed them to pass on. The danger, however, was not over. Behind the rear guard rode the commander of the regiment—a heavy, ungainly, sullen-looking personage, but richly accoutred. With him was an orderly.

"'Tis Old Noll's brother-in-law, Desborough!" whispered Careless.

"I know him," replied the king. "Heaven grant he may not know me!"

Desborough, it appeared, did not mean to let them pass unquestioned. Reining in his steed, he signed to them to stop. At the same time the orderly drew his sword, and called out, in an authoritative voice:

"Stand! Major-General Desborough, Commander-in-Chief of the Army of the West, would speak with you."

Uncovering at this address, both of them remained stationary.

Desborough bent his lowering brows upon them, and fixed his eye upon the king. Charles, however, did not quail beneath his searching glance.

"Look at that man, Colville," said Desborough. "Look at him well. Hast seen him before?"

"I do not think so, general," replied the orderly. "Yet the face seems familiar to me."

It was an anxious moment, for Desborough's brow grew darker, but Juliana interposed.

"You cannot have seen my husband before, general," she cried; "unless you have been to Salisbury, for he has never been further from the city than Amesbury, whither we are going now."

"Is the young man thy husband?" demanded Desborough in a tone that implied some doubt. "Attempt not to deceive me."

"We have been married a twelvemonth," she replied. "And not for a single hour have we been separated since we became man and wife."

"That's much to say," remarked Desborough.

"But there are plenty of persons who can testify to the truth of the statement. My brother Amyas will tell you that Orlando Jermyn—that's my husband's name—and his wife are accounted the happiest couple in Sarum."

"Since you are so well satisfied I will not say you might have made a better choice," observed Desborough. "But I think your husband may esteem himself lucky."

"He tells me so repeatedly," she replied; "and I am bound to believe him. Have you any more questions to ask me?"

Desborough looked again searchingly at Charles, but perceiving no change in his demeanour, and noticing, moreover, that the others seemed quite unconcerned, he signed to them to go on. The orderly sheathed his sword.

Respectfully saluting the major-general, Charles and his attendant proceeded quietly on their way. After a brief colloquy with the orderly, Desborough moved on, to Juliana's great relief.

"At last he is gone!" she exclaimed. "Did I not act my part bravely?"

"Admirably," replied Charles. "You have saved me from the greatest peril in which I have yet been placed. Desborough, I could plainly see, suspected me. But you puzzled him."

Halting near a barrow, they watched the regiment as long as it remained in sight. They then rode on towards Stonehenge, which loomed in the distance.

- - -

## CHAPTER XXV

### THE PARTING AT STONEHENGE.

THERE stand those grey mysterious circles of stones, that for centuries have braved the storms that have beaten upon the wide dreary plain on which they have been placed - none can tell how, or when. There they stand—stern, solemn, hoar, crusted with lichens, incomprehensible, enigmatical as the Sphinx ; muttering tales of days forgotten, and of a people whose habits, customs, and creed, are no longer understood. So strange and mysterious are the old stones, that no wonder the wildest fables have been told of them. Some have thought the pile was reared by magic art, others have deemed it the work of the Evil One, intended by him as a temple where unhallowed rites might be practised. But by whatever giant hands the mighty pile was reared, in whatever age and for whatever purpose—hallowed, or unhallowed—whether as an altar for human sacrifice, as a court of justice, or as a place of execution, all is now dim conjecture. There the huge stones stand as of yore, but their history is clean forgotten.

Though a couple of centuries are little in the history of Stonehenge, a great change has taken place since Charles visited the wondrous monument. A change for the worse. The mighty stones are there, but the aspect of the spot is altered. The genius of solitude that brooded over the pile has fled—fled with the shy bustard that once haunted its mystic circles, and with the ravens that perched on the stones. The wide rolling surface of the plain was then wholly uncultivated. Nothing was to be seen except the clustering barrows, and the banks that marked what is now called, with what truth we know not, a Roman cursus.

Charles approached the pile by an avenue edged by grassy banks, gazing with wonder, not unmixed with awe, at the gigantic circles. As he rode slowly on he came to a single upright stone, and paused to look at it

Familiar with the legends of the spot, Careless informed the king that the stone was called " The Friar's Heel."

"The tale runs," he said, " that while the Evil One was engaged in constructing those mysterious circles, a friar passed by, and was indiscreet enough to make some disparaging remark upon the works. Having done so, he fled. The Demon, in a rage, hurled a huge stone at him, and grazed his heel, but did not check him. There stands the stone, deeply plunged in the earth, to prove the truth of the legend."

Passing through the outer circle of smaller stones, they dismounted, and fastening up their horses to an obelisk-shaped fragment, surveyed the mighty ruin, examining the trilithons and monoliths.

" There is a superstition," observed Careless, " that these stones cannot be counted alike twice."

" I have heard it," replied Charles ; " and I remember what Sir Philip Sydney says of it on the subject :

> " Near Wilton sweet huge heaps of stones are found,
> But so confused, that neither any eye
> Can count them just, nor reason reason try
> What force them brought to so unlikely ground."

" Let us make the attempt. 'Twill serve to pass the time till our friends arrive. Do you think you can count them ?" he said to Juliana.

" I will try, my liege, she replied. " Where shall I begin ?"

" With the altar-stone," replied Charles.

Juliana then commenced her task, going carefully through the different circles, and not pausing till she reached the last stone.

" How many do you make them ?" asked Charles.

" Seventy-seven," she replied.

" My reckoning agrees with yours," cried Careless, who had followed her.

" So far good," observed Charles. " But you have not included the recumbent 'slaughtering stone' near the entrance, nor the 'Friar's Heel' in the avenue, nor the two small stones near the earthen bank. Those will increase the number to eighty-one. Now for the second trial. Start from this stone."

Very carefully Juliana performed her task. When she had reached the altar-stone, a smile lighted up her charming countenance, and she exclaimed joyously :

" Seventy-seven ! I have counted the stones alike twice—and disproved the fable.

After congratulating her on her success, Charles observed :

" I wonder whether a loving pair were ever betrothed at this altar ?"

The significance given to the words, and the look that accompanied them, made Juliana cast down her eyes.

" 'Tis strange that the same thought should have occurred to me," remarked Careless. " How say you, sweetheart?" he continued, taking Juliana's hand. " Shall we plight our vows here, in his majesty's presence? You know that duty calls me hence, and that I may be long detained in France. Let me feel certain I shall not lose you."

" You need not doubt me, Careless," she rejoined, tenderly. " I shall ever be constant to you."

They then bent before the king, and Careless, still holding her hand, exclaimed;

" Bear witness, sire, that I solemnly plight my faith to Juliana Coningsby."

" And I as solemnly plight my faith to William Careless," she added.

" I cannot pronounce a benediction upon you," said Charles. " But I can bear witness to your betrothal. May your union speedily take place; and when it does take place, may you be happy!"

The betrothed pair had just risen, when the trampling of horse was heard.

" They come! they come!" exclaimed the king, joyously. " You were only just in time."

And he hastened to the entrance of the pile.

When he reached the outer circle he perceived Lord Wilmot, accompanied by Colonel Wyndham and Colonel Philips, galloping towards the spot. With them was a fourth Cavalier, whom he doubted not was Colonel Gunter.

In another minute the party came up, sprang from their steeds, and advanced towards the king, who could not fail to read good news in their countenances.

" Welcome, my lord! thrice welcome!" he cried to Lord Wilmot.

" Yes, I bring you good news, my liege," replied his lordship. " But it is for Colonel Gunter to tell it."

Colonel Gunter was then presented to the king, and after making a profound obeisance, said:

" Your majesty will be pleased to hear that I have succeeded in hiring a vessel at Shoreham, to transport you to Dieppe. She is only sixty tons, but a good, stout, well-built bark, and her master, Nicholas Tattersall, is perfectly honest and loyal. The vessel is laden with sea-coal, and bound for Poole, and Tattersall will at first stand for the Isle of Wight, but when he has been out at sea for a few hours he will alter his course, and make for the French coast. The skipper will be ready to sail as soon as your majesty and your companions reach Shoreham. With your permission I will attend you thither."

" This is good news indeed!" cried Charles, transported with delight. " All my difficulties and dangers seem now at an end."

" The only difficulties and dangers your majesty has to apprehend may occur during our journey to Shoreham," observed Colonel Gunter. " But I trust we shall avoid them all."

" Yes, sire, I firmly believe the worst is past," said Colonel Wyndham. " Providence, who has hitherto watched over you, will guard you on your journey, and bring you safely to the coast. You need not fear the repetition of such an untoward circumstance as took place at Lyme. Would I could see you embark, but I should only endanger you if I went with you !"

" No, thou hast done enough, Frank," cried the king, patting him affectionately on the shoulder—" far more than I ever shall be able to requite. We must part here—not for long, I trust. Thou shalt lend me thy horse, and take that which I have ridden. He will bear thee and Juliana back to Trent. Fail not to give my adieux to thy most amiable wife, and to thy venerated mother, whom I love as a son !"

He then turned to Juliana, and found that her bright eyes were dimmed. She had just parted with Careless.

" Be of good cheer," he said. " I promise you he shall soon return."

" Your majesty, I fear, promises more than you can perform," she sighed. " But I will hope for the best."

" I cannot thank you sufficiently for all you have done for me," he said. " But you will always have a place next to Jane Lane in my regard. How I shall prosper when I have lost you both Heaven only knows. Farewell !"

He then pressed her hand to his lips, and springing on the steed from which Colonel Wyndham had just dismounted, he called to the others to join him, and was soon afterwards seen careering at their head across Salisbury Plain.

**THE END.**

www.ingramcontent.com/pod-product-compliance
Lightning Source LLC
Chambersburg PA
CBHW031018120726
47905CB00007B/1961